FiRE&
FLOOD

FiRE&
FLOOD

VICTORIA
SCOTT

SCHOLASTIC INC.

This book was originally published in hardcover by Scholastic Press in 2014.

ISBN 978-0-545-73048-8

12 11 10 9 8 7 6 5 4 3 2 1   15 16 17 18 19 20/0

Printed in the U.S.A.   40
This edition first printing, February 2015

The text type was set in Adobe Garamond Pro.
Book design by Nina Goffi

FOR MY SISTER, WHO KNEW THIS WAS THE ONE

THE PROPOSAL

CHAPTER ONE

If my hair gets any frizzier, I'll shave it to the scalp.

Or light it on fire.

Whichever is easier.

I stare at my reflection in the pond and run my hands through the bane of my existence. For a moment, I seem victorious; my chestnut curls wrangled into submission. But when I drop my arms, the curls spring out, worse for the wear. I point an unmanicured finger at the water. "I hate your face."

"Tella," my mother yells from behind me, "what are you looking at?"

I spin around and grab a handful of my hair. Exhibit A.

"It's beautiful," she says.

"You did this to me," I tell her.

"No, your father gave you curly hair."

"But you dragged me to Middle of Nowhere, Montana, as a sick experiment to see just how hideous I could become."

Mom leans against the door frame of our craptastic house and nearly grins. "We've been here almost a year. When are you going to accept that this is our home?"

I walk toward her and punch a closed fist into the air. "I'll fight to the death."

A shadow crosses the deep lines of her face, and I instantly regret bringing up The Subject. "Sorry," I tell her. "You know I didn't mean —"

"I know," she says.

I rise up on tiptoes and kiss her cheek, then brush past her to go inside. My dad sits in the front room, rocking in a wooden chair like he's two hundred and fifty-six years old. In actuality, I think he's a couple of years shy.

"Hey, Pa," I say.

"Hey, Daugh," he says.

Ever since my mom insisted we move out of Boston and into no-man's-land, I've insisted on calling my dad Pa. It reminds me of those old black-and-white movies in which the daughters wear horrendous dresses and braid one another's hair. He wasn't a fan of my new name for him, but he accepted his fate over time. Guess he thought I could've rebelled a lot more following our relocation to purgatory, all things considered.

"What are we doing tonight?" I ask, dropping down onto the floor. "Dinner at a glam restaurant? Theater in the city?"

Dad's mouth pulls down at the corner. He's disappointed.

That makes two of us.

"Humor me and pretend you're happy," he answers. "That'd be entertaining as hell."

"Language," I tsk.

He waves me off, pretending he's the man of this house and can say whatever he damn well pleases. I laugh when seconds later he glances over to see if Mom heard.

"I'm going to my room," I announce.

Dad continues to stare outside like he's comatose. I know that's exactly what I'll do when I get to my room, but at least I can do it in private.

The floorboards creak as I head down the narrow hallway toward my personal dungeon. A few feet from my room, I pause outside an open bedroom door that isn't mine. I can't help moving closer to the bed inside. Leaning over his sleeping frame, I check to see if he's still breathing. It's my twisted ritual.

"I'm not dead."

I jump back, startled by my big brother's voice.

"Shame," I say. "I was hoping you'd kick off so I could have the bigger bedroom. You take up way more than your fair share of space, you know."

3

He rolls to face me and grins. "I weigh, like, a hundred pounds."

"Exactly."

It kills me to see Cody sick. And it doesn't feel great ripping on him when what I want to do is ugly cry and beg him not to die. But he likes our back-and-forth. Says it makes him feel normal. So that's what we do.

"You look old," Cody tells me.

"I'm sixteen."

"Going on eighty." He points to my face. "You have wrinkles."

I dash toward the mirror over his dresser and look. From the bed, I hear Cody laughing, then coughing. "You're so vain," he says into his fist, his chest convulsing.

"Jerk face." I move to his side and pull the heavy blanket to his chin. "Mom wants to know how you feel today," I lie.

"Better," he says, returning the favor.

I nod and turn to leave.

"Tell her to stop worrying," he finishes.

"I doubt she seriously cares."

I can still hear him laughing when I get to my bedroom, shut the door, and sink to my knees. My breath whooshes out. He's getting worse. I can hear it in the way his words quiver. Like speaking takes everything he has. In the beginning, it was just the weight loss. Then it was night sweats and shaking hands. Then the fun really started. Seizures. Thinning hair. Slurred speech that started one Wednesday and ended with a coma on Friday. He came around three days later. Mom said it was because he didn't want to miss a football game. Not that he played anymore. That died a long time ago.

Now he's down to this: pretending. Pretending to be the brother who swung a right hook in my honor. Pretending to be the son who danced a jig in the end zone that his dad taught him. He's still the guy who isn't afraid to write more than his name in a greeting card. Still the guy who loves redbrick buildings and cars that growl and Cheez Whiz sprayed straight from the can into his open mouth.

He is still my brother.

He is not my brother at all.

I don't know why Mom thought this place would help. A dozen doctors couldn't figure out what was wrong with him, yet she thinks Montana's "fresh air" will do the trick. The look in her eyes while we packed the moving truck still haunts me. Like she was waiting for something.

Or running from something.

I pull myself up and walk to the window. Outside, I can hear yellow-headed blackbirds calling. I rarely noticed stuff like birds in Boston. In Boston, we lived in a brownstone that wasn't brown, and I had friends two doors down. Our family owned three floors of sparkling space, and we could walk to restaurants.

Here there are rocks. And a stream that runs near our home that's free of fish. The sky is empty of rooflines and overstuffed with cotton-ball clouds. There are no neighbors. No girls my age to discuss the joys of colored tights with. A single, lonely road leads from our house into town. When I look at it, I want to strap a bag to a stick and limp down it hobo style.

Tall pine trees surround our house, like their job is to hide us from the world. I imagine running toward them wearing a hockey mask, swinging a chain saw over my head. They'd probably uproot themselves and squash me like a bug. Bury me beneath their twisted roots.

That's how I want to go when it's my time.

With a bang.

I slide the window open and stick my head outside. What I wouldn't do to see my friends again. To get a mani-pedi or a blow-out. Or a Greek salad. Oh my friggin' God, Feta cheese and

5

kalamata olives. I wallow in self-pity for another moment before remembering my brother. Then I spend exactly three minutes feeling like the World's Biggest Ass.

We're here for him. And I'd give anything to see my brother get out of bed and dance in the street like he did on Halloween two years ago. Or even just sit up for a few minutes without coughing.

I motorboat my lips and spin in a circle like a ballerina. I spin and spin until everything becomes a blur. When I stop, my room continues to rush past me, and I lunatic laugh that this is what I do for fun now.

My vision finally returns to normal, and my eyes land on the bed. Sitting on my white comforter is a small blue box.

CHAPTER TWO

I snap my head from side to side, searching for someone in my room. But of course no one's there. Then I realize what's going on. Mom and Dad know how hard this relocation has been on me, and now they're trying to buy my happiness. Or at least a break from my complaining.

Am I really this easy?

Please. They could have tied little blue boxes to the back of the moving truck and I would have chased after them until my feet bled.

I fly across my room and leap onto the bed, a smile spread across my face. I've spent these last nine months with no Internet or cell phone, and right now I feel like a wild dog eyeing its prey.

Holding the box to my lips, I tell it, "You're mine, precious. All mine."

I'm about to tear in when I stop myself. This moment of wondering what's inside will be over so quickly. And once it's finished, I'll have nothing to anticipate. Perhaps I should postpone gratification, hold off until I can't stand it any longer. I could be happy for days just knowing I have something to look forward to.

I pull the box away from my lips and give it a small shake.

Put the box down, Tella, I tell myself.

"Screw that," I say out loud.

I close my hand around the lid and pull it off. Inside is a tiny pillow. I imagine all sorts of miniature animals using it in their miniature beds. But that's dumb, because how would they ever find a pillowcase to fit?

My fingers pinch the pillow, and when I lift it up, I'm surprised by what I see sleeping beneath it. Flicking the pillow onto my bed,

I reach into the box and grab the small, stark white device. It's no longer than a nickel and curves in all sorts of funky ways. It looks . . . it looks like a hearing aid.

My nose scrunches up as I turn the device over in my hand. Then I nearly squeal with excitement when I see a raised red blinking light on the other side. Blinking lights are cool, I decide. They indicate technology and advancement and maybe a connection to the outside world — to my friends. Or maybe it's music. Who knows what wild stuff they've come out with in the last year? I bet this baby holds, like, a billion songs. And I'm going to listen to them. Every. Single. One.

Vowing to give a solid, halfhearted apology to my parents and hoping I'm about to hear Lady Gaga's latest, I stick the device into my ear. Hallelujah, it fits! I couldn't be happier if my Boston boy toy just gave me diamonds.

I fumble for a second before my fingers land on the red blinking button. Annnnnd . . . give it to me, baby.

Once I've pushed the button, I hear a clicking noise. The sound goes on for several seconds. Long enough that I start to feel all kinds of devastated. But then the clicking turns to static, like someone on the other side of a radio is tuning in.

Jumping from the bed, I walk around the room, tilting my head like I'm searching for a signal. I feel like a moron, and it's the most fun I've had in forever. I shoot straight up when I hear a woman's voice. It's a clear, crisp sound. Like this lady has never mispronounced a word in her entire life. My eyes fall to the floor in concentration. And I listen.

"If you're hearing this message, you are invited to be a Contender in the Brimstone Bleed. All Contenders must report within forty-eight hours to select their Pandora companions. If you do not —"

"Tella?" my dad asks. "What are you doing?"

I spin around and do a little happy dance. "What is this thing?"

I point to the device in my ear. "Where did you guys get it? Because it's fan-friggin'-tastic."

"Get what?" My dad's face goes from confused . . . to alarmed. For a moment, I feel like a little kid. Like, any second, I'm going to be placed in the time-out chair and fume while Cody flaunts his freedom like back when we were four and seven. "What's in your ear?" My dad sounds strange. His words are calculated, slow to leave his mouth. "Give it to me."

"What? Why?" I say.

Dad holds out his hand. "Now."

There's no room for argument. My dad's a fairly small guy, but right now he seems enormous. I pull the device from my ear and drop it into his palm. As he closes his fist, I'm certain my new toy has been permanently confiscated.

"Why'd you give it to me if you were just going to take it away?" I ask.

Dad looks at me like he's going to say something profound, but then he mutters, "Your mom needs help in the kitchen." He walks out of the room, my only source of excitement for the next eon tucked in his pocket.

I grab the sides of my door frame and hang my head. My dad's freak-out tells me he's not the one who left the talking hearing aid in my room, which makes me wonder who did. Then it dawns on me. Passing Cody's room, I yell, "Nice joke, ass hat." Even as I say it, I imagine what it would be like if it *wasn't* him. Nothing exciting happens to me. Ever. But that doesn't stop me from daydreaming.

I've got a world of possibilities ticking away in this noggin. And right now I've all but decided the leader of an underground cult has recruited me to be a part of the Brimstone Blood. Or Bleed. Or whatever Cody named it. Either way, it sounds kind of gruesome. He's apparently gotten more twisted in his sibling brutality. And I do count getting my hopes up as brutality.

The real question is how he recorded that woman's voice. Apparently, the kid's been holding out on me. Mom insisted Cody relax once we moved here, hence the Technology Prohibition, but he must have stashed something away. A laptop. A smartphone. Something.

Just thinking about it makes me foam at the mouth.

I briefly wonder if I might be coming down with rabies.

Mom isn't in the kitchen, but I do spot her standing in her bedroom, talking in a hushed voice with Dad.

"You promised!" my dad hisses. "You promised that they wouldn't find her here."

"I'm sorry. It's too late now."

"Not yet, it's not —"

When my mom sees me, she holds a hand up to shush him.

"Tella," she says, "I want you to finish making dinner and meet us in Cody's room." Then she closes the door.

"Jeez, rude much?" I say, mostly to myself. For a moment, I wonder what my parents were talking about. I can't say what I heard didn't unnerve me, but when you live with a chronically sick sibling you get used to overhearing your parents say weird crap behind closed doors. So I dismiss their crankiness and turn my attention to my marching orders.

Tonight is Sunday Funday, which my dad made up, and which equates to eating spaghetti in Cody's room. We all sit around his bed and dine off paper plates, and no one's allowed to say anything negative. All it really means is that everyone saves everything terrible they have to say for Monday, which kicks off the week real positivelike.

I drain the spaghetti and pour in a can of marinara. Then I do that finger-kiss thing that Italian chefs do on TV. Tipping the oversized chrome pot, I cover four plates with pasta and top them with packaged Parmesan cheese and a slice of freezer-stored garlic bread.

Everything we eat is made with love and kindness, and packed with as many preservatives as humanly possible. Living thirty miles from the nearest grocery store pretty much guarantees we'll never eat fresh again, unless we grow something ourselves, and that so isn't happening. My parents have always chosen their wallets over manual labor; another reason why we shouldn't have left the city.

Walking toward Cody's room, I carry a tray covered with plates and glasses like a well-tipped waitress. I even keep one hand cocked on my hip so I can sashay past our too-expensive-for-this-house furniture. When I get to the hallway, I overhear Mom and Dad whispering hurriedly to Cody. I make a point to stop and eavesdrop, but the floorboards choose this exact moment to creak beneath my shoes.

Everyone stops talking.

"You got the spaghetti?" my dad asks. The way he says it sounds like he's digging for information beyond dinner.

I turn the corner and do my best sashay yet. It's so good, I almost lose the tray altogether. Still, if it's between sashaying and keeping spaghetti off the floor — I choose the former. "Dinner is served, my fine patrons." I steady the tray and pass the grub out to my family. When I hand my dad his pasta, I pause and search his face. I know it was Cody who planted the box in my room, but it bothers me that my dad got so weird about it. He hates when Cody and I play-fight, and I guess he just wasn't in the mood. Still, I want to know he's not mad anymore. Even more, I want to steal back that talking device in his pocket. Prank or no prank, it's a lifeline to fighting boredom and isolation.

While we eat, Mom talks ad nauseam about what's on the agenda for tomorrow's classes. I want to remind her that Sunday Funday outlaws talking about anything negative, but I hold my tongue. It's August, which means exactly two things: A) It's a new semester in the Holloway household, and B) Mom's on a steady diet of overeagerness. And maybe crack.

Mom started homeschooling Cody and me once we moved here. It was a huge blow to my social calendar, second only to *Guess what? We're moving to Montana*. I never thought my mom was the relocate-to-the-wilderness-and-homeschool-my-kids kind of person, but turns out she's full of pleasant surprises. I'll admit that, as far as teachers go, she's the best I've had. Maybe because she glows every time I get an answer right, or that she dances when we ace our tests.

Cody sits up in bed and nods as Mom talks about lesson plans. Something about her voice is too eager tonight, like she's trying too hard to get the rest of us to smile. I glance at my dad and realize she's failed to amuse at least one of us. My dad's fork twirls in an endless circle, turning my spaghetti masterpiece into reddish-orange mush.

I can't stand the look on his face any longer. "Dad, you okay?"

His head snaps up, but it takes a while for his mouth to form a smile. "Yeah, everything's great."

Great? Now I know something's up. Without meaning to, I eye the pocket where I know he stashed the device. He places a hand over it, and our eyes meet.

"Let's do the dishes, Andrea." Dad looks away from me and to my mom. They couldn't be more different tonight: Dad with his somber twitchiness and Mom with her pageant smile.

My mom nods and collects our paper plates. Then she leaves, giving my dad a final look. These trippy vibes are killing me, so I open my mouth to say something, anything. "Nice prank, Cody. Too bad Dad killed your punch line." It's not the best I've got, but I feel like my dad's bad mood started with the blue box. Why not lay it on the table while he's still in the room?

Cody is in the middle of pulling himself farther up in bed but stops when he hears what I've said. He looks down and bunches the blanket into his fist. His face looks almost pained. A shiver works its way down my spine. What if Cody didn't put that box in my room? But if he didn't, then who did? Dad's too pissed to have done it, and Mom would never do something like that. At least, I don't think she would. She's surprised me too much this last year to know for sure.

The shiver sneaking down my back starts to morph into goose bumps. But right then Cody raises his head and grins. "Took a lot of brainpower, baby sister," he says, tapping his temple. Then he shakes his head as if I've been a huge disappointment. "Would have been so great."

I sigh with relief. Adventure sounds a whole lot more enticing when it's safe inside my head. For a minute there, I was thinking he might be like, "What are you talking about?" And then I'd have to decide if I really did want something exciting to happen, or if I just liked to dream.

Rolling my eyes, I say, "More like lame. It would have been so *lame.*"

I head toward the door, surprised Dad hasn't spoken. If this is what he's mad about, why hasn't he piped in? As I'm heading out to help Mom in the kitchen, I look back over my shoulder. I catch Dad giving Cody a nod. It's just a nod, nothing special. But something passes between the two of them during the exchange. They both look relieved, and it's the most unsettling feeling — not knowing what they were so worried about.

Walking down the hallway and toward the sound of my mom humming, I can't stop thinking about the device. What it really is. How Cody got his hands on it.

If it even *was* Cody.

The look on his face when Dad nodded makes me question everything. I set my glass down on the kitchen counter, and though I know my mom is talking to me, I don't hear a single word. Because all I'm thinking is that I've got to get that little white device back. Tonight.

CHAPTER THREE

That blue box was meant for me, and my dad stole it. Even if Cody did plant it in my room, which I'm starting to doubt he did, my dad had no right to take it away. What am I — five?

I sit in the living area with my mom and dad, staring at the book in my hands. I'm not reading — I'm masterminding a complicated escape plan for my device. So far, I don't have much in the escape department, but I've come up with plenty that could be classified as *complicated*.

The only thing I hear — and it's driving me crazy — is the sound of my mom and dad turning the pages of their own books. God forbid we buy a TV for this house. Wouldn't want anyone to have a link to life beyond the Holloway household. I swear, the second Cody got sick, my parents lost all sense of reality.

But right now none of that matters. The real reason I'm irritated with my parents is because I want them in bed. Asleep. Where they can't watch me slink around the house, looking for my device. And I am going to slink like nobody's business.

I glance at the clock. It's ten at night, and my parents look like they could run a marathon. I stare at them as they stare at their books and will them to become tired. After five minutes of mental warfare, I give up. But just then my dad yawns. Victory is mine!

"Think I'm going to hit the hay," he says.

"I'm right behind you," my mom answers, not even looking up. She doesn't move.

Hoping she'll be swayed by numbers, I stretch my arms over my head and announce, "I'm exhausted. I think I might turn in, too."

That does the trick. She runs her finger down the page. It's her telltale sign that she's finding a stopping point. She reaches for the busted-up bookmark I gave her for Mother's Day when I was, like, nine, and slides it into place.

"You going to bed, too?" I ask.

She looks up at me and smiles, but it doesn't quite reach her eyes. I suddenly wonder if my parents were doing the same thing I was — pretending to read.

"Yep" is all she says. Then we begin a Mexican standoff: me waiting for her to get up and her waiting for . . . what?

"Okay," I say, caving. "Guess I'm going to go now." I stand up and walk toward my room, throwing the book I wasn't reading onto the couch. Right before I leave, I glance back. She's watching me go, so I throw a little wave. Mom waves back, but her smile is long gone.

Something is definitely up.

That or my family is auditioning for a remake of *The Shining*.

I stop by Cody's door on the way to my room. I want to keep walking, to pretend for once that he's okay and everything is back to the way it used to be. But I can't. So I pad into his room on tiptoes and lean over his bed. Now I'm the one being a creeper.

Once I'm certain my brother is still breathing, I go into my room and collapse onto the bed. One hour. That's how long I'm waiting before I search every corner of this blasted house. Then the contents of that mysterious blue box will be mine.

Four hours later, I wake up.

So much for Operation Sly.

I push myself up from the bed, rubbing my face and berating myself for falling asleep. I'm, like, the biggest weakling on planet Earth. Sliding my shoes off so I make as little noise as possible, I create a mental list of where to check first: the coat closet, the hallway bathroom, maybe the kitchen. The kitchen. I wonder if there's any cherry cheesecake left in the fridge. No. Find device. Then cheesecake.

I'm about to open my door, but something stops me.

It's smoke. A lot of it. And it's coming from outside my window.

Crossing the room, I keep an eye on the smoke as my scalp tingles with nerves. I start to imagine my house catching on fire. Or one of my parents' cars. How would anyone find us out here? I like to think someone would, eventually. Probably a fireman who happens to be my age and carries an ax over his left shoulder like a Greek god. Fire would rage behind him as he saves us all and he'd smile to reassure me and, my Lord, he has dimples.

I slide open my window and the smell of burning wood fills my room. Though I'm terrified that something horrible is happening, I can't help but relish the scent. It reminds me of being home in Boston, of cold nights when Dad would make a fire in the fireplace and we'd drink cocoa with pastel-colored marshmallows.

The smoke billows from left to right and leads me to believe the fire is coming from in front of our house. I'm about to wake up my parents when I see a flash of red and black. I'd know that shirt anywhere. It's the plaid flannel my dad wears when he goes hunting with Uncle Wade.

What is my dad doing in front of our house at two in the morning?

I contemplate going out the front door to ask him. It'd be a reasonable question. No one wants to wake up in the middle of the night to find her dad embracing a new pyromania habit. But something stops me. Maybe it's the way he's been acting since he saw the talking device, or the weird way he whispered with my mom before dinner, or even the way he nodded at Cody like there was something big the two of them were hiding. Regardless, I decide to move in closer without revealing myself.

Crawling out the window, I think of how ridiculous I must look. How if my best friend back in Boston, Hannah, could see this, she'd be laughing like a lunatic. Thinking about her laughing in turn makes me laugh, and I have to cover my mouth as I drop down on the side of the house. This afternoon, I was bored to tears, and now I'm acting like a friggin' CIA agent.

I really am losing my mind out here.

I creep along the wall toward the front of our house and hold my breath as I peek around the corner. My dad is standing in front of a bonfire, just staring into the flames. He looks like an assassin, all crazy in the face. The fire is actually much farther from our house than I originally thought, which makes me even more nervous. It's like he's covering up something. Just doing a bad job.

Running a hand through his thick curly hair, my dad sighs. Then he opens his other hand and looks at something in his palm. I narrow my eyes to try to see what he's studying, but I can't make it out from here. Whatever he's holding has a short life span, because he pulls in a long breath and tosses it into the fire. It arcs in the air for only a moment, but it's long enough for me to see the flash of white.

It's my device.

And now it's gone.

I lean back against the side of the house in a panic. Now I'm certain this was no practical joke. There's no way my dad would go to such lengths to get rid of something trivial. And in the dead of night, no less. Something was on that thing, and now I'll never know. I rack my brain, trying to remember everything the woman had said.

The Brimstone something or other.

An invitation.

Forty-eight hours.

When I peek back around the corner, my dad's eyes meet mine. I slam back against the house and mutter a string of profanities. From far away, I hear the sound of his footsteps. They come closer and I squeeze my eyes shut. I'm like an ostrich, hoping if I can't see him, he can't see me. Seconds later, the front door opens and closes. My muscles relax and I almost laugh at having escaped being caught.

I'm not sure what I'm so afraid of. It's not like I did anything wrong. *He* stole the earpiece. *He* acted weird about it. *He* built a fire and burned what was mine.

Anger surges through my veins. That blue box was meant for me. And now a strange sensation tells me whatever was in it was extremely important. How dare he rob me of knowing what that was?

I wait for a long time, longer than I think I'll be able to, and then head toward the fire. The white device will be burned into a lump of plastic goo, but I want to see it with my own eyes. I wonder if maybe I shouldn't pick it up and storm into my parents' bedroom, demand to know what's going on.

As I near the fire, I realize it's diminished considerably. Only a few flames lick the cool night air, while the rest of the wood glitters red, fading quickly into ash. Coming to a stop where my dad had stood, I inspect the area. When I see it, I take a step back.

The device is nestled in a pile of ash and embers. It doesn't look melted or disfigured at all. I grab a stick and try to flick it out. After a few tries, it lands near my bare feet with a small thump.

Crouching down, I reach out a finger and poke the device. It's not hot. In fact, it's not even warm. I gather it into my hand and stand up. I've forgotten my surroundings. Forgotten that my dad could be inside watching me. All I can do is marvel that the device is untouched by the fire. I turn it over to inspect the other side and my mouth drops open.

The red light.

It's still blinking.

I don't think; I just run. Back to our house. Back to my window. Back to my room where I can listen to this message uninterrupted.

I pray it's still there. For some unknown reason, I can't imagine not hearing what the woman wanted to tell me. I need to know — *have* to know.

Inside my room, I close the window and crawl into my bed. I turn off the lamp and assume a sleeping position. If anyone comes in, they'll think I'm in never-never land. Hesitating only a moment, I slip the hearing aid–looking device into my ear. My fingers find the tiny, lit-up button, and I swallow a lump in my throat.

I push.

At first, there's nothing but dead air, but after a few moments, I hear the same clicking sound. *It's working,* I think. *It's still working.* The clicking turns to static, and I cover my ear with my palm so I can concentrate.

"If you're hearing this message, you are invited to be a Contender in the Brimstone Bleed. All Contenders must report within forty-eight hours to select their Pandora companions. If you do not appear within forty-eight hours, your invitation will be eliminated."

I'm so happy the message is still there, I can hardly contain myself. I sit up and glance around the room for a piece of paper, thinking maybe I should be writing this down. But before I can decide what to do, the woman continues.

"The Pandora Selection Process will take place at the Old Red Museum. The Pandora you choose is of the utmost importance, for it will be your only source of assistance throughout the race.

"The Brimstone Bleed will last three months and will take place across four ecosystems: desert, sea, mountains, jungle. The winning prize will be the Cure — a remedy for any illness, for any single person."

I cover my mouth, trying not to cry. A cure. A cure for Cody. I'd do anything for that. I listen as the woman pauses.

"There can be only one champion."

CHAPTER FOUR

I leap out of bed, heart pounding. This must be a joke. A prank. It can't be real.

Can it?

If this is a joke, it's the worst kind. Because I'd do anything to save Cody's life. And this device — this woman — just told me there's a way. Did my dad listen to this? My mom? Do they know what she said? If they did and they thought there was even a possibility of its being true, why would they ever try to destroy it?

I don't know. I don't care. This is about me now. The blue box was on my bed. I'm the one who received the invitation.

But this can't be real. Can it?

My heart aches as I consider my brother. What's crazy is — as absurd as this race sounds — I can't stop thinking, *What if it's true?* I want to believe it's real. I want to believe there can be an end to Cody's blood tests and MRIs. That my mom will learn to sleep again, and that my dad will stop quietly raging. I don't want to smell antiseptic anymore or meet another kindhearted nurse who's great at hitting a vein on the first try. *How about, instead, you leave Cody alone?*

How about, instead, you make him better?!

Driven by raw emotion, I weigh my choices. Ignore the woman's message and go back to bed.

Or.

Take the chance, the miniscule chance, that my dad knew there was something to hide.

The realization that I may be onto something slams into me. My parents tried to conceal this. My brother passed it off as a joke. But I'll be damned if I'm going to let anyone in my family stop me from helping Cody.

Assuming this is all real.

"It has to be," I whisper in the dark.

Anger coils in my stomach like a serpent. My dad didn't think I could do this. That's why he tried to destroy the device. But maybe he doesn't know his little girl as well as he'd like to believe. Because when it comes to doing something for my family, I'm not just his daughter.

I am strong.

I will be strong for my brother.

My hand grips the device I've removed from my ear. The woman said I needed to get to the Old Red Museum within forty-eight hours. How long has it been since I first saw the box? How long did it take to get to me?

Grabbing my old backpack from my closet, I think about what to pack: clothes, food, water, the device . . . maybe some nail polish. Just because I'm entering a race doesn't mean I don't want to look magically delicious. I throw on a black, long-sleeved T-shirt, jeans, and yellow ballet flats. Then I jam things into my bag as quickly as I can, knowing I want to leave before the sun rises and my parents wake up. The first thing I've got to do is figure out where the Old Red Museum is. We don't have an Internet connection here, but some place in town will. I'll be able to look it up there. At least I hope so.

A lump forms in my throat as I think about leaving. My parents will be fine, but what about Cody? Will he be okay while I'm away? I stare at the bag in my hands, then drop it onto the bed. I'm not even sure of what I'm doing when I leave my room and head to Cody's. I stop in his doorway and listen to his even breathing.

I'm glad he's asleep. There's no part of me that wants to banter with him right now, even if he does like it. I just want to tell him I love him. So I do.

"I love you, Cody," I say. And then, "Please don't die."

21

Tears sting my eyes as I run toward my bedroom. I want to keep this picture of him in my head, his sleeping chest rising and falling under the heavy blue blanket. This race may be a crock, and I may only be gone chasing a phantom for one day, but I'll still miss him.

When I'm almost back to my room, I hear a creaking sound. Crap. Someone's coming. I manage to wipe the tears from my eyes and throw my backpack into the closet, but I don't have time to jump into bed before my mom appears in the doorway.

She walks over to my lamp and flips the switch. Warm light washes across my room. She looks at me for a long time, so long that I wonder if she's forgotten who I am. Then she sits down on the bed.

"You're awake," she says. She doesn't sound surprised. It's more like a statement.

"Yeah," I say, not sure what else *to* say. I consider asking her about the device, if she knows what is on it. But I'm afraid of what she'll admit.

"I heard you moving around," she continues. I notice that she's holding something. Her hands work their way across it like she's smoothing it out. She sees me looking and holds it up. In the lamp's glow, I make out that it's a feather of green and blue and is attached to a thin leather string.

"This was my mother's," she says. "I don't remember much about her." My mom has rarely spoken of her own mother, and it's almost surprising remembering she had one. But of course she did. Her mother died when she was young. But that doesn't mean she didn't exist. Mom holds the feather up to her head and smiles. "I remember she used to wear this in her hair."

The smile slips from my mom's face. I sit down next to her on the bed. I'm about to tell her what I know, but she holds up a hand. At first, it's like she's stopping me from speaking, but then she moves to touch my hair. She pets the back of my head, and I can't help but close my eyes. For the second time tonight, I feel like I might lose it.

"You have your father's hair," she says. Then she looks me dead in the face. "But you have my eyes."

I don't know exactly what she's implying, but it's not that we share the same eye color.

Mom moves the hair off my neck and onto my shoulder. Then she lifts the feather to the bottom of my scalp. Tingles shoot across my shoulders as she ties the leather twine attached to the feather into my hair. When she's done, she lets my curls spill across my back.

"You look beautiful, Tella."

I stand and look in the mirror. The vibrant green-and-blue feather lies over my right shoulder, mixed with a bit of my thick, curly hair. I look at my big brown eyes and wonder what she sees in them. Besides fear.

My mom stands suddenly and crosses the room. She wraps me in a hug and holds on to me for several moments before letting go. I think she's going to confess something, but she only says, "Good night."

I lie down on the bed, pretending I'm going back to sleep. At the door, she stops and glances back. Her eyes flick toward my open closet, where my backpack lies exposed. Her gaze returns to me and her face twists. "Your mama loves you."

Then she's gone.

I choke on her final words, willing myself to crawl back out of bed and grab my backpack once again. Stuffing the clothes down, I decide not to get any food from the kitchen. I need to leave now, and I can buy some in town. But I do grab the stash of money I have from months of unused allowance. I'm sure I must have almost two hundred dollars at this point. Because I have no idea of what I'll need, I also throw in random things from my desk: pens, paper, scissors, tape. The last thing I pack is a photo of my family that's stuck in the edge of my mirror. I can't bear to go without taking a piece of them with me. That and my glittery purple nail polish.

When I leave, I go out the front door. There's something definitive about it. Like if I use it, then I'm making some sort of statement. Even if I have no idea what it is.

We don't have a garage, so my parents park in the driveway, on the opposite side of the house from my bedroom window. I round the corner and deliberate on which car to take. There's the sleek black 4Runner with the navigator and off-terrain tires that I always pestered my parents about driving when I first got my license, and there's Bob. Bob has been with us for a while, like, since I was born. And after almost two hundred thousand miles, the car is an utter embarrassment to the auto community.

I decide to take Bob. My parents will wake up to find their daughter gone. I'd hate to have them left with the crap car, too.

Grabbing the extra keys from the breaker box, I reason that if I gun it, I can make it to town in about twenty-five minutes. Not too bad. I hop inside the car, throw my bag in the passenger seat, and start the engine. As I'm rolling down the dirt driveway, I glance into the rearview mirror. The house is still cloaked in night, and all I can think is: *My family lives there.*

Driving away, I suddenly realize the house isn't so bad. I spent more time with my family in the last nine months here than I did in ten years living in Boston. And as it turns out, my people are pretty awesome.

I pull into the parking lot of the only diner in the area that's open twenty-four hours and glance at the dashboard clock: 3:37. I made it in twenty-three minutes. Not too shabby.

The door of the diner chimes when I walk through. Exactly two people turn in my direction: a trucker-looking dude with Popeye-sized forearms and his female friend, who finds her inebriation hysterical. They're a flawless match in this decrepit town of Montana.

A waitress in bad khakis appears from the back and strolls toward me, holding a discarded tray in her right hand. Watching her walk, I decide I could teach her a thing or two about sashaying.

"Can I help you?" she asks.

"Yeah." I pull myself up, trying to appear adultlike. "Do you guys have a computer I can use?"

The waitress cocks her head. "You buying something?"

"Um, yes?"

"You know how to tip?" she asks.

Oh, real classy. "Thirty percent. That's the standard, right?"

She smiles and nods. "You can use the one in the office. Just make it quick."

I go behind the counter and find the computer. After a little googling on their dial-up Internet connection, I find that the Old Red Museum is in a city called Lincoln. And, good Lord, it's seventeen hours away. What if I miss the selection process for the Pandora — whatever that is?

I print off directions and buy several sandwiches and bottles of water on my way out. I leave more than the 30 percent I promised the waitress, hoping it'll put a little sashay in her step.

Then I get on the road and drive like a demon toward Nebraska, wondering if I'm a naïve idiot for doing this.

Almost twenty hours later, I'm nearing the middle of the city. I'm exhausted after the drive, and by now the whole wide world feels surreal and disconnected. Everything is fast and slow at the same time. I follow the last of the directions until I see it — the Old Red Museum. The picture Google provided matches the enormous redbrick building, which looks more like a medieval castle than a museum. At almost midnight, the place looks particularly eerie.

I find a parking spot and walk up the short flight of stairs. Rubbing my arms to fight off a sudden chill, I stop in front of the enormous double doors.

What the hell am I supposed to do now?

There's no way this place is open this late. And by the time they do open, it'll probably *be* too late. It's probably too late as is. I hold my breath and tug on the door. It doesn't budge. I pull again and again, and scream when it still doesn't open.

I drove across the US of A, left my family without an explanation, and now I'm either too late or there was never anything here to begin with. Ef my life. Rearing back, I kick the door as hard as I can. Then I wrap both hands around the door handles and let out a noise like a wild banshee as I pull back.

The doors swing open.

I'm not sure whether to celebrate or freak out. I decide to do neither and slip inside. As I walk around the inside of the museum, listening to the sound of my footsteps echo off the walls, I imagine I am moments from death. It's sad, I think, that this is all it takes to break my sanity.

Two curling flights of stairs bow out from the first-floor lobby, and red and white tiles cover the floors. There are gilded picture frames everywhere. So many that I think the placement of the frames — and not their contents — is the real art. Everything, absolutely everything, smells like wax. I mosey up to an abandoned reception desk and leaf through the glossy pamphlets littering the surface. I hold one of the pamphlets up to my nose. Yep, wax.

I glance around, having no idea what to look for. Will there be a sign like at school registration? Students with last names starting with *A–K* this way?

On my left, I notice a long hallway dotted with doors on either side. Nothing looks particularly unusual. But when I glance to my right, I spot something. There's a door at the end of the corridor that has a sliver of light glowing beneath it. I'm sure it's just an administration office, one where someone forgot to flip the switch. But I've got nothing better to go on, so I head toward it.

I pause outside the door, wondering if I'm about to get busted for B and E. Then I turn the handle and find myself at the top of another winding staircase.

You've got to be kidding me. What is this — Dracula's bachelor pad?

I've watched a lot of scary movies, and I've learned nothing good is ever at the bottom of a winding staircase. Pulling in a breath and preparing myself to be eaten alive, I head down. My shoes are loud against the steps. So loud, I imagine they are intentionally trying to get me killed.

When I reach the final few stairs, I ready myself to look around the bend. My heart is racing, and I secretly pray the worst I encounter is an angry janitor with a wax addiction. I turn the bend — and my eyes nearly pop from my skull.

The enormous room is perfectly circular, dotted with candles to light the space. Surrounding the walls are rows and rows of dark, rich mahogany bookshelves. A large round table stands in the center of the red-and-white-tiled floor. The room is spectacular, but what it holds is so jarring, my ears ring.

Across every shelf, every spot on the table, every tile on the floor — are small sculptures of hands. And in a few of those hands — the ones still performing their duty — are eggs. There are only nine eggs left, it seems. For a moment, I imagine how amazing it would have been to see each hand holding an egg, but it's enough just to see these nine.

The eggs seem to dance in the candle flame, and as I move closer, I realize why. The surfaces of the eggs are almost iridescent, their colors changing depending on how you look at them. They are different sizes, too; some as big as a basketball, others as small as a peach.

I don't need the device in my pocket to tell me what my gut already knows.

This is the Pandora Selection Process.

CHAPTER FIVE

If this race isn't real, I think, *I give the prankster mad props for enthusiasm.*

The eggs look fragile, like if I touch them, they'll shatter into a million pieces. I remember when I was small and we would go to my grandmother's house — the grandmother I knew — there were always things I was allowed to touch and things I was not. These eggs would have definitely made the Do Not Touch List. I walk around the room slowly, bending down or reaching up on tiptoes to look closer at each one. They're like nothing I've ever seen before, and it feels almost like I've stepped onto the set of a sci-fi flick. I don't understand how these things got here. Or how this is even happening.

Some eggs seem brighter than the rest, while others seem a bit sturdier. I'm not sure how I'm supposed to pick, what characteristics I should look for, or how I'm supposed to announce my decision.

As I'm about to touch an egg, a thought occurs to me. What if the first one I touch defines my choice? Yes, this whole thing may still turn out to be a hoax, but it sure as hell doesn't seem that way, and I want to be careful in case it's not. I yank my hand back and bite down on my fist. Decision making has never been my strong suit.

I lean in close to a rather large egg, my breath causing the colors to swirl and change. It's so beautiful, and isn't it always more fun to have the bigger present at Christmas? A decision must be made, and if I let myself contemplate what's inside each egg any longer, I'll never make one.

"Eeny, meeny, miny . . ." I point to the large egg in front of me. "Moe."

My hands are almost on it when I hear a thundering on the

stairs behind me. I spin around and listen. It sounds like hail during a bad storm. And it's getting louder, and closer. Moments later, people of all ages spill into the room in a frenzy. They race toward the eggs, their eyes wide and their hands outstretched. Unlike me, they don't hesitate. They snatch the first eggs they come to and race back up the stairs.

My face burns when I realize what's happening. They're taking all the eggs. There won't be enough for everyone. I can't wait any longer.

Someone has already grabbed the egg I'd intended to take, so I dash toward another one. A man in his midtwenties cuts me off and swipes the egg in one graceful movement. Then he tucks it under his arm like a football and makes for the stairs.

Three more people rush toward two eggs. They claw and kick and scream until two girls, no older than thirteen, slip away from a portly man and sprint toward the stairs. I see an egg toward the room's entrance and hurry toward it, but I'm not aggressive enough, and when it comes down to me and another girl with wild eyes and big shoulders, I falter. She sneers at me and grabs the egg. Then she's gone, flying up the stairs two at a time.

Everything has happened in a matter of seconds. As I look around the room, I realize with a bolt of fear that there's only one egg left. I'm closest to it, and the girl closest to me realizes that. She narrows her eyes in my direction and darts toward the egg. But I'm faster. The people behind us don't move, or at least I don't hear them move. It's like they know it's too late. That it's between me and this girl, and they might as well pack it in.

I'm so close to the egg that a smile curls my lips. I'm going to get there first. Then it's just a matter of getting past her and back up the stairs. I reach out to grab the softball-sized egg, and then I feel it — a shooting pain ripping across my scalp.

The chick has ahold of my hair and she's pulling me down,

down. I crash to the floor and she leaps over my body. Instantly, I reach for her legs. If I have to fight her on the ground, I will, because suddenly I remember Cody the way he was before I left, the steady rise and fall of his chest.

The girl anticipates my grabbing for her, so she makes a hard left, races around the circular table, and it's over. She's gone. At some point during the mad dash, I realized with overwhelming certainty that this race is real. That the Brimstone Bleed is *real*. And now I try to swallow that I've already lost.

I beat my fist against the ground and look up. Three people remain in the room with me. They looked equally dazed, searching for an egg that isn't there. One of them hangs his head and ascends the stairs slowly. Like me, he seems petrified to return home and admit failure.

The back of my head aches, and when I reach around and touch the throbbing spot, I feel something wet and sticky. Though I know I'll be sick if I look, I almost want to. Like seeing my own injury will be partial punishment for failing my brother.

I look at my hand. Sure enough, my fingers are coated in blood. It's bright red, which I think is good. Dark blood means it's coming from somewhere deep. I glance up to — what? — show the two people left my wound?

But when I look up, there is only one person.

My heart stops.

The guy looking down at me is very tall, or maybe he just seems so because I'm still on the ground. He appears to be about my age, though the broad width of his shoulders tells me he may actually be a couple of years older. His eyes are blue. Not in the way that makes me buckle at the knees and start naming our children, but the kind of blue that makes my breath catch. A cold, hard blue that looks more like a statement than a color — one that says, "Back the fuck off."

His hair is so dark, it looks like wet ink, and is spiked around his scalp in soft tufts. He has a strong jawline, and right now that jaw is clenched so tightly, I'm afraid this guy is about to kick me when I'm down.

"They're all gone," I whisper. I hadn't thought to say anything, but it just slips out.

He narrows those chilling blue eyes at me, and in an instant, they flick toward the floor near one of the bookcases. He looks back at me, and I wonder if maybe, even though he looks a little like a serial killer, he's going to help me up.

His gaze lands on my hair, on the feather woven into it. Then he turns and walks toward the stairs, carrying a colossal egg under his arm. I contemplate fighting him for it; it's easily the biggest egg I've seen tonight. Then I realize it's pointless. I'm dizzy from hitting my head, and this guy looks like he works out for a living. But I think about the way his eyes flicked toward the bookcase. It makes me wonder . . .

Treading softly, I move toward where he had looked. But there's nothing there. I grab on to the top of the bookcase, as far as I can reach anyway, and step up. Then I climb the shelves like they're a ladder until I can see over the top. There's nothing there and — when I look around the room from this elevated height — I don't see anything anywhere else, either.

I crawl down the shelves until I'm standing on the floor again. Then I get onto my hands and knees. When I lay my face against the cool tile and peer under the bookcase, I have to bite my lip to keep from whooping.

I see an egg.

Pressing myself flatter against the floor, I stretch my arm out. I hold my breath as I retrieve it, afraid if I fill my lungs, I'll drop my prize. Once the egg is safely out, I study it closely. It's the size of a watermelon, which I guess is okay, but the coloring is all wrong.

It's not like the others, with the remarkable sheen that changes when you turn them over in your hands. This one is dull, and when I hold it up, I see there's a fracture the length of my finger running across the bottom.

It must have dropped onto the floor and rolled beneath the bookcase. Looking at it, I wonder if whatever's inside is still alive. My guess is no, but I have no other choice than to hope it is. I stand up, pull out my shirt, and lay the egg in like my shirt's a nest.

Then I smile. This egg is ugly, and if I'm not mistaken, it's got a little stank rolling off it. But it's mine. And I'm going to take care of what's inside.

I wrap both arms around the bottom of my egg and hurry up the stairs, out the front doors, and into Bob. Slamming the car door, I glance around. I've got to find a safe place for this thing. I grab my bag from the back and pull out anything sharp. When all that's left is soft clothing, I nestle my egg inside, take one last look at it, then zip the bag back up.

Opening the glove compartment, I start to toss in all the remaining items from my bag. When I get to the device, I notice the red light is blinking. My shoulders tense. Will it be the same message as before? Or will there be new information that helps me find the race? I hadn't even stopped long enough to wonder what I was supposed to do now that I had this freaky egg in my possession.

I slip the device into my ear, close my eyes, and push the button. Silence — clicking — static.

"*Congratulations. You have chosen Pandora Companion KD-8. Each Pandora is unique in its design, and your Pandora is no exception. Please stay tuned for a message from the Creator of KD-8.*"

She knows. She knows which egg I took. Opening my eyes, I place a hand on my bag, imagining the egg safe inside. My knees bounce as I anticipate hearing someone new on the device. I don't have to wait long.

"Hello?" an older male voice says. "Hello? Okay. I'm Creator Collins, and I generated Pandora KD-8. I cannot tell you much about my — er, our — Pandora, as there are strict rules about such things." The man pauses, as if he's afraid to say too much. "But I can tell you I've spent my entire professional life conceptualizing KD-8's capabilities, and I hope you find them useful inside the Brimstone Bleed. While you must discover KD-8's abilities for yourself, please know I have the utmost faith in his ability to reveal his strengths when the time is right. Good luck to you, Contender. And . . ." The man hesitates again. "And I hope you care for KD-8 as I have."

My mind buzzes thinking about the man who created my Pandora — Creator Collins. He sounds like an okay guy. His voice is that of a man who owns too many sweaters. I like the way he seems to care about KD-8. It makes me think there might be something special about my egg. I wonder if he made other Pandoras, or if it's only one Creator per Pandora. Something about the way he hoped I would care for KD-8 the way he did makes me think it's a one-to-one situation. And who are these Creators anyway? I instantly picture mad scientists with big white hair and plastic goggles. Insert flash of lightning.

I keep listening, and within seconds, the woman whose voice I've already memorized returns. "Please report to Lincoln Station and take the train to Valden. You have one hour."

The deadlines thing is already getting old. I'm a girl who doesn't like to be rushed. But apparently that's a big thing in this race. I'm quickly learning that I'll have to adjust, be someone who rolls with the punches.

Pulling Bob's visor down, I check myself out in the mirror. Mascara runs down my cheeks, and heavy bags droop beneath my eyes. My hair is everywhere, but when I touch a hand to the back of my head, I don't find any more blood. Win.

It almost pains me to see myself this way. Even living where no one could judge me besides my family, I prided myself on looking fabulous. And now I look like the bride of Frankenstein. Running my fingers through my hair, I think about how I should be racing toward Lincoln Station. But the compulsion to repair my face is too strong.

I grab my makeup bag — the one I never leave home without — and fix what I can. What I really need is twelve hours of beauty rest and a Swedish massage, but something tells me that ain't happening. My hair also needs way more than I can do from inside a clunky car. And that's when I remember Cody on Christmas.

My curly hair has a will of its own, and while I sleep, that will grows and grows so that when I wake up, I resemble a wild animal. Cody refers to my hair as a lion's mane. And last Christmas — when he'd only been sick a few months — he constructed an actual mane from faux hair and a headband. Then he wrapped it as a gift from me to him. When he opened it, he acted all blessed to receive this gift I hadn't given him and read the card (which he wrote) aloud. "Dear Cody, I want nothing more on this Christmas morn than for you to join my pride. Roar." At *roar*, he clawed the air.

At the time, I hated him for it. But thinking back on how much time he put into being an ass, I can't help but laugh. Because I know now, if he really hated me, he wouldn't have bothered.

I pull my hair in front of my face and study it up close. It's the hair my father gave me; the hair my mom thinks is beautiful. I've always had a love-hate relationship with it. But some girl yanked it to bring me down tonight. And now that I know the race is real, I can't let anything stand in the way of me winning. My brother's life — *Cody's* life — depends on it.

Before I can stop myself, I grab the scissors from the glove compartment and start slashing. I cut a huge chunk of hair from the base of my neck and work my way up until it's almost all gone. Tossing the scissors onto the seat next to me, I run a hand over my head. Crap.

When I look back into the mirror, I grow cold. It's gone. My hair is gone. I mean, all over, there are small pieces of hair curled close to my head — but the length, the heaviness have vanished. I almost cry looking at myself. Almost. I've always hated my hair, but now I don't even look like me. My brown eyes — my mother's eyes — look bigger, and my lips fuller. It's like now that the hair is gone, everything else can breathe. That's nice, I guess. But it isn't all good news. My hair has always pulled attention away from the thing I hate most. My freckles.

Even my brother has never made fun of the freckles that cross my nose and stretch out along my upper cheeks. He knows that I — like everyone else — have a breaking point. And that if he brought them up, I would end him.

Now it's like they're mini-cheerleaders, picking up megaphones and refusing to be ignored. I press my lips together in irritation, but my face softens when I see my feather. I was careful not to cut it when I hacked my hair off.

I lean my head back and reinspect my reflection, try to see things in a new light. With curls trimmed close to my head and a roguish green-and-blue feather dangling over my right shoulder, I decide I just might seem like someone who would enter a daring race — and win.

CHAPTER SIX

Lincoln Station, I discover, accommodates both trains and buses. I have no idea which I'll be taking, but I know I'm going to Valden. I decide I'll just tell the person at the ticket window where I'm headed and let them figure it out.

The station is surprisingly busy for this late at night, or early in the morning, or whatever you call it. The floor is covered in small white tiles, and overhead, there are vast skylights that would probably be pretty awesome during the day. Big round benches dot the floors for people to lounge on, and because the ceiling is high and the floor is tile, every little sound morphs into something like an elephant stampede.

Eventually, I stumble upon the check-in area. It consists of a skittish guy in his midthirties standing behind a large, plasticky counter. He's wearing a navy suit with a crisp white dress shirt. His tie is yellow, which pleases me to no end. The guy spots me approaching and runs a hand over his canary-yellow tie. Then he does it again. And again. It's either his first day on the job, or my being a girl makes him extremely uncomfortable.

"Hi," I say to the nervous guy. "I need to go to Valden." No point in beating around the proverbial bush.

My request pushes Yellow Tie Man over the edge. His eyes get enormous and he actually starts to sweat. "Valden?" he croaks.

"Yeah, Valden. I'd like to go there." I lay my allowance on the counter as proof of my seriousness.

The guy looks around like a SWAT team is about to bust up this convo and pushes my money back toward me. "Are you *sure* you want to go to Valden?"

"Uh, yeah. I'm sure." But now the guy's glistening brow has become a *dripping* glistening brow, and I'm suddenly not sure at all. Maybe Valden *isn't* somewhere I want to go. Maybe it's in the center of a volcano, and that's something I'd like no part of. "Can you remind me what state Valden is in?"

The yellow tie trembles, and so does the man behind the shoddy counter. "It's not a place. It's just a word to let me know —" He stops to wipe his forehead, and I feel my own brow prick with sweat. This explanation does not make me feel better about things.

Eyeing my backpack, he slides a ticket across the counter. I expect it to be laced with acid that'll burn my skin off, but as I take it, I realize my fingers will survive. And so will my allowance, since this dude is apparently giving me a free ride. I shove the cash back in my pocket.

"Where do I go?" I try to sound more confident than I am. Which is not at all.

"You'll take train 301. Down that way." He points over his shoulder to the right. Then he backs up, like he can't wait to get rid of me. As I start to head in the direction he indicated, he throws his hands over his face. "Oh my gawd. I almost forgot. Why do I keep forgetting?" His hands fall. He searches for something under the table, looks around again, and reaches across the counter. "Put this on your shirt."

It's a small gold serpent pin, and it's fairly heavy. When I attach it over my heart, it tugs the cloth of my long-sleeved shirt down, and the snake glares up at me with a glittering green eye.

"It will identify you," he says.

I had figured as much, but it relieves me to hear him confirm my suspicion. As if my figuring out this one thing is a sign from the universe I'll be okay. "Thanks," I say. "Nice tie."

The guy smiles, but I'm not sure I've made his day any better. I want to tell him he didn't exactly soothe my nerves, either, but he clearly wants nothing more to do with me, so I yank my backpack straps tighter and head toward the platforms.

To my astonishment, I get myself onto the appropriate train without killing myself, though I'll admit it's far harder to fall onto the tracks than I'd originally thought. A woman wearing way too much rose-scented perfume shows me to my seat, which turns out to be in a sleeper car. When I first get inside the tiny room with a mini window and cute bunk beds on both sides, I can't help but do my happy dance. Then I wonder exactly how long I'll be on this train and why I'll even need a place to sleep. The question doesn't bode well for my sanity. I mean, trains are cool and all. But not when a small white device has told you to board one to a city that doesn't exist.

I hear a sharp snap and turn around. A girl my age pushes into the room, acting very much like she owns this sleeper car and all the contents in it — including myself. She has short dark hair, with hard bangs cut razor straight across her forehead. Her eyes dart around, looking everywhere but at me. Seconds later, another girl walks into the room. This one looks a bit younger and a lot less hostile. She's got long, wavy hair and big blue eyes, and she stares right at me.

"Hi," Blue Eyes squeaks.

"Hey," I say with a nod. Then I notice a glint on her blouse. It's a serpent pin — the same as mine. I glance at the aggressive girl and notice she has one, too. They're each carrying a bag, and I suddenly realize they're also packing Pandora eggs.

They're Contenders, I think with relief. *I'm not alone.* Then I remember they're my competition. I wonder how these girls got invitations, and if they also have someone they're trying to save. I wonder how any of us were chosen to compete in the race. Did whoever's running this show choose only contestants with sick family members? Do they all have the same thing?

These thoughts make my head spin. Regardless, there's no reason not to be polite to these girls, no matter why they're here. We're all going through this together.

"I'm Tella," I say to Blue Eyes.

The girl looks at me with such relief that my heart aches. She opens her mouth to respond, but stops when someone new comes through the door.

The first thing I see is a shock of color. The woman's dress is so bright and so devastatingly green that I almost forget my name. It curves around every bit of her body and ends at the knee. Her bright blond hair is pulled back into a tight twist, and her lips are painted a flashy shade of red. In her left hand is a gold clutch. She's my kind of girl — a fashion guru, if you will — and I feel underdressed and underkempt in comparison. I wonder where she found her shoes.

"Please, sit." The woman waves a small hand toward the bunk beds. Her voice is perfectly even, perfectly calm. I wonder if anyone has ever told her no. My guess is if they did, they quickly changed their minds.

Blue Eyes sits on a lower bunk and I sit across from her on the other. Aggressive Girl jumps onto the top bunk above me, her legs dangling in my line of vision. I press my lips together in annoyance and move over so I can see.

The woman closes the door behind her and locks it. Never a good sign. She reaches into her gold clutch and pulls out three blue boxes, exactly like the one I found on my bed but much smaller; so small, I wonder what could possibly be inside. The woman hands a blue box to each of us. When she gets to me, her fingers brush mine. My muscles tighten, but she only smiles. I realize the woman must work for this . . . race. I eye her closely, looking for clues that'll help me understand what I've gotten myself into — that'll help me win.

"Open them," she says.

I lift the lid of my blue box. There's no miniature pillow this time — only a single green pill. I remove it from the box and lay it in my palm. It's the kind of pill that looks like it has liquid inside. It's actually quite beautiful, and I find the desire to take it compulsive.

"Swallow the pill immediately. If you do not, you will be disqualified." With that, she unlocks the door and leaves.

I glance at Blue Eyes and wonder if she can hear the hammering of my heart. It pounds so hard against my chest, I imagine I might be having a heart attack. How did this happen? How did I go from homeschool and teasing Cody and Sunday Fundays to this? *I could back out,* I think. *I could just throw up my hands now and decide this is all too friggin' psychotic.*

But then I think of Cody. I know he would do this for me. He wouldn't even hesitate. Despite all his irritating qualities, I've always thought of him as courageous.

"Damn Pharmies," the girl above me says. "Bottoms up."

Blue Eyes gasps. Then she looks at me. "She took it."

I shrug, trying to act like it's all cool even though I'm about to pass the hell out. Glancing down at the green pill, I make a decision. I will not abandon my brother. I pop the pill into my mouth and swallow. It goes down easily, but I still reach for a water bottle in my bag. I take a few pulls, then hand it to Blue Eyes.

"Here, it'll help."

She takes the water with a shaking hand. When she looks at me, the pill close to her lips, I nod. I don't know why I'm helping her. I probably shouldn't. There's no telling what we're taking. I could be helping her sign a death sentence, for all I know.

The thought sends shivers down my body. I tremble so hard, I have to lie down. Turning my head on the overstuffed pillow, I watch Blue Eyes swallow the pill and then two gulps of water. She lies down on her bunk, keeping her eyes locked on me the entire time.

I look above me and wonder what Aggressive Girl is doing. Her legs have disappeared from over the side of the bed. "What did you mean?" I ask, tapping the bottom of her bunk.

"About what?" Aggressive Girl says, though her voice doesn't sound quite so aggressive anymore. It sounds more . . . drained.

"You said something about Pharmies," I say. "What is that?"

"Not what — *who*," she answers, though I can hardly understand her. It sounds like she's slurring her words.

I move to sit up, to drill her with questions since she seems to know what's going on. But as soon as I do, the room spins. I drop back down onto the bed and glance over at Blue Eyes. She's looking at me, her face a mask of fear.

"Who are the Pharmies?" I ask aloud. My voice sounds strange. I'm not sure if I'm talking strangely, or hearing differently.

The girl above me doesn't respond, and slowly, I begin to sink. Blue Eyes and I hold each other's gaze for several seconds, like if we can just keep eye contact, we'll be okay. But then her lids flutter closed and open. Once. Twice. Her cheek presses deeper into the pillow. She doesn't open her eyes again.

My own eyelids feel like they're weighted. *It's just a sleeping pill,* I assure myself. *That's all we took.* Since I haven't slept in I don't know how long, I close my eyes for just a moment. I fully intend to reopen them, but once they're closed, it feels so good.

"Can anyone hear me?" I ask, my eyes still shut. My voice sounds like it's coming from the other side of a wall. Though my arms feel heavy, I manage to tug my backpack onto my chest. I wrap my arms around it, praying my egg is safe inside. When my feather falls over my neck — tickling my skin — it reminds me of my mother.

I pull her face into my mind, and I let go.

CHAPTER SEVEN

The first thing I become aware of is the sound. It's a low rumbling and seems to be coming from beneath me.

I open my eyes and immediately close them again. Everything in my body screams for more sleep. I almost give in to the temptation but know I shouldn't. There's something I'm forgetting. I force my eyes back open and this time, I take in my surroundings. Or at least I *try* to take in my surroundings. There's hardly any light to see, and a slow panic twists in my stomach.

Where am I?

Pushing myself up from the fetal position, I feel smooth wood beneath my hands. I throw my arms out and find four walls. They're close, way too close. My throat tightens when I begin to understand.

I'm in a box.

I go from mild anxiety to full-fledged mania in a matter of seconds. Pounding my fists against the boards, I scream. I swallowed the pill. I'm in a box. How stupid could I have been? I left without telling my family where I was going, got on a train to a city that doesn't exist, and swallowed a foreign object. Oh yeah, and I also picked up a rotting egg along the way.

My egg.

I feel along the bottom of the box and my fingers touch a corduroy bag that's not my backpack. Stuffing my hand in, I sigh with relief when I find my smooth egg tucked safely inside. I pull the bag over my crossed legs and into my lap and wrap my arms around it.

"It's okay. We're okay," I say. I'm not sure who I'm talking to, but I guess it's my egg. I gently lift it out of the bag and lay it in my lap. "Everything's going to be okay." I stroke the outside of the shell and glance around. The rumbling sound outside is steady. It'd almost be soothing if I weren't in a friggin' box.

I consider screaming until someone lets me out, but I'm afraid I'll lose my mind if I do. I'm also concerned with how long I've been in this thing and how much air is left. I don't see any air holes, and I know screaming will cause me to use what little air there is quicker. Thanks, horror movies.

I try to steady my breathing and calm my thoughts. It's not working. I rub my hands over my egg and think that this would be a really good time for this thing to hatch and help a sister out.

I lean over as best I can and whisper, "Please come out."

Nothing happens.

Rubbing the fabric over my knees, I suddenly realize my jeans don't feel right. I grab at my legs and stomach. These aren't my clothes. Oh my God. Someone changed my clothes while I was asleep.

My first thought is: *What creepazoid takes someone's clothes off while they're sleeping?* The second is what undies I'm wearing — whether it's an old skeezy pair or my good Victoria's Secret stuff. I'm not proud of this last thought.

My box suddenly jerks and a loud hissing sound pierces the air. I've heard the sound somewhere; I just can't quite place it. For several minutes, nothing happens. I continue stroking the egg, reassuring whatever's inside that everything's going to be okay. Even though I'm not at all sure it is.

When my box jerks again, I scream for the second time. My hands fly out and I push against the walls beside me. I close my eyes and breathe through my nose. Then the box, and me, and my egg start swinging. It's not much, but the sensation is undeniable.

"It's okay, it's okay, it's okay." I repeat it like a mantra as the box continues to sway side to side.

The box jolts to a stop. I feel like something's going to happen, so I tuck my egg back into the new bag. Then I look around, waiting. The front of my box slides open and light blinds me. I blink several times, my arms shading my face. When I lower them, I see dozens of people wearing what look like brown scrubs and tan boots, all standing in a forest-like area. Looking down, I realize I'm wearing the same thing. With the light, I'm able to look around the box. My backpack is gone. I figured it was, but now I know for sure. The food, the water, the cash . . . the photo of my family. Gone.

Afraid I'll be stuck forever inside this box, I grab the corduroy bag and scramble outside. When I turn around, I gasp. Two enormous semitrucks are parked several yards away. A hundred or more boxes are stacked on the semis, and someone operating a crane is lifting each one off the bed and placing it on the ground. The semis' and crane's windows are tinted, so I can't see who's inside, but I do spot two men opening each box that the crane sets down. They're wearing green, collared shirts and jeans, and they look like they could live in a suburb outside of Boston. One man is tall and lanky, with thinning hair and enormous ears. The other looks almost pregnant with his protruding belly and twiglike extremities.

I turn in a circle and watch as people of all ages, races, and genders crawl out of the boxes. There's an older woman with short blond hair, who folds her arms across her chest and scowls, and a girl with a determined expression, who can't be older than twelve. I spot a man who looks like he's never seen the inside of a gym and young woman who could pass for a physical trainer. Everywhere I look, people. These are the Contenders — I realize. But they're treating us like livestock.

"Crazy, huh?"

I spin around and see a man twice my age with dark skin and enormous eyebrows.

"What's going on?" I ask him. I don't wonder why he's speaking to me; I just want my questions answered.

"You don't know?" he asks.

"No. You do?"

He makes a face like he's sympathetic. "I don't blame your parents for trying to hide this. I would have done the same for mine."

I'm guessing he means his own children, but all I can think about is what he's implying. That my parents knew about this and didn't tell me. I decide that's impossible. They wouldn't do that to me; they certainly wouldn't do that to Cody. Maybe they knew something might happen. Why else would my dad try to burn the device? But they couldn't have known . . . everything.

I notice the man's brown shirt has the gold serpent embroidered onto the pocket. When I glance down, I realize mine has the same.

"Where are we?" I ask him.

He waves an arm behind him. "The starting line."

I really study the area for the first time. Trees tower overhead, growing so close together that their leaves create a thick canopy. When the two men let me out of my box (did I really just say that?), there seemed to be so much light. But now it doesn't seem that way at all. Though there is enough light to see, everything is cast in shadows. A heavy fog lounges above the trees, not helping matters. Even the air feels different, like oxygen is more abundant here, but also somehow thicker.

The thing that shocks me most is the plants. They are everywhere, in every shape and color imaginable. I have trouble finding a spot that isn't covered by long, looping vines or fat palm leaves. The forest is entirely carpeted in green — a canvas of life. I breathe in the rich scent of earth and vegetation. The woman's voice inside the white device said we'd compete across four ecosystems. Remembering this, I suddenly realize this is no mere forest — it's a jungle.

"We're in a jungle," I say to the man with the eyebrows. But he's already gone.

I turn in a circle and count more than a hundred people in brown scrubs. Some have small tan bags, like mine. Others have enormous bags, and some have none at all. The ones with no bags carry eggs in their arms. I glance down at my own bag. Then I hook the single strap over my head and hang it over one shoulder. Sticking a hand into it, I rub the egg and try very hard not to feel claustrophobic among these trees. Many of the people around me seem okay with what's happening. Not me. Every muscle in my body aches for home. Since the race hasn't even started, I feel this doesn't bode well for my competitive edge.

I hear a hissing sound that I recognize from inside the box. Spinning around, I realize it's a semi's brakes clicking off. The two men are climbing inside the crane. All the boxes have been removed from the beds of the two semis, and now the vehicles and monster crane are rolling away from us — going somewhere that isn't here. I have to fight the impulse to race after them, begging for a ticket home. I'm not cut out for this, I realize. I should be in my lavender-painted room, giving myself a milk-and-avocado facial, wrestling my hair into a messy but fashionable updo. My hair, which is completely gone now.

The two semis pull away and follow the crane at a snail's pace. They're leaving us here. What if this is all a sick experiment in which someone somewhere gets off on ripping people away from their homes and dropping them in precarious situations with no hope of survival? How do I know the Cure is real? And is everyone else here racing for the same thing? We're all totally susceptible, the perfect targets to scam. Just dangle a cure no one knows anything about and say, "Run, monkey, run!"

The woman from the device didn't begin to answer the questions I have, and I'm guessing no other Contender knows much about this race, either. Yet here we all are.

I have to leave this place. Now.

I push my way past a blur of faces and race toward the retreating trucks.

"Wait," I yell. "Wait!" The Contenders turn and watch me with visible disgust, but I don't care. I can't be left out here with nothing to go on besides *the winning prize will be the Cure.*

I'm only a few yards away from the semi in the back when a commotion ripples across the Contenders. They're all moving, shifting their weight, and searching their bags. When I spot a handful of people near me place white devices in their ears, I realize what's happening.

I stop running and gasp. It isn't hard; it's like the air wants nothing more than to fill my lungs. This is the jungle, and apparently its goal is to make everything *grow*. I fumble in my bag, pushing my egg to the side, until I feel the smooth plastic. Pulling my device out, I see the light is blinking. It taunts me to make a decision: keep chasing down my only way out of this hellhole, or stop and listen.

Blink.

Blink.

Blink.

Around me, more than one hundred people raise their arms and press the buttons. I wonder what the message is. Turning back to the trucks, I realize they're moving too quickly. I could catch up, but I'd have to run and I'd have to run *now*.

As the trucks pull farther and farther away, noises from the jungle amplify. I turn and face the lush, green landscape. In the mid-day heat, I make out birds calling to one another, and a long, sharp, whooping sound. I can hear the foliage rubbing together, even though there's not a trace of wind. A short, low *roo-mp, roo-mp* sound repeats over and over, and somehow, while listening to all the different melodies, a small smile parts my face. This place . . . it's miraculous.

Cody would love it.

In a daze, I place the white device into my ear.

I push the red blinking button. When the woman speaks, she sounds almost excited. It's eerie to hear her normally robotic voice so animated.

"We'll wait a few more seconds while everyone tunes in," she says.

I wonder how long she's been saying this, and how she could possibly know whether everyone is tuned in. There must be some sort of tracking capability built into the device. Glancing over my shoulder, I note that I can see still the trucks. I could still make it out.

"All right, I think that's quite long enough."

Was that a few seconds? I need her to wait. I need more time to decide. My pulse quickens and sweat beads across my arms.

"If you are hearing this message, then you have successfully completed the Pandora Selection Process. It also means you are now at the official starting line."

Around me, Contenders whoop with excitement. Seriously? They're about to plunge into a wild jungle, and *that* brings them happiness? Once again, I realize how out of my league I am. I don't even have a change of clothes, for crying out loud.

"As you may have realized, you are on the outskirts of a rain forest. This will be the jungle part of the course. You will have two weeks to arrive at the jungle's base camp. You will find this base camp by following the path of blue flags."

Contestants glance around, immediately looking for the first blue flag. As for me, I'm watching the taillights of the semi and having a massive coronary.

"If you are the first to encounter a blue flag, you may remove it, but you may not remove the stake it is attached to. Doing so will result in immediate disqualification."

I wonder why anyone would want to remove the flag to begin with. No one else seems concerned by this.

"While the Cure will be awarded to a single winner at the end of the last ecosystem, we will bestow a smaller prize for each leg of the race. The prize for the jungle portion will be monetary." The woman pauses dramatically. *"I'd like to officially welcome you to the Brimstone Bleed. May the bravest Contender win."*

That's it? That's all she's going to say? Because it seriously sounds like she's wrapping up. So why aren't I running after the trucks? Why am I not chasing after my only way out of this jungle like my life depends on it? I know the answer — though I wish I didn't. Cody would do this for me. I am his only hope. I have to believe his cure exists. My only other option is to return home and watch my brother die. If I could even get back home.

I glance around frantically, looking for someone to tell me what to do. The Contenders have formed a long line, the kind you see at the start of a marathon. A few yards down from where I stand — I see him. My throat tightens when I realize his cold blue eyes are locked on me. It's the guy from the Pandora Selection Process. The serial killer–looking dude who I thought was going to kidney punch me. He glares in my direction like he might take this opportunity to finish what he never started. I raise my hand in a small wave, hoping it says something like: *See? Look how friendly I am!*

He lifts his own enormous hand. For a moment, I brighten. I think maybe that — even though it looks like he hates every fiber of my being — he's going to wave back. But he doesn't. He holds up two fingers — his pointer and his middle — places them under his eyes, and then points in front of us.

Oh no he didn't. I think he basically just told me to pay attention. I'm still processing this when the woman's voice rings in my ear.

"Go!"

CHAPTER EIGHT

It sounds like a stampede.

The Contenders run fast and hard, and the sound makes me feel drunk with energy. If I don't start running, I'll be trampled. Someone shoves me from behind and I almost fall. I don't need another push.

I run.

I forget every fear I've held on to, and I run.

Breath rushes in and out of my lungs and my legs burn beneath me. I have no idea where I'm headed, and I'm sure no one else does, either. Somewhere out here is a blue flag, and I need to find it. The woman said the flags would lead to base camp and that we have two weeks to get there. Base camp sounds good, like it might have hot food and soft beds. So I run toward what I imagine could be the direction — straight ahead.

It seems many others have the same idea. Some race beside me, but most race before me. I don't worry about catching up. Not yet. I just keep a hand on my satchel, ensuring the egg isn't hurt by slapping against my thigh. It helps if I imagine I'm running for us both. If I imagine that right now I am my Pandora's protector and maybe if I do well, someday soon the tables will turn.

After several minutes, Contenders start to slow. I begin to feel my first shock of confidence as I pass one person after another. No one would ever accuse me of being an athlete. I was always the girl who'd rather cheer from the sidelines than participate in something that'd make her sweat. I'm not a softball star or a volleyball champion or someone who knows her way around a basketball court.

But I can run like the wind.

I use every bit of speed I have to gain the only edge I may ever get. It isn't long before there are only a few people left in front of me. I push myself harder, flattening my hands and slicing the air.

I pass a few more people, leaping over dead logs and the widest array of plants I've ever seen. Large leaves brush against my ankles and smaller ones kiss my cheeks. I wonder what creatures call this jungle home and how many of them rest beneath the same plants I'm stepping on. There are so many things to be afraid of in this jungle, but as I run, my blood pumping hard in my veins — I feel no fear.

I run for what feels like two hours before slowing, even though I know it can only have been minutes. Sweat pours down my face and drips onto my brown scrubs, leaving dark starbursts in their wake. Gross. I hope there's laundry at whatever base camp we're supposed to find. I throw my hands behind my head and try to walk off the stitch in my side. I'm not sure whether this actually helps, but I've seen runners do it, so what the hey.

When I glance around, I see only two Contenders. They're fairly far away from where I've paused. For a moment, I'm thrilled. I left most of them behind, and for the first time, I feel like I may actually have a chance. I may be small, but I'm fast. And this is a race, after all. But when they both disappear into the foliage, a bolt of panic shoots up my legs.

I'm alone.

I think about chasing after the last person I saw. There's no reason we can't travel together for two weeks, then run for the finish line at the last minute, right? I run my hands over my freshly shorn hair and drop down onto my knees. Even if one of the other Contenders agrees to search for base camp with me, could I even find a fellow Contender at this point? Best bet is I'll race after them and end up getting myself lost. I decide to stay put but reason that if I see another Contender soon, I'll run my tag team idea across them. Deal? Deal.

Oh Jesus. I'm already talking to myself. Or thinking to myself as if there are two of me. Is that the same thing? I'm not sure. But I do know I've been alone for two minutes and I'm already losing my shit.

I slide from my knees onto my butt and nestle the egg into my lap. I've got to think. If I were a base camp, where would I be? I can only imagine that we're on one side of this jungle, and it's on the other. So we'd have to cross through the jungle in order to get there. That's exactly what'd they want. To drag the Contenders through the worst of the jungle — the middle.

I don't know who "they" are, but I feel like I'm onto something. If the camp is on the other side of the jungle, then I can just as easily get there by going *around* the jungle as I can by going through it. The trek may be longer, but I won't encounter as many obstacles staying on the perimeter. At least, I think. No, that sounds right. It does.

Hot damn! I have a plan!

Wiping the sweat from my brow, I stand up. Holy mother of God, it's hot up in here. It's not a sweltering heat. In fact, it's probably less than ninety degrees. But it feels like a *wet* heat, the kind that makes you perspire just by breathing. None of that matters, though, because I have an idea on how to get to base camp that doesn't involve getting killed. Every few minutes, I have to laugh at what I'm planning. Because I used to sit on our blue-and-yellow, floral couch eating cheese and crackers and laughing at those *I Survived* shows in which people would take vacations to the jungle and end up fighting off wild animals.

"Idiots," I'd say, crunching another cracker. "Who tafes vaca to the friggin' hungle?"

And now here I am. Some people say life has no sense of humor. Please.

Something snaps and I freeze. A few yards ahead, I swear I see a man. It looks like he's wearing face paint and trying hard to remain hidden. A second bolt of fear blasts up my spine. I glance around to see if there are others, and when I look back, he's gone. Or he was never there to begin with. Which is probably more likely. A half hour into this race and I'm already hallucinating things.

I rehook my bag over my chest, repeat that there's no strange man, and walk toward my right. Before, I ran straight ahead. But now that I have the plan, I need to cut across the jungle and find the perimeter. I'm not sure how I'll know when I've reached this so-called perimeter, but I'm guessing the foliage will be thinner. Yeah. I'm going with that.

As I march across the jungle, lifting my knees high to keep from stumbling, I begin to list just how many things can end my life. If I eat the wrong thing . . . death. If I don't find water . . . death. If a saber-toothed tiger stumbles upon me on an empty stomach . . . death. Granted, I don't think saber-toothed tigers actually exist anymore. But if they do, they live here.

Sound is everywhere. Some I recognize: birds calling and bugs buzzing. Others, I'm uncertain of. Like the rustle the ground makes when something is slithering beneath it, and the high-pitched scream of an animal I can't name. Even the trees seem to whisper as creatures dive into their leaves. The smell of earth fills my nose, and everywhere I look, pops of color rest against green. There are flowers the color of ripe oranges growing along a thin, spiraling vine. Other flowers are purple and yellow, and there's a robust spray of something blue that's shaped like avocados. I want to touch everything and nothing at once.

I make it about a half mile before the sky splits open. There's no lightning, no thunder. Just rain. I run for cover, certain I can find something to use for shelter. But everything I think can work looks terrifying to crawl beneath. There's a wide plant that can do the trick if it weren't decked with black needles. And another that shoots up and over like an umbrella that I'm certain shelters killer somethings or others. I imagine all sorts of insects and animals have the same idea I do — seek shelter — and I suddenly realize rain's not so bad. Not in comparison anyway.

It seems there is less green growth near the base of some trees. I suspect that has to do with lack of sunlight. Whatever the reason, I crouch down and lean against a tree trunk, the wet bag heavy in my arms. Rain still pelts me, but it's not as harsh here. I think about continuing to walk while it pours, but something tells me staying dry is important. Reaching my arms out, I gather some rain in my cupped palms and quench my thirst.

I sit for what feels like hours. The rain doesn't cease. As best I can, I try to cover my bag with my body, shielding it from getting too wet. Already, it feels like the egg and device are my ticket to winning, and I can't risk either getting damaged. When I can no longer handle the shaking in my arms — or the anxiety that threatens to overwhelm me — I close my eyes. And despite all odds, I fall asleep.

When I wake, everything is blanketed in dark. It's a dark like I've never experienced. I can't see what's five feet in front of me, but I can hear the rush of rain and smell thick, musty scents I don't recognize. My head starts to pound. I didn't think about this part of the race — the night.

I've never liked the dark. Not as a child, not now. And this . . . this is almost unbearable. Blood pulses in my ears, and I push my hands over them to stifle the sound of my own heart thumping.

Within seconds, I've imagined every worst-case scenario. Most of which involves being eaten by something.

Once, when we still lived in Boston, my mom took me to hot yoga. It's normal yoga, but for masochists. In it, they teach you to retain control of your mind and body in uncomfortable situations. This is as uncomfortable as I've ever been, so I swing my legs beneath me to sit cross-legged. Then I place my hands on my knees and breathe. In. Out. In. Out.

Something tells me this doesn't work when you're in the middle of a jungle at midnight.

An ear-piercing shriek penetrates the night. Though it sounds like it's a mile away from where I sit, I imagine it's only inches. Moments later, another shriek emanates from the opposite side of the jungle. The two animals call to each other. Back and forth, back and forth. If I were watching this on TV, I would find it awe inspiring. But here — sitting in my damp clothes on the forest floor, blind to what's around me — it's so overwhelming, it makes me cry.

I brush tears from my face and think of Mom. When Cody and I were little, she would sing to us. It was a special occasion, her singing. She'd only do it when we were sick. Not for a sore throat or a bruised knee, but for the bedridden times when even soup and hot tea and warm blankets didn't help. I can't count the number of times Cody or I feigned an illness to rope my mom into singing.

There's nothing else I can think to do.

I pull my egg out of my bag and nestle it in my lap. There's no telling what this thing holds, and part of me is afraid to find out. But for now I try to forget that and just imagine it's something normal, like a chicken.

I draw in a big breath.

I'm not the world's best singer, but I'm not the worst, either. And so I sing for my Pandora, blocking out the sounds of the jungle, forgetting why this may be a bad idea. I just run my hand gently over the dull shell — and I sing.

Because I can't see anyway, I close my eyes and picture my family as I'm singing. I remember the time my parents brought home a blue parakeet, and Cody and I released it six days later. I almost laugh when I think about the face my Boston best friend, Hannah, made when I told her I loved the goth kid from biology class.

I lift up my Pandora so that my lips brush its shell. I sing every song I can remember the words to. And when I can't sing any longer, I lie on my side, keeping my arms wrapped tightly around my egg. When I feel myself drifting off once again, I nuzzle my head against my egg and imagine how wonderful it will be when my Pandora hatches. How I won't be alone anymore.

I don't care what it will look like.

Or what it will do.

I just want it to be here, now.

"Good night, little Pandora," I say. Then opening my eyes and looking straight at the smooth, fragile egg, I add, "Good night, Madox."

I don't so much sleep as drift in and out of consciousness. And when the sun finally creeps through the canopy of leaves overhead, I chalk it up as a job well done. I managed to live through a night in the jungle. How many people can say that?

My Pandora is in my arms when I wake. I rub my hands over him and stretch my legs.

"Ready to get moving, Madox?" I say.

I don't feel ridiculous in the least speaking to my egg. I've gotten it in my head that if I'm nice to him, then maybe he'll come out quicker. Or she. Or it. I wouldn't judge. I place Madox into my bag, thinking I really like his name. Madox. I'm not sure where I got it from. Some movie or TV show, no doubt. Either way, I like the idea of him having an actual name. I mean, *KD-8* is cool and all, but *Madox* sounds less like an alien species.

Running my tongue over my teeth, I cringe. What I wouldn't give for a toothbrush and a shower . . . and a turn-of-the-century toilet. Turns out I never properly appreciated the awesomeness that is toilet paper. Next time my mom asks me to pick up a jumbo pack at the store, I will hold my head high.

"I think if we only stop once to rest," I continue, "we might make it to the jungle's perimeter by nightfall." I have no idea if this is accurate, but I'm trying to make Madox feel better. As if he understands. "Want me to sing to you again?" I pause and imagine him/her/it skipping around and nodding. "All right, already. Calm yourself."

As I walk, I begin to repeat all the songs from last night. My clothes are still drenched from yesterday's shower, but I'm certain they'll dry as I move. It's amazing how optimistic I feel this morning. *This race lasts only three months,* I reason. If I can make it one night, I can make it two. Et cetera, et cetera.

When my stomach growls, I'm not surprised. The last thing I ate was a PB&J yesterday morning. The more I think about it, the hungrier I get, until at some point, my brain is pounding against my temples.

As I'm walking from plant to plant — wondering which will kill me fastest if I consume it — I hear a muffled, snapping sound. For the last eighteen hours, I've heard more coinciding sounds than I could have thought possible. They never stop.

But this one is close.

I wrap my arm around Madox, mentally telling him that everything is going to be okay. It's amazing how fast I've become attached to my Pandora. One night alone, and I'm more afraid of losing him than I am of starving. But I guess whoever created this race knew this is exactly what would happen.

When the sound comes again, closer, I pull Madox onto my chest and protect him with both arms.

The noise is behind me now. I whip around to face it, shaking so hard, my teeth chatter. A sharp caw rips right above my head and I glance up. When I look back down — an enormous beast is staring right at me, hunger storming in its yellow eyes.

It lowers its head, touching a pink nose to the ground. A low growl builds in its throat. The animal stalks closer, eyes locked on my face. I try to stand perfectly still, but I'm hyperventilating and it makes holding myself together extremely difficult.

As the animal moves in, its shoulder blades rise and fall like waves in an ocean. I allow myself to believe for one fraction of a second that it's only curious. It'll see that I'm not a threat, that I'll give it no chase, and will tire of me and leave.

But then the beast lifts its enormous head and releases a blood-curdling roar only the king of a jungle can.

CHAPTER NINE

The lion rushes toward me in an instant, and all I can think about is how I once heard that lions don't actually live in jungles. Today, I will die at the hands of a misconception.

My legs shake as the animal closes in, his muscles rippling as he moves. There's too little time to dream of fleeing. No chance to react, to run for my life. I close my eyes and wait for the impact. But at the last minute, I can't help but peek. It's the wrong move. My eyes fall on the lion's open mouth, on the dark shadows cast by his ivory teeth.

I choke on a scream as the lion leaps.

"M-4," I hear a deep voice bark.

The lion touches down an inch away from me and stops cold. Then he glances over his shoulder.

From out of the brush, the serial-killer guy strides toward me. He slaps his thigh once. "Now." The lion pads toward him and stops near the guy's leg, turning to keep both bright yellow eyes trained on me. When the guy steps closer, I notice he has a scar cut through his right eyebrow and that the bottom of his left earlobe is mangled.

He's wearing the same brown scrubs I am, but he also has two straps across his chest that attach to bags at his hips. When I see what's in the bags, my stomach rumbles. They are both overflowing with some kind of fruit, and I even catch the scent of raw meat. I have no idea where he found food or how he knew what was safe to eat, but I consider taking on him and the lion for just a taste.

"What are you doing here?" The guy's voice is as sharp as it is rough, and he steps toward me when he speaks. An intimidation factor, no doubt. His shirt pulls tight against his chest, and I realize just how easily this guy could kill me. Muscles bulge beneath the fabric, and thick veins run along his tanned, sculpted arms. I yank my eyes away from his shoulders to meet his gaze.

"What do you mean?" I clip. "I'm in the race, same as you." The lion at his side stirs, licks his chops. "What is that thing?" I should be more afraid, but I'm still too weak from exhaustion and hunger to run, and it seems this guy has a handle on the animal. The answer hits me when I realize he's not carrying his massive egg. His Pandora hatched. My brain stutters trying to comprehend this, that a *lion* was inside an *egg*. I glance at the animal and wonder at the possibility. He's bigger than I ever imagined a lion would be in real life. For one small moment, I feel envy.

The guy's got a good Pandora.

Shame fills my chest, and I absently stroke Madox's egg inside my bag.

His eyes travel down the length of my body, and I recall that my wet scrubs still cling to my skin. His gaze finally lands on the feather in my hair, and his eyes narrow. Looking up, he jabs a finger at me. "Stay away from me."

I plan to do just that, but when the guy turns to leave, I spot something in one of his bags. It's electric blue cloth, and I know instantly what it is.

He's found a flag.

"Wait." I remember the deal I made with myself, that if I found another Contender, I'd suggest we search for base camp together. This isn't exactly the kind of person I'd hoped to partner with, but it's better than traveling alone.

"Wait," I repeat, stumbling after him. "Maybe we can, you know, help each other." The guy walks quicker, but I keep talking to his broad back. "I mean, when we get close, it's every person for themselves, but in the meantime, why not have company?" I pause, trying to think of what skills I possess. "I can be funny.

I mean, I used to make my best friend, Hannah, laugh so hard, she'd pee. I can entertain you while we walk."

The guy flicks his hand and the lion at his side turns on me. He throws his head back and roars so loudly, I can feel it in my bones. I see every thick tooth in his mouth, and a bolt of fear twists my stomach.

I raise my hands slowly. "Okay."

The guy moves away and the lion trots to catch up with his owner.

I'd like to yell how sorry he'll be, how when my Pandora hatches, he'll beat up his Pandora. I look into my bag and smell the sour odor. It's getting stronger, and I wonder if Madox is already gone. If he never hatches, I'll be alone. And as much as I hate to admit it, I fear isolation worse than the jungle itself.

The guy has food, but more important, he has a flag. Maybe he already knows the way to base camp. He certainly looks like the kind of guy who treks through jungles for fun. I remember once, in my Business Basics class at Ridgeline High, my teacher got on this rant about research and development. I don't remember the details of his spiel — I was more concerned with the text Hannah had sent me about a jewelry sale at Forever 21 — but it was something about how McDonald's puts all this time and resources into finding the absolute perfect location for a new store. They believe if they buy the right real estate, the burgers will sell themselves. The kicker was that other burger joints just watch to see where McDonald's puts a store, then they plop a store nearby and save themselves a boatload of cash on all that blasted research.

At the time, this story seemed pretty shady; I mean, those other stores seemed like copycats, and that's just lame.

. But now I'm standing here in a jungle in the middle of God knows where, watching a convict and his lion tramp through creepy-looking plants and all I'm thinking is: *Homeboy's got a flag.*

He's got the right *real estate*. So maybe all I need to do is follow his ass.

And so I do.

For two days, I follow this guy . . . and I learn that I have no business competing in this race. Not when Green Beret is here, sniffing out berries that I assume are safe to eat, or listening for strange sounds I don't recognize, or finding safe places to sleep I never would have seen.

To give myself credit, I don't think the guy knows I'm following him. I've stayed far enough behind that the jungle masks the sound of my footsteps. I eat what he eats (which is Disgusting with a capital *D*), I drink from the streams he stops at, and I sleep when he sleeps. Each morning, I wake up to the sound of him moving about. Though he's quiet most of the day, in the morning, he's louder than any alarm clock I've ever owned.

For the most part, following him is working out all right. The problem is the guy hasn't found any more flags, and I'm starting to wonder if maybe finding the first one was a fluke.

Night falls quickly in the jungle, which isn't good. I hate the night, the time when I feel utterly alone, even though Green Beret is only a few yards away. Plus, it gets cooler at night, and for some reason, my skin is doing something funky that worsens in the evening. It feels and looks thinner where the brown scrubs touch my body, and a pink rash covers my chest and back. It freaks me out to no end, but I can't tell what the issue is. I think maybe I'm allergic to walking this much.

I watch the guy find a place to rest. Last night, he slept in the trees, which I find wildly disturbing. But tonight, he pulls up plants by the fistful and lays bark and twigs onto the ground he cleared. Then he covers that with dead leaves. Finally, after he's been working and inspecting the site for several minutes, he sits down. The lion pads toward him and leans back on his haunches. The guy rubs the lion under his chin, and a warm, rich purr erupts from the animal's throat. A small ache twists through my chest. I'd do almost anything for that kind of companionship right now.

It fascinates me, watching this guy and his Pandora. I still haven't gotten over the fact that we're in this race and that we have these animals to help us through. Thinking about the other Contenders, I wonder if their Pandoras have hatched, too.

Am I the only one left with an egg?

I try not to think about it as I watch the guy move around, finding a comfortable position to sleep. He's extremely tall — well over six feet — and it seems every inch of his frame is covered in muscle. I knew guys like him in school. The ones who spent every waking hour pumping iron so they could stare at their sweaty masses in the mirror. I do wonder about his disfigured ear, though, and the scar over his eye. And I wonder about other things, too: the way he circles his makeshift beds like the lion beside him, or the way he rubs his left elbow when he's thinking. And, good Lord, how many times does one person need to crack his knuckles in a day? Only the knuckles over four fingers, though, never the thumb.

Crack your damn thumb, I think every time he does it. *You're forgetting your thumb!*

Watching him has been my entertainment for over thirty-six hours, a distraction from a cruel realization — my Pandora may never hatch. At times, I imagine him seeing me in the distance and welcoming my company, but I know that won't happen — not with this one.

The dark, shadowed jungle of the day has morphed into the black hue of night, so I don't see any harm in inching closer. Last night, I slept as far away as I could while still keeping him in my line of sight. Tonight, I can't bear to be more than a few feet away. He may hear me, but with this cloak of darkness, he'll never see me.

Folding my arms around my knees, I close my eyes. Inside my head, I'm back home in Boston, sitting in front of the TV with a bowl of kettle corn. My dad is talking football with Cody, and my mom is harping on us to come to the table . . . and for me to lay off the popcorn before dinner. I picture us sitting down to my dad's meat loaf, the kind with the red gravy. Cody will make a remark about Brad Carter sucking face with a new girl, and I'll sock him in the arm. Mom will get mad. Dad will laugh.

Before I can stop myself, I start to hum to Madox. It's the tune to my mom's bedside song — our sicky song. I hum for several seconds until I hear a cracking sound. When I open my eyes, I spot Green Beret staring in my direction.

Crap!

Oh well. It's not like he can see me. It's too dark. But then he stands up and steps closer. I hold my breath, willing him to look away. He lifts his chin and leans toward where I'm sitting. Shaking his head, he runs his hands through his dark hair. Then he lets out a long sigh that says in no uncertain terms that he's wildly irritated.

I'm not sure whether it's his bed made of sticks that has him pissed, or if he's spotted me. I lock my muscles in place and pretend I'm a lifeless stump. Nothing to see here, folks. He looks in my direction for a long time, then turns to his Pandora.

"M-4," he says. His voice startles me. He hasn't said a single word in the two days I've followed him. It's amazing really, because I've got a novel's worth of backlogged dialogue waiting in my head. My ears strain to figure out what's going on, but I think I hear him tap the ground twice. It's so dark, I lean forward to try to see what's happening.

Then light springs forward from the lion's mouth.

What the —? I gasp when I realize. The lion breathed fire. My skin buzzes from what I just witnessed. Maybe I'm hallucinating? But even from here, I can feel the warmth of the flames. Before I can comprehend how this guy's Pandora — M-4 — created fire, the guy packs up his two bags, hooks them across his chest, and motions for M-4 to follow him. He's leaving his campsite, I realize. He's almost out of sight when I see him turn and look in my direction. His face is stone, his eyes hard as iron. He steals a glance toward the fire, then turns to go.

For several minutes, I wait, watching the fire. I'm afraid the fire will consume everything, but it doesn't spread. The surrounding wood is too damp to catch, I guess. Everything here is always damp, including me. My clothes never dried from the rain two days ago. I slowly realize why the rash is spreading across my skin.

I haven't been completely dry in days.

The air is too muggy here, and there's hardly any sunlight below the canopy overhead. Once it rains, the moisture stays. I'm afraid if I don't dry my clothes now, I may never get another chance. I wait a bit longer, then creep toward the fire. When I don't see the guy or his Pandora, I sit down on the twig pallet and pull off my boots. My feet are wrinkled and swollen and covered in red patches. The rash has spread. I tug off my shirt and pants, and dry everything by the dancing flame. Then I curl into a ball, my Pandora pulled closed to my stomach, and I sleep.

When a small noise wakes me hours later, I try to block it out. I need sleep if I am to survive out here. But a strange cracking sound comes again, which I can't ignore. Even stranger is the crawling sensation along my bare stomach.

My eyes snap open and I glance down.

My Pandora — it's hatching.

CHAPTER TEN

I bolt upright and the egg rolls away from me. I reach for it, and freeze when a small black paw strikes out of the shell like it's grasping for something.

I can't help the tears that sting my eyes.

Covering my mouth, I watch as my Pandora pushes his way out of his egg, piece by piece. He's alive. All this time, I feared he was never going to hatch, that the smell wafting from the egg was from decay. But it's happening. He's here.

My Pandora, my Madox, kicks the last piece of shell away. He's covered in a thick, greenish slime, but he doesn't seem to mind one bit. He stumbles onto his back, his four legs kicking the air like an overturned turtle's. When he rights himself, he circles twice, his small pink tongue dangling from his mouth.

I study my Pandora: his black fur; his four, pawed feet; his pointy, alert ears. When his eyes find mine, I draw in a quick breath. Madox's eyes are brilliant green, so bright, they seem to glow radioactive in the night. My Pandora looks, in every way, like a baby fox.

When Madox sees me, he takes two quick steps back.

"It's okay," I tell him. His ears perk at the sound of my voice, but he seems unsure. "You are KD-8. You're . . . my Pandora."

I keep waiting for some supernatural crap to happen, like for him to grow wings or speak. But I don't hear a thing. I pull myself up, and the fox backs away farther. It's enough to make me want to sob. I've waited so long for him to arrive, and now he's afraid. Not that I blame him. I wonder if he knows what's happening or why he's here.

Racking my brain, I try to think of something to let him know it's safe. That I want so badly for us to be allies. The only thing I can think of is my mother, so instead of speaking to Madox, I try humming. I start low and hum louder when he cocks his head and listens.

I laugh, seeing him with his head turned, but then I gather myself and keep humming. I decide to try singing. A few notes in, Madox rights his head and his green eyes widen. His mouth falls open and, I swear to God, he seems to smile.

Opening my arms, I pray for a miracle. That Madox and I can skip the days of awkward companionship and sail right to friendship. The black fox takes a tentative step toward me. I hold still.

Wishing he could understand me, I think, *I'm not going to hurt you.*

He takes two more steps, then he trots toward me until I run my hand over his wet, sticky fur.

It's a scene right out of a friggin' Disney movie. Minus the green slime.

I manage to get most of the goop off him by using large palm leaves. He helps the process by offering me places he's still coated. When he rolls onto his back, I spot something on his right back paw. With one hand, I scratch behind his ears, with the other, I lift his leg. The other paws are black like the rest of his fur, but this one's pink. I notice there's a tattoo on the soft pad. It reads *KD-8*.

They mark their Pandoras. It's not surprising; I imagine they want to keep track of their inventory. Madox wiggles his leg free and takes a cautious step into my lap.

"Come on." I open my arms, leaving my lap wide open. "It's okay." He crawls all the way in, circles four times, and lies down. My heart swells as I look at him. He's my Pandora, and I am his Contender. I can't help wondering about all the cool things he might be able to do. But mostly, I'm just happy he seems to trust me.

I glance around and notice I'm not sure where the guy and M-4 went. I know I should venture into the brush to look, but I'm still so exhausted. Also, I don't want to move. Madox looks so serene, asleep in my lap. For a long time, I pet him and sing. He seems to like the sound of my voice. When he starts kicking in his sleep, I have to bite my lip to keep from laughing.

"We've had a long day," I whisper to Madox. Then I lean back, careful to keep my legs crossed, and I fall into a deep slumber.

I dream I am running from a monster. The creature has yellow eyes and a bow slung over his right shoulder. Every few minutes, he strings an arrow into his bow and aims it in my direction. I run faster, weaving between gnarled trees and boulders the size of elephants. Everything is so dark; I can't imagine how he can see me. But he does. I feel an arrow strike my skin and I cry out. I run faster, but it isn't fast enough. Over and over, the arrows pierce me until it feels like there are thousands hitting me at once. I drop to my knees and roll from side to side, trying to escape the pain, but nothing helps.

When I finally wake up, Madox is yelping. I shoot up to see what's wrong with my Pandora, but agony blinds me. My skin stings so badly, I believe I must be burning alive. When I look down, I see hundreds of red ants crawling over every inch of my skin. They aren't built like the ants in Boston. These suckers are the length of a quarter, and each sting is enough to make me nauseated with pain. I jump to my feet, screaming, swiping at the insects. They crawl over my arms and legs and hands, and even across my scalp.

I brush them off hurriedly, then lean over to rescue Madox. There are still dozens of ants trailing across my bare skin, but I've got to help my Pandora. Madox darts into the ashes from last night's fire and rolls around. I flick off the ones he doesn't get, then brush off the remaining ants still left on my legs. When we've rid ourselves of the insects, we move away from the campsite.

My bag, the one I carried Madox in, is covered in ants. I grab the device from the inside of it, then drop the bag onto the ground and leave it there. My Pandora licks himself, whining. I place my device into my pocket, pick Madox up, and stumble farther from the site. This is why the guy sleeps in the trees, I suddenly understand. Thinking back on the three nights I've spent on the jungle's floor, I can't believe this hasn't happened before. How could I be so stupid? The ants probably felt like they hit the jackpot when they stumbled across an almost naked girl and her fox.

Though the stinging sensation along my skin is almost unbearable, I know I have to grab my clothes and boots. Ants crawl across them in organized rows. I put Madox down and take four more stings in order to shake everything off and get dressed. With all the insects gone, I can finally inspect the damage they've done. Glancing at my arms, I decide I look like I have chicken pox. It's disgusting, and I'm certain I'll have nightmares about this long after the race is over. In a strange way, it makes me mad, too. These tiny little creatures just treated me and Madox like an early-morning snack.

I see a flash of red. Before I can stop myself, I start stomping across the site, the ants squishing beneath my thick boot heels. A wild scream escapes my throat, and I sound more animal than I do human. Madox trots behind me, licking up two or three ants at a time and gnashing them between his teeth.

Laughing, I point at Madox's mouth. "Hell yeah. Eat those effers." Then I stop. "Wait, Madox. No. I don't know if that'll hurt you." I scoop him up as he swallows down another mouthful of ants, smacking his jaws together.

"Let's just go," I tell my fox. "We need to find the guy I've been following. You may not like his Pandora, but I think he might know where we're headed."

After walking for several minutes, Madox trotting by my feet, I still can't find any trace of either man or lion. At first, I'm devastated, but then I remember that I followed him for two days and he never found another flag. Plus, now I have Madox, so I don't feel the desperate need to be near another person.

As Madox and I trek through the jungle, I notice the plants are taller. Three days ago, they reached my ankles. But now, now they brush my knees, my hips, and in really dense areas, they even graze my shoulders. I feel like I'm being swallowed alive and realize that by following the guy, I've been heading deeper into the jungle. He obviously wasn't following the perimeter plan.

At some point, I stop and listen. I hear a screeching sound. It's not a sharp caw like some of the birds make. This one is lower and carries farther. Madox cocks his head. He hears it, too.

"What is that?" Madox circles my ankles, and I crouch down to stroke the fuzz behind his ears. "It's okay," I tell him. But the sound grows closer, and it's clear now the noise isn't coming from a singular animal, but many of the same kind.

I stand up, rubbing the searing pink bumps along my skin. My lungs pull in quick darts of jungle air, and a cold sensation blooms in my belly. The calls are so loud now, they feel like they're coming from inside my head. Madox barks and backs up. Before I can rejoice in the fact that my Pandora just barked for the first time, the brush opens like a velvet curtain.

A dozen chimpanzees move toward us, swaying side to side as they walk. One near the front, the biggest one, stops suddenly. He didn't expect to see me here. I pray I've startled him enough so that he'll turn and flee. My heart skips a beat, then another, as he studies me.

Another chimpanzee moves forward. She has a baby chimp in her arms. The sight is eerily human. The large chimp near the front holds out an arm to stop her from going any farther. The gesture pushes me over the edge; it's too much like something my father would do to me or Cody. I don't know much about apes, but I know I'm outnumbered.

I take a small backward step.

Moving is the wrong thing to do, I realize too late. The large chimp pulls himself up to standing and beats a single fist against his chest. *My land,* he seems to say. Maybe I've shown submission when I should have been aggressive, but it's too late now. He screeches loudly, and the chimps behind him follow suit.

"Run, Madox!" I turn and race away, glancing down to ensure my Pandora is by my side. He's little, but he's good at finding small spaces in the foliage to dart through, and so he keeps pace. My blood is ice in my veins. I pray that the chimpanzees will be content that I've fled, but soon I hear the unmistakable sound of being pursued.

They scream over one another, and creatures in the canopy overhead cry in return, anxious at what is happening below them. The chimps are gaining on me. Of course they are. They've lived in this jungle all their lives.

Thorns tear into my clothing as I race. I have no idea what they'll do if they overtake me, and I cry thinking about it. Wiping the tears from my eyes, I run faster. Madox is still at my feet when the foliage begins to clear. The plants that were thigh-high thin and shorten, but I'm not sure this will help. I need to move quicker, but I also need the jungle's natural cover. Balling my hands into fists, I push even harder, and for a few seconds, I am filled with triumph as I gain a solid lead on the chimps.

The black hole comes out of nowhere.

One moment, I'm whipping past trees and overgrown vines, and the next, I'm throwing myself back to keep from tumbling to my death. Madox stops just in time and comes to rest nearby. The chimps are growing louder again. I know it won't be long before they find me. I can't run forever. I can hardly catch my breath as it is, and fear is making it hard to think.

I glance down into the enormous pit, maybe forty feet down, noting the thick vines along the sides. If I'm careful, and if the vines can hold my weight, I can scale down into the cave and wait until the chimps pass. I'll have to be quick, though. If they see me, they'll follow. I'm certain of it.

"Come on," I whisper, scooping Madox into my arms. Stuffing the bottom of my shirt into my pants, I tuck Madox in between my shirt and chest. Then I grab on to the thickest vine I see, tug it twice to ensure it'll hold, and step over the side. My brain screams that this is not the alternative I want, that there's no telling what lurks inside this cave. But I have no choice, so I push those thoughts aside and descend into darkness.

For having never climbed anything before, I think I'm doing pretty well. I use my legs to balance my weight against the rock wall, and test my footing before I step. I'm halfway down when I hear the chimps closing in. I have to hurry. Glancing beneath me, I note there are still ten feet left before I reach the cavern floor. In a panic, I try sliding down the vine. My feet slip out from under me and before I can regain my balance — I'm free-falling.

The breath is knocked from my lungs when I hit the ground. Instantly, I check Madox. He pulls himself out from my shirt, and when I realize he's okay, I lie back and cringe against the shooting pain in my lower body. I know I have to check for broken bones, but right now I'm still more afraid of the chimpanzees. Grabbing Madox, I pull him onto my chest and press my head into his damp fur.

Please don't let them find us.

I pray for several seconds before I'm brave enough to glance up. The chimps' cries are directly above the cave, and I know they're standing dangerously close to the edge. Sucking my bottom lip, I lift my head from Madox's warm body and peer upward.

A chimpanzee stares down at me.

I start to scream, but cover my mouth to stop myself. My body shakes with fear, and I forget all about the pain in my back and legs. The chimp raises its hands and intertwines its fingers over its forehead like it's worried. A sharp call nearby steals its attention, and it looks away. It glances back at me once more, then turns and flees.

CHAPTER ELEVEN

For a long time, I don't move. I can't. Each time I consider sitting up, I imagine hearing the chimps' calls. But when Madox starts licking my face, I know I have to keep going. This is a race, and I can't stay down here forever.

As I pull myself up, I feel wetness on my back. For a fleeting moment, I'm terrified it's blood. But when I search further, I realize it's only water. Madox scurries beneath me and drinks from the narrow stream. I suddenly realize I'm incredibly thirsty, and before I can wonder what kinds of terrible things call this stream home, I get down on my hands and knees and drink. The water is cool and tastes like nothing I've experienced before. I've never had water this pure, untouched by humans. It's almost too much, and I close my eyes against the euphoric feeling of meeting such a basic human need.

There are moments in the jungle where I can't help but laugh at how my life has changed in these last four days. Drinking from a stream, in the belly of a cave, is one of those moments. Yesterday, if this had happened, I would have daydreamed about my leopard-print house slippers and my grandmother's crocheted blanket that I've kept at the end of my bed since forever. But today, I just glance at Madox drinking beside me (downstream, thank God), and I'm thankful for his presence. I was afraid that after he hatched — *if* he hatched — he would leave me. But so far, Madox has been faithful, and I feel another stab of affection for my little Pandora.

Using the stream, I bathe like a New World pioneer, splashing water over my skin and hair. Then I do my best to rub my teeth clean with a finger and some more water.

When I finish, I inspect the cave, searching for other hidden secrets that'll help me win the race. It's dark down here, darker than the jungle itself. But I can still see the lichen growing along the bottom of the cave, and now that I'm paying attention, I can hear the slight gurgle of the stream. Mostly, though, there is mud and rocks. It seems this might be a good place to sleep and stay hidden from larger animals like the ones I escaped less than an hour ago. But surprisingly, I'm fairly well rested, and I know I need to keep moving if I want to find base camp.

Hitching Madox inside my shirt again, I scale up the side of the cave. Going up is way harder than going down, but I manage it after several failed attempts. Before I crawl up onto the jungle floor, I peer over the lip of the cave to ensure the chimpanzees are gone. When I don't spot them, I release a shaky breath. Then I pull myself over and stand up.

Today, I need to find a flag. I spent my first day in the jungle panicking. After that, I spent two days and one night following the Green Beret. Now it's just me and Madox. The fourth day. That means I have ten days left to reach base camp. I'm not sure if there's a certain hour we have to arrive, so I cut it to nine days to play it safe. The flags will be hard to find. I know because I haven't seen one yet. But then, I'm not sure I was ever looking that hard. Not until now.

"Want to find a flag, Madox?"

My Pandora barks in response, and I wonder if maybe he can understand me after all.

I narrow my eyes and kneel down. "Madox, roll over." He stares at me. I try something else. "KD-8, roll over." He sits down on his haunches and glances away, like he's bored with the nonsense spewing from my mouth.

"All right, guess you don't speak human," I say. "We still need to find flags." Briefly, I wonder why the crazy guy's lion seems to understand English and Madox doesn't. I guess it's just not one of his capabilities. No biggie.

As Madox and I make our way through the jungle, my stomach growling, I make a game out of my Pandora's inability to understand me. "Madox, climb a tree," I say. "Madox, fetch us lunch." "Madox, give me a hot-stone massage and serve me green tea. Iced, not hot."

My Pandora barks every time I make a request, like he's participating in the conversation. In reality, I wonder if it's his polite way of telling me to shut the hell up. As the sun begins to set — and I still haven't spotted a blue flag — my spirits plummet. I was certain if I focused on where I was going and used my gut as a guide, I'd find a flag. Now I have to decide whether to keep looking for one tomorrow, when the sun rises, or resume the perimeter plan and hope I find base camp without the flags.

Glancing up, I wonder if I can make a bed in the trees like the guy did. My guess is no, but I have to try. I turn in circles, inspecting the trees, deciding which would make the best starting point. But as I spin, something catches my eye.

In the distance, I see a soft, dancing glow. I recognize instantly what it is — a fire. And I know what maniac's Pandora probably created it. Ensuring Madox stays nearby, I creep toward the surge of light. When I'm within a few yards, I begin hearing voices. Not the kind that worry psychologists, but the real kind. The ones that tell me this isn't just the Green Beret and his lion, but *people*. I briefly wonder if I'll see the guy I spotted my first afternoon in the jungle, the one whose face appeared painted. Then again, I'm not entirely certain that wasn't just my imagination.

I move closer, hoping to get a look at them while staying hidden. Madox seems to sense we're prowling, so he mimics me, staying close to the ground and taking careful steps. The voices grow louder as I settle behind an enormous tree trunk. Pulling a deep breath, I peek around the side and take in the view.

Three people squat around a small fire. There's not a lot of light radiating from the flames, but inside the dark jungle, it's more than enough. They're all wearing brown scrubs with a single pocket — and a serpent embellishment — on the chest. Some of their pockets protrude, and I can only imagine they're storing their devices in there as I am.

The first person I notice is a woman maybe in her midthirties. She has prominent cheekbones and long black hair. There are small laugh lines around her mouth, and the way she keeps folding and refolding her hands tells me she isn't any more comfortable with this jungle than I am.

Beside the woman is a young boy. He has thick, curly hair, and I instantly like him. I know what it's like to wake up to *that* nightmare every day. He smiles easily at what the woman is saying, and I notice he's drawing something into the dirt with a long stick. I'm terrible at guessing kids' ages, but I'd put him at probably about eight.

The last girl I see, I want to strangle. Like the woman, she has long hair. But instead of dark, it's blond — no, honey gold — and shines like that of a Broadway starlet. I can't see her eyes from here, but I'm sure they're some stunning shade of blue. She has cream-colored skin and a body that belongs in a magazine — the kind for guys, not girls. I hate her with everything I have as she laughs her perfect laugh and tosses her perfect hair and crosses her to-die-for legs. The girl seems to be about my age, or just a few years older. We could be friends, I realize, if I weren't so over-whelmed with the urge to end her.

My legs ache from bending down, and when I stand to relieve them, Goldilocks glances over. I freeze as she gets up and walks toward me and Madox. The woman starts to stand, too, but the blonde holds out a hand to stop her. Her eyes narrow as she searches the area. Then she glances directly at me.

Green eyes, not blue.

The girl motions for me to come out. "I see you, Contender. Identify yourself or I'll send my Pandora after you."

Inspecting their campsite, I don't see her Pandora. Or any Pandora, really. I contemplate coming out like she asked. From what I can tell, none of them carries weapons, and I'm sure I can flee if the need arises.

Picking up Madox, I stroll out from behind the tree trunk. "Hey" is all I can think to say.

Goldilocks tilts her head at me. "Who are you?"

"My name's Tella Holloway," I answer. She seems to be waiting for something else, so I add, "I'm a Contender."

She nods like she assumed as much but is relieved to hear me say it. Pointing at the feather over my shoulder, she says, "Nice hair flair." I smile cautiously as she motions toward the fire. "Want to join us?"

I can't help the spike of excitement in my chest. For four days, I've had no one to talk to except a mute fox — God love him. And now this girl — who I'm hating less — is offering her company. "Yeah," I say, setting Madox down and moving toward the fire. "Thanks."

The girl sits down on a log and scrutinizes me. "Have you found any flags?" she asks, her brow lifting.

I shake my head. "No. You?"

She doesn't answer, but the drop in her shoulders tells me she hasn't. "My name's Harper. This is Caroline," she says, flicking her finger toward the woman. "And this is Dink," she adds, referring to the kid.

"Hey." I sit on the ground and try to act as unawkward as possible. "It's nice to meet you guys."

"Do you want something to eat?" Harper asks.

My stomach growls when I think about food. I want to be self-sufficient, to show these people I can fend for myself. But I nod anyway, then watch wide-eyed as Harper reaches into a bag and pulls out a sliver of charred meat wrapped in a palm leaf. "Don't eat the leaf, just the meat."

Though I know I should be offended she thinks I'd eat the leaf, I'm glad she clarified. I don't ask what I'm eating. I don't want to know. The meat is tasteless, but it still feels so good to chew, I can hardly contain myself. As I eat, I wonder why this girl is being so nice. There can only be one winner, so why is she helping me?

I think I have the answer when I notice her eyeing my Pandora, who's currently lying on his back, four legs kicking at the sky. She wants to know what he's capable of, which immediately fills me with anxiety. My fox had yet to demonstrate any of his skills. Maybe hers hasn't, either. "This is Madox." I nudge my Pandora with my boot and he bites at it.

Harper's face opens. "You named it?"

"Well, yeah." So much for not feeling awkward. "His original name was KD-8, I guess."

"You shouldn't do that," Harper says.

"Why not?" Caroline's voice surprises me. It's low and gentle, and I get the sensation she doesn't ever raise it. "Why can't she name her Pandora?"

Harper bristles. "It's not right. They're here to help us survive. Not be our pets."

Caroline presses her lips together. It seems she disagrees, but doesn't want to push the issue.

"What's up with its eyes?" Harper asks suddenly. "They're trippy-looking."

I glance at Madox's electric-green eyes. It's something I'd assumed all Pandoras had — unnatural eye color.

Instead of waiting for an answer, Harper asks another question. "When did it hatch?"

"Last night," I say. Then to emphasize I'm my own person, I add, "*Madox* hatched last night."

Harper looks confused. "Hasn't grown much, huh?"

I glance at the baby fox. Had he grown at all? I didn't think so. Shaking my head, I ask, "Did yours grow?"

She laughs. It's a short burst of sound. "From the second it hatched, it wouldn't *stop* growing. But I think it's done now." She looks at Madox. I can tell she thinks my Pandora's a dud. It's decent that she doesn't voice the thought, but a knot of fear still twists my stomach.

Is there something wrong with Madox?

"Speaking of, where *is* my Pandora?" Harper says, interrupting my slide into hysteria. "It should be back already." She stands and places her two pointer fingers into her mouth. Across from her, the young boy — Dink — plugs his ears. Seconds later, I learn why.

A sharp whistle sounds from Harper's mouth. Madox jumps up, startled. I pull him into my arms and wait for whatever Harper called to show. There are a few seconds of silence in which my ears ring. Then I hear a whooshing sound. Something flashes across my line of vision, and moments later, an enormous bird lands on Harper's outstretched arm.

Its beak is a brilliant shade of yellow, and its head is masked in white. The rest of its body is deep brown. "That's a bald eagle," I say, proud of myself for knowing.

"So it is." Harper lowers her arm and the eagle hops off onto the ground. It's holding something in its right foot. Upon closer inspection, I realize it's a large fish. Harper points to the catch. "Clean it so we can cook it over the fire."

The eagle drops the fish and slices it open with a razor-sharp talon. Then it proceeds to rip out pink, fleshy entrails with its beak. I might be disgusted if I weren't so happy that Harper's Pandora knows how to scavenge food. No wonder the others travel with her.

"What is its name?" I ask.

"RX-13." She taps its head once. "Hatched less than an hour after the race started." Harper holds out her hand to Dink, and he offers her the stick he's been drawing with. She spears the cleaned fish and holds it over the fire, smiling. "You should see the things she can do."

So much for my theory that her Pandora hasn't displayed any capabilities. I want to ask her exactly what RX-13's skills are, but I'd rather not admit Madox hasn't shown any himself.

My Pandora is struggling against me. I'm not sure whether it's to run from the eagle or to check her out. I decide to take a chance and put him down. I'll have to at some point, I reason. As soon as he's on the ground, he races toward the oversized bird and barks. I can't help wondering why both M-4 and RX-13 understand their Contenders, but Madox doesn't understand me. I refuse to believe anything is wrong with my Pandora. Even if there was, I wouldn't care. He's mine, and I'll never be sorry that I'm the one who got him.

I watch my Pandora try to make friends with the bird. He barks and pushes down on his front legs, asking her to play. In response, RX-13 sweeps a wing back and knocks him across the campsite. He squeals and runs toward me. The bird chases after him — half flying, half jumping — and snaps at his tail. An overwhelming need to protect my Pandora slams into me as I scoop Madox up and glare at the bird. Harper doesn't seem to notice what's happened. She's too busy cooking the fish.

Madox lays his head against my shoulder and I keep an eye on RX-13, who looks as if she'd like nothing better than to clean him, too. When I realize Dink is eyeing Madox, I say, "Want to hold him?"

The boy looks at Caroline, and when she nods, he does, too. I walk around the fire, wondering how they got it started with all this damp wood, and place Madox in his arms. The black fox reaches up to lick the boy's chin and the boy giggles.

Thinking I should say something to Caroline, I ask, "Is he yours?"

A strange expression shadows her face, but it quickly vanishes. She offers me a warm smile. "No, we're just traveling together."

I rock back on my heels and smell the scent of fish cooking. "Is your Pandora hunting, too?" I ask, trying to keep the conversation rolling.

Caroline looks at Dink, then shakes her head. "We lost our Pandoras early on. Mine died after a day, and his never hatched. Isn't that right, Dink?"

The boy nods and continues playing with Madox. I wonder if his name is really Dink. Maybe he gave himself a new identity at the start of the race. Seems like something an eight-year-old would do. The woman on the device never mentioned if we had to cross the finish line with our Pandoras alive, so I guess we don't. But I can't imagine doing this without Madox.

"So all of you travel together?"

Caroline shrugs. "Until we near the end."

I smile. "I thought about doing that. Finding others to partner with along the way."

"And so you did," Harper says from behind me. Her voice is teasing, and she grins when I glance at her. Then she turns her attention back on the fish. Pulling it from the flames, she lays it along a flat rock and instructs RX-13 to slice it into six pieces. I'm wondering why we need six when two more people appear from the brush.

CHAPTER TWELVE

The two boys look like copies of each other. They're both on the short side — only a few inches above five feet — and have oversized ears and red hair. I glance at Dink for reference, then decide these boys must be about thirteen years old. One carries a spear in his hand, and the other is holding something above his head and waving it around. A collective gasp springs from the group when we realize what he has —

A bright blue flag.

"I found it," the boy holding the flag cries.

The twin next to him jabs an elbow into his side. "*We* found it."

"Whatever. Same difference."

Harper crosses the campsite in a flash and holds out her hand. The boy lays it in her palm and mock bows as if she is their queen. "Where did you find it?" she asks.

"Not far from here," he says. "We can show you."

Harper turns and inspects the flag in the fire's light. I can see it clearer this way, and I notice the flag isn't really shaped like a flag at all. It's more of a long and narrow strip of cloth. Harper grins and wraps it around her hand. Then she unwraps it and hands it back to the boys. "Show me tomorrow," she says. "Tonight, we sleep."

"We can wear it, right?" one of the boys asks Harper.

"Split it," she answers.

I'm not sure what they're talking about until I see them tearing the fabric lengthwise. They each take a piece of the blue flag and tie it around their upper arms. Then they dance around the fire. So that's why people remove the flags? To wear them as trophies?

"Have you seen anyone else wearing the flags?" I ask.

The boys stop dancing and look at me. "Who's this?" they ask together.

"Her name's Tella," Harper answers for me. "She's a Contender. She wants to travel with us."

Though I never actually said that, she's right. I'd rather be with a group than go this race alone anymore. "Nice to meet you."

"You haven't met us," one says.

"Not yet," the other finishes.

"I'm Levi," the boy with the spear announces. He elbows his twin. "And this is my brother, Dick."

"Yeah, my name's not Dick. It's Ransom."

I laugh and the boys seem pleased.

"Want to meet our Pandoras?" Ransom asks.

Though I'm not sure I can handle any more strange animals tonight, I say, "Sure, bring 'em on."

"Yep-yah!" Levi jabs his spear into the air while Ransom walks to the edge of the bush and calls out. It isn't long before the vines rustle and two Pandoras stroll toward us, one after the other.

The first is the largest raccoon I've ever seen. Its eyes are cloaked in black, and its tail is striped black and white. The rest of its fur is gray. Its whiskers twitch as it hurries toward Ransom. "This is DN-99," Ransom says, bending down to run his hand over the raccoon's back. "He's hella cool."

Behind the raccoon is a much larger animal. It's built like a huge deer but has great, curling horns above his eyes. A ram, I realize. Levi steps forward. "And this is G-6. And he's cooler than DN-99."

"You wish," Ransom says.

"Where's your Pandora?" Levi asks me.

Almost as if the other Pandoras are responding to the question, they move toward Madox. The raccoon, DN-99, reaches up on Dink's legs and sniffs Madox. The ram looms over all of them and presses his muzzle closer. I'm hoping these Pandoras are nicer than RX-13. In case they aren't, I start to stand.

"Is it still a baby?" Levi asks.

"We've been over that already." Harper's tone says not to bring it up again, and I'm thankful she's ended the subject.

"Can I set him down?" Dink asks me. It's the first time he's spoken. His voice is rougher than I'd imagined.

"I'm not sure. I don't know if —"

Before I can finish speaking, the raccoon nips Madox. The fox struggles, then falls from Dink's arms. As soon as my Pandora hits the ground, he rushes toward me. But before he can get there, the raccoon bites him hard on the rear. Not wanting to miss out on the bullying, G-6 attempts to slam the fox with his horn. I hear Dink screaming as I reach my fox and hoist him up.

I dare these animals to get through me.

"It's okay," I tell Dink, who's crying now. "You didn't do anything wrong." Caroline pulls the boy close but stops when the ram rears up on his back legs.

"Oh crap," Levi yells. "Hold on."

The ram slams his horns into the ground and the earth trembles beneath us. It's like a small earthquake ruptures the jungle. Trees shake, leaves fall in a shower, and the place where he hit splits open and groans. I try to hold on to Madox, but the ground won't stop rocking. My Pandora tumbles from my arms and hits the dirt hard. On one side of the fire is the ram; on the other is the raccoon. Madox chooses to run toward the raccoon.

The ram races after him, and when Madox gets within a few inches of the raccoon, sharp spikes burst from his gray fur and pierce my Pandora.

"No!" I scream as Madox yelps.

Ransom and Levi bark orders for their Pandoras to stop. Immediately, they do. But now the eagle, RX-13, is swooping in from the trees, talons stretched toward Madox. I get there first, pulling Madox up with my left arm — and when the eagle gets close enough — I swing a right hook and collide with the bird. She slams into the ground and slides for several feet.

I'm waiting for Harper to jump me. But she doesn't. Her eyes are big with approval. "Nice hit."

I'm having trouble catching my breath, but I still find a way to yell. "Nice hit? That's what you have to say? Why are your Pandoras intent on killing mine off? What's wrong with them?"

Harper shrugs. "Never seen it happen."

I look at the twins, and they shrug, too. Ransom tugs on his enormous earlobe. "Maybe they smell something on him."

"What could they smell?" I ask.

His forehead scrunches. "I don't know. What did you do today?"

What did I do today? I got eaten by ants and attacked by King Kong.

I don't answer. Instead, I watch as the eagle flies back up into the trees, and the ram and raccoon settle down. Inspecting Madox, I don't see any permanent damage, but he still whimpers in my arms. I don't know what's normal with Pandoras, but I can't travel with these people if I'm constantly worried about his safety.

As if Harper can read my mind, she walks over and offers me a piece of fish. "It's okay; we'll watch them from now on." She turns to the twins. "Right?"

They mumble a response, drop down, and sit cross-legged.

I'm not sure I believe them, but I'm happy Harper addressed what happened. Trying to move past the fear I felt for my little fox — and once again deal with the knowledge that these animals have *powers* — I study the fish in my palm. For one glittering second, I think about swallowing it whole. But then I see Madox and know he probably needs it more than me right now. I hold the fish up to his nose and laugh when he eats it straight from my hand.

When I glance up, the twins and Harper are staring at me incredulously.

"What?" I say. "You saw what just happened."

"You're a strange one, Tella," Levi says.

I tilt my head, stick my tongue into my bottom lip, and roll my eyes inward. It's the most horrendous face I can make. I know, because I once spent an hour practicing in the mirror.

Montana. Not much to do there.

Ransom points to my face. "That is terrible."

I laugh and so does everyone else. My ugly face is pretty awesome, but not enough to warrant this kind of reaction. *It's the jungle,* I decide. *We're desperate for normalcy.* For the next hour, we swap stories and laugh until our sides ache. We talk about the jungle, and the flag the twins found, and how terrifying being in the box was.

We don't discuss the reason we're here. I guess it feels personal.

When the fire gets too small to see well, Harper speaks up. "Levi, Ransom, feed the fire and then we'll sleep." The twins leave and return moments later with twigs and dried leaves. They toss them into the fire and the flames kick higher, sputtering sparks as they climb. I breathe in and relish the smell of ash. It reminds me of when I was home, of when I found my device in the dying fire my dad built. It seems like an eternity ago.

"We take turns keeping watch," Harper tells me. "For animals and insects and such. I'll go first, then the twins, then you, and finally, Caroline and Dink take the last shift. Thanks to you, we'll all get to sleep a bit longer tonight." Harper brushes clear a spot on the ground and motions for me to lie there.

"Thanks," I mumble. Harper is the obvious leader of this

group. I wonder if she likes the position or resents it. I can't get a solid read on her. Pulling Madox close, I lie down in the dirt and watch Caroline fold and unfold her hands. I listen as Dink's breathing becomes deep and steady. And I close my eyes and sleep.

———————————

When Ransom wakes me hours later, the first thing I do is look for Madox. He's there, sleeping along my arm, his head lying across my wrist.

"It's your turn," Ransom whispers. Behind him, Levi is already settling along the ground. "Can you stay awake?"

"Yes," I say quickly. I want these people to know I'm more than willing to do my part. Pulling myself up, I breathe in the smell of wet soil and smooth my hair. It still shocks me to feel so little of it there. Ransom lies down close to his brother, and only a few moments later, I hear the twins snoring.

I feel alone again. I know I could wake any of them if I need to, but somehow, it isn't enough. When I was by myself in the jungle, I thought constantly of staying alive. But now that I'm among others, it's like the weight of survival has been lifted and loneliness for my family fills its place. I run my fingers along my feather and think of Mom. Of what she's doing now. And if she wonders where I am . . . or if she knows.

I look at the Contenders and notice their Pandoras sleeping close by. The ram and raccoon rest a few feet from the twins, and the eagle stands near Harper, eyes closed. I narrow my own eyes and notice Harper's hand is resting over RX-13's feet. A smile finds its way to my lips. I suddenly wonder if Harper exaggerated her indifference toward her Pandora. She may never admit it, but there's often more truth found when we sleep than when we wake. Dad used to always say that.

Pulling my knees forward, I allow my mind to drift. I think of Mom and Dad and Cody. Somehow, staring into the fire, I enter a sort of trance. I don't know how long I stay that way, lost in my thoughts. But at some point, I snap out of it. When I look up, I notice Madox is inches from the raccoon.

"Madox," I whisper, alarm lacing my voice. "Get away from it."

That's when I notice my Pandora's face. His normally brilliant-green eyes are . . . *glowing*.

CHAPTER THIRTEEN

Madox is staring at the raccoon so intently, I think he's having a seizure. His little legs are locked in place, and he's leaning forward. From across the fire, I can see his eyes burning green like he's some sort of alien.

"Madox," I whisper again. "What are you doing?"

My Pandora is actually starting to freak me out. I move to stand but stop suddenly when Madox relaxes out of his crazy stare. His eyes return to their normal, nonglowing green and he trots over to where the ram sleeps. Then his muscles tighten, his eyes flick back on, and he studies G-6 like the ram holds the answers to the world.

I can't speak anymore. I'm too terrified of what will happen if the others wake up and see this. But I'm also afraid of what Madox might be doing to these creatures. I need to *do* something. Pulling myself up, I head toward my Pandora. I've almost got him when he breaks his trance, slips between my legs, and heads toward Harper.

The eagle. He's doing something to the eagle this time.

His eyes are still glowing when I scoop him up. Turning him around, I watch as they dim to their normal green hue. I'm breathing hard, and I feel a little unsteady on my feet, but I pull him to my chest and squeeze him tight.

What were you doing?

I glance at the other Pandoras. They seem to be fine, so I try to calm down. It feels like a few hours have passed since I've been keeping watch, so I decide to wake Caroline and Dink. Also, I want to know if they feel like anything is off. Starting with Caroline, I gently shake her shoulder until her eyes open. Then I move to wake Dink.

"No," she says quickly. "I'll wake him."

I nod, wondering about their relationship. Dink may not be Caroline's son, but she treats him as such, and I'm sure there's a story there. As the two pull themselves up and dust off their brown scrubs, I study their faces. They don't seem to sense anything strange, and Madox's eyes haven't flicked back on.

Caroline glances at me. "It's okay," she says, seeing the worry in my face. "We'll keep watch."

I force a smile and lie down on the hard ground. Madox circles three times and then plops down, his side pressed against my belly.

What did you do? I think again. For some reason, I feel as though I'm failing as a Contender because I don't know. With my left hand, I stroke his soft black fur. My Pandora closes his eyes, and his body relaxes. For a long time, I study Madox, the way his chest rises in quick bursts. I don't know how I'll ever sleep, but I know I need rest. So I close my eyes and try.

I wake to something splashing over my face. Dink giggles as we all sit up and realize we're being rained on. Leaning my head back, I open my mouth and drink in the cool liquid. It's not as hot in the jungle early in the morning, and with the rain pouring down my back and over my cropped hair, I feel invigorated.

"Why you smiling, loony?" Ransom asks.

"Because she's thirsty and it's raining," Levi answers for me. He opens his own mouth, and Ransom copies him.

Soon, we're all standing there, drinking the rain. We look like idiots. Every last one of us.

Madox jumps around and splashes in the quickly forming puddles, and the other Pandoras chase and snap at him. He dodges them and continues playing. I restrain myself from picking him up. I want so badly to rescue him from the bullying, but I have to start letting my little fox fend for himself. And I'm honestly kind of relieved the other Pandoras are okay after Madox's glowing-eyes attack.

Ransom plucks his device from his pocket and stares at it. I know what he's wondering — whether an electronic anything could still function after this downpour. It's the same thing I wondered the first day of the race, when the rain had lulled me to sleep. Ransom sees me watching him. He gives a halfhearted smile and drops it back into his pocket.

The rain continues as we stretch and yawn and listen to Levi tell us where we're headed. "Toward where they found the flag," Harper explains to me, as if I hadn't heard him. We walk for what feels like two miles, and the rain never stops. At one point, I do pick up Madox. I can't help myself. He looks so small in the mud and rising water.

"There," Ransom yells, running forward.

We run after him, Dink ahead of us all. When I see the pole the flag was attached to, I grimace. There's no way I've accidentally missed flags. The pole itself stands seven feet tall, six inches wide, and is painted bright blue to match the flag.

"How did you reach it?" Caroline asks. I was wondering the same thing.

Ransom looks offended. "Uh, what are you implying?"

Caroline blushes, but Harper just says, "You're short. The pole is tall."

Ransom crosses his arms. "We're not that short. In fact, we're —"

"It was tied to the middle," Levi interrupts. "Right there."

We all stare at the middle of the pole and nod our heads. Dink reaches out to touch the pole, and right as he's about to brush his fingers along it, Levi grabs his arm and yells. Dink jumps, and Levi laughs.

Caroline pulls the boy to her, but maybe she shouldn't, because Dink is laughing, too.

Harper glances around. "We need to keep track of them." I think she means for Levi and Ransom to not lose the flags on their arms. "RX-13," she calls. The bird swoops down and lands on her arm. She lets her onto the ground and kneels in front of the eagle. Then she pulls the front of her shirt up, enough so that I can see her bra is a perfect shade of pink. Of course it is. I'm relieved to see that she has the slightest hint of stretch marks on her belly. Though they're hardly visible, I'd like to imagine she was once enormous.

"Make a mark in the center of my stomach. Deep enough to scar, but not so deep that I won't heal," she tells her Pandora.

"Harper, what are you —" I start to say.

The bird raises a talon and makes a tiny slice three inches above her naval. Blood drips from the wound when the eagle removes her claw.

"Jesus, Harper," Levi says. "Couldn't we have used something besides your body?"

"My stomach is a map, see?" she explains, ignoring Levi. "When we find another flag, we make a new mark in relation to this one." Harper points to the bleeding cut. "It needs to always be with us," she says. But what she means is: me. It needs to always be with *me*.

Levi rolls his eyes. "You're frackin' bananas."

I stare at Harper as she bunches her shirt up and presses it against the wound. What I want to know is how her Pandora knew how deep to cut. Is the bird suddenly a doctor now? *Maybe Harper's lost her mind,* I think, *but at least she's making decisions.* "Let's keep moving," she says.

"Which way?" Ransom asks.

"It doesn't matter," I answer. "As long as we keep track of the direction."

Harper glances at me and nods. "Exactly."

"South?" I want for it to sound like a statement, but it's clearly a question. One directed at Harper.

She looks in front of us and nods again. "South."

We push forward through the morning. At about midday, the rain turns torrential. The twins pull off their shirts and pants, then rinse them out in the rain. They wipe their arms and legs and anywhere else there's caked-on dirt. Ransom and Levi are only thirteen or so, but it still feels odd seeing them in only boxers; their thin, pale bodies so . . . exposed.

I startle when Harper pulls off her own shirt and pants and tries to get the dirt out. She continues walking in her heavy boots and matching pink bra and undies. When she sees me watching, she laughs. "We'll never see these people again."

She may be right, but I'm pretty sure from the way Levi and Ransom are staring that they'll remember this forever. I decide to remove my shirt, but leave on my pants. Caroline still has her clothes on, and it makes me wonder what she's thinking. What my mom would think about me showing my goods in the middle of a jungle.

I think she'd tell me to stew in my own filth. That's what I think.

As I hike between towering plants, trying to pull my shirt back on, I notice something on my side. It's thin and black and slimy-looking. Because it's pouring, I can't quite tell what it is. But when I touch it — I know.

There is a leech on my body.

Oh my God. Oh my friggin' *God.*

Strangely, my first concern is to not let anyone else see. I just want to handle it and then have mild panic attacks for the rest of the day. Then chase it with a thousand nightmares while I sleep.

I pull my shirt the rest of the way on. Then I reach my hand up my side until I feel it. When I realize how plump it is, I almost lose the charbroiled meat-in-a-leaf Harper gave me last night. Biting down, I dig my nails beneath it and rip outward. The leech comes away in my hand and I throw it to the ground without looking. Making sure no one is watching, I tug the side of my shirt up and glance down. There's still a piece attached to my skin. The head, perhaps.

I vomit.

Ransom hurries over to me and rubs my back while I retch water. He's so distracted with my being sick, he doesn't notice when I reach up my side and pluck the last of the leech away. Thinking back, I know it must have attached when I was lying in the cave's stream yesterday. I mentally add caves to my Terrible Jungle Things List.

"I'm fine," I tell him.

"I shouldn't have given you that meat," Harper says, appearing sincere. "It may have been too old. It's my fault."

"It's not that," I say. "I just drank too much rainwater." I feel like we're yelling through the heavy downpour when I'd like nothing better than to *not* talk about this.

Harper seems to understand because she asks, "You okay to keep moving?"

"Harper." Ransom says her name like she's being cruel.

"No, I am," I say. "Let's keep going." Ransom stares at me, so I raise my voice. "Please."

He grins and punches my shoulder. "You so crazy, girl."

"Yeah, thanks for helping me puke. You lead, I'll follow."

Ransom kicks his leg into the air for whatever reason, then jogs toward the front of the group. Once everyone's past the spectacle of me barfing, I slide my hand up my shirt and feel stickiness.

It's not blood, I chant over and over. *It's just rain.*

Madox watches me carefully for the next few minutes, like he's afraid I'm going to eat it any second. I kick rainwater on him every once in a while, and he bites at the air. But he still watches me.

When we reach the only clearing I've seen in four days, everyone's spirits lift. It appears that a few trees died and fell to the earth recently. Now there's a big open space in the canopy above. Though the rain still comes in violent sheets, it's wonderful to see the sky.

"Let's break here and send RX-13 hunting," Harper says.

"How will we light a fire to cook?" Caroline asks, folding her hands extra hard.

Harper shrugs. "Let's just see if she can find something. Then we'll figure out how to eat it."

Levi and Ransom are already settling down on one of the fallen trees when I hear it — a low, rumbling sound. I'm about to check if anyone else heard anything when Caroline asks, "What was that?"

"Excuse me," Levi says, holding his stomach.

Ransom shoves him. "Shut up, idiot. That wasn't you." He glances around. "I heard it, too."

The sound comes again from the nearby foliage. It's louder now, loud enough so that I know it's not thunder or branches rubbing together or Levi's stomach. It's an animal. Though there are six of us and four Pandoras — standing in this clearing, blinded by the rain — it suddenly feels like we're prey.

CHAPTER FOURTEEN

The ram, raccoon, and eagle Pandoras seem to sense danger is near. They circle around us and back up, pushing us closer together so that we — the Contenders — form a close knot in the middle.

The eagle stands on the ground but snaps her wings open wide. The ram huffs sharply through his wet nostrils, and even the raccoon pulls up on his hind legs like he's readying himself for battle.

"Look at them," Levi says. He's talking about the Pandoras — their stances, their fearlessness of what's prowling the dark perimeter of this jungle clearing.

My heart throbs against my ribs, and I glance down to ensure Madox is still close to my ankle. He is. The other Pandoras may have bullied him last night, but they may very well help save him today.

"It's probably just a jungle animal," Harper says, though she sounds unsure. "We have it outnumbered. It's going to leave once it gets a good smell."

I don't like what she just said. That it's *smelling* us.

I can hear our collective breathing; Dink's sounds almost labored. Taking his hand from behind me, I squeeze, trying to reassure him it'll be okay.

The growl comes again. Deep. Close.

And then the animal erupts from the foliage and launches forward. Caroline screams, and as the sound pierces my ears, I make out what's charging toward us — a grizzly bear.

It runs on four legs, jaws open, black eyes set on the ram. Inside its ear, I can see a tattoo. It reads: *AK-7*. Seeing the bear coming, the ram rears up on his back legs. I know what to expect this time, so I grip Dink's hand tighter and feel other hands grab on to my arms. We brace ourselves for the ground to shake.

But the hit never comes.

The bear plows into the ram and the two roll in a heap. Somehow, the bear manages to land on top of the ram and opens its jaws wider. As it brings its head down, I realize the bear is going for the ram's throat.

"No," Levi cries. He starts to run toward his Pandora, but Ransom holds his brother in place. Like Levi, I want to help. To do something. But we have no weapons, nothing to defend ourselves with.

The raccoon races toward the bear — and seconds before the bear's jaws hit their mark, the raccoon jumps onto the creature's back. Spikes shoot out from the raccoon's fur and embed into the bear's brown hide, piercing the flesh below.

Pulling up onto two legs, rain washing over its massive body, the grizzly bear releases a bloodcurdling roar. Then the bear reaches around and bats the raccoon away with its massive paw. DN-99 flies across the clearing and its spikes retract into its fur.

The bear falls onto its four legs and turns its attention on us. I brace myself for the worst — but as it moves closer, nose raised, RX-13 takes to the sky and sets her target on the bear. The eagle flies faster and faster, her talons stretched in front of her.

And then she is gone.

Seconds later, she reappears, her talons mere inches from the bear. They plunge into the bear's flesh, just missing its eye. The bear howls.

"Holy crap," I say.

"Yeah," Harper says, and though I can't see her, I can hear the enthusiasm in her voice. "Invisibility."

Just like with the raccoon, the bear tries to slam the eagle away. But the eagle vanishes before that can happen, only to reappear behind the bear for another attack. Rearing back, the bear swats at the eagle. Blood drips from the animal's back as it moves. The eagle tears at the bear's flesh, but eventually, she gets too close, and the bear catches the bird between its claws.

Now the ram is back, and behind him, the raccoon.

They fight the bear like this, in rotations, for what feels like an eternity. In actuality, it's probably only a few minutes. When Dink squeezes my hand, I know what he's saying. *The bear is winning.*

Watching the fight, I know we don't have much time to make a plan. We must escape while the Pandoras attack one another, but each time someone in our group moves, the bear charges toward us. *We're the ultimate target,* I realize.

"What are we going to do?" Caroline asks through her tears.

Harper shakes her head, like she can't believe our three Pandoras are being taken down by this one.

Next to my ankle, Madox barks. It's just a small sound, but it pains me inside. If the bear gets to us, he may be the first to go. I have to do something.

Before I can make a decision, my Pandora rushes forward.

"Madox," I scream. I go to chase after him, but Harper grabs both my arms.

"You can't, Tella," she says, struggling against me. "We have to get out of here."

Madox races toward the bear and stops a few feet away. He barks again. The bear stops fighting the ram and looks at the small fox. My head pounds inside my skull as Madox's eyes flick on, burning bright green.

"What's he doing to it?" Ransom asks, astonished.

I shake my head and bite my lip. *Get away from it, Madox. Just get away from it.*

The bear moves toward my Pandora, transfixed by the glowing light.

And then Madox begins to change.

His head falls back and his spine ripples. Beneath him, his legs and arms stretch longer and wider, and his black coat begins to thicken. My Pandora grows massive muscles and new body parts — morphing into something I don't immediately recognize. His ears pull in to form neat half-moons, and his muzzle lengthens. And then understanding shakes me to my core.

The baby fox has transformed into a carbon copy of the grizzly bear before him.

And my Pandora — my sweet Madox — rears up, opens his great jaws, and roars.

In that moment, my heart swells with so much pride, I fear it will burst.

Madox doesn't wait for an invitation to fight; he just storms toward AK-7 and attacks. Rising up at the last minute, he bites down on the bear and takes it to the ground. They fight in the lashing rain for several seconds. It's hard for me to tell at one point which is my Pandora. One bear gains the advantage and readies itself to go for the other's throat. But before it can, the bear beneath it ripples and changes until all I see is a flutter of feathers and wings. The top bear fumbles backward when it realizes it's no longer fighting a bear — but an eagle.

Madox has changed again, taking the form of RX-13.

As if the other Pandoras suddenly understand what is happening, they leap into action. RX-13 dives toward the bear beside Madox and together they sink their talons into its flesh. Before, when the three Pandoras fought, they had to take turns attacking and recovering. But with Madox's help, they can now fight alongside one another.

The ram and raccoon rush forward to assist the two eagles' assault. Somehow, though the eagles are quick, the bear manages to pin one to the ground. The eagle between its claws changes yet again to take DN-99's form. The raccoon replica shoots his spikes out and the bear howls and drops him to the ground.

Amazingly, the bear still charges forward. It's like it can't stop until we're dead. I almost break away from Harper when I see my Pandora, back in his fox shape, race toward the perimeter of the clearing.

"Let me go," I scream. "I've got to see if he's hurt."

But Harper won't release me, and now Ransom and Levi are helping her hold me in place.

When Madox reaches the perimeter, his eyes flick on. He's staring at something in the bush, but I can't tell what he's copying now. Until he starts changing.

His body widens and grows taller, and his black fur pulls in and lightens in color. His tail lengthens, and a shock of hair fluffs out from around his head. Madox swishes his tail, turns back toward the bear, and locks his lion eyes on him.

As he prowls toward the bear, keeping close to the ground, I notice something appearing from behind him. A shiver works its way up my spine. It's M-4, and from the look in his yellow eyes, he's come to help.

The grizzly bear spins in a circle. It can't win. There are too many surrounding it. But there's determination in its rigid stature, and I know it won't stop until it's dead. As the Pandoras close in on it, Harper whispers, "Let's go. There's no use in watching."

"What are you talking about?" I hiss, spinning to face her. "The bear can still hurt one of them. We can't leave until we know they're okay."

"Damn it!" Levi yells.

I turn back around and hear the bear release a roar that confirms my earlier suspicions: It'll fight to the death. It drops onto its paws and races toward the ram.

"Say it!" A new voice crashes through our clearing. "Stop him."

When I see who's appeared, I can't help but smile.

He's got *psycho* written all over him.

CHAPTER FIFTEEN

Green Beret is holding another guy in front of him. Or rather, he's holding his head. And he's holding it in a way that makes me think he could seriously hurt him with a simple movement.

The grizzly bear has stopped attacking and is staring at the guy in front of Green Beret.

"Say it," Green Beret repeats, and his voice raises goose bumps on my arms. There's no way in hell I'd think about going against that order.

The guy in the headlock apparently agrees, because he opens his mouth and says, "AK-7, stand down."

The bear sits on its haunches as if that was exactly what it wanted to do this entire time. It begins licking its wounds as Green Beret shoves the guy in front of him. Scurrying over to the bear, the guy inspects it closely.

"I had no idea," the guy says. "He got away from me somehow."

The guy has blond, chin-length hair and sun-kissed skin. He looks older than me but younger than Green Beret. Like my own, his brown scrubs are battered and torn. But that's not what has my attention — it's the blue flag wrapped around his bicep. Even as Madox resumes his fox form and allows me to baby him, I can't stop staring at it.

"He's yours?" Harper asks the guy with the flag. She raises her chin, and I envy the way she can immediately regain control. I, on the other hand, feel like I'm going to pass out.

"Yeah, he is." The guy straightens and moves toward Harper, his hand outstretched.

"Pass," she says, eyeing his muddied palm. As he stands near Harper, I notice he's almost as wide as he is tall. Built like a wrestler. "Did you sic your Pandora on us?"

"Why would I do that?" the Contender asks, a hint of a smile on his lips. He brushes off his hands and looks at each of us, waiting for someone to come to his defense. No one does.

"You'd do that so there's less Contenders to compete against," Green Beret growls. I glance at him and notice he's staring at me, even though he's speaking to the new guy.

"That's insane," the guy says, shaking his head like we're idiots. "Who would do that?"

Harper grabs his beefed-up arm and eyes the flag. "Where did you get this?"

The guy beams at her, and the sight makes me squirm. There's something not quite right about him. "My name's Titus. Thanks for asking."

"Duly noted. Flag?" Harper pushes.

Titus seems to calculate his options, as I try to fathom why Green Beret is staring at me. His dark hair is still spiked, and I wonder where he's getting his gel. I try not to notice the way his cold blue eyes study my face, but it's hard to ignore. Swallowing my fear, I turn and meet his eyes. I smile. He doesn't.

"I can show you," I hear Titus telling Harper.

"Then do it." Harper nods to us like the matter is settled. We'll follow Titus, who may or may not have tried to kill us, to locate where he found the flag.

"Are you coming with us?" I ask Green Beret. My voice is barely a whisper. I have this strange half fear, half fascination going on with this guy. Like I'm not sure whether I want to watch the sun set together, or sleep with one eye open.

Green Beret's face pulls together. I realize it then — he hates me. And not in the way in which I find out later that he actually liked me the whole time.

"O-kay." I think it's clear he wants no part of this travel entourage. But then as I'm turning toward Harper, I hear him speak.

"Yes."

I spin around. "Yes? Yes, you're coming with us?"

He yanks on his left earlobe — the mangled one — and walks by me, nearly bumping my shoulder as he passes.

"My name's Tella," I say to his back. He stops for one second, then keeps walking.

Harper turns to face him. "Who are you?"

"Guy Chambers," he answers.

What the hell? Why doesn't he hate Harper? I look her up and down. *Oh, right.*

Harper glances at his lion, then back at him — at his broad shoulders and towering height. I imagine she's noticing the way his eyes don't dart, but lock on their subject. "Okay," she says. "Welcome. We're following Titus here to see where he found his flag."

Guy reveals his own flag and balls it in his fist.

"Where?" Harper asks. She seems to know better than to grab him.

"At the start of the race. About two miles northwest of here." His voice is deep and steady, like he's never been unsure of anything in his whole entire life.

"RX-13," Harper yells. *Oh God.* I wince as the eagle makes a new mark on Harper's stomach northwest of the one the twins found. Guy nods his approval. They're a good match. The two nutcases.

Harper presses her palm to the wound. "Let's move."

And just like that, we forget about nearly getting killed. About how minutes before, our Pandoras were fighting for our safety.

The grizzly bear is near the front by Titus's side. The other Pandoras eye the bear as they move, but for the most part, they stay near their Contenders and remain calm. Madox bounces around near my ankle, biting at my bootlaces.

Shaking my head at him, I try to hide my glowing admiration. *You could have told me you were a total badass.* I imagine him shrugging. *Yeah, I know. You're not the talkative type.* Clenching my hands together is the only way I can keep myself from trying to pick him up every five seconds. I'm just so damn happy to call him mine.

I walk near the back and watch Guy move through the jungle. He's in front of me, and Caroline, Dink, Harper, and the twins are sandwiched between Guy and Titus. For several minutes, we walk in silence. Then Guy turns and faces me. He holds a finger to his lips and points at my feet. He's insinuating I walk like an ogre, heavy and loud.

"What?" I cock a hand on my hip when I say it, because it's honestly kind of belittling. "Sorry, I don't slither like a *snake*."

He looks me over for a moment too long. The others continue walking, oblivious that Guy is staring me down, running his eyes over my face . . . my neck. "Pick your legs up higher," he says before returning to the hike.

I glare at the back of his head but decide I'll try the whole picking-up-my-legs thing. It causes my thighs to burn, and at first, I'm certain the only thing it's doing is making me work harder. But then I realize I'm not stumbling anymore, and, yeah, I guess I sound a little less like a bulldozer.

At one point, Ransom jogs over to hang out with me. "Going to puke again?"

I see Guy tilt his head and realize he's listening. My face burns. "No, I think I'm retch-free," I answer.

Ransom nods toward Madox. "Dude," he says.

I smile. "Dude."

"Did you have any idea?"

I pretend to brush the front of my shirt so Ransom doesn't see how guilty I look. It's not like I knew exactly what Madox was capable of, but then again, I certainly hadn't admitted to what happened with his glowing eyes last night. "Um, sorta."

Ransom grins. "Way to play the underdog."

"I wasn't —" I start to say, but Ransom is already jogging toward his brother.

"Let us know if you need to ralph," he yells. "We'll make a pit stop."

I'm mortified. Though I don't know why. Who cares if the two new guys know I got sick?

After what feels like another half hour, Titus points in front of him and says something. I'm too far back to hear, but I see the pole and connect the dots. We've found it. Again, we stand in a circle and stare up at the flagstaff. I half expect us to take hands and sing "Kumbaya" while swaying side to side.

We don't. But Harper does practice the art of self-mutilation via eagle talon for the third time today. The third small gash along her stomach indicates this flag is southeast of the one the twins found. And the one the twins found is southeast of the flag Guy found. The three marks make a diagonal line starting at the bottom left of her stomach and continuing to the top right.

"Is it a pattern, you think?" Levi asks.

"We have nothing better to go on," Harper says. She looks at Guy, and I wonder when he suddenly became her collaborator. He nods and then pitches his head to the east. "Yeah," she says. "Let's head east for a while. We'll camp there for the night, then head south later."

I agree, but secretly resent I'm not the one giving orders. Five days ago, when it was my first day in the jungle, I would have *loved* for someone to take charge. Now I feel an itch to be a part of the decision making.

I'm not sure we're headed exactly east. Who could tell? We more just hang a left and start walking. At some point, the rain finally relents. The brown scrubs cling to my body as we move, and my boots are heavy. I run a hand over my head and figure that with my short hair matted against my scalp, I probably look less like a girl and more like an emaciated, prepubescent boy. Hot.

Though we're all dragging our feet through the mud and probably driving Guy crazy, we're making good progress. Walking in a group helps. No one wants to be the person to slow the rest down.

At some point, I tire of being at the back of the pack. So I quicken my steps — passing Guy and fighting the urge to stick my tongue out at him — and catch up with Ransom and Levi. The first thing I notice is Ransom holding his left hand with his right.

"Are you okay?" I ask.

Ransom drops his hand and presses it against his side. "Yeah, it's nothing."

I circle him and grab his arm. There are a dozen dots of blood springing up across his palm. "What happened?"

Harper pauses and motions for the rest of us to stop. She trudges over and inspects Ransom's hand. "Does it hurt?"

"No," he answers, though he says it through his teeth and is obviously lying. Below us, Ransom's Pandora is going crazy, circling his feet and reaching up like it wants to say something. "I grabbed ahold of a vine to keep from slipping in the mud." He shakes his head. "It was covered in spikes."

Guy appears and takes Ransom's hand from me. He rubs his thumb over the puncture wounds. Then he glances around like he's searching for something. "You need to disinfect the area. There's a plant that can help. I'll keep an eye out for it as we walk." He nods to Harper.

"Let's keep moving," she says.

Titus, who joins our huddle, tilts his chin in her direction. His eyes keep shifting toward the jungle, as if standing still is physically painful.

"Wait," I tell Harper, though I'm watching Titus. "We need to do something for him. He's in pain."

"It's okay," Ransom says.

"No, she's right." Levi studies his brother's face. "He's hurting."

Ransom tears his hand away from Guy. "I'm going to keep walking. The rest of you can stand here and discuss whether I feel up to it or not." Ransom turns and walks in the direction we've been heading. He doesn't want to be the weak link, and I don't blame him.

Levi shakes his head and follows after his brother. Before he gets too far away, I hear him mutter, "Damn this race."

I couldn't agree more.

When the sun begins to set, Harper indicates we should stop and set up camp. The twins plunge into the jungle to look for moss and twigs, things to help start a fire. When they return, they hand what they found to Dink. I have no idea what this eight-year-old is going to do with this stuff, but he begins rubbing the bark between his hands with surprising confidence.

Guy walks over to Dink and looks him up and down. Then he reaches his hand out. "It's okay, M-4 can handle it."

I really want to see what Dink was about to do, but the boy just hands the bundle to Guy and watches him set it on the ground. Guy waves M-4 over, and the lion breathes fire over the twigs and moss, lightly at first until they're dry, then harder to make them catch.

Harper grins, watching the lion's skill. "Very nice," she says. "He'll be a good asset to our team."

Guy doesn't acknowledge her, and I'm kind of glad. There's a part of me that doesn't like her considering us tools in this race. I just want . . . for these people to be my friends. Watching the fire grow, I silently kick myself. I can't afford to think this way. I have to remember my brother.

I have to be more like Harper.

CHAPTER SIXTEEN

As we sit around the fire, Titus tries to make conversation. He jokes about how unpredictable Pandoras can be, but no one humors him besides Caroline. Next to him, his bear shifts and then disappears into the jungle night. I don't like his Pandora being out of sight or how easily Titus lets him venture off without saying anything.

Grabbing a dead leaf, I try to entertain Madox. He jumps after it a few times as I swish it back and forth, but then he collapses and closes his eyes. I smile to myself and stroke his fur. My fox has had a big day.

"He was pretty impressive." Titus's voice makes me flinch. "The way he changed shape."

I look at him for a long time while I pet Madox. "How do you know he changed shape?"

Titus grins so that I can see every tooth in his mouth. "He was a lion when I got there."

Glancing around, I notice everyone else is watching him speak. I wonder why he's still with us. We already found his flag location. I wait for Harper to say something, but she doesn't.

"Where is your Pandora?" I ask him.

Titus shrugs like he couldn't care less. "Probably went hunting." As if on cue, the bear peeks out from the brush. He studies his Contender for a long moment, then saunters over to sit beside him. All along his great shoulders are strange lash marks. I wonder if he got them from the fight or from something else. My curiosity over his injuries is severed when I see what's between the bear's jaws. I gasp with surprise.

The rabbit struggles against the bear, and already I can see blood dripping from its back legs. AK-7 opens his mouth and drops the rabbit to the ground. The creature immediately tries to run, but the bear pins it down. Then he drags a single claw lightly along his prey. He does it over and over again as the rabbit squeals. The animal's entrails begin to bulge from its belly, but still the bear torments it, and still the rabbit screams.

"Stop him. He's torturing it," I tell Titus. The other Contenders shake their heads and mumble their own protests.

"Why?" he asks, laughing. "He has to eat."

Titus watches with fascination as the bear places a giant paw over the rabbit and presses down. I jump to my feet and rush toward AK-7, but it's too late. The rabbit's skull cracks with an audible snap.

"Oh God." I turn away and feel tears burn my cheeks. When I glance back, the bear is ripping the rabbit's leg off and shoving it into his mouth. Red flashes before my eyes. "What is wrong with him?" I rub my tears away. "What is *wrong* with you?"

Titus holds his hands up, but I don't miss the smirk on his bronzed face. "Calm down. This is a Pandora, not a teddy bear."

I storm toward him, but two strong hands grab ahold of me. "Tella." Warm breath tickles my neck. "Go sit down."

Craning my head, I see Guy standing behind me, feel his fingers burning against my skin. "*You* go sit down." I glare at the other Contenders, and finally, Levi speaks up.

"Seriously, man," he says. "Why don't you ask it to eat that somewhere else?"

Titus tucks his blond hair behind his ears. "I don't understand what the big deal is."

Guy lets go of me and steps toward him. "If you want to travel with us, the bear eats somewhere else."

"Exactly," Harper says, nodding.

Titus holds his hands up, surrendering. "Fine. AK-7, eat that away from here."

The bear looks at him for a moment, then gets up and leaves, rabbit carcass dangling from his jaws.

Guy faces Titus for another moment before turning to me. His eyes search my face, digging for something. "You can sit down."

"What's in your hand?" Caroline asks. I glance at her and notice she's directing the question at Guy. That's when I notice the two snakes he's holding.

I stumble backward and land hard on the ground. He watches me bust it, then picks up a long twig from the fire and drives it through the snakes.

"Dinner," he says finally. "They aren't venomous."

"I usually make RX-13 hunt," Harper says, and I'm surprised to find even she appears uncomfortable. "But I guess I could give her the night off." Harper waves a hand at the eagle. "Go hunt for yourself."

Levi and Ransom do the same for their Pandoras, though Ransom's is slow to leave. The raccoon seems upset by something, but I can't tell what that might be. Before long, the three animals vanish into the jungle. I should send Madox after them. He should learn to get along with the other Pandoras. But I can't help wanting him close.

My stomach turns as Guy cooks the cleaned snakes, then hands each Contender a piece. When he offers Titus a helping, Titus says, "Is that all I'm supposed to eat?"

In response, Guy tosses the piece of charred snake into the dirt at his feet. "Overeating will make you sleep too heavy."

"We take shifts," Harper breaks in. "We can sleep heavy if we need to."

Guy looks at her and then tilts his chin toward the snake, saying she can have more if she wants it. I decide to follow Guy's lead and eat only what he gives me.

There's an uncomfortable silence as we chew the tough and

bony meat. I gag four times but somehow manage to get the meal down. For some reason, the only thing I can think while I'm swallowing a hunk of snake is that I am the type of person to have three glittery feather boas draped over my dresser mirror at home, purple, pink, and red. And now I am eating snake.

Everyone watches Titus as he shoves the charred meat into his mouth and chews. I don't like the way his eyes flick over my body as he eats, or the way he eyes Harper as she tends to the fire.

Caroline senses the need to break the awkwardness. "We did well today, huh?"

I smile in her direction. Her eyes are a soft gray, and they tell me everything I need to know. She is kind and giving . . . and she will not win this race.

Harper hands Dink a stick from the fire, and the boy uses it to draw bunnies in the dirt. "We did do well," Harper says to Caroline, returning to her seat. "We'll do even better tomorrow."

I want to ask how she can be sure. But then I realize she can't be. It's just what leaders say to inspire the troops. Harper twists her long blond hair into a bun and spears it with a thin twig. Her green eyes dance in the firelight, and I wonder what she's like when she's at home. Whose child she is. What her room looks like. I wonder if we had gone to the same high school, if we'd be friends, or if we'd ignore each other, too different to connect outside of this race. I'll tell you one thing, I bet having a friend like Harper would have made life at Ridgeline High a lot more exciting.

"Do you think we'll —" Caroline starts to say.

"Guys," Levi interrupts. "Look at this."

We all look at his open hand. He's holding his white earpiece.

The red light is blinking.

No one says anything for a long moment, then everyone fumbles into their pockets or bags for their own devices. When we've each retrieved them, we hold them out on display. *They still work. Even after all that rain.* I breathe a sigh of relief, then wonder whether this should actually worry me rather than provide peace of mind.

Seven lights blink, creating a circle of red flashes around the fire. I count the devices. There are too few, I realize.

Dink starts crying softly.

"It's okay. It's fine." Caroline pulls him into a hug. "We'll tell you what it says."

"What? Did you lose your device?" Titus asks Dink, laughing. Though I'd also like to know, I want to slap him for asking.

Dink cries harder, and Caroline gives Titus a look that's supposed to shut him up.

"And where are your Pandoras?" Titus adds, looking back and forth between Caroline and Dink.

"They didn't make it," she says for them both. "And Dink did lose his device, but it was an accident."

Titus tilts his head and presses his lips together, like he's being sympathetic. "It's not his fault. This race isn't cut out for *certain* people."

Caroline's face reddens. She jabs a finger in his direction. "Listen, kid —"

"Guys." Levi lifts his hand and refers to the device. "Can we listen to the message now, please?"

Titus shrugs like he doesn't care, and everyone starts to put their devices into place. But me . . . I can't stop watching Caroline glare at Titus. Maybe I underestimated her. Each of us has a reason back home to fight through this jungle. Caroline has one, too, I'm sure. But she also has a reason sitting right next to her.

I feel someone staring and glance over to find Guy studying me. I make a *what?* face. He points to his ear as if to say I'm lagging behind. I roll my eyes and shove it into place.

As soon as I do, a wave of anxiety rolls over my shoulders. Harper gives us a thumbs-up. Everyone besides Dink touches the red blinking lights. The clicking and static noises begin, and I feel my body tighten with anticipation. I know that across the jungle and here in front of me, other Contenders are probably hearing the same message. But for some reason, it's as if the woman is speaking directly to me.

"If you've been keeping count, you'll realize this evening concludes day six of the race. You have until noon on the fourteenth day to arrive at base camp. Therefore, you have approximately eight more days remaining to reach your destination."

My skin crawls thinking about spending another eight days in this place. I don't know how I will do it. As I look around the campsite, I understand now more than ever that I may not have had a prayer before I met these people.

"We are so very proud to have such a diverse group of Contenders this year. It will make for an exciting race." The woman pauses and I hear paper rustling. *"You may be interested to know that exactly one hundred and twenty-two people entered the Brimstone Bleed."*

A hundred and twenty-two people? I think back to the first day at the starting line, to all the nameless faces. I wish I knew them. I wish I knew where they were now. A new thought occurs to me: If we had all decided to race as a team and *demanded* to share the winning prize, could these people have created enough of the Cure for everyone?

The woman shuffles more papers.

"There are currently one hundred and fourteen Contenders competing in the Brimstone Bleed."

CHAPTER SEVENTEEN

The Contenders around me remove their devices, but I stay still. I keep waiting for an explanation. Why are there fewer Contenders now than there were six days ago?

You know the answer, my mind whispers.

The device suddenly feels too large. It's going to grow until it splits my ear wide open. I snatch it out and throw it to the ground. "What happened to them?" I yell to no one in particular. "Where are the other Contenders?"

Titus chuckles. "Seriously?"

My head turns in his direction. "Yeah, seriously. Spell it out for me."

"Okay, they're dead." He slides his hand across his throat. "Jungle meat."

"Real nice," Harper says, looking disgusted.

"Yeah, you know what, why don't you take a walk?" Levi adds.

"You going to make me?" Titus asks, laughing.

"Yes, *we* might," Ransom says, next to his brother.

"Please." Titus snorts. "I'll whip you both and wipe my ass while I'm at it."

Guy stands up.

Titus sizes him up for a long moment, then opens his arms out wide. "I don't know why everyone's jumping on me anyway. The girl asked a question."

"And you answered it," Guy says. He nods his head toward the jungle. "Go blow off some steam."

Titus's mouth quirks on one side like everything's a big joke. "I'll go. But I'll be back." Before he leaves, his eyes land on me. He searches my face and then looks down into my lap where Madox is sleeping. Titus narrows his eyes.

I clutch Madox closer, and Titus laughs.

"See you later, compadres."

After Titus disappears, Guy turns around. He doesn't look at me. Instead, he eyes the same thing Titus did — Madox. *They want him,* I suddenly realize: *It's why they're both traveling with us.*

The thought makes my stomach turn. For a minute there, I figured they wanted the same thing I did during this race — the comfort of companionship. But they only want what will help them win.

Is that so terrible? I wonder. *That they want to save the life of someone they love?*

The things I'm thinking feel too big for my head to hold, like they need somewhere to go.

"I'm here for my brother," I blurt out.

Guy's eyes flick from Madox to me. His face stays hard and unreadable, but he sits down. I imagine it's the best invitation I'll get from him.

"He's nineteen years old. Only three years older than me." When I glance around, I notice Harper is looking at me with a strange expression. Envy, maybe. "He likes these glossy comic books about aliens?" I say it like a question, because I'm not sure how everyone is taking my verbal vomit. But no one stops me from continuing. "And he still has these action figures that my grandma gave him. They're from a fast-food joint by our old house. Which means they're worthless, you know? But he keeps them anyway." I pull in a long breath. "He likes vanilla pudding, but only if it's really cold, and he has about thirty different colognes that are half used."

I have no idea where I'm going with this, but once I've started talking about him, I can't stop. A million fun facts about Cody Holloway fill my brain, itching to be released into the jungle. I open my mouth to continue, but Ransom jumps in.

"We're here for our sister," he says, and Levi nods. "She's a year younger than us. Mom says she got so lucky with Levi and me that she had to keep going while her luck was hot."

Levi laughs, like he remembers his mother saying this.

I'm so happy Ransom is sharing his own story that I can hardly breathe.

"Josie, our sister," Ransom continues, "has this boyfriend we give such a hard time. But I guess he's all right, really. She texts him so much that we joke and say she has an addiction. So now my dad has been researching texting rehabilitation clinics. Seriously. They have those." Ransom gives us all a look so we know just how serious he is. "Anyway, she's obsessed with her boyfriend. And mood rings. And these dumb mint cases that you can only buy online." Levi nudges Ransom, like he's forgetting something. Ransom shakes his head like he doesn't understand, but when Levi rolls his eyes, Ransom laughs. "Oh, I guess she likes us all right, too."

For some reason, we all look at Caroline. She seems like the next-most receptive person to this little share-and-tell thing we have going on.

"Oh, my turn?" she asks, placing a hand to her chest.

"Spill it," Levi says.

"Okay, well." Caroline adjusts herself on the ground, crossing her legs tighter. "I guess I'm here for my mom. I mean, I *am* here for my mom. She just turned fifty-five. We had a birthday party for her before we left. My son and I made this cake . . . but she refused to eat any." Caroline shakes her head. "My mother used to be in the movies. Not like those big-budget films, just some of the ones that go straight to DVD. But that doesn't stop her from acting like a big-budget actress, right down to the no-carb, no-sugar diet." She laughs to herself and rubs the back of her neck. "My mom carries around these markers in her purse, just in case someone asks for her autograph. And then if no one does, she'll just sign something anyway — a napkin or ticket stub or whatever — and hand it to them with this smile . . . this smile that says she's *somebody*."

Dink tugs on Caroline's sleeve and she wraps her arm around him.

"I never really knew my mom that well. But she says if I win, she'll spend the rest of her life being friends with her daughter."

The first thing I think is that her mother is lying. That she's saying whatever she needs to motivate Caroline to win. The second thing I think is . . . "How does your mom know about the race?"

Caroline glances at me. "Because her uncle was a Contender."

I feel like someone has kidney punched me. "So she *knew*? She knew about the Brimstone Bleed? Did she know you'd be invited to become a Contender? Does she know about the Cure?" I know I'm grilling her with questions too quickly, but I can't help myself. I'm dying for more information on how this happened to us.

"No." She shakes her head. "She just knew the stories about her uncle. She only told me about them after the blue box — er, the device — appeared on my windowsill. Mom says she would've told me sooner if she thought there was any truth to his stories. But I'm not sure she would have. It seemed like she was nervous telling me what little she did know."

"So what did she tell you exactly?"

"Only that he competed in something called the Brimstone Bleed to save his wife's life." She looks at Dink before adding, "He left after the second leg of the race."

I want to ask why her uncle gave up, but I don't want to pry in case it's a reason she doesn't want to share. Instead, I ask, "Did she say anything else? Like what to expect or how this all started?"

Caroline thinks for a moment, and then shrugs with one slender shoulder. "That's all she really told me. That her uncle entered and that he didn't win." Her eyelids flutter. "Maybe she didn't want to scare me."

Glancing around, I notice that Harper and the twins are just as eager for information. Guy, however, looks like he knows something. "Guy, do you know anything else?"

He looks slowly from Caroline to me. Then he shakes his head.

But I can see it all over his face.

He's lying.

Harper interrupts my train of thought and speaks to Caroline. "Are you sure that's all your mom told you?"

Caroline nods. "I'm sure."

"So this race has happened before," Harper states.

Ransom crosses his arms. "This crap is so messed up."

I wholeheartedly agree. Somewhere out there is a person, or a group of people, running this thing. How can they do this to us? How can they play with our emotions — and our lives — this way? I look up at the people sitting here with me. We're not so different. We're all here out of selflessness. Here to save someone else's life.

Glancing at Dink, I wonder who *he's* here for. Titus is a prick, but he's right. This race isn't for children. "Dink," I say softly. "Who are you trying to save?"

The boy's head snaps up. He looks at me with big brown eyes. Somehow, though I hate my own curly hair, on him, I find it adorable. It makes him appear even more innocent. So I can't bring myself to push when he just shakes his head.

"That's okay," Harper says. "You don't have to tell us if you don't want to." When I look at Harper, she makes eye contact with me for a second, then glances down. It's obvious she won't be sharing a story tonight, either.

Everyone looks at Guy.

He pulls in a long breath. "No."

We all stare at him, thinking he may say something else. He doesn't.

The silence among our small campsite is ruptured when the raccoon and ram return. Behind them are Titus and AK-7. I cringe, thinking Titus is going to pick right back up where he left off. That he's going to confront Guy. But he just sits down and leans back, like he couldn't care less that we're here. His grizzly bear shakes like a wet dog, then lies down beside him, muzzle still coated in blood.

DN-99 runs circles around Ransom, and again I wonder what's going on with this supersized raccoon. Finally, Ransom pays attention to him. "What?" he says. "What on God's green earth are you so wound up about?"

When Ransom reaches out to stop his Pandora from racing in circles, the raccoon leaps onto his left hand and pins it down. "What the hell?" Ransom says. He tries to jerk his hand back, but before he can, the raccoon begins licking his puncture wounds. Ransom's eyes slip closed and he groans with pleasure. Then his eyes snap open. "Wow, that was embarrassing." He laughs. "It just — it feels really good."

Levi leans forward and looks at his brother with disgust. "All right, man. Can you stop with the animal porn? Get him off your hand."

"No," Ransom says, shaking his head. "I can't."

"Dude," Levi yells. He grabs his brother's left hand and yanks it away from the raccoon. Then he narrows his eyes. "Holy crap."

Ransom pulls his hand away from his brother and inspects his palm. "The wounds," he says quietly. "They're healing."

We all rush over to see it happening — the small, round holes squeezing closed. I feel like I'm imagining it and wonder if maybe that snake was venomous after all. When the wounds have completely healed, we all take turns pressing on his palm to make sure it's real.

Then we stare at the raccoon.

So *that's* why it'd been acting strange all afternoon. Then again, what is strange for a Pandora?

Glancing up, I notice Titus licking his lips. Harper notices him ogling, too. She makes a face like she's uncertain of what to do next. Finally, she says, "So the Pandoras haven't shown us their full capabilities yet."

"Maybe they aren't even aware of them themselves," Caroline muses.

Ransom turns his hand over several times in front of his face, while the rest of us pull away and try to relax on the ground. Even though it feels like something truly mind-bending has just taken place, we settle down to sleep. It's the only thing we can do for now. Dink yawns, and Harper stretches out onto her back, gazing up into the canopy.

"Ransom, how about you and your brother take the first shift?" Harper says, her eyes still locked on the trees. "Caroline and Dink can go next, then I'll go, then Guy and Titus, and finally, Tella." Harper tears her eyes away from the jungle and looks back and forth between Guy and Titus. "We take shifts when we sleep, looking out for predators and insect hordes." She glares at Titus. "And stray Pandoras."

Titus doesn't acknowledge her remark. He just lies back and folds his thick arms beneath his head. Even though he looks about eighteen, his enormous frame makes him appear much older. But right now — lying in the dirt like the rest of us — he doesn't seem very menacing.

I watch as Guy stands up, dusts himself off, and searches for a place to sleep. I'm not sure why. There's no magical spot that feels better than the rest. My heart picks up when he moves closer to where I'm sitting. He inspects the area only three feet away, kicking at rocks and pulling up stray vines. Then he sits back down. His eyes flick in my direction and a chill races over my arms. He nods his head, lies down, and closes his eyes.

Did he move next to me on purpose? Is he offering his protection? Or am I his first target?

My God. I am in the epicenter of hell, and I'm trying to psychoanalyze some guy. Pathetic. Shaking my head, I lean back and try to find a comfortable position to sleep. Right as I'm about to drift off, I hear Caroline's voice.

"I just don't like that there aren't any rules," she says. "There should be rules."

No one responds. I know she's talking about the race. I'm sure everyone does.

We just don't know what to say.

CHAPTER EIGHTEEN

I wake up and am surprised to find I slept deeply, despite the small portion of delicious snake I ate. As I'm stretching, I glance up, thinking it might be morning. But that would mean I missed my shift for keeping watch.

Surveying our campsite, I note Guy sitting straight up, staring into the fire. I look around. Everyone else is asleep. I'm not sure why he's ignoring me. It's obvious he knows I'm up.

"Hey," I whisper. He turns and looks at me. "Why isn't Titus awake?"

Guy looks back at the fire. I'm not sure he's going to answer. It certainly wouldn't surprise me if he didn't. But then he says, "Harper only woke me. Maybe she thought I would wake him up myself."

He doesn't finish his thought. That he *didn't* wake Titus up.

"How long have you been keeping watch?" I ask.

Guy scratches his cheek. "A while."

"It's my turn, isn't it?" I say. "You didn't wake me up, either."

He doesn't respond.

"Okay, well. We need to get something straight." I straighten and look directly at the side of his head. "You may think I'm weak, but I'm actually pretty damned determined to win this race. And I am going to do my part as long as I'm traveling with these people." I gesture toward the sleeping Contenders. "It's only fair."

Guy cranes his neck. Not enough so that he's fully looking at me, but enough to let me know he's listening.

I reach down and pet my Pandora, who's lost in dreams. Guy and I don't say anything for several minutes. I'm trying to prove that I'm a contributing team member, and Guy is trying to prove . . . what? That he doesn't trust me?

"You needed sleep," he says suddenly. His voice, normally so deep, is almost jarring when he's making an effort to keep it low.

I attempt to process what he's saying. "So, you didn't wake me up because you thought I needed more rest?"

Guy doesn't move for a moment, but then he nods slowly.

"Because you think I can't handle this race like the others can?" There's a defensive edge to my words as I recall my dad trying to burn the earpiece. He didn't believe I could handle this race, either.

He looks me dead in the face. "Because you looked tired."

I hold his gaze for a moment, and as I do, a shiver shimmies down my spine. His eyes are the most phenomenal shade of blue I've ever seen. They're not beautiful, exactly. More . . . startling. And the way he looks at me now — as if he sees through to the other side — makes him seem wildly unpredictable. I wonder about the deep white scar cutting through his right eyebrow. For some reason, it seems to say more than even his eyes do.

"Oh," I manage to say. "Thanks, then. I guess."

Guy looks up at the canopy and puts one hand on his lion. "Your Pandora is extraordinary."

If I didn't know better, I'd say Guy just initiated a conversation. It stings that it's only to dig for information. "Yeah," I mumble. "The other Pandoras were picking on him a couple of days ago. I'm kind of happy he was able to prove his worth. Not just for my sake, but for his own."

"You care about it," Guy says. It's not a question. He's seen the way I cling to Madox.

I nod and wrap my arms around my waist.

Guy rubs his jawline. "The other Pandoras were intimidated."

I glance at him, curious as to where he's going with this. Shadows cast by the fire dance across his face. "What do you mean?"

"They must have" — Guy flicks his fingers near his nose and breathes in, like he's sniffing something — "smelled it on him. They must have sensed his ability to replicate them. That has to be intimidating, knowing their only job is to help their Contender win and running into another Pandora that can do what they can just as easily."

I watch Guy saying this, the sureness with which he speaks. "Maybe you're right," I say. He seems to be intuitive about a lot in this race. He found a flag within the first twenty-four hours. He knows how to handle himself in the jungle. And I'm certain he knows much more than he's letting on. "Guy," I say gently, "how much do you know about the Brimstone Bleed?"

The muscles in his arm tighten, and I'm sure I've heard the last I'll hear from him today. But he surprises me again.

"I know some things," he says. Then he looks at me. "But it isn't anything that will help me or you win." He clenches his fists. "Our families, even if they knew, weren't allowed to tell us anything before we received our devices. If they had, there would have been consequences."

I search his face and feel sure he's telling the truth. There are so many questions I want to ask him, but I think he's told me everything he's willing to share for now. So instead, I try something different. "Do you think we'll make it to the other side of the jungle in time?"

He tilts his head and studies me with what, strangely enough, looks like sympathy. "Tella, they're not leading us to the other side of the jungle. They're leading us to the center."

I let my gaze fall to the ground. Of course they are. The jungle must get much worse the farther you get inside. "I don't understand what the people running the Brimstone Bleed get out of this," I mumble, shaking my head. "They seem so *cruel*."

"It's complicated," he says quickly.

Everything in me wants to shoot questions at him like rapid-fire, but I can't speak. Because Guy is staring at me in a way that makes my cheeks flush. He puts his palms against the ground and moves closer. When he's only a breath away, he lifts a hand and runs it over my side. Every rational thought in my mind vanishes.

"What happened here?" he asks.

Glancing down, I notice he's thumbing the quarter-sized stain of blood on my shirt. To my surprise, there's a fainter, larger stain circling the center one, as if the blood has seeped outward. Guy pulls the side of my shirt up and I gasp when I notice the small wound the leech left. It's pink and puffy, but the most alarming part is that it's *still* bleeding.

Guy presses near the wound and blood oozes out.

I fight the urge to faint.

"This is from a leech." He looks at me for confirmation, and I nod. "When they bite, they inject you with venom that prevents your blood from clotting."

I am going to bleed out from a leech. And die.

That is how I take this news.

"You'll be fine." Guy lets my shirt fall back into place and stands up. "I need to go find something to stop the bleeding, though. I'll be right back." He taps the lion's head. M-4 springs to his feet. "Come on, boy."

For fifteen minutes, I plan my funeral. My pastor will give my life eulogy. He'll say I wore way too much makeup and that I had a borderline obsession with sticky notes. They'll serve Greek food at the wake, because Mom will insist it was my favorite, and Cody will ask why he has to eat this crap even after I'm gone.

But that's not right. Because if I'm gone, then Cody . . .

I hear a rustling nearby and am so relieved to see Guy, I almost hug his legs. He's holding a fistful of leaves in one hand and two stones in the other. Sitting next to me, he grinds the leaves between the rocks.

"Is that going to save me?" I ask.

Guy stops grinding. "Save you?"

I realize in this moment that my life is not dangling by a thread. I laugh. "I'm kidding."

He goes back to grinding. Seconds later, he lifts my shirt back up. Despite what we are treating here, I can't help but get goose bumps. Because he's, you know, *lifting my shirt up*. I watch as he gets some of the leaf pulp between his fingers and spreads it over the wound. As he works, I don't even think about what he's touching. Instead, I concentrate on the way he chews his bottom lip in concentration. Guy is so distant and cold, but right now he's something different.

"Why are you traveling with us?" I ask suddenly.

He stops applying the makeshift medication and looks up. And, my God, he is so damn close. Guy's eyes travel from my eyes to my lips. He presses his own together, and then pulls away. "Your Pandora is very powerful," he says. "I can't imagine there was a better one created than him. I know if I stay close by, your Pandora will remove most roadblocks from here to the Cure."

I swallow. He told the truth. I had expected him to lie. Then I'd expected to wrestle the rest of the day with whether to believe him. But he told the truth. I run a hand over my head. "Thanks for telling me, I guess."

"You already knew," he says.

I look at him. "I suppose I did."

Guy returns to medicating my side. When he's finished, he moves away, but only a little. "You look different," he says.

My face scrunches with confusion. "How so?"

He touches a calloused hand to his head and tugs on a spiked clump of his own dark hair.

Oh.

"Yeah, I probably do, huh?" I say. "I forgot you saw me at the Pandora Selection Process." I lean back on my hands. "There was a girl that dragged me down that day by my hair. I decided it had to go." What I want to also say, for some asinine reason, is: *Don't worry, it'll grow back. I won't always look this hideous.*

Guy studies the feather lying over my shoulder, then nods to himself. If I didn't know better, I'd say I just got an official nod of approval. Not sure of what to say next, I ask, "Do you think the raccoon would have done this? Healed my wound?"

He shakes his head. "Not for you, no."

It's what I figured, that each Pandora looks out only for its own Contender. Still, I wonder how he knows for sure.

Guy cracks his knuckles like he wants to say something, but doesn't know how. When after several seconds he still hasn't spoken, I decide to take a gamble. "Guy? Will you tell me about this race?" I swallow hard and add quietly, "Please."

"I told you it wouldn't help."

"Tell me anyway," I say, hoping my voice is steady.

Looking toward the sky, he seems to think. He pulls in a breath and lets it out. He does it again. And again. His broad chest swelling like a bird's, then flattening. Then to my astonishment, he speaks. "There are different people running it. Different . . ., names for them." He stops suddenly, like he can't believe he's said anything. I stay quiet. So quiet, I can hear my heart pulsing in my ears. Guy wets his lips. "There are the Creators, the ones that made your Pandora. They're more commonly referred to as Pharmies."

My mind spins. I know that word. The girl in the train car with me said it.

"They work in pharmaceuticals, of sorts, and ensure the Cure is available to the winner." He taps his temple lightly. "These guys are brilliant. They were experts in genetic engineering by the early 1950s, two full decades before the public started reading about it."

Guy looks at me, but I avoid his eyes. I don't want him to see how enraptured I am by what he's saying. Instead of asking him to clarify, and before I can really think, I ask, "Who are you here for, Guy?"

He turns away from me. I've asked the wrong question, and now he's shutting down. To my surprise, he looks back at me with a mischievous glint in his eyes. "You owe me a favor for treating your wound." He says it so even keel that I wonder if he practices speaking without emotion.

"A favor?" I ignore the fact that he's avoiding my question, or that he's just told me half a story. "What kind of favor?"

He looks at Madox, and my stomach plummets. No. I won't give him my fox.

"I want you to sing that song," he answers.

"What song?" But as soon as I ask, I know. He heard me singing to Madox when I was following him. Which means he *knew* I was following him. "Oh God." I cover my face with my hands. "You mean the sicky song."

When he doesn't say anything, I realize he really, truly means for me to sing it. Like, now. "You can't be serious," I say.

Nothing.

I roll my eyes. This will be the most embarrassing moment of my life. But he touched my leech wound, for crying out loud. And I have so many more questions I need him to answer. So if he wants the sicky song, he gets the sicky song.

I clear my throat like a professional might do. Then I open my mouth and sing. It lasts for ninety humiliating seconds. I can't even look at him when I'm done. But when he doesn't say anything, I can't *not* look at him.

Glancing over, I notice he's just staring forward.

"You are a horrible singer," he says.

My jaw falls open. The friggin' nerve. I'm about to tell him where he can shove it, but then I see it — the smallest of smiles tugging the corner of his mouth up. And I can't help myself. I point at his face. "You're smiling," I say while laughing. "You're totally smiling."

The grin slides from his face, and he shakes his head as if he doesn't know what I'm talking about. But I totally busted him and he knows it. Mr. Stone Cold just *broke*.

He lies down and closes his eyes. "I think you're well rested enough to watch on your own now."

"I was to begin with," I retort.

He's quiet for a full minute before I hear him speak again. "My cousin," he says. "I'm here for my cousin. Because he'd have done it for me."

I smile to myself.

I know he won't say anything else.

CHAPTER NINETEEN

Our group hikes through the jungle for five days, our Pandoras trailing nearby. We face problem after problem: falling trees that nearly flatten us, unrelenting rain, chronic fatigue, insect stings . . . the list feels never ending. The *race* feels never ending. Mostly, we do what we can to survive each day. We eat and drink what the jungle provides. We share stories and memories from home as we hike to keep our spirits up. And we locate two more flags: each southeast of the one before it.

At night, we set up camp and take our usual shifts keeping watch. Guy continues to not wake me when it's my turn, and I continue to wake up on my own through sheer determination.

We talk during this time. Me more so than Guy, but still, he has his moments. There's never any divulgence about the race, not since that first time. But it feels good to have a moment that's stolen. As if we carve it out of the jungle night and say, *This belongs to us.*

I learn that Guy actually enjoys the wilderness, and if it weren't for the race, he might be having the time of his life. He's from Detroit, which I find insanely cool, and he has three younger brothers. Though he'll never admit it, I know he also worships his father. Oh, and he likes newspapers: not to read, just the crinkling sound the pages make.

Five days. Ten stolen hours. And that's all I know.

Every day now, Guy hikes behind me. It makes me super paranoid. Mostly, I think about the size of my butt and its general flatness versus roundness. At least it keeps my mind off more serious matters. Like the fact that my hands have started trembling, or that Dink hasn't said a word in three days, or that Titus grows more agitated and aggressive by the day. I once asked Guy why we let him stay. He said something about it being better to have him in sight.

Today is day ten. And behind me I can hear Guy's steady steps. They are faint, but the sound still soothes me. Just like every other day, I puzzle over what Guy told me about the race. About why the Pharmies created the Cure, and the Pandoras, to begin with. Four days ago, I thought about telling the others what Guy told me but decided I'd better try and get the full story first. Because God knows if they all start asking questions, he'll clam up for sure. But once I do find out, I'll share what I know. It's only fair.

"Everyone still good for another hour before we rest?" Harper asks, rupturing my thoughts. She cranes her head skyward as she speaks, searching for her eagle.

The other Contenders and I mumble an affirmative response.

"Okay, I'm going to ask it," Ransom says. "How much friggin' farther do you think base camp is from here?"

"Forever," Levi answers, one hand on his ram's curled horn. "It's forever from here. That's what it feels like anyway."

"Ten days," Caroline says quietly.

I know what she means. We're starting to cut it close. We have only four days left.

"What if," Ransom says. "What if there really isn't a base camp?"

Harper stops suddenly, and Ransom slams into her back.

"God, Harper," he groans. "Walk much?"

She spins to face him. "Don't say crap like that. We don't need it. Understand?"

He looks off to his right. I can't see his expression from here, but I imagine it's one of irritation. Our fuses have become shorter with each mile we hike. Ransom rolls his hand as if to say, *Whatever, let's go.*

We keep walking, and I fight the urge to look behind me. To see what Guy is doing. Maybe he's building binoculars out of bark or a cell phone out of vines. Madox trudges through the jungle near my right ankle. He's been a trooper during this race, though I can tell even he is beginning to tire.

We walk in formation for another few minutes until I hear something. Everyone stops and listens. This is what this leg of the race can be summarized as: listening. There are sounds that tell us a foreign animal is near, and others that the rain makes. When it's morning, there are sounds that entire armies of insects create, and different sounds for when we're near a stream.

The sound I hear now is not an innocent one.

It's heavy and slow, and my mind begins to fill in the blanks. It must be large, and it's either hunting for something or already on the prowl. As the noise grows louder, I know it's closing in, and because it doesn't slow, I determine it's not here to attack us. Titus's grizzly takes a step forward and lifts his muzzle into the air, smelling. M-4 mimics him from a few feet away.

I startle when I feel something behind me. Craning my neck, I find Guy standing so close that his arm brushes my back. He's looking over my shoulder, watching intently, like he's waiting to take those last two steps so that he's in front of me. I want to tell him I can take care of myself. That *Madox* can take care of me. But the truth is I like that he's there, just in case. So I turn and face the sound.

Narrowing my eyes, I can spot two animals heading toward us. As they tread closer, I notice there is a third smaller animal and three people following behind. I wonder if they are Pandoras or jungle creatures. But as I get a better look, I know it's the former. The animal in front is a zebra. Its stripes change colors as it walks so that it blends almost seamlessly into the green and brown foliage. Behind it is a rhinoceros, a thick ivory horn growing from the tip of its nose. Hanging near the back, close to the three Contenders, is a kangaroo. Its long tail drags behind it as it hops along.

The Contenders don't notice us, and I'm not sure if that's for the best. I can't help wondering who these people are, where they came from. The cluster of travelers is made up of an older man, maybe in his midforties, and two younger girls who appear dangerously thin.

Harper takes a few hesitating steps toward them, and then raises her arm. She's going to let them know we're here. But before she can, Titus grabs her wrist and yanks it back down.

"What the hell are you doing?" he hisses. "Trying to get us killed?"

Harper gives him a lethal stare before ripping away from him. "There's no reason we can't help each other until the end." I still don't know how I feel about Harper, but I can't help agreeing with her on this point.

Though I know she's fuming, she looks away from Titus and back at the strangers. No one else says anything as we watch them pass. When they're out of earshot, Guy steps beside me and speaks to our group.

"Running into other Contenders may mean we're getting close." His brow lifts. "And it probably means we're headed in the right direction."

Levi points toward where we spotted the Contenders and their Pandoras. "Look, something else is coming."

We watch and wait. The vines and plants rustle, but we never get a clear view of who's there. I make out that they're human — that there are maybe six of them — and that they aren't Contenders. Their clothing is also brown, but it's too dark in color. As they move, they stay close to the ground, their heads snapping this way and that. A sense of foreboding brews in my stomach, and even the birds overhead seem to hold their breaths. Though my brain demands my silence, every muscle screams for flight.

"They're following the Contenders," Guy says quietly.

Watching them, I know he's right. There's an odd, jerky manner to the way they move. These people, though I can't fully see them, are like nothing I've ever known.

Except.

I think back to the man I saw the first day of the race. The one I thought I imagined. Maybe he's one of these men. I wonder what they're here for and whether they've been following us. Madox whines below me . . . and my legs begin to shake. I tell myself it's because we've walked for too long this morning and that I'm exhausted. But I know it's something more. That it's fear.

Guy looks into my face. I wonder if he sees how this race is beginning to take its toll on me. I think for a moment that he's going to suggest we stop here to rest.

"We should walk through the day," he says. "We can rest tonight."

I close my eyes against the disappointment. But I won't be the one to suggest we stop. So I clench my fists, remember why I'm here, and hike to the front of the group with Madox at my heel. "I'll lead," I announce. "We're all tired, but I expect you to keep up."

For one single moment, I wait for Harper to protest. To stake her claim as leader of this troop. But when I glance at her, she has a look of relief in her green eyes. She doesn't smile at me, or even nod. She just gets in line behind me and starts walking.

We've been heading east, but it's nearing time for us to turn and trek south. I'm still at the front, hiking through thick jungle plants, a film of dirt and sweat across my brow. Every few minutes, I scan our perimeter, searching for more Contenders and their Pandoras. We'd seen more over the last three hours. There was a teenage boy with a tortoise, a man with long black hair and a yellow snake wrapped around his arm, and two women in their forties with a pair of owls. Most Contenders traveled alone, but some, like us, hiked together. It's reassuring to see them. A lot better than seeing the strange men, who we keep an eye out for but haven't spotted again.

My boots begin to feel heavier as I walk, and I cringe from the blisters that have formed along my Achilles tendons. I look up to ensure the path ahead is free of logs or dense plants, and notice the ground seems darker. I realize then that my boots haven't gotten heavier, but rather the earth has become softer, making it more difficult to walk.

"The ground," I say. "It's getting muddy."

Guy walks up next to me, and his lion shadows him. He crouches down, digs his fingers into the wet dirt, and rubs them together. "We're nearing a body of water."

Over the last week or so, we'd crossed many streams that allowed us to quench our thirst. But at night, Guy tells me about great, rushing rivers that live inside most jungles. A tickle of excitement creeps through me, imagining his river.

"Let's keep going," he continues. "We have to stick to the plan."

This is fine by me. I'm eager to see what's ahead. So I plow onward, even though the dirt gets thicker and harder to trudge through the farther we go. Soon, the sound of rushing water is unmistakable. My tickle of excitement morphs into full-body exhilaration. Ever since that day in the clearing, where Madox shifted into different Pandoras, I haven't seen anything but dense vegetation and tall trees. And right now the desire to see the sky or a river or something *different* is overwhelming.

I rush forward. After several more feet — and a few stumbles — I see it. The river. It's wide and caramel brown and there are bright white clouds floating overhead. A grin sweeps across my face, and when I turn to see the other Contenders, I'm thrilled to see they are smiling, too.

Everyone except Guy, that is.

I'm suddenly furious that he can't appreciate this, the whispering water and cool air. "What's wrong with you?" The bitterness in my voice surprises me. "Why aren't you happy?"

His eyes stay on the river, searching. "Because it's time to go south."

I turn back to the water and dig my nails into my palms. He's right, of course. We've spent about six days traveling east, so it's time to turn. Scanning the thick mud along the bank, I know it'll be impossible to hike alongside the river and make enough progress.

We'll have to use the current to carry us south.

We'll have to go into the river.

CHAPTER TWENTY

The river seems so vast, a winding, curling snake in the heart of the jungle. I can't imagine how we'll ever use it to travel. Or what creatures live in its dark belly.

"Do you . . ." Caroline says slowly, eyeing Guy. "Do you think we should swim?"

"I'm not swimming in that shit-stain water." Titus snorts. "Do I look like someone who wants Ebola?"

I have no idea whether you can get Ebola from swimming, but I sort of agree. This water doesn't look like something I want to submerge myself in.

Guy walks away from us and comes back a few seconds later, holding various things. He moves closer to the water and throws the first item in. I'm not sure what it was, but it now lives at the bottom of the river. He throws the second thing, and it plays follow-the-leader, sinking fast. I watch as he throws in two more things. They all plunge into the river and drown.

His back rises and falls like he's taking a deep, frustrated breath. Then he cracks his fingers — all but his thumbs. I picture racing over and cracking those blasted thumbs for him, but before I can, he says, "We need something that floats."

"Okay," I say quickly, turning to browse the vegetation around the riverbank. This feels good, like we have a plan. *We need something that floats,* he said. Fine. Everyone in our group searches the jungle floor for several minutes while our Pandoras watch. We look like a crew from one of those murder movies. Like we're searching for a body. It's a twisted thought, but it makes me laugh.

"What's so funny, Looney Tunes?" Levi asks.

I shake my head. "This is the crap I used to watch on TV.

People searching through wooded areas, wearing horrendous clothing. I mean, how is this happening to me?"

Levi's brows pull together like he's thinking really hard. Then he looks at me and his face splits into a smile. "I have no idea."

Ransom stands up like something huge has occurred to him. We all look in his direction.

"What is it?" Levi asks.

Ransom glances around. "I'm in a jungle. A. Freaking. Jungle." he says. "With a magic raccoon."

Dink giggles, and the sound surprises us so much that we all stare at him.

Ransom points at Dink. "I made the kid laugh."

"People," Guy says. "Floating objects."

We all look at Guy, then make faces to one another like he's our overbearing dad. Secretly, though, I love that he's so focused and reliable. His steadfastness is what allows the rest of us to let loose. Even Harper, who days ago was the epitome of seriousness, now shakes her butt at him.

"That's great," Guy says, watching her. "Thanks for your help."

"Okay, okay," I say. "Let's help Boy Scout find something that works."

Minutes later, we're standing along the bank, our arms overflowing with random jungle foliage.

"All right," Guy says. "Throw them in."

Everyone tosses their arms up, and down rains the most useless crap ever.

Except for what Caroline throws — which, thank the sweet heavens, actually floats.

"Yep-yah!" Ransom shouts, pointing at the long, thin tube surfing the river.

We all dance around like idiots at Caroline's success. Levi and Ransom pick her up, and the three nearly tumble into the river.

We are delirious from exhaustion, but I'm relieved that something has worked and that we're doing our best to stay optimistic.

Titus glares at Caroline.

Lost in the moment, I stick my tongue out at him. "Cheer up, Grinch."

He crosses the distance between us in a matter of seconds. His hands wrap around my waist and he jerks me against him. "Stick that tongue out again," he whispers against my neck, "and I'll show you what I want to do with it."

Titus flies away from me and lands hard. Guy stands over him, face twisted with rage. He points a densely muscled arm at him. "I need your help with this river, so I'm going to let you pick yourself up out of that mud." Guy bends down and gets in his face. "But if you touch anyone else here, I'll hold you underwater until the last breath leaves your body." He stands up. "Do you understand? I will *end* you."

Titus's eyes are large with surprise, like he has no idea how he ended up on the ground. But then his eyes change. They fill with fury. And the smile that crawls over his face in no way resembles the wrath lacing his voice. "Sure, buddy," Titus says, grinning. "I was just messing around."

The look on Titus's face says there's no way he'll let this slide. Afraid of what Guy will do, I eye him with alarm. But Guy does something that surprises us all. He offers Titus his hand.

Titus, still sticking to his innocent facade, takes Guy's offer and pulls himself up. He looks at me and his grin widens. "You know I was just playing, right?"

I nod, because I don't know what else to do. In my peripheral vision, I spot Titus's grizzly bear. He never moved to protect Titus, which surprises me. Madox, on the other hand, is at my feet, hackles raised, a small growl in his throat as he eyes Titus.

No one speaks for the longest moment of my life, and then Caroline says, "So what do we do now, Guy?" It's a reasonable question, but it still feels odd after what happened. Guy tears his gaze away from me and looks at Caroline. He seems equally confused by how to respond. Rubbing the back of his neck, he glances at the water, like he just remembered it's there. "We have to build something so that we can ride the river."

Everyone kind of looks around, eager to have something to do that isn't standing here uncomfortably.

"Caroline, where did you find the thing that floated?" Guy asks. "That piece of bamboo?"

She points upriver. "It's down that way. Along the bank."

"Okay, good." Guy knits his eyebrows together, and the scar over his right eye deepens. "Titus, Ransom, and Levi, you guys come with me and we'll get as much bamboo as we can. The rest of you need to look for vines that don't break when you tug on them. Does that sound good to everyone?"

Harper glances at me and says, "We got it on our end." I nod to let her know I agree.

Titus salutes Guy. "Happy to help, General."

Guy ignores the comment and starts walking, M-4 at his side. The rest of us head back into the jungle foliage. A half hour later, we're on the riverbank again. We made out like bandits in the vine department. It was Harper who found the best kind. We tried everything to get it to break, but short of RX-13's eagle talons, nothing worked. We have our winner.

The boys appear minutes later, carrying their last armfuls of long bamboo shoots. M-4 and AK-7 walk beside their Contenders, holding their heads high. I imagine it was them who cut the shoots down and then sliced them into equal lengths.

Ransom lines the bamboo stalks side by side as the guys lay

them down. Harper, understanding what is happening, goes to one side of the bamboo and begins tying the ends together so as to create a long and narrow raft. I take her lead and begin working on the other side.

As I'm winding the vines around the bamboo, I notice Madox is watching me. Thinking about riding the river creates a nervous rumbling in my belly. But I smile at my Pandora and pretend everything is as it should be. He climbs onto the raft and cocks his head to the side. I imagine he's saying: *Let's* do *this thing*.

Guy tugs on the bamboo and tries to separate the stalks. They don't budge. He looks at Harper and me, and gives us a thumbs-up. I light up like the sun, then feel like a chump for being so desperate for approval. "Are you all ready?" He doesn't actually wait for an acknowledgment. Just starts positioning us on the raft. I suddenly realize there's not enough room for our Pandoras. Not even close.

"What about our Pandoras?" I ask him.

"They can travel faster without us." He motions farther up the bank. "We'll have them follow our progress along the river."

"No way," I say. "I'm not leaving Madox behind."

"Tella," he says. Warmth fires across my skin when I hear him speak my name. I shake my head against the reaction, and he mistakes it as disagreement. "Yes. They have to stay here. If we try to put them aboard, the entire thing will capsize. We have a lion and a bear. Think about it."

He's right. I know he is. I want to insist there's at least enough room for Madox and perhaps even RX-13 and DN-99. But I know it'd be unfair. I swallow down the fear of losing my baby fox and gently nudge him off the raft. "KD-8," I say. "I want you to follow the raft from the bank. Understand?"

Madox looks at me with confusion, and Titus snickers. I fight the urge to yell at Titus.

Please do it, Madox, I silently plead. *Just go with the others.*

I sigh with relief as my fox chases after the other Pandoras, whose Contenders have given them similar orders.

"Okay, everyone off." Guy waves his hand to hurry us along. "Titus and I will move the raft into the river, and then everyone needs to get on exactly as before."

We all step off and watch as Titus and Guy maneuver the bamboo raft into the water and hold it into place. Then we carefully step back on. Surprisingly, the raft doesn't rock too much, and we're able to get on without too much trouble. Right before Levi steps on, he grabs a spare bamboo shoot. He holds it as Guy gets on behind Titus, who's in the very front. Guy takes the bamboo shoot from Levi and pushes us away from the bank.

As we float toward the middle, I spot something moving in the brush.

"Look," I say, pointing to where we just were.

A man dressed in strange brown clothing peers out from behind the trees. His head darts side to side as he inspects us. He acts just like the men we saw following those Contenders earlier today. And he looks like the guy I spotted my first day in the jungle. The one I thought I'd imagined.

There's a long, spear-looking object in his left hand, and he raises it to point in our direction. Moments later, two more men come to crouch beside him. Their faces and lips are painted with vibrant red streaks and their heads are adorned with bright feathers. The effect is nothing if not creepy.

Inspecting the feathers closer, I notice they are green and blue like the one I wear in my hair. I touch it absently, running my fingers down the soft bristles. "Who are they?" I ask.

"I don't know," Harper answers. "But I'm glad they're there and we're here."

The men cock their heads like birds, then disappear into the jungle. I watch the spot for a few seconds longer until we've floated so far down the river that I can't remember where I'd seen them. An icy chill swirls inside my chest, and I wonder if the men will follow. I don't like the way they watched us — like they'd missed a crucial opportunity.

Dink raises his arm and points. We all look up and see RX-13 flying overhead.

Harper — who is standing next to me — grins.

I look toward the bank. I pray Madox is keeping up with us and that the other Pandoras are, too. Though I remember these people are my competition, I don't want them to lose their companions.

When I don't see any sign of Madox, I stare down into the river. It's dark, too dark to see much of anything beneath the surface. Gazing into it, I can't help wondering what animals live in the current. Piranhas? Do they live in jungle rivers? What about crocodiles?

"Titus, I need you to steer me in the right direction." Guy uses the bamboo paddle to keep us floating in the center of the river. I wonder why he chose Titus to take the lead. *Maybe to keep an eye on him,* I think.

Though we are all behind Titus and Guy, I can see the way Titus pulls himself up taller. "So far, so good, General."

We float for about fifteen minutes before the sun begins to set, and it starts to rain.

"Rain. How original," Levi mutters.

Harper presses in close to me. I look at her in surprise, but she won't meet my eyes. I press back against her and try to hide my smile.

The rain isn't anything new, but the fact that we're on the river while it pours down is. I watch as the river slides farther up the banks and notice that the water under the raft is rushing much faster than before.

"Guy," Caroline says from behind me. There's a question in the way she says his name, and I realize I'm not the only one who's growing more afraid of the rising river.

"Titus, guide me toward the bank." The muscles in Guy's back tighten as he works to get our raft stable. "We'll continue after the rain stops."

Titus yells over his shoulder, but because the rain is coming down harder, I can't make out what he's saying. Guy switches the bamboo paddle from his right side to his left, and back again. Then he looks back and motions for us to crouch down.

We don't wait to be told again. Soon, everyone besides Guy and Titus are on their knees, holding on to the bamboo as best they can. The river rages beneath us, and I can't fathom how this happened — how the river changed from frightening to lethal.

The sound is almost deafening. It's like a white noise, and it is everywhere. The rain pours over our scalps and shoulders, and the river sprays across our bodies. I see white tips form along the river surface and though I've never floated on a river — not once — I remember they're called rapids. It's a strange word, I think. Rapids. *Rapids.*

My thoughts are shattered when I hear a high-pitched scream. I spin around and my stomach plummets.

Caroline is gone.

I stand on unsteady feet and search the river. The scream grows louder and I realize it's coming from Dink. Next to me, I see Harper get to her feet and rock unsteadily. She moves to the side of the raft and I realize suddenly what she's going to do.

"Harper, don't," I yell.

Above us, RX-13 screeches. Harper's concentration breaks and she glances up. I do, too.

The eagle glides through the sky, beats her wings once, then folds them against her body and dives down. The Pandora crashes into the river, vanishing beneath the surface.

"No," Harper screams.

Though the water is murky and the sky is growing dark, I spot the eagle just beneath the surface. She's flapping her wings as though it's the most normal thing in the world — an eagle swimming. Seeing this, Harper pauses. But only for a moment. Then she readies herself to dive in.

The eagle breaks through the river and opens her great wings in front of Harper like a shield. Every time Harper tries to dive in, the eagle blocks her advance.

"Stand down, RX-13," Harper cries.

But I know if the Pandora can help it, she won't let that happen. Because her job is to protect Harper, and no one else.

I know what I have to do.

I close my eyes, pull in a breath — and jump.

The last thing I hear is Guy calling my name. Then there's nothing but the river.

CHAPTER TWENTY-ONE

My body is pushed forward so quickly, it's like I threw myself in front of a moving car. My legs and arms splay out in a panic and I wonder if maybe this wasn't the best idea I've ever had. But then I remember why I jumped. That Caroline is in the river, and that I have to help her.

I somehow gain control of my body and break the surface. Guy peers over the edge of the raft, a hand raised to his eyes. From the angle of his body, I can tell he wants to jump in, but he's trying to determine where I am before he leaps. Maybe I should have done the same. Now I'm being dragged downstream, with no idea of where Caroline is.

Diving under the water, I search for her. My eyes fill with the murkiness, and I don't see her anywhere. I come up for air and then dive back down. Underwater, I hear a sort of ringing in my ears and the dull *thump-thump-thump* of my heart. Though it's chaotic above the surface, it's strangely peaceful below it.

I swim in a circle — and see Caroline. She floats like a broken angel — long, dark hair forming a halo around her face. I yelp with surprise and bubbles burst from my mouth. Taking another breath from above the river, I dive down and swim toward her. How long has she been underwater? A minute? Two?

My fingers brush her skin. I've almost got a good hold on her when something large appears in the corner of my vision. My heart flies into my throat and I imagine this is it, that I'm going to spend the rest of my days in a crocodile's gut. But when I look closer, I realize it's Dink, swimming toward Caroline like he was born with fins. He wraps his arm across her chest and pulls her toward the surface with ease. I follow him, gasping for air. When his eyes find mine, I point toward the shore and he nods.

We swim hard toward the bank, Dink doing a far better job than me. The closer I get, the faster the river seems to go. I watch as Dink gets on dry land and drags Caroline behind him. My arms and legs grow heavy, and that's when a new fear washes over me — one that says I'll drown in this river. Behind me, I see the raft pulled up onto the bank. The other Contenders look like blurry dots in the rain. Closer to me, Dink is bending down over Caroline, breathing into her mouth. But even he is moving away much too quickly.

My head bobs above and below the surface, and each time I draw in a breath, I wonder if it'll be my last. Everything is happening so fast. I have no idea how I went from hero to victim, and I'm not sure how I'll ever get to shore when I can hardly use my legs.

I feel something break through the water behind me and then brush the top of my head. I glance up and almost cry with relief. *RX-13!* The bird latches her talons on to my shoulders. I bite down against the pain as her nails dig into my skin. The bird flaps her wings hard in the rain and moves toward shore. I do what I can to help the momentum, but I'm running out of energy.

Little by little, the eagle gets me closer to land until finally I feel the earth beneath me and am able to walk up the bank. I collapse onto the ground and breathe hard. When I turn to see the eagle drying her wings, I realize her eyes are bright green.

"Madox," I croak, spitting up water.

Pain shoots through my ankle and I realize my foot must have caught on something in the river. I reach down and grasp it. The pain worsens beneath my touch. I have no idea how I'll keep moving on a bad ankle, but there isn't time to feel sorry for myself —

Because I hear something.

It's a sound — careful, deliberate steps — that lets me know I'm being watched. Madox shifts into fox form and stands between me and the sound. A low growl erupts from his throat. The noise causes a bolt of terror to strike through me. My gut says it isn't the other Contenders from my group. But then, what could it be? It's the strange men, I realize suddenly. They followed us.

New sounds crash around me, and I glance away.

Contenders.

Everywhere.

They're running, sprinting toward something, with looks of horror twisted across their faces. Or maybe they're running away from something. Not waiting to see what's coming, I grab Madox and run in the direction the other Contenders are. Pain rips through me as I step down on my injured ankle, but I will myself to race through it. Pandoras of all shapes and sizes run beside their Contenders — and if it weren't for their anxious howls, I'd be filled with awe.

I look over my shoulder and gasp. The strange men are chasing us. Each holds a long spear, and they're making odd chanting noises. Nearby, I notice a girl a few years older than me. She's running hard, her hands splicing the air. For one moment, our eyes connect. Then she hits the ground hard. I stop, thinking she fell and I'll just pull her back up. But when I get closer, I spot the spear protruding from her back. Her head is turned sideways, and her face is vacant.

"Oh God." My whole body begins to shake.

I hear my name being called, but I don't look up. I can't do anything but stare at the girl. Someone grabs my arm and yanks me forward. It's Guy. He's tugging me onward and screaming at me to move.

But the girl.

"Tella," he yells, shaking my shoulders. "Run!"

Madox wriggles in my arms. It's enough to bring me back to reality. I nod at Guy and we race forward. Beside us, I see Levi and Ransom and wonder where the others are. Maybe they've found a safe place to hide. I tell myself this as I run, pain tearing through my ankle.

Up ahead, I see a flickering orange light. As we get closer, I discover that the light is coming from lit torches and that the torches form a massive circle.

"It's base camp," Guy yells through the rain, through the night. "It has to be."

I run harder, but when I look over my shoulder, I realize the men are closing in. From this distance, the red stripes on their faces look more like blood than paint.

I concentrate on keeping my legs high so I don't trip. It's no use, though. Because the men are gaining on us, and I know it's only a matter of seconds before they take one of us down.

I glance back one more time and scream when I see a man with green face paint reaching toward me. In the same moment, I feel Madox fight against my arms and fall to the ground. The second his body hits the wet earth, he begins to shift. The man slows enough to watch Madox transform into a lion, and he stops cold when my Pandora opens his mouth and roars. I try to stop, too, but Guy grabs my hand and pulls me along.

"Keep moving, Tella," he growls.

I try to keep running, but when the man recovers his senses and aims his spear at Madox, I stop and cry out. Madox spins away from the man and races toward me. I think he's going to barrel into me, but instead he digs his head beneath my legs. I realize what he's trying to do — that he intends for me to ride him — so I grab on to his mane with my left hand. My right hand is still holding Guy's, but when Madox launches forward, we're ripped apart.

"Guy!" I yell.

He runs after me, but Madox is too quick, and it isn't long before I can hardly see him. The camp ahead grows closer. When

I turn back, I can just spot Levi and Ransom running toward us. Behind them is the man with green face paint who almost grabbed me. He raises his spear — and throws.

Levi hits the ground.

I can still hear Ransom screaming when we fly between the torches and into base camp.

CHAPTER TWENTY-TWO

I scrabble off Madox's back to rush to Levi, but my Pandora blocks my way. I've never been angry with him, but right now I'm so furious, my vision blurs.

"Move, Madox," I scream. "That's an order. Get out of my way."

He either doesn't understand or isn't listening, because he continues to ensure I stay put. Moments later, I see Guy and M-4 race past the torches. He turns around to look behind him and gasps for air. Then he sees me.

"Are they here, too?" he asks. "Are the men inside the camp?"

I shake my head, but not because I know one way or another. But because I can't speak, thinking about what happened.

"Tella, are you okay?" he asks, moving toward me. "Are you hurt?"

I shake my head again and begin to cry.

Over Guy's shoulder, I see Harper, Caroline, and Dink cross into base camp. Minutes later, Titus arrives. Through my tears, I watch them catch their breaths and gather around Guy and me.

"Is she hurt?" Harper places a hand to her chest and rubs, like she's willing her lungs to fill with air.

"I don't know," Guy answers.

I'm so relieved to see Caroline okay, but it does nothing to stop the things I feel after seeing Levi fall.

"Where are Levi and Ransom?" Harper asks, glancing around.

Everyone stops and looks for them. Everyone but me.

"They got him." My voice breaks. "This man threw a —"

I can't finish my sentence. It's too hard. Especially when I see Ransom approaching base camp. His cheeks are streaked with tears, and his chest and arms are coated with blood that I know isn't his own.

I rush forward to help him, but the others beat me there. Harper puts her arm around him, holding him up as best she can. Caroline gets the other side. Titus just stares at us. He doesn't help, and he doesn't say anything. He just watches.

Guy looks away from Ransom and back at me. His eyes run over my face, but he speaks to both of us. "You couldn't have saved him."

I cover my eyes and press them, but a sob still pours from my body. I feel someone's arms around me. They lift me up and carry me somewhere warm. They lay me down and tuck a heavy blanket around my shoulders. I only know for sure that it's him when he tells me to sleep, that he'll be right here when I wake up.

When I open my eyes hours later, the first thing I see is Guy. He's sleeping a few feet away on the floor. I glance around and spot several other Contenders, and a few Pandoras, sleeping, too. My heart skips a beat when I see Madox lying over my feet. I'm so relieved to find him there. Then I wonder *why* I'm so relieved.

When I remember what happened, I bolt upright. The girl lying in the jungle with lifeless eyes. Levi with a spear breaking through his chest. The men —

"Guy," I whisper, shaking him. "Guy, wake up."

He moans and then opens his eyes. They go from sleep laden to alert in a matter of seconds.

"Are the men here?" he asks.

"No. Or maybe. I'm not sure." I gaze out a small window and see the same orange lights dancing in the night. The torches are still lit. "How long have I been asleep?"

"A while," he answers. "Some people were already asleep when we got here."

I look down at my hands. "Levi?"

Guy slowly shakes his head.

I expect to feel sadness or depression or even fury. But instead, I feel nothing. It's like I'm empty inside. I came here to save my brother. But how many people have died trying to save one person? I wonder why we stay . . . if we could leave now if we chose to. But then I imagine returning home to watch my parents grieve and Cody die in his bed. And I know there's no way I can stop if there's a chance I can change that future.

"Our devices went off while you were sleeping," Guy says. "We all listened already." I start to dig into my chest pocket, but Guy holds out a white device. "It's yours. I just checked to see if it was blinking."

I feel my eyes glass over. "Can you just tell me what it says?"

He looks at me like I may suddenly break into a thousand pieces. Then he nods. "It was the woman. She congratulated us on completing the first leg of the race and for arriving at base camp."

My face scrunches, and I turn away in disgust. People died in this jungle. *Congratulations,* she said.

"She said there will be a ceremony in four days when the first deadline passes. She called it Shevla."

I hear what Guy is saying, but for some reason, I can't absorb the information. I inspect the interior of where we are. It seems like a cabin, like something made of logs and mud from frontier days. It's a single room with only six beds, which are more like cots. Everywhere I look, I see green-and-blue plaid blankets and fluffy white pillows. The cots remind me of home, of how secure I felt in my own bed with the cool of my pillow beneath my cheek.

I wonder how Guy secured me a bed when so many people are sleeping on the floor.

The cabin has two small windows and only one door. No bathroom, no kitchen . . . no electronics of any sort. Once again, we're completely barred from the outside world, without a clue as to where we are.

"Is this everyone?" I ask Guy.

He pauses, like he's processing that I brushed past the ceremony tidbit. "No," he says, finally. "There are nine more cabins like this one. Most are about half full. This one has more beds than the others."

I glance down at the cot I'm lying on. Then I remember where Levi is lying — dead in the jungle — and I'm overtaken by a wave of dizziness.

Guy stands up and then sits along the side of my small bed. He places a hand on my shoulder and pushes me back down. I don't fight him. I just let my head find the pillow and I squeeze my eyes shut. I hear him get up and walk away, and the sound rips my heart in two. I don't want him to leave me. I know so little about him — about the person he was before this race — but I've come to think of him as a source of stability. With him, we are safe.

I wonder if Levi thought he was safe.

I stuff my mouth against the pillow and cry.

Then I feel someone slip into bed behind me. My head snaps around to see Guy's blue eyes slide over my face. He holds my gaze for a few moments, then lies down and wraps his strong arms around me. He pulls me tight and buries his face in my neck. Madox hardly stirs.

All the fears I've held inside rush out. It's like he's asking for them, saying he'll carry them for me. I press back against him and curl into a ball.

We lie like this for several minutes before I feel his words on my neck. "My cousin loves lemon," he says. I can tell he's trying to whisper, but the deepness of his voice makes it almost impossible. Over the past ten days, I haven't learned many personal things about Guy. But I have picked up on the way he operates. And so I know that if I say anything now, he'll shut down. I stay quiet, and after what feels like ten minutes, he speaks again.

"He has lemon everything. Lemon soap, lemon shampoo, lemon tea. He even let his girlfriend paint his room yellow because the color was called Lemon Laughter." I feel Guy shift behind me. "My brothers and I ragged on him pretty hard about it. But after he got sick, I spent months obsessing over that same lemon crap. Sometimes . . . I felt like if I could find something really great for him, something lemon scented or lemon flavored or whatever, that he'd be happy again."

We lie in the silence, and eventually, I feel his breath on my neck deepen. Before I fall back asleep, I wonder where the strange men are and if they'll enter the base camp. But inside Guy's arms, I imagine it isn't even possible.

For four days, we reside inside the camp. The two men from the start of the race are here, the same ones who helped unload us from the semis. They wear green, collared shirts and gold chains with serpent pendants. Contenders try to ask them questions, but when that happens, the men just glance past as if they aren't even there. The only thing they *will* do is tend to the injured. Apparently, they're part day laborer, part doctor. The men are an odd addition to an even odder situation.

The base camp is made up of ten small cabins, and the ground around and between them has been cleared so that it's just soft dirt beneath our boots. I'm thankful for this, because even though my ankle is improving, I imagine it'd still hurt to walk on uneven terrain.

Torches circle the perimeter, and in the center of the camp is an enormous fire pit — though the men keep us from lighting it. In one of the cabins, there are basic supplies: packs of dried fruits and meats, bottles of water, toothbrushes and toothpaste, deodorant, soap, and even TP. And across the base camp, where no windows face, are three outdoor showers that offer a bit of privacy. I don't know where the water comes from, and I don't care. It feels like heaven on earth.

During the day, we entertain ourselves as best we can — mostly by meeting other Contenders and gawking at their Pandoras — but at night the Contenders pull away into small clusters. Harper, Caroline, Dink, Guy, and I spend most of our time together. I keep an ever-watchful eye on Madox, who seems playful and carefree at times, and anxious at others.

Ransom has become reclusive, and though we try to include him in everything we do, he mostly stares off into space, his face shadowed with rage. It kills me to see him this way. I think the others are getting tired of me talking about it. But I can't forget him, and I know he needs us now more than ever.

Titus also doesn't hang around us anymore. This, on the other hand, is a relief. He seems to have found a new knot of Contenders to group with. They're all guys, ranging from maybe early teens to midtwenties. The pack has swiftly formed an unsettling reputation, and most people stay out of their way as best they can.

Glancing around, I spot three women in their early fifties discussing something. Two of them laugh, while the third frowns. After a moment, the women disperse. Sitting close to where the women stood are a guy and girl pair a bit older than Guy. They stay close to each other, constructing something long and thin out of branches. They don't speak; they just work. On the far side of the camp, children play. A girl Dink's age chases a boy and girl, diving after them and kicking the ground in frustration when they narrowly avoid her grasp. Many of the Contenders have plum-colored bruises or shallow lashes across their extremities.

Others seem untouched by the jungle. But they are all here, seeking some sense of normalcy.

Since it's the last day to locate base camp, I'd expected a constant stream of Contenders to trickle in. But no one has arrived since last night. When the sun nears the middle of the sky, all the Contenders hover around the perimeter, waiting to see who will make it in at the last minute. But as the sun crosses the sky and begins to set, we know it's over. That this is everyone.

The horizon, or what I can see of it, is splashed with reds and pinks. It's so beautiful, and in my stomach, I feel the first twinge of happiness after four days of fear and mourning. I knew Levi for only ten days, but I won't ever forget him. And I'll never forget that he died fighting for his sister's life.

I feel someone standing near me and turn to see Guy watching me.

"Hey" is all I say. Then I turn back to the painted, darkening sky. Guy feels huge next to me, and I fight the urge to lean closer. I don't know how to explain my feelings for him — if they're circumstantial, or something more — but I know it's hurt that he hasn't slept in the bed with me since our first night at base camp. It was the only time I felt any true relief — and though he always sleeps close by, it isn't close enough.

Guy reaches his hand toward me, but when I turn to face him, he lets it fall. His jaw clenches.

"Guy —" I start to say.

"May we have your attention?" a voice booms from behind us. Guy and I spin around to see the two men in collared shirts standing near the fire pit. We glance at each other like we're not sure they just spoke, because before now, you'd have thought they were practicing to enter a Buddhist monastery. "We will now begin the ceremony that marks the completion of the jungle race."

The man on the right has a swollen belly and thin arms. He lights a match with his even thinner hands and tosses it into the pit. Fire bursts toward the sky and sounds of awe ripple across the Contenders. The man on the left, who's sporting a wicked comb-over, raises his arms into the air and his voice rumbles. "Welcome to Shevla!"

CHAPTER TWENTY-THREE

I gasp as men, women, and children dressed in white robes and ankle-high boots pour out of the jungle and into our camp. The women wear huge, bright jewelry and serious faces as they carry platters of food above their heads. And as they move closer, decadent scents roll off the dishes. Every memory of being eaten by ants, of escaping chimpanzees, of being sucked on by leeches and nearly drowning and racing through the jungle with strange, painted men trying to kill me — they vanish when I smell the food.

The women set the platters down onto tables the men carried in on their backs. I laugh with surprise as small children approach the fire and sit with drums between their legs. They begin to play. The beat is contagious, and before long, the women in white begin to sing strange, seductive songs.

Guy takes my hand.

I look up at him, forgetting the trance Shevla has brought.

"Do you want something to eat?" he asks.

I nod like a child on Easter, a yard of candy-filled eggs just beyond my reach. Guy pulls me toward the tables and we get in line. Four women in white tell us about the food as we fill our stoneware plates.

"Smoked over fire," a woman says, pointing to cooked fish. "And here, we roast these with spices from the jungle," she adds, touching a finger to a platter brimming with glistening vegetables.

Guy and I settle in close to the fire and listen to the beat of the drums. The women continue singing, but now they add dancing to their performance. They skip and leap and toss themselves in peculiar patterns around the fire as if the music has possessed them. I glance at Guy, and notice there's a smile on his lips fighting to make an appearance. I want to tell him to let it happen, to not be so serious all the time. But I know it'll vanish the moment I do, so I don't say anything. Instead, I nudge him with my shoulder.

"Pretty cool, huh?" I say, after swallowing down a bit of charred, buttery fish.

He doesn't look at me, but the quasismile leaves his face, as I expected. "Yeah, it's pretty cool." He looks down at his plate. "I don't think these people know about the race. They were probably just paid to bring us food."

That's why I'm able to enjoy it, he means. *Because* they *didn't do this to us.*

Across the fire, Caroline is finger brushing Dink's hair. He pretends to pull away, but the slight grin on his face gives him away. Ransom is nowhere in sight, which worries me, but I do spot Harper a few feet from Caroline. There's a guy talking to her. She ignores him completely. Even so, he continues to chat away as if they're both participating in the conversation. Harper sees me watching and sighs heavily. Against all odds, I smile, and it actually feels authentic.

I'm not sure what Harper's ideal type would be, but I'm pretty certain this guy isn't it. For one, he seems way too happy to be here. Or maybe he's just happy to be near *her.* The guy looks a bit younger than Harper and is extremely tall. His hair falls in messy blond curls that nearly hide his eyes. He uses a lot of dramatic arm gestures as he speaks to Harper, and I can only imagine this annoys her to no end.

"Check out the guy talking to Harper," I say, attempting to discuss anything that isn't the race or Levi or the fact that no one has seen Ransom today. "He seems pretty determined to get her attention."

Guy's brow furrows as he inspects the blond. "Poor guy."

I laugh and punch his shoulder. "Why is he 'poor guy'? Harper is a . . . is a . . ."

"Exactly," he says. "There are no words."

I roll my eyes and try to keep laughing, to hold on to this small moment of joy. An older man sitting on Guy's other side hands him a bottle of something. Guy smells it and raises it to his lips. After he swallows, his face pulls together and he sucks air between his teeth as he passes it to me.

Taking it in my hands, I inspect the bottle. It's round and heavy at the bottom, and flows into a long and narrow neck. The green glass is too dark to see what's inside. I glance at Guy, and he makes a tipping motion with his hand as if to say *Drink up.* I remember all the things I *don't* want to remember, and I stare down into the bottle. For three seconds, I wonder what Dad would say about my drinking to kill bad memories. Or about my drinking at all. But then I decide that the second I joined the Brimstone Bleed was the second I had to learn to survive any way I could. And this . . . this is a ticket to mental freedom.

I tip the bottle back and guzzle until my head swims.

When I lower it and wipe a hand across my mouth, I note Guy eyeing me.

"Great," he says, shaking his head.

"Great what?" I pass the bottle to the woman next to me, who is all too eager to accept it. "What's so great?" I ask this question about a hundred times over the next half hour. Guy just shakes his head, which makes me laugh hysterically and hang on his arm. "What's great, Guy? Me? Am I great? I am, right? Do you want to know why?"

I stare into the fire, transfixed by the flames.

"Why?" Guy says suddenly.

"What?" I turn and look at him.

"You asked if I wanted to know why you're great."

I shake my head and look for the green bottle of magic and awesome. "You're crazy."

He sighs.

I glance back at the fire. All around it, Contenders dance. Most of the men in white have left, but a few children and women stay behind, singing and beating the drums. The smoke from the fire wraps around the arms and legs of the people dancing and eggs them on. Everything seems to go in slow motion: the *thwump-thwump*ing of the drums, the Contenders' easy laughter, the Pandoras howling at the moon.

When I glance at Guy to see if he sees what I do, I realize he's staring at me. "Why are you always watching me?"

His face opens with surprise at my question. I'm a little surprised myself, but mostly, I'm wondering where the damn green bottle is.

"Did you hear me?" I ask.

He presses his lips together and nods his head.

"Then why don't you answer?"

"Maybe I don't have the answer." He leans back onto his hands and looks up at the sky. "Why do you ask so many questions?"

"Because I'm curious," I say.

"About everything, apparently."

"No, just about you." Though I feel relaxed and carefree, this last admission feels like one I may later regret. My eyes find his, but he's not looking at my eyes. He's looking at my mouth. Before I can protest, he raises a hand and runs his thumb over my lips. I close my eyes and shiver beneath his touch. I feel him shift beside me, and then his warm palms wrap around my face. I pull in a breath.

And his lips touch mine.

It's so sudden that I almost don't know how to react. But that's okay, because my body understands *exactly* what to do with him.

My back arches and I wrap my arms around him. His mouth is warm and soft against mine. And when his tongue touches the inside of my lips, a clap of thunder sounds through my body. I realize now that neither the jungle, the leeches, the raft, nor the river posed any real threat. The real fear is here.

That I will surely drown in his embrace.

All the things I question about Guy vanish. I don't care what he's hiding. I don't mind that his hands are calloused and his skin is pricked with sweat. I only care that he's pressed against me. That he's here.

Our kiss has just started — seconds of bliss, maybe only a single moment — when it's interrupted by the men in collared shirts.

"May we have your attention?" one man says. The drums stop. The dancing stops. Guy and I pull away and look at each other, breathing deep. I have a sudden impulse to kiss the scar over his eye, or run my fingers over the mangled part of his left ear. Every last imperfection seems to beg for my immediate attention. "It's time to announce the first victor."

This gets our attention. Guy and I turn and gaze at the man with the comb-over. He holds something in his closed fist, but I can't make out what it is. "One hundred and twenty-two people competed in the first leg of the race," he says. Some Contenders clap and the sound appalls me. "But only one could win the initial prize."

The man holds up his fist. I notice then how large his ears are, how they redden with his excitement. "Rachelle Gregory, please come forward."

A short, robust woman on the other side of the fire stands up. Contenders nearby give her congratulatory pats as she moves toward the man. She appears to be Caroline's age and has feathery red hair . . . and freckles. I wonder if she hates them as much as I do mine. Maybe she doesn't think about them. Maybe I shouldn't think about them.

The woman — Rachelle — stands near the fire and beams. Her smile is so wide, I'm afraid her face will break. But her rigid posture speaks the truth. She hates it here, and I decide then that I like this lady.

Opening his fist, the man stretches a long green ribbon taut. Then he ties it around her upper arm. A hush falls over the crowd. We've been trained so that flags mean everything. They were life preservers in the jungle, something that said: *You're on the right track; everything's going to be okay.* And now, at base camp, they're a status symbol. I spot them here and there tied around the arms of Contenders, young and old. They wear them proudly, their heads held high and their chests full.

But no one has a green flag.

The woman's smile falls as she fingers the ribbon around her bicep. I wonder how it feels. A few days before we found base camp, our group agreed not to wear the flags. Except Titus, who may very well have solidified the trend.

"You worked hard to win this leg," the man tells the woman. "And though our resources are limited, those of us working behind the Brimstone Bleed are doing everything we can to help save lives."

I wait for people to scoff, to mumble smart responses. No one does. I think about what Guy told me, about the Pharmies. Glancing at him, I vow to learn more of the story soon.

"So tonight, we'd like to award you a monetary prize: enough to secure the best doctors in the world. While only the Cure can guarantee health for your loved one, this money will help ensure they get the best care in the meantime."

The man hands her a slip of paper.

She gasps.

Nobody says anything for a few seconds. Finally, a young boy calls out, "What does it say?"

Rachelle looks up. Tears threaten to spill down her cheeks. "It's a check for two million dollars," she says. Contenders who just got done patting her on the back are now looking at her with envy. And hatred.

The man places a hand upon her shoulder. "And now it's time to ask you a question, Rachelle." He touches a hand to his thinning hair, then glances out at the crowd. "Are you going to continue the race? Or will you return home?"

Rachelle looks at him with shock. Before this, I'd often wondered if we'd be allowed to leave if we wanted to. Surely, she must have wondered the same thing. And now here it is — a ticket out of this place. I try to decide what I would choose: to return home with the money and hope better doctors can help save Cody, or to stay and fight for a guarantee. The woman's face tightens, and I can tell she's asking herself the same thing.

"I want to leave," she announces.

The Contenders clap at this, happy to have her out of here. To be rid of a fierce competitor.

A woman in white takes her by the arm and the two disappear outside the base camp. *Where are they taking her? To a village? A small airport outside the jungle?* I have a reckless longing to race after them, screaming to wait up, Madox bobbing in my arms.

A small voice inside my head whispers: *Are you* sure *you're strong enough? Are you sure there's really a cure?* Worse still: *Is your brother's life really worth risking your own?*

I jump to my feet and storm toward the cabin Guy and I have slept in for the last four nights. Behind me, I hear the man saying something else, and the Contenders grow excited. But I block it out and keep moving. I have to get away from here. I need time to think.

Finding my usual cot, I nearly collapse onto it. But I stop myself. What makes me deserve this bed more than someone else does? After questioning the value of my brother's life, perhaps I don't warrant anything more than the floor.

I grab a plaid blanket and a pillow and lie down beside the bed. Curling into a ball, I pray for the sound of Guy's approaching footsteps. I want him to chase after me. I need him to find me and hold me like he did the first night. My face burns as I think about our kiss. I squeeze my eyes shut and think about the feel of his lips, the fleeting touch of his tongue. But what does it matter amid the Brimstone Bleed?

It matters more than anything.

I hear footsteps approaching and watch the door. *Please let it be him. Please let it be him.*

The door creaks open, and Harper steps inside. Somehow, her being here is even better. I watch her search the floor until she finds me. In her hands are two envelopes. "Tella," she says gently. "You left before they made their final announcement."

Madox trots through the door Harper left open and locates me within seconds. He nudges my arm until I lift it and let him snuggle against my chest. I pet his thick black coat and raise my head to look at Harper. Her eyes are red-rimmed and glistening.

I bolt upright. "What is it? Are you okay?"

"I'm fine." She hands me one of the envelopes. The other, the one she's clutching in her left hand, has already been opened. "This is for you."

Harper turns to leave. I want to ask her to stay, to tell me what's wrong. But she's moving too quickly. When she gets to the door, there are two Contenders trying to make their way inside.

"No," Harper says, blocking their way. "Go away. Find another cabin."

"This isn't your —" one starts to say.

"Out," Harper shouts. She looks back at me. My stomach clenches when I notice tears are now streaming down her face. "I'll be right outside." Her voice breaks. "No one is going to come in."

"Harper," I say. But she's already closed the door.

I glance down at the envelope in my hand. It suddenly feels too heavy, too hot. Like it's going to burn right through my palm. Grabbing the corner, I tear it open.

CHAPTER TWENTY-FOUR

The letter is folded three times. So little stands in the way of my reading what's inside, but my hands shake as if I'm hanging from the side of a cliff, seconds left until I free-fall to my death.

I don't have to unfold the snow-white paper to know who it's from. The blocky letters peeking through tell me everything. There's only one person in my family who writes like this. Only one person who uses all caps like they're screaming everything they inscribe. My mom tries to tell him to write like a gentleman.

But my brother never listens.

I unfold the letter and squeeze my eyes closed. A lump forms in my throat. I try to swallow it down, but it's there to stay. When I manage to open my eyes again, the letters are blurred, swimming on the page like they're playing a game. I rub the back of my hand across my face and begin reading.

TELLA,

YOU LEFT BECAUSE OF ME. I KNOW YOU DID. MOM AND DAD TRY TO PROTECT ME FROM WHAT'S HAPPENED, BUT I WISH THEY'D STOP. SOMETHING'S GOING ON, AND I DON'T KNOW WHAT. I ONLY KNOW THAT DAD SAID SOMEONE SENT YOU SOMETHING MEAN. THAT IT WAS A PRACTICAL JOKE, AND I SHOULD PRETEND IT WAS ME TO PROTECT YOU. AND NOW YOU'RE GONE.

THE POLICE OFFICER HERE, HE ASKED ME TO WRITE YOU A LETTER. HE SAID YOU RAN AWAY TO TRY AND FIND SOMETHING TO MAKE ME BETTER. BUT THAT'S CRAZY, TELLA. THE DOCTORS SAID THEY COULDN'T HELP. SO JUST COME HOME. OKAY? JUST COME HOME. I KNOW I ALWAYS GIVE YOU A HARD TIME, BUT I'M JUST PLAYING. YOU KNOW THAT, RIGHT? ~~I'VE NEVER ACTUALLY TOLD YOU, BUT I THINK YOU'RE PRETTY COOL.~~ I'VE NEVER ACTUALLY TOLD YOU THAT I LOVE YOU SO MUCH, IT HURTS. THAT I'D DIE TOMORROW IF IT'D BRING YOU HOME.

WE'RE ALL WORRIED, TELLY. DAD STAYS UP ALL NIGHT PACING, AND MOM KEEPS REPEATING SOMETHING ABOUT YOU HAVING HER EYES. COME HOME. PLEASE.

— CODY

The letter flutters to the floor as I curl into myself. The knot in my throat unties itself, and I choke on a sob. Madox is on his feet, licking my hands, telling me he's here. But right now it isn't enough. I need my brother. My mom. My dad.

I need my family.

I've deceived myself. Pretended I was okay here in this jungle without them. But it's a lie I can't escape. Tears race down my cheeks and tumble to the floor.

I know why the people working this race delivered these letters.

It's to prepare us for the next leg of the race. To provide motivation.

Their plan so works.

Having Cody's words in my head makes everything I've done worth it. He loves me. Of course he does, I know that. But he actually *said* it. My brother and I don't do that. We tease each other, pull harsh pranks, and take every opportunity to make the other look bad. But deep down . . .

And he said it.

I despise the people running this race. But I need them, too. Because I have to win. I have to save him.

The door opens and I wonder if Harper is back. When I glance up, I see Guy silhouetted in the doorway, an envelope crumpled in his grasp. My sobs deepen, and I reach toward him. I'll crumble if he refuses me. If he walks away.

He looks at me for a long time. Even in the dark, his eyes are the same as the first moment I saw him — cold as revenge. I reach toward him again and say his name. He glances away, and his face whispers of torment.

"Don't —" I say, but it's no use.

He turns and leaves.

My heart explodes. My bones break. Tears pour from my body until I'm sure there's nothing left. I pull into myself and clutch the letter to my stomach. My eyes slip closed, and I drown in despair. Madox nudges against my hand, but I don't lift it. I can't. He whimpers softly. It's the last thing I hear as I crash into sleep.

When I wake in the middle of the night, I feel Guy behind me, holding me as if I'm his only path to salvation.

After five more days at the camp, I become restless. The woman from the device said the race would take three months. Harper and I decided this meant two weeks in each ecosystem, and one week of rest in between them. We couldn't decide what the last week would entail. Then again, this was all guesswork.

The other Contenders seem ready for action, too. It's like we've all spent adequate time sulking over our letters, and now we're ready to tackle the next obstacle. But the men in collared shirts don't respond when we ask what's coming. They just wave us away and keep patrolling the area. I begin to wonder if this isn't part of a bigger test. To see who breaks under the pressure of idleness.

As time passes, Guy continues to stay nearby. Rarely close — but nearby. Sometimes he'll grace me with conversation. And on rare moments, a smile. My body aches for him in a way I've never known. I feel like an animal, all muscle and hormones and lust. We never mention the kiss, and it does nothing to quench the strange pull between us. It's odd to feel this way in the heart of the jungle, but I think Guy could probably make me hot in the ninth circle of hell.

I watch as Titus picks on a kid half his age. I'm tired of seeing him bully his way into a position of authority among the Contenders. And I decide since I have nothing else to preoccupy myself with, I'm going to give him a piece of my mind.

Dusting myself off, I head toward him. He's holding the boy around the neck, and I mentally tell the kid to go for the crotch. That'd be my tactic. In fact, it *will* be my tactic. I'm only a few feet away when Caroline steps in front of me. Dink is hanging on her waist, and she's holding her device out so I can see.

It's blinking.

My teeth snap together, and I immediately look for Guy. I don't want to hear the message without him near my side. I'm aware that my feelings for him can't end well, not with us both here as competitors. But those are long-term thoughts. And right now, staring at the blinking light with my heart pounding against my ribs, I'm only thinking in the now.

"Does everyone know?" I ask Caroline when I don't spot Guy.

"Not yet." She places the device into her ear but doesn't press the button. "It won't be long, though."

She's right. Within minutes, every Contender is putting their device into place. I don't want to listen without our group together. It feels like if I do, then maybe we aren't really a group at all. Already, Caroline and Dink stay by themselves, Ransom hides inside the cabins all day, and Guy and I move quietly through base camp side by side.

And Harper. She's still being stalked by the gangly blond. He refuses to leave her alone, and for some reason, she doesn't tell him off. Just continues to ignore him.

I give up hunting the Contenders I've become familiar with and put the device into my ear. Caroline wraps her hand around the side of Dink's face, and nods.

We both push the buttons.

There are a few moments of silence while everyone tunes in, then the woman begins.

"Good afternoon. I'd like to wish everyone well as we close the first chapter of the Brimstone Bleed."

I curl my hands into fists.

"As you know, Rachelle Gregory won the first leg of the race and chose to return home to be with her family. We, at headquarters, fully

support her decision. And now we'd like to offer the remaining Contenders a choice as well."

The woman pauses, and I can almost feel the Contenders around me holding their breaths.

"In a few short moments, the two men who have graciously overseen base camp will leave. If you choose to follow one, you will be led to the next part of the race. If you choose to follow the other, you will be taken home. The decision is yours to make."

Caroline finishes listening to the message and drops her head. When she looks back up, there are tears in her eyes.

I don't know what to tell her. This decision is easy for me. I won't give up. My brother loves me. And I love him right back. But her mother has never shown her enough affection to warrant this kind of personal risk. I'd understand her decision to leave. I grab her hand and squeeze. "It's okay," I whisper. "You don't have to stay. We'd understand."

"Would *she*, though?" Caroline says as Dink tugs on her side and looks up at her. "Would my *mother* understand?"

I shake my head, because I can't find the words. And because, *no*, her mother doesn't sound like the kind of person who would understand. Or the kind of person who'd have ever considered doing for her daughter what Caroline's done for her.

"If I leave, I'm going to take him with me." Caroline pulls Dink in front of her.

"I think that's a good idea," I say, though I'm fighting the urge to beg her to stay. To tell her I can't continue this race without all of us there.

Something brushes my back, and I turn to find Guy. His eyes lock on my face. "Are you ready?" he says. "They're already lining up."

I glance over his shoulder and see that he's right. The two men are positioned ten feet away from each other, and a line of

Contenders stands before each person. There are fewer Contenders in front of the man on the right, and I wonder if that's the leave or stay line.

Guy places his hand on the small of my back and a torrential current rushes through me. I wonder whether Guy is confident I'm staying, or has come to ensure I don't go.

I look back at Caroline as Guy leads me away. I want to tell her good-bye, that I'll never forget her or Dink. But something tells me it's better this way. That I have to learn to move forward without lingering on the past.

Guy moves toward the left. "Is this the stay line?" he asks the girl in the back.

She nods, looks us both over, and turns back around.

Harper comes up behind us. I smile in her direction. She doesn't return the gesture, but maybe that's because the blond guy is still chatting away in her ear. He follows her into line like she's his lighthouse and gives me an excited wave when he catches me watching.

I wave back and laugh despite the situation.

Titus elbows his way past us all and heads toward the front, his pack trailing behind him. He turns once to verify we're watching. When his eyes connect with Guy's, he looks forward and continues on.

Near the front, I see the man in the collared shirt raise his hand to silence us. For the first time, I notice there's a small chest near his feet. It's made from carved wood, and the latch glitters emerald green. When a hush falls over the Contenders, he opens the chest and retrieves a monstrous-sized syringe. It's filled with a green, swirling liquid.

"Right sleeves up." The man indicates the syringe. "You'll only need a little," he adds, as if this is supposed to comfort me. As if the thought of that needle going in my arm isn't enough to make me switch lines. I glance over at the leave line. Yeah, no syringe.

The Contenders begin pulling up their right shirtsleeves. The man injects a small amount into the first Contender and moves down the line.

"Guy," I whisper, sweat pricking my brow.

"It's okay," he says. "They wouldn't kill us now."

Kill us? *Kill* us? I wasn't even thinking that. I was only worried about the syringe. And maybe that it'll make us fall asleep again. But mostly, that the man and his mammoth needle are only four Contenders away now.

Three.

Two.

He gets to Guy, and Guy holds out his upper arm as if he's actually excited about getting injected with a foreign substance. The needle punctures his skin and I see a bit of blood spiral amid the green. *They shouldn't be using the same needle on all of us, should they?* My muscles clench tighter. Madox rears up against my leg and barks.

Yeah, no crap. That's what I'm saying. Why is no one freaking out?

I glance at Harper, but she's facing forward like a marine. I hate her so much right now, I could scream.

Something pricks my arm and I yelp. I turn and glare at the man. He gives me a look that says I'm pathetic and moves toward Harper. *It's over,* I think. *It wasn't so bad.* I glance at Caroline and Dink, and I can't help myself. Raising my arm, I wave. I must tell them good-bye, if only in this small way. Caroline smiles warmly and waves back, her eyes still wet with tears. She raises Dink's arm and waves for him, too. I bite my lip to keep from laughing . . . or crying.

And then Caroline's face begins to blur.

CHAPTER TWENTY-FIVE

When I open my eyes, the sun blinds me. I jerk my face away from the light and gag on a mouthful of grit. Glancing down, I realize what I'm swallowing is sand.

I push myself up as adrenaline courses through me.

The desert.

We're in the desert.

I shade my eyes and glance around. Other Contenders are pulling themselves up and rubbing their faces. The memory of leaving the jungle is hazy. I can only recall the syringe.

Panic strikes through me as I search for Madox. I find him close by, jumping in a circle and biting at the sand swirling around his feet. I scoop him into my arms and glance around, looking for Guy. He's already pulled himself upright and is striding toward me.

As he walks, I notice he's no longer wearing brown scrubs. And neither am I. We're now dressed in white shirts, tan cargo pants with a serpent on one of the many pockets, and brown boots that creep toward our shins. Guy's white shirt hugs every muscle in his chest and arms as he moves. I blush against the desert sun and hope he thinks it's from the heat. My embarrassment serves to distract me from the knowledge that once again, someone has changed my clothing without my remembering. If that's not the epitome of creepiness, I don't know what is. I'm discouraged to see my new threads aren't a wardrobe improvement. I briefly consider making Madox my Toto and clicking my heels together.

There's no place like Nordstrom, there's no place like Nordstrom.

Already, sweat forms along my hairline. It must be a hundred degrees here. Maybe more. The heat isn't wet like it was in the jungle. Instead, it's so dry that each breath I take parches my throat. Realization hits me that I left for the race in August, which means it's probably September by now. September. In the desert.

Great.

Better than August, I guess.

Hills of sand roll across the landscape like waves in an ocean. The sun is enormous, and I imagine if I stretched tall enough, I'd burn my fingertips. With the presence of a never-ending sun and the absence of heavy foliage, it's like I can see forever. My eyes ache from taking in the vast emptiness. In the jungle, I was always seeing, always exploring something new. But here, my mind is clear. There's a kind of beauty in the stillness. In the quiet.

Guy and his lion circle around the Contenders and move away. I'm not sure where they're going until I see a mess of bright orange packs along the ground. The people working the race obviously dropped us here with supplies. Maybe that's good. Maybe that means this leg will be easier.

After taking three steps toward the bags, I stop. The tanned muscles along Guy's arms work as he pulls not one but two packs over his back, and then he heads over.

He hands me one of the backpacks and I put Madox down to slip it on.

"Thanks," I mutter. I've accepted that I'll never figure Guy out — the way he helps and protects me, then leaves when I need him most. I know he's here to save someone, and that I'm probably confusing him. But I wish he'd open his mouth and say so.

Reaching into the pockets of my cargo pants, I feel the white device and relax slightly. "Do you have your device?" I ask Guy.

He nods and turns toward the desert. "I'm sure it'll go off soon enough."

I watch him watching the sand, then I turn and look for Harper. She's heading in our direction, the blond boy at her heel.

"Hey," she says. "You guys getting ready?" She seems unsure for some reason, and I wonder if she's questioning whether we'll continue to travel together. I know it's what I've been thinking.

I decide to rip the Band-Aid off.

"Ready, now that you're here. Took your time sauntering your tush over, didn't you?" I bump her shoulder and smile, all while holding my breath. "Want to lead for a while when we kick off?"

She turns away and peers into the sun, but I don't miss the relief dripping from her face. "Sure, whatever."

"Hey-o, I'm Jaxon. With an *x*, not a *cks*. Pleased to make your acquaintance. Harper's told me so much about you." I look at Harper. She shrugs. Jaxon throws a long, thin arm around her shoulder and she brushes it off. "I'll be traveling with you guys, but don't fret, I'm good company. Whoa, rewind. Let's go with *outstanding*. Don't want to shortchange myself."

"Traveling with us, huh?" I can't stop smiling at a fuming Harper. It's obvious she's found some redeeming quality in the guy, or she wouldn't have ever agreed to this. Which I'm actually only guessing she has. "Well." I glance at Guy, then back at Jaxon. "Welcome, I guess."

A young girl with red cheeks steps out from behind his legs. She looks to be about ten years old and is every bit as round as she is tall. Her brunette hair is pulled back into a ponytail and small wisps of hair curl around her face. The overall effect is beyond endearing.

The girl straightens. "I'm Olivia. I'd like to come, too. If it's all right."

Jaxon musses Olivia's hair and more wisps spring out from her ponytail. "'Course it's all right. I can't go anywhere without my sidekick." The girl grins up at him.

"You're more than welcome to join us." No one contests what

I've said, so I assume the matter is settled. We'll have two new Contenders to add to our group.

"Are we being replaced already?" a soft voice asks from behind me. I freeze, but a slow smile crawls across my face. As I spin around, my heart leaps.

Caroline and Dink are trekking through the sand toward us.

"Knew you couldn't stay away," Harper says.

I throw my arms around the woman I hardly know, almost giddy with relief. "You came," I say. "You changed your mind." I try hard not to do my happy dance, to keep my arms at my sides and my feet on the ground, but my body wins out. I jump in a circle, pump my arms, and shake my butt. I'm so obnoxious.

"What the hell are you doing?" Guy asks.

"My happy dance," I respond, as if it's obvious.

He shakes his head, but I can tell he's pleased we're all together. But we aren't, really. Our group falls quiet and it's like we've suddenly remembered who we're missing. One brother is gone forever. But the other . . .

Our heads turn as we seek him out. At first, we don't see him, but then Dink raises his arm and points.

"I'll talk to him," Guy says. No one fights him for the job. He walks away and approaches Ransom. We watch without speaking as Ransom shakes his head. His mouth never moves. Guy returns and when we look at him for confirmation, he shakes his head once. We don't ask for details, but I can't help feeling like I should try. I swallow my apprehension and move toward Ransom.

Guy grabs my arm. "Let him be, Tella," he says. "He's not ready for anyone's companionship."

I hear Guy speaking, but I can only study Ransom's slim body. He looks like he's lost a lot of weight, and his Pandora watches him carefully, as if he knows something is off with his Contender. *So young,* I think. But then I remember that he's only two or three years younger than I am.

"I'll give him space today," I say, mostly to myself. "But I won't stop trying to reach out." I know by saying this, I'm letting go of the fantasy that our old group will travel together. And I suppose I'm praying now for another chance to see him at the next base camp. Maybe after some time alone to mourn his brother, he'll be more willing to let us in.

"What's inside the packs?" Caroline asks. "I haven't looked yet."

Instead of answering, I look more closely at Dink. His face appears flushed, and I wonder if he's okay. "Dink, are you feeling all right?"

"Oh, he's fine," Caroline says, pulling him against her. "I think the serum they gave us just affected him more than most." She looks down at him. "He's so small."

"And inconsequential, which is exactly why he shouldn't be here," a new voice says. His words grate my nerves, and before I even turn my head, I know it's Titus. His blond hair is slicked back, and he's wearing a painted-on smile. "Tella," he says, cocking his head up.

"What do you want?" I ask.

"To make you a proposition." He looks at the pack of guys behind him, then back at me. "I've chosen the best Contenders to travel with. And I assure you, one of us will win this race." Titus glances at the fox at my feet. "I'd like to offer you a position with us . . . with the Triggers. And with it, a chance to win."

"Pass," I say.

"Reconsider," he growls, stepping toward me.

Guy shoves him backward. "She said pass. Now get the hell out of her face."

Titus looks alarmed, like he never expected Guy to challenge him in front of his followers. But once again, he fakes a smile and opens his arms, as if everything is one big joke. "Have it your way. Die in the desert, assholes."

When he swivels on his heels to move away, I gasp. I notice for the first time that he's holding the end of a rope in his left hand. Attached to the opposite end is G-6, Levi's ram. I go to snatch it from Titus, but he jerks his arm away like he has eyes in the back of his head.

"See you noticed I went Dumpster diving," he says over his shoulder. "He's not the most impressive Pandora, but then again, I'm not done collecting yet."

At this, Guy attempts to grab Titus, but AK-7 barrels forward and growls. In response, M-4 leaps in front of Guy and swipes his paw just shy of the bear's face.

Titus roars with laughter and leads the clan of guys — the Triggers — and their Pandoras away. I catch Ransom staring Titus down and wonder if he has a plan to get his brother's Pandora back. If he does, I certainly wouldn't mind being included.

I glance at Guy. "He's after Madox. That's what Titus was saying, right?"

Guy rubs his jawline, considering. "Yeah, but I think he'll be looking to pick up any Pandora he can along the way."

"We've got to take that jerkoff down."

We all turn and look at Jaxon.

"What?" he says. "That guy's a grade-A douche."

The corner of Harper's mouth hitches up, and Guy offers his hand to Jaxon. "Welcome to our group."

Jaxon laughs and pumps Guy's hand. Then he says, "The Triggers. How friggin' pompous is it to give yourselves a name?" He sighs. "What's ours?"

"No," Harper says. "We're not naming our group."

"I know. *The Bombs.*" Jaxon makes a falling motion with his fist, then explodes it against the palm of his other hand.

"Dumb," Harper says.

Jaxon thinks. "The Machines?"

"Nope," I tell him.

"The Brimstone Bosses!"

"Guys," Caroline says softly. "The light is blinking."

My shoulders tighten, and I dig into my pant pocket, searching for the device. When I find it, I fit it into my ear. My eyes never leave Guy's face. He puts his own device into place and holds my gaze. After three weeks in the jungle, his hair still springs toward the sky in dark spikes. It's like it's determined to hold its style regardless of what happens. As opposed to my own hair, which curls closely against my scalp in chaotic patterns. For a fleeting moment, before the woman speaks, I pray that the orange pack I'm wearing holds Chanel makeup. And a brush. And a mirror.

Clicking.

Static.

"Welcome to the second leg of the Brimstone Bleed. As you're probably aware, this portion of the race will take place across the desert. Just as before, you will need to find the flags in order to locate base camp. And once again, you will be allocated two weeks for completion."

The sun beats down on the sand dunes, and I can see the air vibrating. It's almost like I'm underwater. There are sporadic bushes and sparse trees sprouting from the sand, and I wonder how it's possible they grow in this heat. How anything can survive it. How I will survive it.

"One hundred and twenty-two people entered the race," the woman says proudly. *"And seventy-eight Contenders remain."*

I'm surprised so many Contenders have dropped off. I didn't see that many in the leave line at base camp, which means some

Contenders are still in the jungle. Or worse, they're like Levi. Gone.

"That means your odds of winning this leg of the race are that much better. And this round, we have a very special prize." The woman pauses, and I imagine how strangling her might feel. *"The winner will receive a small dose of the Cure. Enough to ensure your loved one lives for a minimum of five years."*

All around me, people gasp. As for myself, I'm too shocked to move. My insides roil with conflicting emotions. One is hope, that I can win Cody a guarantee of five healthy years. Another is anger, that the people working this race can do this to us. Surely, if they wanted to, they could create enough of this cure for everyone. The last emotion is the hardest to face — doubt. Doubt that any of this is real. That there's really a cure that can save Cody. Or anyone else, for that matter.

Still, I have to try. I have to fight for the *chance* to help him. Besides, Guy did say the Pharmies existed. And I trust him.

Right?

I notice Jaxon waving down two animals, which I assume are Pandoras. The closest one, a cheetah, sprints over to Jaxon and rubs against his leg. Behind the cat, taking slow, heavy steps, is what looks like a baby elephant. The creature moves toward Olivia and wraps its long gray trunk around her waist. The girl scratches beneath the elephant's chin and stares forward.

Beyond the Pandoras, my eyes connect with Titus's. He raises a thick arm and points in my direction. Ice courses through my veins at the sight.

The woman's voice continues.

"The best of luck to you, Contenders," she says. *"Now run!"*

I can almost imagine her arm punching the air. In the same moment as the woman tells us to run, the ground shudders.

Seventy-eight Contenders and their Pandoras rush forward. Guy grabs my arm and holds me in place. I'm not sure what he's doing, but I take his lead and do the same to Harper. One by one, we pull ourselves together to avoid being trampled.

We don't run. We don't panic.

We just watch.

CHAPTER TWENTY-SIX

The Contenders race in all different directions, and Pandoras fly, crawl, and slither behind them.

There are so many different creatures that the sight is astounding. It wasn't as startling at base camp, seeing them all lounging along the ground, cleaning themselves, and snoozing in the wet heat. But this, watching them plow through the sand, grunting from the strain, their bodies rigid — it's spectacular.

After the sound dies down, and the Contenders and animals become a blur in the distance, Guy speaks. "We need a plan."

"Right-o," Jaxon says.

Guy looks at him for a long minute before continuing. "Last time, there was a pattern to the flags. I think we can assume as much here, too. Otherwise, it wouldn't be a game of skill." He pulls his pack off and drops it into the sand with a thud. "We also need to dump these. They're too bright, and they'll alert our presence to other Contenders." Guy crouches on the ground and unzips the pack. As he works to pull the contents out, I wonder how he got this way. How an eighteen- or nineteen-year-old could prepare himself for conditions this extreme.

Guy separates the things in his pack into piles. On one side are what looks like a rolled-up tent, a sleeping bag, and a thick length of rope. On the other are a large switchblade and a canteen, which I imagine is full of water. The chrome side of the circular bottle gleams in the sunlight, and I wonder if the race peeps didn't answer my prayer for a mirror after all.

"Hey, this canteen could be used as a signal to each other," Olivia says, turning hers so it flashes. "Wouldn't that be cool?"

As I stare at my own bottle, my tongue swells. I've been conscious for ten minutes in this blasted desert, and already I could drink my body weight in water. Or Lake Michigan. I think I could drink that, too. Or maybe the water from that jungle cave, complete with slimy leeches.

"Are you sure we should leave everything? What if we need it later?" Caroline asks. "Surely, they wouldn't give it to us if we didn't need it."

"No." Guy wipes his brow. "We leave it."

"Could we carry the stuff in our arms?" Jaxon glances at his cheetah. "Or could our Pandoras carry it?"

"We'll be too tired to carry anything," he answers. "So will they."

Normally, we follow Guy blindly. But right now the group seems to hesitate. Maybe it's the heat or the fact that the desert looks so barren. I imagine these people are wondering how they'll replace the things they need if they leave them behind. In the jungle, there was stuff to use. If you could find the right stuff. But here, it's a blank sheet of paper.

I understand Guy wants to remain invisible to the other Contenders, but I'm not sure why it's so important. Is he afraid they'll follow us to the flags? Maybe he's concerned others will want to join our group. If so, what's the harm in that? I'm beginning to wonder if this is a good idea. Until I remember Titus. The way he said he'd be collecting Pandoras. And the way he looked at me right before the desert race began.

I remove my pack, pull out the canteen and knife, and toss the bag away.

Harper's eyes widen slightly, but she quickly follows suit. As soon as she acts, so does Jaxon. Olivia goes next, followed by Caroline and Dink.

"Okay." Guy points to the sky with his canteen, and the lion at his side glances upward. "We can use the sun as a compass. It rises in the east and sets in the west. I suggest we head east."

"But that was the pattern last time," Harper argues. "Won't they change it?"

"That's what they'll expect us to think," Caroline reasons. We all look at her, but she doesn't notice because she's messing with Dink's hair. When she looks up, surprise crosses her face. "What?"

Guy grins.

My heart bursts.

"That's exactly what I was thinking, Caroline," he says. "I believe we should start east, then try going north from there."

"Right on," Jaxon says with a nod. "When do we get to drink the water?"

I wait for Guy to scold him, to patronize his need for hydration so early on. At the least, I expect Guy to ignore him completely. Instead, he screws the cap off the canteen and tips it up. We watch as his throat works up and down. He must have drained half the water as the rest of us licked our lips. Pulling it away, he sighs with pleasure. "Now. Drink it now."

"Won't we need it later?" Olivia asks, one hand pressed against her elephant.

"It's more important to prevent dehydration." Guy loops the canteen's strap across his chest. "So drink as much as you need to feel content. Not satisfied, just content."

I want to ask about three hundred questions on exactly what *content* entails. But when Harper raises the canteen and starts drinking, human nature wins out. I open my canteen and nearly die with euphoria as the cool water rushes down my throat. For a moment, I imagine pouring it over my head and then stealing everyone else's for the same luxury. But I don't. I just drink until I'm *content*.

Then decide I loathe the word.

After pouring a little in my hand, I bend down to let Madox drink some. He pulls away like he detests the stuff, and the rest of the Contenders watch me like I've lost my mind. I drink the water in my palm, and wonder why my Pandora wouldn't take it. Does he not need it, or is he sacrificing himself in order for me to have more?

When we're each done drinking, we strap the canteens over our shoulders like Guy does. We all want to be like Guy. Go, Team Guy.

"Everyone ready?" he asks.

Harper steps forward. "Tella said I could lead."

My jaw struggles to fall open, but I somehow manage to keep it closed. Since when did what I say become law? I try to maintain a face that says: *Yes, that is what I said. Let it be known to all who travel this desert dune. Hear, ye.* I mentally stab a staff into the ground and realize Guy is staring at me.

"All right, that's cool," he says, still watching me like maybe I'm the serial killer now.

Harper tells RX-13 to take to the sky, and the eagle opens her wings in flight. The sun is already skydiving toward the earth, so we head in the opposite direction — which I guess is east. Walking is like a nightmare all its own. When I first saw the sand, I thought it was beautiful. Like maybe it'd be fun to just roll around in and make sand angels. Now I know the truth, that sand is actually the love child of proud parents Marie Antoinette and Joseph Stalin.

I march behind Harper and am surprised by the bitter wind. I wonder if it's always this way, or just a today thing. Regardless, it's wildly annoying. Every few seconds, I wipe sandy sweat from my face, to have it replaced moments later.

I eye Harper's canteen. *Could I drink her water before she takes me down?* I wonder.

I'm not proud of this thought.

In the jungle, it felt as if the rain was never ending. I grew to hate it with a wild passion. And now . . . now I ache for it.

We walk for what feels like years and stop only when the sun vanishes over the dunes. Our clothes are soaked through with sweat and cling to our bodies like a second skin. Harper stops walking, and we all follow suit. I crumple to my knees, and Caroline drops down beside me. Guy was right. There's no way I could've carried anything besides the knife and canteen.

I glance at him to see what Man o' the Wild is doing now. Just rubbing a random leaf along his arm and inspecting the results. Right. Nothing too strange.

"What are you doing?" My throat aches asking the question. I decide then that if Guy says we shouldn't drink the rest of our water tonight, I will kill him in his sleep, lion or no lion.

He continues rubbing the leaf along his arm and watching his skin like a maniac. A hot maniac, mind you. But a maniac nonetheless. "We can't sleep on the sand."

Caroline looks at the sand, and I can almost see the fear fill her eyes. She folds and unfolds her hands. "Why not? What's wrong with the sand?"

Guy stops rubbing and glances around. "It's going to get cold. And the sand will rob our bodies of warmth," he says. "We have to find something to sleep on."

The promise of colder weather is almost as wonderful as what's left in my canteen. And now that he's mentioned it, I realize it's not nearly as hot. In fact, it almost feels a little cool already. My white shirt and khaki cargo pants, still soaked with sweat, nearly make me shiver. In a weird way, because it feels so good compared to the heat, the sensation is almost erotic.

Guy gathers branches from the small bushes spread across the desert and asks M-4 to light them. He does, and Jaxon and Olivia provide the appropriate amount of verbal awe at the lion's skill. Then we all huddle close to the flame, though what I'd like to do is douse the fire and relax in the dropping temperature.

"Take off your clothes," Guy says quietly.

Five heads whip in his direction. Well, four. Harper's already peeling her clothes off and drying them by the fire. Jaxon watches her, eyes as big as Saturn.

I quickly understand Guy's reasoning. The clothes have to dry out so we don't freeze in our own sweat. That's it. *Chillax, Tella,* I lecture myself. It's not like Guy was talking just to me.

"Seriously?" Caroline asks.

Guy doesn't answer; he just tugs his shirt off and turns his back to remove his pants. That's when I see his scars. They're pink and raised and hug his rib cage. Partially covering them is a tattoo of a large bird facing forward, its wings stretched open.

"You have a tattoo." As soon as the words leave my mouth, I cringe. The scars seem too personal, but I couldn't stop myself from asking about the ink. Now he knows I've been watching him undress. And everyone else does, too. Great, I'm the official creeper in the group.

Guy glances over his shoulder at me. Then he looks off in the distance and kind of nods to himself.

Since I'm already a creeper, I decide to go full-fledged and dig deeper. "It's a bird, right?"

He pulls his cargo pants off, and before I turn my head, I notice he's wearing black boxer briefs with a red waistband. Even though I'm light-headed with thirst, right now I can think of nothing else besides the way he's built: the hard muscles across his back, the bronzed glow of his skin. When he turns around, I can't help but peek from the corner of my eye. The flames throw shadows across his broad chest and tight stomach. My own stomach fills with butterflies. I decide as long as his clothes are off, I won't kill him in his sleep . . . regardless of what he says.

"Tella?" He speaks my name as if in a question, but all I can do is watch his full, pink lips move around my name. The

198

way his tongue quickly touches the top of his mouth when he says it. He sits down next to his lion. "You need to take your clothes off."

And I die. Right there in the sand.

I glance around and notice even Caroline is removing her shirt. She's avoiding anyone's gaze, and I don't blame her. Slowly, I stand up. My fingers find the hem of my shirt and I start to pull it skyward. I can't help looking up, and when I do, I find Guy watching me.

I stop cold.

His eyes travel to the band of skin I've exposed above my hips, then they move up to my face. I take a deep breath, hold his eyes — heart pounding inside my chest — and gently lift the shirt over my head.

Guy sucks on his bottom lip and it's nearly my undoing.

He's only watching *me*, I realize. Not Harper and her perfect body, or Caroline and her beautiful complexion and dark hair. Only me. Confidence builds in my belly. I have not a spot of makeup on my face. My thick, chestnut curls are gone. And my skin is bright red from the desert sun.

But he thinks I'm beautiful.

I pull in a ragged breath and undo the button on my pants. Moving my hips, I allow them to slide down the length of my legs and drop into the sand. I step out of them, wearing nothing but my mismatched bra and underwear, and my brown combat boots. The flame feels delicious against my skin. Even better is the way his eyes take in every part of my body.

My hands rub along my hips, and my lungs cease to work.

Guy stands up.

He moves so very slowly toward me.

When he's only inches away, he raises his hands and wraps them around my face.

He's going to kiss me. Oh God, he's going to kiss me in front of everyone.

Guy's eyes dart over my face, and the look on his own is filled with confusion, like he's not sure how this is happening. He presses his lips together. He closes his eyes. And he pulls me against him.

I fold into his warm chest as he cloaks his arms around me, pulls me tight. His hand strokes the back of my neck, and he lays a small kiss on the crown of my head. I know I lust for Guy. That my body yearns for his touch. But I've always attributed it at least partially to circumstances.

Now I'm afraid it isn't so simple. That this thing —

May not be mere lust after all.

"So . . ." Harper says slowly. "Are you guys, like, doing it?"

"Seriously." Jaxon laughs. "Awk-ward."

I glance away from Guy and realize they're all staring. Of course they are. There's nowhere else to look. A blush brightens my face, but Guy tips my chin up to look at him. He's a full foot taller than I am, and I feel incredibly small in his arms. I wait for him to say something, anything. But he only pulls me back against him.

CHAPTER TWENTY-SEVEN

Guy guides me to the ground and we sit side by side.

"You didn't really answer my question," Harper says, flashing a grin.

"Jeez." I cover my face.

"No," Guy says. I can still feel his eyes on me. "We're not . . . doing it."

Her voice changes, humor mixing with concern. "How will it work for you two? In the end?"

"Harper," Caroline scolds. "We may be traveling together, but we're still allowed our privacy. Let them figure it out."

I can't believe this is happening. That this thing between Guy and me is public knowledge. Surely, they've seen the way we paired off at base camp. But maybe they thought it was a strategy thing. I guess I always figured the same. Even now Guy doesn't say what's on his mind. He's only hugged me. And kissed me the once.

Uncovering my face, I meet Guy's stare. He's close enough so that I can feel the warmth rolling off his body. I wish he were closer. I wish his hands were still on me, his arms still wrapped around my waist. But I'm slowly growing accustomed to his sudden bursts of affection. He reaches over and runs his fingers along my feather. He narrows his eyes as he inspects it, then lets it drop against my shoulder.

"Where'd you get that thing?" Harper says, obviously still watching us. "I never asked."

I grasp it in my palm. "I'm not sure. My mother gave it to me before I left. Said it was her mother's."

"Maybe her mom competed in the Brimstone Bleed."

Even though the desert night is quickly becoming too cold for comfort, my skin flushes with heat. I've secretly wondered the same thing. If my mom knew what she was doing when she gave me the feather. If she knew details about the race but told me nothing.

Except that I have her eyes.

Whatever that means.

Guy mentioned that our families may have known, but if they'd told us, there would have been consequences. I wonder about those consequences. I want to ask him, but I'm afraid he won't say anything in front of the others, so I decide to wait until we're alone.

"We need to find something to cover the ground," Guy says. I realize he kind of interrupted Harper and wonder if he did it on purpose.

"What's the plan, Stan?" Jaxon asks.

"I think we need to use these bushes." Guy glances at the arm he was rubbing the leaf against, and seems satisfied. "They're all over the place. Why don't you, Dink, and I go collect them and the girls can ensure the fire stays lit."

"Oh yeah. That's all we're good for," Harper says. "Why don't we watch the sand while we're at it? Make sure it doesn't blow away."

Guy turns and looks at her, exasperated. "You want to come? You're more than welcome."

She looks past him and into the dark mouth of the desert and hesitates. "I'll watch the sand."

"Thought so." He stands and offers Dink a hand.

"Why does Dink have to go?" Caroline asks, reaching out to the boy as Guy pulls him up.

Guy doesn't answer for a long moment, and I can't see what look he's giving her. "You know," he says, finally.

I glance at Harper, my face scrunched with confusion. She shrugs.

After they leave, I ask Caroline, "What did Guy mean? When he said, *you know*?"

She presses her lips together and shakes her head like she *doesn't* know, but I can tell she's lying. I add Dink to my list of things to ask Guy about tonight.

Nearly an hour later, the boys come back with armfuls of small branches and leaves. They spread them out for us. It isn't enough to stretch out on, so we all curl up in balls. It feels like I'm sleeping on bones and needles. Overall, a pleasant experience.

"This is terrible," Jaxon says. "I want one of those number beds old people sleep on."

"I want my pillow-top mattress," Caroline adds.

Olivia, who has hardly said anything today, shifts on her twig pallet. "I want a water bed. And then I want to suck every droplet out of that bastard."

Harper and I look at each other, our eyes wide. Then we burst out laughing.

Guy sits up and opens his canteen. He takes a long pull of water and then lies back down. When he realizes we're staring at him, he says, "It's not like you need my permission."

We all move at once, bolting upward and reaching for our canteens. I tip my bottle back and close my eyes against the goose bumps rolling across my skin. It's like heaven in my mouth. Once again, I attempt to give Madox, who's sleeping nearby, some water. He turns his head away.

I decide to treat the water I'd reserved for him as an unexpected gift and rub it over my face. The sensation is amazing, and I feel like maybe I could walk through the desert for another two hours if need be. No sooner do I think this than I feel myself lying back and my eyes closing. Harper is rattling off the keep-watch shifts, but I can barely make out what she's saying. It's like the words are coming from behind a wall.

I have to wake up when it's Guy's turn, I tell myself. I need to ask him what else he knows about the race. And about Dink. And if he's being generous with the convo, maybe about that sexalicious tattoo on his back.

Someone takes my hand in theirs, and though I want so badly to open my eyes and find out who it is, I tumble into sleep.

———————————

The next morning, I wake to Madox licking my face. I have to admit, with my skin feeling like crispified meat loaf, it isn't the worst sensation in the world. Without opening my eyes, I turn my cheek and allow him access to the other side. My mind is still hazy with sleep, so I don't think to check if someone is watching — until now.

My eyes snap open.

I find Olivia looking at me with sheer disgust dripping from her face.

I push Madox away gently and pull myself up. She's the only one awake. I'm thankful for that, at least.

"It's not what it looks like," I say.

"That makes it sound so much worse," she responds, shaking her head. Her elephant is sleeping next to her, its legs folded beneath it. It sounds like it's snoring.

I glance down at Madox, whose body is writhing with excitement. He's thrilled that I'm awake, and I love him so much for that, it nearly hurts. Looking back at Olivia, I try again.

"I was half asleep," I say. "I would never make him —"

Olivia smiles, and I realize she's messing with me. "Sorry, I got bored keeping watch all alone. Humiliating you is the most fun I've had all morning."

I breathe out and kind of half laugh. "I thought you were serious."

"Nope."

I survey our campsite and spot Jaxon spread out on his twig bed. His left hand twitches. "I would've thought Harper would assign you two to keep watch together."

"She did."

"Oh." I fight the urge to smile, but lose the battle. The corner of my mouth tugs upward and Olivia matches the gesture.

"You're all right, Tella." Olivia stands up and walks over to Jaxon. As she nears him, I think about what a grown-up thing that is to say. *You're all right.* The chubby girl squats down and gets close to Jaxon's ear. She fills her lungs, opens her mouth, and yells, "Heeeeeey, Jaxon."

He doesn't move.

Olivia looks at me. "I think he's dead."

"I assure you, I'm not," Jaxon mumbles.

The girl smiles and slaps him on the back. "Up and at 'em."

Jaxon lies still, but the rest of the Contenders begin dusting themselves off and putting their clothes back on. When Guy glances at me, I silently kick myself for sleeping through my shift. I know Harper must have assigned us to keep watch together, and I know he didn't wake me — as usual. I had so many questions to ask. Questions that'll have to wait another day.

When Guy takes a pull on his canteen, we all do the same. There's hardly any water left in my chrome bottle, and I assume from the concerned looks on the other Contenders' faces that I'm not alone in this predicament.

"We should keep heading east," Guy says. His voice is rough from sleep, and I have a strange urge to lay a kiss on his throat. "Harper, you want to continue leading?"

Harper avoids his gaze and instead stares at her Pandora, who's flapping the dust from her wings. She couldn't send a clearer sign; she's too tired from yesterday to lead today.

"No, I want to lead," I say. "It's my turn." As soon as I speak the words, I regret them. My skin is raw and blistering, and my legs are sore from trudging through the sand. I'd actually rather pour the remaining water from my canteen into the wind than lead this group. But I don't want Harper to be embarrassed.

Harper shrugs. "Fine. Whatever."

Before we head out, RX-13 and Jaxon's Pandora, Z-54, hunt for food. They return with bitter green fruit and we force it down. Guy says it's good they found this, that the fruit is mostly water and will help quench our thirst. I seriously doubt that.

Just as it did yesterday, the sun beats down with a vengeance. It's like it has a personal vendetta against human beings and wants nothing more than to fry our asses like bacon. Which I could totally go for about now. And pancakes. Powdered sugar, blueberries, syrup — the works. Ugh. My skin feels like it's on fire, and every breath I take burns my throat. The Pandoras hike alongside us, and I can tell that even though they were designed for this race, they're struggling in these conditions.

Z-54, the sleek-bodied cheetah, strides along in front of me. The design of his body allows him an ease of movement the rest of us don't have. Every so often, it's like the animal catches himself and slows to match our pace. And each time he turns his head, I see his mouth hanging open, panting in the sweltering sun. I follow his paw marks in the sand, leading our group across the desert dunes, thankful for the guide.

After three hours of hiking, I hear something drop behind me. Turning around, I notice Dink slumped into the sand. All of our faces are coated in sweat and grit. But his looks different, almost swollen. "He needs water," Caroline says, flustered. She pulls the canteen from across his shoulders and opens it. Holding the bottle to his lips, she tips it upward. He doesn't react, and I soon learn why.

There's nothing left inside.

"Oh my God. I knew this would happen." Caroline looks at me — brow furrowed — as if I have the answers. "How are we supposed to survive out here?"

Olivia drops down and covers her face, like she's been fighting the urge all morning. I glance at Guy, who looks every bit as concerned as Caroline does. I give him a look that says, *What are we going to do?*

He bites the inside of his cheek, thinking. "We need to find a body of water."

"No shit, Sherlock," Jaxon says, kneeling to rub Olivia's back. "But that doesn't exist in the desert."

"Actually, in many deserts, it does." Guy massages the back of his neck. "Some deserts have streams running through them, and others lie adjacent to oceans or snow-capped mountains."

"But an ocean won't help us," Harper says.

"No." Guy looks at me. "But a stream or snow will."

I can't fathom being anywhere near snow. It doesn't seem possible. Jaxon stands and squints up at the sky. "Maybe we should travel at night," he says. "It wouldn't be as hot."

It seems like a brilliant plan, but Guy shakes his head. "That's what's easiest, so it's what other Contenders will do. We need to travel during the day if we want to circumvent . . . conflict. Also, too many predators come out at night. We won't be able to avoid them if we can't see."

Jaxon's face drops with defeat. "Then what are we going to do? We'll die in this heat, or we'll die from predators. How do these pricks expect us to live?"

"Guys," Caroline says, her voice cracking. "We have to give Dink our water or he's not going to —" She stops and weeps into her hands. Her back convulses, but when she pulls her palms away, they're dry. We can't even cry anymore, we're so dehydrated.

Olivia flops onto her back and squeezes her eyes shut. "I finished my water, too," she says in almost a whisper. "And I don't think I can survive this day without more."

Olivia's Pandora — which she told me this morning is named EV-0 — startles like it heard and understood her. In a flash, the elephant stomps away from Olivia and rears its head back. The Pandora raises its trunk into the air and then drives it into the sand. Madox barks and jumps in circles as the elephant blows through its trunk and sand showers the air. The Pandora blows again and again, and more and more sand sprays up, creating a cloud of yellow.

"What's it doing?" Harper yells, waving her arms in front of her face.

"I — I don't know." Olivia stands. She goes to move toward EV-0, but Jaxon grabs the back of her shirt and pulls her against him. Harper watches the way Jaxon shields Olivia with a strange look on her face. One I can't quite read with the airborne sand blurring my vision.

The elephant stops blowing through its trunk, and when the cloud settles along the ground, I see that a small pit has been created in the earth. Other than that, nothing spectacular has happened. Olivia breaks away from Jaxon and throws her arms around her Pandora, which still has its trunk buried in the sand.

Bending down on its front legs, the elephant blows one last time into the earth — and the shallow pit fills with water.

"Get the heck outta here," Jaxon says.

CHAPTER TWENTY-EIGHT

The water gurgles from beneath the pit, and soon there's a miniature pond of clear water reflecting the burning sun. Caroline doesn't hesitate. She drags Dink to the side of the water and splashes it across his face and over the sweat-soaked curls on his head. His eyes stay closed, but a low groan escapes his throat. Keeping an arm around his shoulders, Caroline fills the boy's canteen and brings it to his lips. He drinks greedily.

After that, it's a mad dash to the water.

Guy and I fill our canteens as Olivia drinks straight from the pool of water. I'd find it a bit gross that she's drinking straight from the source we're filling our bottles, but she's beat out on the grossness scale by the lion, eagle, cheetah, and fox tongues lapping up the liquid.

So Madox was *thirsty,* I realize. *And he was reserving what water I had for me.*

I know my Pandora's been programmed to help me win, but I can't help feeling like he did it for more than just that reason. My heart aches watching him drink with insatiable thirst, and I pledge to force him to share my water going forward. 'Course, I guess that won't be an issue since this baby elephant can apparently find water from inside the earth via its magical trunk.

Caroline and Jaxon fill their canteens last, and we all lounge in the sun, drinking water until our bellies are full. Olivia scratches her Pandora behind its ear; it has withdrawn its trunk from the ground and is drinking the water itself now.

"So . . ." Jaxon says. "Did that elephant just spit up water and we all drank it?"

"Don't think about it," Harper says.

Immediately, Jaxon nods. *Of course,* I can see him thinking, staring at her. *What an idiot I am to have thought that. You are so wise and beautiful and perfect.* Harper doesn't seem to realize he's studying her. That he seems awfully close to eating her face to see if it tastes like happiness. Knowing Harper, it probably does.

Before we leave the pit, we each take a turn washing the stank off our bodies — something we're all thankful for. And then, with thin limbs and protruding guts, we continue walking through the desert. Olivia leads, with the elephant by her side. Guy suggested the idea to have her at the front, and ever since, the portly, frizzy-haired girl has trekked at the top of our group with her chin tilted toward the sky. I have to admit, I'm quickly becoming a devout Olivia fan. And her elephant? Any Pandora that can produce water in this hellhole is A-OK by me.

Madox circles my ankles and looks up at me so intently that he trips over his own feet. He seems to be saying, *It wasn't* that *cool, Mom. I can do anything it can do.* I want badly to pick him up, but even though I've had my fill of water, I'm exhausted after walking so far today.

When the sun begins to set, we do exactly as we did the night before. Caroline fusses over Dink. Jaxon ogles Harper. The boys gather desert carnage for our beds. Guy watches me undress. I imagine our wedding.

We gather around the fire M-4 lights and talk for a few minutes. Everyone is fatigued and it isn't long before I hear Jaxon snoring.

"Guess Jaxon can take the late shift," Harper says, rolling her eyes. She assigns our shifts, and Caroline, Guy, and Olivia speak over her, echoing her words.

"We know our shifts," Caroline says, grinning. She fingers Dink's curls as he closes his eyes. It's obvious he's not quite asleep, but he seems to be fading fast. Though he drank as much water as we did, he still seems . . . off. Usually, he'd be the last to lie down, and only after he'd drawn pictures in the dirt or sand for a half hour or so.

I lie down, keeping my eyes on Guy. He's stretched out on his back, his hands folded beneath his head. I realize I've hardly ever seen him sleep. There was this morning, and also when I followed him in the jungle and he slept in the trees. Maybe he doesn't need sleep like the rest of us do. Maybe he really is a machine. I'd like to cut him. Just a little bit. Just to see if he bleeds. Then I'd like to kiss the spot and take the hurt away.

What is *wrong* with me?

Guy turns his head and looks in my direction. Just as I suspected, he isn't asleep. Instead, he's studying my face, like he couldn't fathom succumbing to slumber before I do. I smile at him. It isn't something I do much anymore, but right now, feeling his undivided attention — I give in to temptation.

He doesn't smile back, and an unreadable expression shadows his face. I can't quite interpret what it says, but I know it's mixed with worry. For some reason, it makes me furious. I don't need his concern. I can take care of myself, and I think I've proven that.

Turning away from him, I shut my eyes. I think of my brother and realize with stinging guilt that it's the first time I've thought of him since arriving in the desert. I've been too occupied with the man who's here now. And for the first time, I wonder — if that's exactly what Guy wants.

I wake to someone rubbing my upper arm. When my eyelids lift open, the first thing I notice is the dark stubble along Guy's jaw. He shaved at base camp, but it's already grown back, casting a shadow on his wind-worn face.

His steady blue eyes watch me as I pull myself up.

"You woke me," I say quietly. "I can't believe it."

He shrugs one shoulder and turns toward the fire. It's roaring and crackling in the cold desert night, and I imagine he must have had M-4 relight it moments before. Scooting close to him, I feel the heat rolling off the flames.

"I'm glad," I finish.

"You didn't seem as tired tonight." Guy rubs his hands together, then places them on his knees. He seems nervous, but I don't think it's because he has something to say. It's more like he seems embarrassed to have woken me up. Like he's afraid I'll realize he wanted company.

That he was actually lonely.

I know he's not going to initiate a conversation, so I decide to ask him the questions I've been harboring. I start with the easy stuff. "Guy?"

He looks at me.

"What did you mean when you told Caroline, 'you know,' after you said Dink should go with you guys?"

Guy stares into my eyes for a long time, searching. Then he says, "I just meant that he's got to start doing things for himself. Caroline is stronger than she appears, but no one's survival is guaranteed out here. If something were to happen to her —"

"There'd be no one to baby Dink anymore," I finish.

Guy nods.

I'm not sure I believe what he's telling me is the truth, but I have no reason to think he's lying. Running my hand over Madox's sleeping body, I ask my next question. It's not the one I'm most curious about, but I'm going for easier banter before I pull out the big guns. "When did you get that tattoo?"

He swallows and glances toward his lion. "A few months before I left."

This surprises me. I thought maybe it'd been something he did right after he received his invitation. As a let's-get-ready-to-rumble

212

symbol. But then, I guess it'd be all scabbed over like the minia-ture one my BFF from Boston, Hannah, got on her ankle. Of her own name.

"It's a bird, right?" It's the second time I've asked this, but I feel like maybe he'll answer now that we're sort of alone.

Guy runs a hand over his fresh stubble, and I'm suddenly envi-ous of that hand. "Yes, it's a bird."

"Any particular kind?"

Guy looks right into my eyes, and my heart stops. I imagine I'm dead, and this is what heaven feels like. The way he's staring at me makes me think I'm missing something important. "It's a hawk," he says slowly, so quietly I almost don't hear him.

"Oh" is all I can think to say.

He looks at me for another full minute, then glances back at the fire. Guy is a mystery. From the way he speaks to the scars and disfigurements across his body. And I'm ready to get answers. *Real* ones. I swallow the lump in my throat. Last question. "You know more about the race than what you've already told me." I squeeze Madox's short tail in my palm. "I want you to tell me the rest. Everything."

"That's not going to happen," he says.

Anger boils inside my chest. He's harboring information that could help the rest of us. We've all agreed to aid one another until the end, yet he's not doing that. Not really. What upsets me most is that I know I'd tell *him*. "You act like you're a part of this group. But as long as you're withholding information, you're not." I lie back and roll onto my side. "I can't trust you if you won't trust me."

He stares straight ahead, but even from here, I can see his face soften. "The only things I know . . ." He pulls in a breath. "The only things I know are what my parents told me." Guy glances at me. There's fire burning in his eyes. "I won't tell you anything that could bring you harm."

I sit up, hands on my knees. And I wait. I know to wait.

"It started with a man named Gabriel Santiago. The Pharmies worked for him." Guy fills his lungs like he's preparing to fill in the holes in the info. "Some of the Pharmies were scientists who worked in genetic engineering. Others worked in medicine. But they were all creators of sorts. And Santiago, he had the kind of money that could make things happen.

"He was a gambling man. He loved watching his money grow without his lifting a finger. Santiago believed he was born lucky and maybe that he was born smarter. Smart enough to know it's easier and more exhilarating to earn money from being *right*. So he sought ways to gamble: cards, hounds, horses. He loved discovering grander and riskier bets. Because Santiago believed he couldn't lose. And if he *was* losing, he had a crew of guys who'd ensure it didn't last long. Gabriel Santiago wasn't the kind of boss you disappointed." Guy rubs the back of his neck like he's thinking. Or maybe like he's trying to decide how best to tell the story.

"Santiago had a young daughter named Morgan. She was . . . she was his everything. He'd lost his wife years before, and Morgan was all the family he had left. He gave that little girl everything. Anything she asked for, and anything else she didn't. Some said he was a cold man, others called him a criminal, but for her, he melted."

Guy narrows his eyes at the sand between his knees.

"One day, one of Santiago's guys told him that this firm, Intellitrol, was looking for financial backing. Said these guys were playing with genetic engineering and making huge discoveries in medicine and that there was a fortune to be made. That they just needed direction and cash . . . and someone willing to take a chance. To Santiago, it sounded like a different kind of gamble, and he couldn't help being intrigued. So he agreed to meet with them, and before you know it, Gabriel Santiago had these guys working on all kinds of crap. And in general, things seemed to be going smoothly.

"But one day, when Morgan's birthday was rolling around, Santiago jokingly asked one of the scientists at Intellitrol to make a puppy for his daughter that can fly like a sparrow. At first, they were all laughing, but then the Pharmies started thinking about it. Why couldn't they make something from two different animals? Or from different elements that existed in the world? This was when genetic engineering was first being discovered, right, so there was a lot of excitement at Intellitrol about it. And they had Santiago's resources to play with. . . . So they *did*."

Guy's eyes meet mine, and my stomach clenches.

"When Santiago saw the animal they created for his daughter, and when he witnessed how much Morgan loved it, he saw a business opportunity that dwarfed anything else he'd done before. So he told these guys to start making more of these animals . . . fast."

I glance at Guy's lion and think about the fire it created hours earlier.

Guy hesitates again, and I get the sudden sensation this isn't going somewhere good. "But soon, Santiago started pushing the Pharmies to take more and more risks with these creatures. And as the animals started increasing in numbers — kept in cages below a warehouse Santiago bought — the scientists started worrying. See, none of this research had been approved by Intellitrol. Or anyone. And the public tends to rebel when something unnatural — something *ungodly* — is created. Plus, these scientists weren't exactly supposed to be taking orders from Santiago, their investor, when it was a public company and whatnot." Guy bites the fleshy part of his thumb, like he's debating telling me more. When he looks at me, I know he's decided to continue.

"So the scientists decided they'd approach Santiago and tell him they didn't want to make these animals any longer. Well, the guy went apeshit. Threatened to go public with their research and tell Intellitrol, the FBI, the CIA, whoever what they've been working on. In truth, Santiago never would have reported them, not with his past. But the scientists didn't know this, so they came up with a plan: burn the building down and call it an accident. The other Pharmies, for one reason or another, agreed it was the best way out. So they started the fire. But they didn't realize . . ."

Guy wipes a hand across his brow. He flinches.

I put my hand lightly on his thigh and hold my breath.

"Santiago's daughter, Morgan, she was in the building. She was . . . she was down near the animals' cages, probably playing with them and crap when the Pharmies started it." Guy swallows and says in a rush, "She died."

"Guy —" I start. But he shakes his head and I can tell the conversation is over. I want to push for more. I want so badly to know how this story ends with us *here*. With me and Guy and Harper and the rest of the Contenders fighting to save the lives of the people we care about. But I know it won't get me anywhere. So I make a promise to ask him later. Maybe then he'll share the rest of his secrets.

As my mind wraps around the horrific story he told, I lie back down. This time, I don't turn away from him. After a few moments, he reaches out and lays his enormous hand against my cheek, cupping my face. I press against it and close my eyes, thinking of Morgan, of how she burned to death.

Maybe Guy is filled with lies. Or maybe he has an ulterior motive in telling me what he has. But just for tonight, I decide to throw caution to the wind. And trust him completely.

Even if he does break my heart.

CHAPTER TWENTY-NINE

The next morning, we are rejuvenated. Already, we've learned how to sleep in the cold, on twigs and leaves. We've adjusted to the desert quicker than we did the jungle, though the desert is crueler. Still, it shows surviving the wild is a learned skill. That we can apply tricks from one ecosystem to another.

Caroline says she'll lead, and Guy quickly agrees, though the rest of us are worse at veiling our surprise. The daughter who came to save her mother has shocked me more than once. Guy was right when he said she's stronger than she appears. I'll have to keep an eye on her. Although last night I lost myself in Guy, in the story he told me, today I remember my brother — that I'm here to save him.

That Guy is temporary.

And Cody is my family. My blood.

This morning, I'm near the back. It allows me to move slower, knowing I won't hold anyone up besides Olivia, who's behind me. It also allows me to think about what I've learned. That Santiago had a daughter and that scientists accidentally killed her. Did Santiago find out what the Pharmies did? Or did he die an old man still thinking it was an accident? Regardless, I need to find out the rest. About how all this leads to the Brimstone Bleed. I know now how the Pandoras were first created, but why a race today when this happened sixty years ago? And when am I going to tell the others about the things I've learned?

I look at Guy. A few more days, I decide. Just a few more questions answered before I risk the others jumping on him. It isn't fair that I'm keeping this from them, but I tell myself it's because I want to get the full story first. That it'll help them more if I do.

I glance around and notice Madox is trudging along near the lion this morning. M-4 wants no part of the baby fox, but my Pandora is insistent. Overhead, RX-13 screeches and glides through the sky, wings spread open, riding the wind.

I pull my canteen off and take a long drink. The water feels incredible washing down my throat, and I pray today won't be as hard, knowing I can drink when I need to — which is about every ten minutes.

Behind me, I hear Olivia's stomach growl. *You and me both, sister.* For the last three mornings, we've eaten a steady diet of bitter green fruit. I'm about ready to stir-fry Madox just to get a little meat up in this joint. Madox looks up at me and whimpers, like he can read my mind. I hold my hands up in claws and act like I'm a monster. He trots ahead of the lion.

God, I'm such a jerk.

I stop when I don't hear Olivia or her elephant trudging behind me. Turning around, I notice she's about ten feet away, bending over at the waist. She's going to be sick, I realize.

"Jaxon," I say, because it seems right to tell him. "I think Olivia needs you."

Everyone stops, and Jaxon moves toward Olivia. That's when I see the girl reach a hand out toward the ground. *She isn't sick,* I gather suddenly. *She sees something in the sand.*

"Olivia," Jaxon barks, his voice cold as steel. "What are you doing?"

Guy races past me so quickly, a breeze blows across my skin. But it's too late.

The sand beneath Olivia's hand shimmies and a thick brown snake thunders into sight, pink tongue tasting the air. Above its eyes are two perfect horns. The sight sends a shiver down my body, but I don't move. No one does. Not even the Pandoras. Olivia has frozen solid, her hand still outstretched toward the snake.

"Olivia," Guy says beneath his breath. "Do not move."

A hissing, crackling sound emanates from the snake in a crisp warning, and the girl begins to cry silently. Her arm shakes, and tears drip down her cheeks, drying before they reach her jawline.

"I want you to listen to me." Guy is a statue of muscle and bronze in the scorching sun. I want to believe he can help her. He has to. "I'm going to tell you exactly what to do."

"Don't let that thing touch her, Guy," Jaxon snarls. "Don't you dare fuck up on this."

"Olivia, open your eyes." Guy's voice is smooth as milk, but each word feels like a gamble. Like something that may startle the snake and put Olivia at risk. "That's good," he says. "Now, I want you to take a very small breath. Very small. And at the same time, I want you to step backward. Pull your right foot back first, then bring your left back to meet it."

My head is pounding. My heart is thumping. I'm afraid I might scream from pure anxiety.

Olivia pulls in a small breath and steps back with her right foot. *Should she have moved so fast? Why is she moving so fast?!*

The girl brings her left foot back to meet her right, and I can see her body relax just a bit. The snake watches her carefully, tongue flicking, body arching.

"That's good," Guys says. "Now, when I tell you to, I want you to do the same thing again. Another small breath, another step back. The rest of you, stay still. Don't approach Olivia. That means you, Jaxon."

Jaxon doesn't respond, but I recognize the fear twisting the features of his face.

Olivia sucks in a short breath and steps her right foot back. Flawless.

She brings her left foot back to meet it —
And stumbles.

Her hands splay out and she falls forward. Jaxon runs toward her, and Olivia's Pandora makes the most terrible sound through its trunk. But nothing helps.

The snake strikes.

Caroline screams, or maybe it's Harper. My heart is pounding so loud in my ears, I can't tell where it came from.

The next thing I know, Jaxon is carrying Olivia away and the elephant is stepping on the snake's head. Guy withdraws his pocketknife and swiftly cuts a clean slice behind the snake's head. When the elephant pulls its foot back, Guy kicks the head away from us and rushes toward Olivia.

"Give her to me," Guy tells Jaxon.

"Screw you," he says.

"Give her to me!" I've never heard Guy so much as raise his voice. So the sound of his shouting sends waves of hysteria rolling over me. This is serious. Oh my God, this is *serious*. I can't lose someone else. Olivia can't die.

Jaxon's eyes are wide with uncertainty, but he hands a sobbing Olivia over. Guy drops to the ground and holds her against his chest. He looks her over before announcing, "It struck her on the hand. On her pinkie." He sighs with despair and adds quietly, "A horned viper." Guy searches the desert, and his eyes land on her elephant. "Olivia," he barks. "Tell your Pandora to help you."

Olivia stops crying for a moment, sniffs, and looks at the elephant. "EV-0," she says, her voice shaking so much, my heart clenches. "Please help me."

The elephant takes two steps in her direction and stops.

"EV-0, help me," she repeats.

Her Pandora's head drops ever so slightly.

Olivia looks at each of us and then back at her elephant. "Help me, you worthless animal! Help me! Help me, damn you! Help —"

She stops screaming and sobs into Guy's chest. Jaxon points at Guy, tears streaming down his face. "Do something," he says. "You do something or I'll kill you myself."

Guy didn't put the snake there. He didn't make Olivia stumble. But we depend on him. And now that something terrible has happened, we expect him to make it better.

"Take off your shirt," Guy says, staring directly at Jaxon.

Jaxon rips his shirt off like it's made of acid. He drops it in front of Guy.

"I need yours, too, Dink." Caroline helps Dink — who appears even paler than he has the last two days — remove his shirt. She tosses it to Guy. He lays Olivia flat on her back in the sand, and she curls into a ball, sweating and crying without end. He takes Dink's shirt and twists it into a long rope. "Open your mouth, Olivia."

"What are you doing?" Jaxon says, pacing.

Guy ignores him, and Olivia opens her mouth. "Bite down on this," he tells her.

She does, and my stomach turns as I realize what he's planning.

Guy wipes his switchblade along his pants to remove the snake's blood. He looks up at Jaxon, then at Harper. "The two of you need to hold her down."

Olivia squeezes her eyes shut and moans into the shirt. I know she's thinking the same thing I am, that this isn't going somewhere good. Looking at her now, I briefly wonder if Santiago's own daughter, Morgan, was much younger than Olivia.

Harper grabs Olivia's arms, and Jaxon holds her legs.

"Tell me what you're going to do, asshole," Jaxon spits.

Again, Guy doesn't answer. And I still don't move. But when he grabs Olivia's hand, and lays the blade at the base of her finger, I turn and vomit into the sand. I'm still emptying the water in my

221

stomach as Olivia's muffled screams reach my ears. When I finally stand up, I'm shaking so hard, I almost collapse. I know what's happening behind me, but I can't look. I can't.

Eventually, Olivia's screams stop. Someone else is crying, but I know it's not her. At some point, I'm going to have to help. We're here for one another . . . until the end. And I've done nothing but nurse my own fear while Olivia lives a nightmare. I pull in deep breaths of dry desert air and turn around.

The world spins as soon as my eyes land on Olivia. Her body has crumpled in on itself. She looks lifeless, but I can see her chest moving, so I know she's not gone. She must have just lost consciousness. Harper is rocking herself and staring at her own boots, and Jaxon is crying into his hands. Guy kneels over Olivia, his hands covered in blood. His eyes are glassed over, like he's having trouble grasping what he did. But he shouldn't. It isn't hard to understand when the truth is lying in the sand —

As Olivia's severed pinkie.

Though Guy seems helpless, I notice he's wrapped Jaxon's shirt around the girl's hand and is pressing down. I don't know if he'll be able to stop the blood. It's a finger, not a skinned knee. A friggin' *finger*. I remember when Hannah and I used to play those would-you-rather games.

Would you rather kiss Curtis O'Brian with tongue, or get a hickey from Mr. Davidson?

Would you rather go three days without makeup, or get kidney punched by that girl who only wears lip liner?

Would you rather discuss sex with your mom, or cut off your own pinkie?

In any situation in which losing your pinkie was an alternative, the finger always got the ax. But that was in theory. Not in real life. Not in an Olivia's-finger-is-lying-in-the-sand-and-turning-blue kind of way. In this case, I'd choose the other option. No matter what.

Guy speaks and it startles me in the way a shotgun firing might.

"We need to rest here for the remainder of the day," he says. "If she's okay when she wakes up, we'll travel through the night." No one responds. I'm sure we're all thinking the same thing. That we don't want to make her travel at all, but that we also need to find base camp or we're all dead.

The cheetah moves toward the finger and sniffs. My heart beats in overtime praying he has some skill that can help. I know Pandoras usually help only their own Contenders, but maybe because Jaxon is so upset, Z-54 will do something anyway. Harper raises her head to watch, and even Caroline stops rocking Dink to see what the creature will do. We all hold our breaths.

The Pandora continues to sniff it for a few seconds, then lifts his head . . . and bats at the finger like it's a toy.

"Oh my God," Jaxon says. He jumps toward his cheetah. The Pandora snatches the finger between his jaws and trots away from the group. Now M-4 runs after the cheetah. They fight over the finger in a way that's almost playful. *This is a game for them,* I realize. They love us, are built to help us survive, but they also have instincts. And right now they smell blood.

The lion steals the finger away and pops it into the air. From behind the lion, the cheetah leaps up and bites down on it.

"Jesus," Guy says. "Someone get that thing away from them."

I try not to think about what's happening, and instead race toward the two cats. Right as I reach them, the cheetah closes his mouth over the finger. And swallows.

Squeezing my eyes shut, I fight the urge to get sick again. Seeing a cheetah eat a child's finger is not something I ever thought I'd need to be equipped to handle.

We find a small tree, which offers almost no shade, and carry Olivia beneath it. And then we wait. At first, we watch the girl, but she never stirs. Then we watch the cheetah to see if it gets sick from the venom, but it doesn't.

When the sun finally sets, and Olivia still hasn't woken up, Guy says we need to bring her around. Jaxon agrees and shakes the girl gently until she stirs. "Heeeeey, Olivia," he says, though nowhere near the way she did to him this morning. "Heeeeey, Olivia." The girl's eyelids flutter for a moment, then she raises them completely.

The first thing she does is puke.

I bite my lip watching her, hoping this is a good sign. Guy doesn't seem too concerned, which I take as promising.

"Give her water," Guy tells Jaxon.

Jaxon retrieves his canteen and tips it so that Olivia can drink. She takes a few pulls and then pushes it away.

"Olivia," I say. Jaxon, Guy, and the girl all look at me. "Is there anything we can do? Anything?"

Her eyes fall to the sand. "Is it gone?"

Guy hesitates, then says, "Yeah, I had to remove it so the poison wouldn't get in your system. We probably got the majority out."

"My body hurts and my head feels funny," she says.

"That's the venom." Guy glances at her hand, still wrapped in Jaxon's blood-soaked shirt. "It should wear off over the next several hours."

Olivia closes her eyes and swallows. "Where is it?" she asks. "My . . . my finger."

Everyone looks at Jaxon.

"Don't look at me. It's not like I made him do it." Jaxon's already sunburned face reddens deeper. Though he acts upset with what's happened to Olivia, he also seems relieved that she's okay now. "Stop looking at me. All of you."

"Jaxon," Olivia says. "Where is my finger?"

Harper snorts, and now we look at her. "Oh my God," she says. "I'm so sorry. I didn't mean to . . ." She shakes her head, covers her mouth, and waves her hand as if to ask us to stop staring.

"Will someone tell me what's going on?" Olivia sits up and holds her injured hand in her lap. "I just got bit by a snake with horns, got my finger cut off with a switchblade, and I'm in so much pain, I feel like I could die."

"Does your hand hurt?" Guy asks.

"Actually, no," Olivia admits. "It's throbbing, but it's numb."

"Probably the venom, but maybe it's because of blood loss." Guy narrows his eyes, thinking. "Maybe it'll stay numb until we can —"

"Where is my finger?" Olivia screams.

Caroline bolts to her feet. "The cheetah ate it."

Olivia's eyes get so big, I'm afraid they'll burst. "The cheetah. Ate. My finger." The girl looks at each of us. "That's what you're telling me? That Jaxon's Pandora ate the pinkie from my right hand? My *writing* hand?"

"To be fair, he won it from M-4." Harper looks like she's about to explode from laughter. I'm not sure whether I feel like laughing, too, or punching her in the ear. "They battled for it."

Olivia's gaze turns wild, and she stares off into space for a minute. Then a small smile crawls over her lips. "That is, like, *the* best way for my finger to go." She looks at Jaxon. "Ever."

CHAPTER THIRTY

Soon, we start walking. Olivia seems to be doing better, but the pain in her hand is now full force. Jaxon sets her atop the elephant and stays close by to ensure she doesn't slide off as we travel. Every few minutes, the girl whimpers in agony. The sound gives me a nervous tic, and I find myself anticipating it, my hands balled at my sides.

As the last of the day disappears behind the sand dunes, I think about what Guy said. That we shouldn't walk at night because of predators. A chill rushes down my spine — not only because of the plummeting temperature, but from thinking about what might be lurking nearby, invisible in the night. The smell of Olivia's blood wafting around us can't be good.

"Are we sure this is a good idea?" Caroline asks. Her voice startles me. It feels too close and too far away at once. It's been night for all of ten seconds, and already I can hardly see anything.

"We have to find base camp." It's Guy's voice. I'd recognize it anywhere. And I know exactly what he's implying: that if we don't find base camp, Olivia may not make it. The poison is mostly gone from her body by now, but she's clearly still losing blood.

I stop when I hear a scuttling sound nearby. "Did you guys hear that?"

"Oh God," Caroline moans.

Everyone stops walking, and the sound continues. It doesn't grow louder, but it doesn't go away, either. I hear Guy sigh and know he's contemplating what to do. Something brushes my ankle. I'm seconds from screaming bloody murder until I realize it's Madox. Crouching down, I run a hand over his sand-filled coat.

"Everyone needs to ask their Pandoras for help," Guy declares.

Immediately, there's a chorus of voices as Contenders call out demands. I speak directly to Madox, who ignores me as usual. I still can't figure out why other Pandoras seem to understand their Contenders and Madox doesn't. Maybe he just wasn't built with that skill. Thinking he's incapable of doing something the others can pains my heart. Not because I want him to be the best for me, though there is that. It's more that I can't help but think of him as anything less than perfect.

Before I can reflect more on Madox's inability to comprehend English, a flash snaps over the area. I shade my eyes for a moment, and when I pull my hand away, I can see everyone in our group and all our Pandoras clearly. When I spot Z-54, my mouth tugs into a smile. Jaxon's cheetah stands a few feet away, his eyes shooting out twin beams of red light. I survey the area and don't see anything. Whatever the sound originated from is now gone.

"Wicked cool," Jaxon breathes, approaching and then petting his Pandora. He looks up at us. "Do you see this? Do you freaking *see* this? I never knew."

"Perfect," Guy says, as if this is the most normal thing in the world. "I just wish we had another set to light our rear as we travel." Guy looks in my direction. Understanding floods over me.

"Madox doesn't understand me," I say quietly. "Or I'd tell him to."

I wish he could understand me, I think to myself. *I wish I could just ask him to listen to Guy and mimic the cheetah, and it'd happen.*

Madox chases the beams of red light for a moment, like it's a game. Then his eyes flick on. They scan the cheetah, and seconds later, my baby fox morphs into a large spotted cat.

"Holy crap." Jaxon points at Madox, but looks at me. "No way."

I pull a Guy and shrug like it ain't no thang. "He does it all the time."

"He rips off other Pandoras?" Jaxon says. He inspects Madox closer. "He's like a fugazi."

"A what?" Harper says.

Jaxon tosses the curly blond hair from his eyes. "A fake."

"He's not a fake," I say. "He's brilliant."

"Fugazi," Olivia croaks from the elephant.

Jaxon nods toward Olivia as if that settles it.

"Does anyone know anything else their Pandoras can do?" Harper says. "If so, spill now. These revelations are taking up way too much time." Everyone stays quiet, and Harper waves a hand ahead of us. "Let's roll, then, shall we?"

As Madox heads toward the back, his red-flamed eyes pass over Caroline and Dink. In that small moment, I notice just how terrible the boy really looks. His skin is ashen and coated with sweat, even in the cool air. And his chin touches his chest as if it's too much to hold up his own head.

I move toward him. "Dink, are you okay?"

"He's fine," Caroline snaps, pulling him to her.

"Yeah, he's clearly not," I say.

"Tella." Guy speaks my name in a way that says to drop it, but I'm not about to.

"What?" I tell him. "Why can't I ask what's wrong?"

Harper takes two steps toward Dink and then freezes. "Oh God. He's really sick. Caroline, why didn't you say something?"

"Everyone needs to leave him alone," Caroline says in a whisper.

"You mean, leave *you* alone, right?" Harper cocks a hand on her hip, like she's ready to go twelve rounds. "You seriously need to —"

"Just shut up!" Caroline screams so loudly, her words seem to echo for miles. Bathed in red light, her shaking body looks almost explosive.

Harper steps backward and holds her hands up. "Okay, sorry. Jeez. Freak out much?"

"Let's keep moving," Guy says, interrupting the weirdfest.

Madox, dressed as a cheetah, strides behind us as the real Z-54 takes the front. We move through the desert like this, ignoring what just happened, four beams of red light paving our way. For the first couple of hours, I can't stop thinking about Dink. Then I start thinking about Cody and the prize. And how if I can make it to base camp first somehow, then I can make my brother healthy again. If only for a few years.

I'm not sure if it's the lights or the sound of our steps shuffling through the sand, but I never see any predators. Not that I want to make night traveling a habit. Then again, we've been walking for an eternity and I don't feel like a puddle of sweaty filth. So that's something, I guess.

When we finally stop, Guy and Jaxon gather a few twigs — only enough for a small fire — and M-4 lights them. Then we squat around the flames and warm ourselves. Walking heated our bodies fairly well, but now that we've stopped, the perspiration lacing my skin causes me to shake.

Jaxon, Olivia, and Caroline drift off to sleep, even though there's little time before the sun rises. Even Guy closes his eyes. Maybe he's asleep, though I like to imagine he's not. It makes me feel better about the strange way Dink is staring at me.

"Can I do something to make you feel better?" I ask the boy.

He doesn't answer, just wraps his arms around his legs and sticks his head between his knees. I glance at Harper to see how she's handling this. From the looks of it, she's not. She glances everywhere but at Dink, and I realize it's the most nervous I've seen her. I don't think she knows what's going on with him, but it certainly makes her uncomfortable.

"Harper," I whisper. "What do you think we should do?"

Her head snaps in my direction. "How should I know?" she says. "He's just a kid. Why is he even out here?" She shoots up and walks away into the darkness.

"Harper," I yell-whisper. "Harper!"

But it doesn't matter. She keeps moving. I think about waking up Guy and ordering him to do something. But it's obvious she wants to be alone, so I inch closer to him and keep my eyes trained on the boy. My chest aches as I watch him. I want to do something to help. We've been so focused on Olivia ever since the snake, but now I'm wondering if Dink didn't need our attention just as much. The only thing I know for sure is that we have to get to base camp soon. For both their sakes.

I must have drifted off, because when I open my eyes, I see Harper smiling over me.

"Wake up, woman," she says. "I found a flag."

"Really?" My voice sounds like a truck driving over gravel. Nice.

"Yeah, hop to." Harper moves away and rouses everyone else. I wonder if her waking me up first is her attempt at an apology. I decide to think it is, and accept it as an early-morning gift.

"You found a flag?" I hear Jaxon saying over and over. The pride in his voice is evident, as if Harper's success is partly his own doing. He lifts her up and spins her in a circle.

She shoves an elbow into his chest. "Let me down or I'll aim lower."

He sets her on her feet. "You're sexy when you threaten me."

"You disgust me," she retorts. But I don't miss the blush that brightens her cheeks. Harper looks at me and Guy, and attempts to hide her reaction to Jaxon's words. "It's this way."

Guy glances at me, and I notice his skin has become even bronzer in the desert. It's like his body is made to withstand any situation, while the rest of us wither like dried cranberries.

I hate him.

The corner of his mouth quirks upward.

Or love him.

Jaxon checks on Olivia, who mumbles that she's *still in pain, thank you very much. And keep your idiot Pandora away from my other fingers.* He seems pleased that the girl is well enough to be difficult and nods to Harper that the two are ready to travel. Caroline puts an arm around Dink and signals that they'll follow.

Harper straps her canteen across her chest. "Great. Let's get going. We can have RX-13 catch us some breakfast after I show you where the flag is."

Oh, the anticipation.

It takes about a fifteen-minute walk before we get to the blue flag, which lies lifeless against the tall rod. My fear that we'd trudge through a *windy* desert every day was obviously unfounded. I bet RX-13 hates days like this, when she has to beat her wings often in order to fly. Then again, maybe that's the fun part. Who knows.

"Why didn't you take it down, champion?" Jaxon asks Harper.

Harper shrugs.

"If I were you, I'd strap that baby around my head like Rambo." Jaxon looks at Guy. "Have you ever seen *Rambo*? It's an old throwback action movie where —" He pauses, and his face brightens. "Hey, that's it. Let's be the Rambos. Yeah, we're *totally* the Rambos."

"That's the worst one yet," Harper says, her eyes trained on the flag.

Jaxon looks at me. "You like it, right?"

"Actually, I kind of do." And it's the truth. I could totally sport a flag around my head and Rambo out if someone threatens us. "Maybe we should vote on —" I stop when I notice Guy bending down a few feet away. "What's going on?" I ask. "What do you see?"

"Footprints," he answers.

Caroline moves closer, leaving a red-faced Dink behind. Harper is nearest Dink, though I don't expect her to offer support. Watching her shy away from the boy, I wonder again who she's here for. She and Dink are the only ones of the old group who haven't volunteered the information. I move next to the kid and wrap my arm around his shoulders. He leans against me and makes a low, guttural noise. Something dies inside me when I hear it.

"Maybe the prints are from Harper," Caroline offers.

"No, there are different sizes." Guy sweeps the sand with his fingers and looks over his shoulder at Jaxon. "Did you come here last night? Did you follow Harper?"

Jaxon holds his hands out. "What am I, some sort of stalker?"

"You're totally stalking her," Olivia mumbles from atop the elephant. We've had to move slower since EV-0 is carrying the girl, but I'm just thankful we can get her across the desert. Though I wonder how long the elephant will be able to continue with the extra weight, especially if we travel in the heat.

"There's nothing wrong with a little infatuation." Jaxon raises a single eyebrow at Harper, and she pretends not to notice.

"If someone else was out here, they would have seen the flag," Harper says. "And they would've taken it."

Guy's shoulders drop. He stands up and glances at me, then at Madox. "Maybe they weren't interested in the flag."

"Oh snap." Jaxon tugs the flag off the pole, wraps it around his forehead, and ties the ends behind his head. "The Triggers tried to jack our Pandoras. But never fear, the Rambos are here! Am I right?" A huge grin stretches across his mouth.

Guy shakes his head at Jaxon, then looks back at me. "It may not be him."

But we both know it is.

"Just in case it is," Guy continues, "we need to travel through the day."

"But we've hardly slept." Caroline eyes Dink with worry.

"And they probably haven't, either." Guy looks around the desert like he's already searching for the next flag. "Which means they'll be stopping soon to rest."

"It's the only way we can try and lose them," Harper says, finishing his thought.

Guy nods to himself. "We agreed to go north after we headed east, but this flag was directly east. So what do we do? Continue east or head north?"

I glance up into the sky and locate the sun. It's the morning, which means the sun is currently east. Which also means . . . I look in the northern direction. On the horizon, I see something. Squinting, I can just make out a different sort of landscape. It appears almost darker. "Look," I say, pointing. "Do you guys see that?"

Everyone stares into the distance.

After a moment, Jaxon looks at me like I'm crazy. "Uh, yeah. It looks like sand."

Caroline shakes her head. "I don't see anything, either."

"That's because there's nothing there." Jaxon takes a drink of water from his canteen. "You people are dehydrated. Seeing visions and shit."

"No, farther out," I say. "There's something there."

"I see it, too." Harper steps toward the blurry shape as if that'll help.

Guy starts walking. "We head north."

I look at Caroline. She shrugs and takes my place next to Dink. "I guess we're going north," she says.

Getting in line behind them, I pray what I'm seeing is something worth pursuing. Otherwise, I could be the reason we perish in this desert. But right now all I'm worried about is getting as far away from those footprints as possible.

CHAPTER THIRTY-ONE

After trudging through the sand for half a day, we find another flag. I gloat. I point fingers in people's faces. I tell anyone who will listen that I know this desert like the back of my hand.

Harper almost slaps me.

I don't blame her. I almost slap me.

I'm just so happy what I saw pointed us in a direction that didn't lead to certain death. Then again, there's still a ways to go before we reach the thing I discovered, which has more or less turned out to be rock formations.

"So we just keep on heading north, right?" I ask.

Guy nods. "We keep heading north."

"And why is that?" I twist side to side, a huge grin splitting my face. "Because we found another flag?"

My dark-haired, blue-eyed, bronze-skinned muscle man rolls his peepers so hard, they nearly fall from his head.

"Okay, but we're going to stop once the sun sets." Caroline places a palm to Dink's forehead. "I mean, we have to."

"Yeah, we'll stop," Harper answers for Guy.

After walking for several more hours, we're still a day or more away from the rocks. It doesn't seem like base camp would be this close, but it still gives me hope. Maybe we found it really quick this time. It's only been, what, five days? That means we have nine left. Piece of cake.

Oh my God. *Cake.*

Once I start thinking about it, I can't stop. I picture chocolate on chocolate and strawberry with pink frosting. Then I think of the more interesting kinds: carrot cake, pound cake . . . German chocolate. And cheesecake. Oh, holy mother. *Cheese. Cake.*

"You okay?" Jaxon asks as we find a place to camp for the night. "You look a little crazy in the face."

"I'm so hungry," I say.

Jaxon holds his hands up and steps backward. "Easy, girl."

"I'll send RX-13 out," Harper says.

Though I'm not looking forward to what the eagle finds in this hellhole, right now I'm too starved to care. "Want me to send Madox with her?" I ask, eyeing my waistline. I'm thinking I could've used the desert diet last swimsuit season. Maybe I could package it and make millions.

The desert diet: Eat whatever you want, as long as it's nondescript green fruit or beetles. If you're hungry, spring for a rabbit. Plain.

"No, the fox will just slow her down. Even if he does change shape." Harper sends RX-13 off in search of food, while I think over the Madox insult she just tossed out. "God, I'm exhausted," she says.

I eye her with amazement. I thought she was like Guy, that maybe she wouldn't know exhaustion if it shaved off her shiny, blond hair. Yawning, I realize I'm also beat. Walking through sand for hours on end has a way of sucking the life — and soul — out of you. For a moment, I imagine winning the Cure for Cody. On one hand, after he's better, I could be all quiet-hero and never mention how difficult the race was. People will talk behind my back and say, *She's so brave. She never even brings it up, but we know it must have been terrible. That Tella, she's amazing.*

On the other hand, I could go for martyr-who-will-never-let-it-go. I could shove it in Cody's face every chance I got. I'd be like, *Hey, Cody, enjoying that doughnut? You wouldn't be if I hadn't saved your ass.* And, *Hey, Cody, nice wedding you're having here. You know what you'd be doing today if I hadn't saved you? Not getting married.*

Lying back and driving my hands beneath my head, I smile at the possibilities. I feel Guy lie down beside me. I wonder if he'll light a fire, now that I can hardly see a thing and the temperature is dropping. Or if he'll get twigs for our beds — God forbid we sleep on something mildly soft. I decide if he does go twig hunting, I'll go with. There's no reason why I can't help.

I'm still puzzling over what Guy will do, and what his bedroom looks like, when sleep takes me.

When I wake up in the middle of the night, the sheer darkness startles me. I'm so used to waking to find sunlight or a fire. I sit up and glance around. I can't make anything out, but I can tell there are sleeping bodies nearby. I assume they're my fellow Contenders and decide I must have missed dinner or that everyone passed out before RX-13 returned. I also determine Guy is human after all — otherwise, I know he would have lit a fire before crashing. I lie back down, scoot closer to where I think he is, and try to fall back asleep.

But before I can, I spot something.

In the distance is a glowing light. Madox is grunt-snoring at my feet, so I know it's not coming from his eyes. I decide maybe it's the cheetah but figure I better check it out. Pulling myself up, I debate whether to wake Guy. If this were a movie, this would be the part where I scream at the girl to not go alone. But this isn't a movie. And if I wake up Guy and it turns out to be nothing, he'll give me another one of those concerned looks.

Running my fingers over my feather, I decide to take a quick gander and come right back. I listen for a moment to ensure Madox is still asleep — and still snoring — and head toward the light.

As I get closer, I realize from the way the light dances that it's a fire. Something is blocking my view of the flames, but I can't determine what it is. In the colorless night and the flickering glow, my mind plays cruel tricks. I slow my stride and stoop closer to the ground, a nervous sensation blooming in my belly.

I should go back.

I should wake Guy. Or Harper. Or anyone.

Though I think these things, I can't help but take one more step. Then another. My heart throbs inside my chest. My skin tingles with energy. I can see the thing in front of the fire better now. It's small. And it's crouched. My face pulls together with confusion.

One more step and I'll be able to see it.

I take the step.

Understanding hits me as the thing turns in my direction. My entire body tightens and something screams inside my head.

The thing is Dink.

His pink mouth and small hands are covered in dark blood. I stagger backward and shake my head when Dink's blood-coated lips part into a spine-chilling grin. Something is wrong with him. Something is *very* wrong with him. And I can't help but notice how close he is. How he could reach me in a few seconds if he wanted. But that's a ridiculous thought. Because this is Dink — the boy I decided is only about eight years old.

Dink stands, and I notice the blood doesn't just paint his hands but stretches toward his elbows. I take another small step back and stop when he holds out his palm. It's like he's asking me to come play. Behind him, there's something lying on the ground.

The blood. That's where the blood is coming from.

I glance around Dink and train my eyes on the thing he's been toying with. The boy brings his outstretched hand to his mouth and licks his fingers. Then his smile stretches farther.

Oh God.

He hasn't been playing with something. He's been eating *it.*

I move to the side, my sight fixed on the boy. Then I glance down.

A scream catches in my throat when I see Jaxon's cheetah lying behind Dink, his stomach ripped open.

Dink makes a loud hissing noise and leaps forward.

He's on me before I can think.

The boy opens his jaws and reveals his miniature teeth, laced with bits of flesh. He jerks his head toward me and tries to bite my neck. I fight to keep the child away from my face. There's no way he weighs more than seventy pounds, but his strength is staggering when he knocks me down into the sand, as if his sickness has made him stronger. I cry out as I shove him away. But as hard as I push, he moves only a few inches back. He's still dangerously close, but the extra space between us gives me the opportunity I need. I use my leg as a slingshot and kick him away. He flies off and lands hard in the sand.

In a heartbeat, he springs onto his hands and feet like a monster and scurries toward me. His jaw hangs open and that same hissing sound emanates from his throat. I crawl backward as fast as I can, but he's coming too quickly. His brown eyes have taken on an almost red hue, and I know if he gets to me again, that this time, he will actually bite me. No matter what, I have to stop that from happening. I can't contract whatever he has. I can't die in this desert. Because if I do —

My brother dies with me.

As Dink races closer, I spring to my feet, look for something to ward him off. Spotting the fire, I decide if I can grab a burning stick, maybe I can use it as a weapon. I dash toward the flames, the sound of Dink at my heels driving me forward. When I get to the blaze, I stop in astonishment. The fire — it's burning without wood. Without leaves. Without anything.

How?

No sooner do I think this than Dink slams into my legs. My knees buckle and I fall to the ground again. He climbs up my back and wraps his hands around my throat. I open my mouth to scream, but he covers my lips. I cry out through his fingers anyway.

Then he starts to push my head toward the fire.

Every muscle in my body tenses as my face nears the flames. I manage to push away from the heat a few inches, but he shoves me back down. The smell of burning hair fills my nostrils. My mind spins when I realize the scent is my own.

Deep in my throat, I scream. The sound is inhuman. I thrust myself away from the ground with every ounce of adrenaline I have. Dink soars from my back. Turning around, I ready myself to fight him. But when I see the boy, he's lying on his back, staring up at Guy.

Switchblade in hand, Guy crouches on one knee and jabs the other knee into Dink's chest. The boy kicks and thrashes and flails his arms. But mostly, he makes that strange hissing noise. Guy raises the knife above his head.

"No!" I scream.

But it's too late.

Guy plunges the blade into Dink's chest. The boy's mouth falls open and his eyes widen. He pulls in four sharp breaths, and then his eyelids slide closed. They stop midway, so that I can still see the red brown of his irises. I cover my face and shake my head. This didn't just happen. It didn't. *It didn't.*

When I uncover my face, tears streaming down my cheeks, I see Guy pulling off Dink's boots.

"Wh-what are you doing?" I choke. "Leave him alone."

He doesn't stop. Just keeps tugging off his right boot and then his left. He rips the boy's stiff white socks off next and leans in. Glancing over his shoulder, he motions me to come closer.

I shake my head.

"Tella, come here," he says gently. But I can't listen to what he's saying when his hands are covered in Dink's blood. I know the boy was trying to hurt me, but he was sick. We could have saved him.

Guy stands up and drags the boy toward me by the ankle.

"Stop it," I say quietly.

But he doesn't. And when he pulls the child close enough so that I can see what he's trying to show me — I gasp.

T-33 is stamped on his foot.

Guy drops the boy's ankle, and his leg falls to the ground with a thud.

Like honey dripping from a bottle, realization trickles through my mind: Caroline saying her and Dink's Pandoras had perished; Dink pretending to have lost his device; Dink saving Caroline from the river with ease; Dink building a fire without the use of anything flammable.

Dink is a Pandora.

Dink is *Caroline's* Pandora.

"No way," I say, tears blinding my vision.

"There's nothing we could have done." Guy says it like I'm feral, like I might bolt into the desert and never return if he speaks too loudly. He reaches toward me, and I curl into myself. I can't look at him right now. He saved me. But he killed Dink. But he saved — "Tella, there was something wrong with it," he continues. "The Creators went too far when they made this one."

"I don't know how I missed it," I whisper. I look up into his eyes. "I don't know how I never —"

I stop talking and a shiver races over my skin.

Titus is standing behind Guy.

"Guy!" I scream.

Titus brings his arm around Guy's throat before he can react. He snaps his head backward and Guy's eyes bulge. I race toward him, but someone grabs the back of my shirt and yanks me against his chest.

"Hey, beautiful," a voice says against my neck. I cringe against the sound and land an elbow in his gut. He releases me, and I turn on the guy. He's easily a foot taller than me, and is no doubt one of Titus's friends, but right now I feel like a weapon. Like I could take down an army of Tituses.

I stomp on the guy's boot and then throw my palm into his nose. A cracking sound splits the air, and the guy crumbles to his knees. I feel another pair of arms clamp down on my shoulders and yet another pair grab my legs. The two guys lift me into the air and I erupt with anger. I kick and scream and bite and tear with my nails. But it's no use.

No use. Until Harper appears with Jaxon and Caroline — and our pissed-off Pandoras — at her heels.

"Get. The hell. Away from her." Harper catches up to us and lands a blow on the guy holding my arms. He releases me and turns to wrestle with her instead. I watch her for only a moment, but it's enough to realize that — though I've always thought of Harper as indestructible — I've grossly underestimated her.

She isn't a Contender.

She's a *warrior.*

Harper takes down a guy nearly twice her size as I wrestle with another who keeps going for my legs. Over my shoulder, I hear the screeches and cries of our Pandoras engaging the Triggers' Pandoras. My gut twists as I think of Madox fighting. But right now I have to concentrate on the guy in front of me. The one sneering like I'm his next meal.

When I hear Caroline wail, I realize she's found Dink's body. I want so badly to go to her. To tell her everything will be okay. But I can't risk turning my back right now.

From the corner of my eye, I spot Titus's grizzly bear limping toward the fire. He opens his jaws and roars. The second time he roars, he also raises his paws, and a driving wind floods from his mouth and paws. I stop, startled, and watch as the fire blazes higher. As more wind pours from the bear's mouth and claws, sand washes over the flames.

The blaze drowns.

I spot Caroline on the ground, Dink's broken body lying over her lap.

And then there is only darkness.

A pair of hands encircles my stomach and hauls me away from the battle. I can hear Harper screaming in agony as I'm dragged away from my friends. Away from Guy.

Away from Madox.

CHAPTER THIRTY-TWO

It's daylight when I come to. My hand flies to my head, and I groan. There's a hard lump beneath my fingers that hurts when I touch it. For a moment, I can't remember why. Then I see Titus squatting by his grizzly bear. He's sharpening his knife against a stone. The steady *slink-slink-slink* it emits makes my head pound.

He stops and looks over. A slow smile parts his mouth. "You're awake," he says, as if we're old friends instead of a guy and the girl he knocked unconscious. "You've been moaning over there for a good hour. Thought you'd never come around." He points the tip of his knife to his forehead. "Sorry 'bout the blow."

Glancing around, I notice six other guys sleeping. They're spread out like skydivers along the sand. All except one, who's curled into a tight ball. It's an odd sight, given that he must weigh three hundred pounds.

I pull myself up and wrap my arms around my waist.

"I took your device and your knife," he says. "And your canteen." Titus stands up and walks toward me. I pull into myself as he crouches down. "Oh yeah. And your *Pandora*."

He points the knife over my shoulder at something.

Spinning around, I spot at least a dozen Pandoras. My eyes scan each of them quickly. "Madox!"

I scramble for my black fox, but Titus grabs on to my legs and drags me toward him. He wrenches me to my feet and presses our foreheads together. "I see you're going to need some breaking," he says.

I jerk my head back and locate my Pandora. He has a rope around his neck that is tied to a tree. Many of the smaller Pandoras are secured in the same fashion. The Triggers must have used all their rope from the orange packs in order to imprison these creatures. A few Pandoras aren't secured, and I wonder why they don't flee. Among them are Titus's grizzly, which I assume stays out of loyalty for his Contender. But the stolen Pandoras should have no such loyalties.

Pandoras like Levi's ram, G-6.

Most of the animals have lash marks across their faces and torsos. Even the bear has a large wound across his midsection that appears infected. Seeing the laceration, I remember the creature had similar injuries when Titus was traveling with us. At the time, I assumed it was from the fight with our Pandoras. But now I'm certain it's Titus's doing, that he's abusing his own Pandora. Though the bear makes me extremely nervous, I can't help but feel a pang of sorrow.

Madox, thank God, appears to be in perfect condition. Surprisingly, he isn't fighting against the rope. It's like he knows not to upset Titus. It seems all the Pandoras think the same thing.

Don't startle the psycho.

I decide to take this as my own personal motto.

"Isn't my collection awesome?" Titus presses his nose to my cheek. "And now I've added one more to my display." I think he's implying Madox, but when he runs his hand over the back of my neck, I realize he actually means me. "Good thing my prized possession comes with the best Pandora on the market."

Letting me go, he points toward the top of the tree. "See what else I picked up?" I glance up and spot RX-13 among the branches, a rope wrapped around her leg. "That Harper bitch sure doesn't need it anymore."

My head wants to snap around to look at him, see if he's telling the truth, but I try not to move instead. He's trying to get a rise out of me, but he won't get it. I know they didn't kill Harper. They couldn't have.

Right?

Titus walks to his guys and kicks them each in the ribs until they wake. They don't even complain. They just pull themselves out of the sand and look to Titus for direction. "These are the Triggers," he says. "But I told you that already, didn't I?" He nods to himself. "But did I tell you that we've been following you since the desert race started? I told my guys, I said, *Stick with me, 'cause I know a girl and her fox who can win this thing for us. And when they do, we'll all share the Cure.*"

"You can't do that," I say. "The Cure is to save one life."

"Who says? A voice from a little contraption?" He scratches his head with the tip of his knife, mussing his slicked-back blond hair. "When I win, I'll make sure my guys are taken care of."

Though I know he's dangerous, I can't help but wonder if he's right. Can the Cure be shared? Can the rules be changed? Looking into Titus's dark brown eyes, I know that even if they can, he isn't going to help these people.

"Tella, listen. I know you may be pissed now, but you'll come to realize I'm your best bet of winning part of the Cure. You'll learn to like me. Hell, you might even learn to love me."

"If you think that's true," I snarl, "then you're even dumber than I thought."

Titus nods toward Madox. "Dumb like a fox."

His guys — the Triggers — laugh like this is the funniest thing they've ever heard. Except the huge one, the one who sleeps like a terrified child. He smiles, but never quite laughs. I wonder if I could find sympathy with this guy. If he might help me escape. But I quickly dismiss the idea. Anyone who sides with Titus is someone I can never trust.

"Thirsty?" Titus asks, holding up two canteens. I assume one is mine. For a moment, I consider refusing his offer. I don't want to take anything from him. But I know if I want to survive this day, this heat, then I have to be smart. I nod. He hands me a bottle and says, "We didn't know what the hell we were going to do about water. Good thing you guys had a Pandora who could create it, or whatever it is that elephant does." His narrow nose wrinkles. "Though I'm not sure I enjoyed drinking after you. Pretty disgusting, actually."

"How will you find water now?" I ask, after I drink from my nearly empty canteen.

Titus smiles. His teeth seem too big for his mouth, but they're alarmingly straight and bright white and not altogether unpleasant to look at. "I guess we'll have to find base camp quickly." He reaches for my canteen, and I shove it in his hand. Behind us, the guys start untying the Pandoras. I hear an animal grunt, and I whip around. One of the guys — who has a severe case of acne — is kicking a stag in the legs.

"Stop it," I yell, but the guy continues his abuse. Turning to Titus, I say, "Stop him or I'll kill you. I swear to God, I'll kill you."

"Oh, I'm shaking." Titus mimics being afraid as I imagine stabbing him in the pectoral. He looks at the guy hurting the Pandora and says, "All right, stop beating on that thing already. We have company. Manners, people."

When Acne Face cuts Madox lose, I run toward him and lift the fox into my arms. Madox presses against me and I whisper in his ear, "I won't let them hurt you."

"How touching." Titus pulls two canteen straps over his head. "Now let's keep moving. We head toward those rocks. That's where you guys were going, right?"

I want to mislead him, but another part of me wants only to rejoin my Contenders. To be with Guy again. Knowing Titus will probably head north anyway, I decide to pretend I'm easily breakable and tell him the truth. "Yeah, we thought maybe base camp was beyond those formations."

"Splendid," he says. "Let's skedaddle."

The guys form a line behind their leader, but Titus insists I walk next to him. As if we are equals. As if we are friends. As if. I squeeze Madox so tight, he yelps and I have to let him down. Several times as we walk, I glance at Levi's Pandora. The ram has cuts along his muzzle and one of his kneecaps seems to be breaking through the skin. Even worse than the sight of him is the groaning sound the animal makes as he walks. Tears burn my eyes when I realize the creature won't make it much farther. It makes me hate Titus so much, it's almost scary. He may not have laid a hand on any creature besides his own, but these guys listen to him, and he obviously allowed this to happen.

As we continue through the worst hours of the day, I question why Titus is chancing traveling while the sun is up. Guy assumed most Contenders would move during the night, but Titus seems determined to get to base camp. Watching him unscrew his canteen and take a pull, I suddenly understand there's a reason beyond winning the five-year cure: We're running out of water.

The stolen Pandoras surrounding us look beaten into submission, but I'm still curious as to why they don't try and escape. It almost seems like once their Contenders were out of sight, they lost track of what their purpose was. Like they've turned into zombie animals or something. Watching Madox trudge through the sand, tongue hanging from his mouth as he pants, I pledge to never let that happen to him.

"Enjoying the weather?" Titus asks. Even covered in sweat and filth, he's not unattractive. His wrestler build, deep-set eyes, and wheat-colored hair make him my best friend Hannah's exact type. But it doesn't take X-ray vision to see that his insides brim with wickedness.

"It's great," I say evenly. If I can play nice and make it to tonight, then perhaps I can escape while they sleep. Even if they take shifts like we do, I'll have a better chance of fleeing when it's one-on-one.

"What exactly is your plan when we get to base camp?" I ask, trying to appear social. "You know my friends will make it there. And there's no way they'll let you hold on to me."

"I don't need a plan. By the time we get to base camp, you'll have realized you belong with us."

Fat chance.

"We'll see."

Titus flashes me another thousand-watt smile. He thinks I'm open to the idea. I can see it written all over his pompous face. The question that nags me is why he cares if I willingly join them. He already has me and my Pandora in his possession.

I feel a hand squeeze my butt.

"What the hell?" I yell, spinning around. The guys keep straight faces and stare forward. Titus stops, and the tin soldiers stop, too.

"What happened?" Titus asks.

I inspect the guys, searching for something that tells me who it was. Then I look at Titus. His face is pulled together in confusion, and he's too far away for it to have been him. I want to spill, but I'm afraid it'll A) cause a commotion I don't need, and B) screw with Mission Escape in the Dead of Night. For now I've got to pretend I'm considering joining his ranks. And part of that is acting like this kind of stuff doesn't bother me. So I feign passiveness.

"Nothing," I say, trying to hide the venom in my voice. "The guys were just messing around." I don't smile. I don't laugh. Doing either might send a red flag. Titus may be nuts, but he's not stupid. I just shrug like it isn't a big deal and keep walking.

Surprisingly, Titus doesn't press. But I see the way he eyes his guys before I turn away.

After we've hiked for another hour — Titus chatting away like we're on a first date — Madox begins to whine. Titus holds a hand out and everyone stops. "What's he doing?" he asks.

I approach my Pandora, but it does nothing to calm his nerves. "I don't know," I answer honestly.

"The wittle fox is all tuckered out," Acne Face mocks from the back. The guys laugh, but the gesture sounds forced.

Titus waves a hand forward and keeps walking. When I go to follow, Madox barks. Once. Twice. Three times. Every step I take, he becomes more and more upset, circling my ankles, rearing up and placing his front paws on my shins. I feel like I'm watching an old black-and-white *Lassie* show.

What is it, girl?

Titus stops us again. Nothing looks strange ahead, but Madox certainly doesn't want me going any farther. Titus looks at Acne Face and says, "Go check things out."

The Trigger seems proud that Titus asked him out of the other five guys. He nods and jogs past us. He searches the ground, looking for whatever it is that's caused my fox to panic. Then he turns and faces us. "I don't see anything," he calls back.

Titus's brow furrows. "Keep looking."

The guy spins around and takes a few more steps. Then he stumbles and falls.

At first, it appears he's just tripped over a rock or something. But as he flails, I start to realize it isn't that at all. It almost looks like he's . . . sinking. Titus waves an arm at the guys behind him, and they race past us to help Acne Face. The Pandoras stay behind, heads hanging. I take a step to follow the guys, but Titus grabs my arm.

He tips his chin up and asks them, "Well, what is it?"

A guy with enormous shoulders and long legs turns around. "Quicksand."

CHAPTER THIRTY-THREE

Titus keeps hold of my arm and creeps toward the quicksand. Madox goes crazy, barking and whining when he notices Titus dragging me behind him. I silently plead with my Pandora to cool it, and miraculously, he does. "Nick," Titus calls. "You sinking?"

"Yeah," Acne Face — Nick — answers. "Get me out of here!"

The guys make way as we get closer. Titus slinks to the very edge of the wet sand and stares down. "How did you not see this? It's clearly darker here."

Nick shakes his head, eyes bulging with fear. "I — I don't know. But I gotta get out." His legs and hips are buried, so all I can see are his chest, arms, and head. The more he squirms, the farther down he sinks. My stomach tightens and I suddenly feel like it's hard to breathe. Like it's not Nick down in that sand, but me. This morning, he beat that Pandora like it was nothing, but I can't watch another person die.

"Help him," I beg Titus. "Please."

He glances at me from the corner of his eye, his face pinched with disgust. It's like he hates that I care.

"We need all the hands we can get if we're going to win." I pull myself up like I'm strategizing. I can't say I'm joining the Triggers — Titus wouldn't believe it — but I can let him read into my statement and form his own conclusion.

A slow smile splits his mouth. He waves a hand toward the guy with long legs. "Get him out."

Long Legs reaches his long arm toward Nick. Clearly relieved, Nick takes hold of his hand and pulls. Long Legs wobbles and nearly falls in until another guy grabs the back of his shirt. "You're going to have to help me," Long Legs tells the guy behind him. The guy nods and reaches out an arm, too. But even together, the two guys can't seem to free Nick from the sand. As time wears on, and Nick sinks deeper, a hysterical sensation washes over me.

What if they can't get him out?

They have *to get him out!*

"Let's try the Pandoras," I tell Titus, worried his patience is wearing thin. I'm afraid of drawing attention to Madox, of involving him in anything that could put him in harm's way. But I know I can't let this person die. Not like this. Not when he's screaming in a way that makes my skin crawl.

Titus glances over his shoulder at the Pandoras and back at Nick, who's now immersed up to the bottom of his chest. Nick cocks his head like he knows what's coming. "No," Titus says. "He let your little friend with the bird kill his Pandora. Why should I risk the rest to save him?"

Even half buried, Nick looks furious. And when I think of Madox behind me, I know why. Losing my Pandora would crush me. I rip my arm away from Titus and lean over to help Nick. Maybe he's the way he is because of Titus. Maybe there's still good I can dig out of him. But whether there is or isn't, I'm going to help him.

Before I can offer Nick my hand, the large guy — the one who sleeps curled in a ball — stops me.

"Let me," he says. I look in his soft brown eyes and some of my fear dissipates. He's built like an SUV, and his head is shaved to the scalp. When I glance at the hand covering my arm, I find it's as wide as a toaster, and that his nails are manicured to perfection, like maybe this Godzilla hit a salon before entering the race.

Stepping back, I allow him to edge closer. He reaches his salami of an arm toward Nick, and Nick grabs hold.

"On three," Godzilla says.

Nick nods.

"One . . ."

"You ask me, he deserves being stuck in that sand," someone pipes in.

"Two . . ."

"Touching Titus's girl that way."

"Three."

Godzilla starts to pull at the exact moment that Titus barrels forward. I move to stop him, but it's like standing in front of a cannon. Titus shoves me to the ground and slams into the guy who has great nails. The big guy hardly moves, but it's enough to cause him to lose his grip of Nick's hand. Titus jabs his boot out and places it on top of Nick's scalp. Without a word, he pushes the guy's head downward.

Nick's chest plunges under the sloshing sand, then his arms. His shoulders. Nick shouts, and I scurry along the ground toward Titus's legs, trying to tackle him. To push him into the quicksand. Something. But the big guy grabs me and tugs me to his chest.

"Stop it," he says quietly. "Stop making a scene." Then he wraps his enormous hand around my face so that I can't see.

I don't have to see, though. Because I can hear. I can hear the way Nick begs. The way he explains his allegiance and that he never meant to touch me. But his pleas must not douse Titus's anger. Because the next thing I hear is the gurgling sound Nick makes when his leader pushes him the rest of the way under.

And then I hear nothing.

The guy covering my eyes pulls his hand away. Titus stands near the edge of the quicksand, staring at the ground like he can't believe what he just did. He glances up at the six of us and tries to offer an explanation. "He touched Tella," he says, focusing his attention on me. "He grabbed you or something."

He's waiting for me to agree. But I don't. I can't even see him through the tears.

"He would have hurt you." He points a limp finger at me. "Probably would've forced himself on you. You saw how he treated the Pandoras."

Titus nods to himself and takes a deep breath, his chest expanding. He tilts his head up and gazes at the sky. Then he peers off to his right. "Would you look at that," he says, flicking his wrist at something in the distance and grinning wide. "A flag!"

After we leave the quicksand, I lose touch with reality. Thoughts of Levi and Dink and Nick swirl in my head like a demonic merry-go-round. Titus leads us to the flag so he can remove it and tie it around his bicep. It's everything I can do to keep walking. To will my body forward.

Godzilla walks behind me. Every few minutes, he touches my lower back. I'm not sure why because I'm not thinking clearly. I just know it's the only thing that reminds me of where I am, and that this is real. And that Titus actually killed one of his own.

Madox keeps close by. He glances up at me, and his ears perk when he thinks I'm going to acknowledge him. But I never do. I can't even feel the ever-present ache in my muscles anymore. It's like my entire body has gone numb.

When the night falls and Titus finally stops, all I can think of is one person — Guy. Where he is now. What he's doing.

If he's coming for me.

He's here to save his cousin. So I'm not sure where that leaves us, especially now. Still, I have to believe that what I felt between us is not just circumstantial. That even though he's here for family, he wouldn't leave me out here with Titus.

I have to believe.

Titus sends his bear to gather food for dinner, and the guys work on building a fire. Turns out Godzilla used to be a Boy Scout and knows how to do such things. It takes him about eighty-seven tries, but he finally gets a small spark to ignite between his blade, a dark rock, and a handful of mossy foliage.

"Fire!" Titus roars, laughing from deep in his gut.

I have no idea what's so funny, and I have no idea why these idiots follow him so blindly.

"You know, Tella," Titus says. "I was never a big fan of fire before Brimstone. I was terrified of it, actually. So wild and unpredictable. But I tell you what, I've learned to respect it. Now, water? That's something I've loved all my life. My old man said I was born with fins. Said even when I was a kid, I took to the sea like a shark. Hammerhead, that's what he called me. 'Cause hammerhead is a type of shark, and he said I wasn't keen on listening." He knocks on his head with a closed fist. "Hardheaded, I guess."

I try to pretend I'm listening. That I care. But it's hard to keep up a facade when all I want to do is wrap my hands around his throat.

Titus unscrews his canteen and drinks for several seconds. The guys around him take the cue to drink as well. My throat burns thinking about water, but I refuse to ask for my own bottle back.

"Here," he says, handing me his canteen. "Have a drink. We can save yours for tomorrow."

I snatch it away like a wild animal and drink until it's gone. Titus doesn't stop me.

"See, everyone loves water best. You just have to be reminded why." A smile plays on his lips, and my insides churn. "Let's hit the hay, shall we?"

It takes everything I have to nod.

Titus moves closer and sits next to me. The guys stay on the other side of the crackling fire, far away from us. I steal a glance at Godzilla — who I've learned is named Braun — and the overgrown pink pig at his side. I'd assumed the Pandora was one they stole from another Contender, but I was mistaken. Because Braun keeps an eye on that pig like I do Madox. It's a funny sight, seeing a guy as large as Braun worried about a pig. Though it feels unnatural, I smile with one side of my mouth — and Braun smiles back.

"What are you smiling about?" Titus asks. I turn my head, and my smile drowns. He's watching me the way Guy does. With questions lingering on his lips. But unlike Guy, he isn't afraid to ask them. "Do you like the fire?"

I nod and run my hands over Madox, who's curled in my lap. Now that he's near me, I feel better. Though most of that security is canceled out with Titus so close. Looking at my small fox, I wonder why he hasn't done anything to get me away from Titus. I reason it's probably because the guy doesn't intend to harm me, that he only wants me to join them.

"Why do you want me to join your group?" I ask suddenly.

Titus tilts his head back, like he's surprised I asked. "It's hardly a group after today," he says, laughing. "We're down to seven, counting you."

My face must show my revulsion, because he coughs into his hand and says, "Bad joke."

I'm surprised that Titus is aware that what he did was wrong. It's like he's two different people: one who's rational and intelligent, and another who reacts on raw emotion without thinking.

Looking at him now, I wonder if he knows about the Brimstone Bleed the way Guy does. I consider asking him. But, no, I decide. I don't think he does, and I won't risk revealing what I do know, which is really just bits and pieces of a story I don't understand.

I breathe in and the smoke rolling off the fire fills my nose. For a moment, it brings me home to my parents' house.

"You remember that night after our Pandoras got into a skirmish?"

I'd hardly call it a skirmish, but I decide to play along and nod.

256

"You didn't like the way my Pandora ate or something." He smiles at me like we've been married for ten years and he's recalling our first kiss. "You really went off about it. You got in my face and just went *crazy*. And as I was watching you get so upset about everything, I said to myself, *There's a girl that's got fire. With that Pandora of hers, she just might win this thing.*" Titus licks his thumb and rubs a blotch of dried quicksand off his boot.

"When I saw your fox fight and change like he does, I thought he might be the best Pandora out there. But I figured you wouldn't be strong enough to survive the race even with a creature like that. Then I saw you that night, though, rage and fear in your eyes and this little feather in your hair." He pauses and touches my feather. I try not to cringe. "I knew I had to partner with you. That I had to —" Titus glances at my lips and I realize he's too close. Way too close. "That I had to be with you."

He leans in and a million thoughts flood my mind. Things like:

Do I let him kiss me so he believes I'm not a threat?

Do I slap his face and drag my nails across his cheek?

Would his lips feel like Guy's?

Guy.

"Hey, Titus." I hear someone say. Titus swears loudly and shoots a death stare at the speaker — Braun. "Just wanted to let you know AK-7 is back with dinner."

Titus sighs heavily and rolls his wrist. "Well, then, bring that fat bear over here."

I breathe out and curl into myself with relief.

I almost kissed someone I'd like to kill.

Inside my head, I scream.

CHAPTER THIRTY-FOUR

I'm still reeling from my near kiss with a murderer when Braun returns. The enormous guy has Titus's Pandora at his heel. Between the grizzly's jaws is something that looks like a spotted dog. Titus claps his hands and says we'll eat like kings, that this doesn't look half bad. I flinch and look away. No matter how long this race wears on, I'll never get used to seeing my food whole. When I get home, I may never eat meat again. Vegetarian or bust.

After the guys have cleaned and cooked the animal, they offer Titus and me a generous portion. I take it, close my eyes, and chew as quickly as I can. The meal tastes bland and tough, and has the distinct flavor only burned meat does. When I'm done eating as much as I can force down, I offer a large piece to Madox. My fox looks me over like he's making sure I'm satisfied, then takes the food from my hand and chows down.

"I can't believe you do that," Titus sneers. "Feed that thing."

"They get hungry, just like us," I answer, keeping my eyes on Madox.

"But they're built to survive without it."

"How do you know?"

"Look at my bear," he says. "It's the same size it was weeks ago. It hasn't lost an ounce. Me, on the other hand, I'm fading in the wind."

Glancing at Titus's swollen muscles and large frame, I find it hard to believe he's lost weight. But his face does appear thinner than it did in the jungle. And my waist and hips have never been this narrow. Inspecting Madox closer, I notice he does seem to be the same size. But when I watch him eating the meat, I know he's happy.

"They enjoy eating, otherwise your bear wouldn't have eaten that rabbit in the jungle."

Titus laughs and points a finger at me. "See, you even know what kind of animal it was. You remember that moment."

Rolling my eyes, I stand up. I'm not sure if what I'm about to do is just to piss Titus off, but once I've decided I'm doing it, I can't stop. Grabbing a hunk of meat off the cooked dog — and nearly gagging — I move toward the Pandoras and provide them each a piece. Most turn away and refuse to eat it. But that's fine, because what I'm doing is more of a statement. These creatures help us, and we need to treat them with respect. I give Braun a piece and he passes it to his pig, all while keeping an eye on Titus.

Finally, I get to AK-7. The bear sits on the ground with his paws in the sand. I step closer to him, and my heart pounds. Out of all the Pandoras, he's the one I'm most afraid of. This is Titus's animal, and there's no telling what it's been trained to do. I bring my hand up and the bear recoils like I'm going to hit him. When I see him pull back, my chest aches. I kneel down in front of the bear and Madox whines behind me.

"Here," I say, holding the meat out.

"Get away from my Pandora, Tella," Titus says slowly, evenly. "You can play nice with the other ones, but that there's mine."

The bear watches Titus speaking over my shoulder, his eyes shifting back and forth between the two of us. I drop the meat between his legs and back away. The creature glances down at the food, then up at me with something that looks like disbelief. But that can't be.

Can it?

"Don't you eat that, AK-7. You hunt for yourself if you're hungry," Titus says.

I spin around and square my shoulders. "Let him eat if he wants to. God, Titus. For once, just be a human being and have some compassion."

Titus's eyes widen like he's surprised I just said that. But then his face changes, darkens. He jumps to his feet and races forward. I cower, expecting him to strike me. But he flies past and slaps the piece of meat from the bear's paw.

"I told you, *no*," Titus yells in the Pandora's face.

All my anger toward him boils over. Before I can think, I shove Titus as hard as I can. He stumbles, trips over the bear's leg, and hits the ground. From across the fire, I see Braun stand up. The other guys stay put, waiting to see what happens.

"Don't scream at him," I yell. "Scream at me if you're so pissed." I hit my chest. "Scream at *me*."

Titus pulls himself up and kicks his bear's leg out of the way. The bear scoots backward and lowers his head.

I ready myself for a fight, but Titus only smiles. "See what I mean?" he roars. "That's the fire I've been talking about!" In a heartbeat, he crosses the distance between us and slams his mouth over mine. I place my palms against his chest and push like I did before, back in the jungle. But this time, he doesn't budge. His tongue slides across my lips, and my scream comes out muffled. Grabbing at my back and waist, he tugs me closer until I feel him press against my pelvis. Because I can't shove him away, I come up with another plan. I'm going to bite his tongue off. I feel the wet slick of it against my mouth, and this time, I open my lips to grant it access.

Titus groans.

"The device," someone calls out. "The device is blinking."

Titus pulls away from me, breathing hard. He wipes his mouth with the back of his hand, completely unaware of how close he just came to losing his tongue. A smile crawls across his face, and I try with everything I have to pretend it wasn't the worst thing in the world. To not show my horror.

To not give away that I will flee. Tonight.

The guy strides to our side of the campsite, holding his device up as evidence. When I look away from Titus, I'm surprised to find Braun nearby, shades of fury stretched across his face. His pig is at his side, grunting and raising its nose into the air.

Was he about to help me again? I wonder.

There's something in Braun's eyes that tells me he isn't like the rest. Already, he's done two things to aid me: He held me as Titus killed Nick, and he interrupted Titus's kiss. I wonder what else he's willing to do.

I startle when I see a second pig nearby. It's identical to Braun's, but this one's eyes are emerald green. If Braun wasn't about to help me, Madox sure as hell was. I almost laugh seeing my fox as a pig. Almost.

Titus digs his device out of his pocket and places it into his ear. The rest of the guys follow suit.

"Give me mine," I say.

Titus pushes the red button and listens.

"Give me my device," I repeat, louder.

He holds his hand up and makes a face like I'm annoying. But he has no idea how annoying I'll become if I don't get that device. I stop bugging him when I notice the way Titus's face changes. The way his eyes widen and his mouth goes slack.

"What is it?" I ask. "What's she saying?"

The other four guys come to join Titus, Braun, and me. They eye the stolen Pandoras. And they eye Madox. A clap of fear strikes through me, and I move to stand in front of my fox/pig.

The guy with long legs and big shoulders pulls out his switch-blade and thumbs the knife into place.

"Now hold on," Titus says. "We're going to do this real calm like."

But there's nothing calm about the way Long Legs creeps toward the Pandoras. And now the guys behind him are pulling out their own knives.

"What's happening, Titus?" I reach for my knife, which of course isn't there. "What are they doing?"

"I said, *wait*," Titus barks.

The guys still don't listen. Long Legs lets out this strangled cry and races toward the Pandoras. He moves quickly, so quickly, madness dancing on his face in the fire's glow. In two calculated movements, he pulls his knife into the air, then drives it into the belly of a Pandora.

The Pandora — a llama — cries in pain and trots in circles, blood painting the sand.

Behind Long Legs, the other guys spring into action. They dart toward the creatures, their knives flashing. But this time, the Pandoras know what's coming. They bolt into the cold night — wings beating, hooves thumping. I almost whoop with joy when Harper's eagle flies into the air and vanishes. The guys pursue the Pandoras as Titus screams.

"I told you to tie them up," he yells. "Every damn night! Tie the Pandoras up before you eat! How hard is that?" Titus paces, hands in his hair. "Now what are we going to do? What are we going to *do*?"

Moments later, the guys return. They pant and bend over to catch their breaths as I try to figure out why they're killing the Pandoras. But they're not trying to hurt all the Pandoras. Just the stolen ones. All that's left now are our own. Slowly, Long Legs raises his head. His eyes fall on something lying on the ground. My muscles clench when I realize what it is.

I thought all the stolen Pandoras had flown. But I was wrong.

There's one left.

Levi's ram.

Instinctually, I race toward it, silently begging Madox to follow. My Pandora stays right by my side as I throw myself in front of G-6.

"I don't know what's happening," I snarl. "But you won't touch this creature." Braun moves toward me, and I jab a finger in his direction. "I'll ask my Pandora to change. He can mimic anything your Pandoras can do. And he will kill you. To hurt this ram, you'll have to hurt me. And then my fox will kill you." I hold both my hands up in front of me, hoping that what I'm saying is true.

"Tella." Titus says my name like I've lost my mind. "Don't be unreasonable. There are six of us, and we each have Pandoras. We can get past you. And we can get past *it*." He nods toward Madox.

I nearly scream when a ball of gray rolls next to my boot and into the firelight. Everyone stops and looks down. Titus cocks his head. "What the hell is that?" he says.

The ball of gray unravels and spikes shoot out from its fur.

"It's my Pandora, asshole," Ransom says, stepping into view. "And the girl's right. You're not killing that ram. Over my dead body."

When I see Ransom so close by, the knife in his hand and the resolve on his face — my heart leaps. My plan was to flee tonight as the guys slept. But now is even better. I step closer to Ransom and we exchange looks. It isn't much, but it's enough to know we're on the same page. That we're going to get Levi's ram and get the hell out of here.

"You're crazy if you think you're leaving with that Pandora," Long Legs says.

"You're crazy if you think I'm not," Ransom answers.

"For crying out loud, can we stop making empty threats?" Titus grins like this is the most fun he's had all year. "Get this joker out of here."

The guys charge us. I think their goal is to hurt Ransom, but they seem much more interested in DN-99, the little raccoon who could. One guy chases the Pandora around the blaze, and in the blink of an eye, DN-99 burrows beneath the sand and is gone. The creature reappears seconds later beneath the guy's feet. Spikes spring out from the Pandora's coat and jab into his boots. The guy hollers in pain and falls to the ground. He tugs his boots off and inspects the damage.

Upon seeing this, the other Triggers become more agitated. They watch as the raccoon disappears once again. And then they wait.

DN-99 bursts from the ground beneath another guy's feet, and down he falls.

"He's like a land mine," I tell Ransom.

"That he is." Ransom smiles in my direction, and I'm so happy, I almost don't see a third guy storming toward me. Luckily, Madox does.

Stop him! I think, though I have no idea how Madox could do that.

My fox — dressed as a pig — races in front of me and oinks insistently. Surprisingly, the guy stops, knife-wielding arm suspended in the air. He meets the pig's eyes dead on, and when he does, an empty expression crosses his face. Then he brings the knife down and points the tip beneath his own chin. Even though the guy doesn't seem to understand what's happening, his whole body shakes with fear. The knife digs into his neck and a trickle of blood escapes the wound.

Understanding crashes over me. "Madox, stop."

My Pandora backs away, and I back away with him. When Madox breaks eye contact, the guy shakes his head like he's confused. It's like he doesn't remember that a pig just mind freaked his ass.

Hearing a loud squealing sound, I spin around. The guy without boots is trying to plunge his blade into Madox. But my Pandora is too quick for him. And now he's got a pissed-off Contender joining the fight.

I leap on the guy's back and dig my fingers into his eyes. The guy howls with pain. My attack ends early when a pair of hands wraps around my waist and throws me to the ground. The guy who assaulted me hurdles over my body and chases after Madox. Everywhere I look, the same thing is happening. Titus is trying to slaughter Braun's Pandora, and Braun is trying to fight him off. Two more guys are crawling after Madox — one on his hands and knees with bloodied feet, and another on two legs. A fifth guy is scurrying after the raccoon, and the last person is wrestling with Ransom over G-6.

With adrenaline coursing through my veins, I grab on to a guy's arm and wrestle him for the knife. There is a moment, as I'm fighting for the blade, when I remember that I own a green, rhinestone-encrusted hoodie that says GIRLS DON'T FIGHT. THEY FLAUNT. I'm wondering if it's still in my closet when the guy pops me in the side of the head.

The world goes blurry.

When I clear my eyes, I notice Ransom has beaten back his attacker. He has one hand around the rope attached to G-6 and his raccoon by his side. All three look ready to retreat. But there's a problem.

Me.

Ransom tilts his head and a pained look crosses his face. I know what he's thinking. He came to rescue his brother's Pandora. After that, he's here for his sister. He also knows if he stays, he's sacrificing his sister. The girl who loves her boyfriend and mood rings and hard-to-find mint cases. And her brothers. One of whom is dead.

"Go," I say. When Ransom doesn't budge, I scream so loud, my throat burns. "Go! Get *away* from me!"

He takes a few steps back, but looks confused.

"God, Ransom. Get the hell *away*!" I yell with conviction. Like I've got a plan that doesn't involve him. "You're screwing everything up. *Go!*"

Something seems to click inside his head. He turns and races into the desert. The guys move to go after him, but I throw myself in their paths. I punch groins and bite into arms and grab ahold of legs and don't let go. I do anything I can to slow them down. And they, in turn, grace me with heavy blows. But not too heavy, because Titus is watching.

"Stop," Long Legs says. "That punk is gone. He's *gone.*"

"Could've predicted that." Titus brushes off his shirt, unruffled. "That's what happens when there's no structure." He looks at his crew. "Complete idiots."

"The woman said we have to —" someone begins.

"I know what she said," Titus interrupts.

Long Legs looks at Madox, his lips curled back. "I'm going to get the shape changer. The rest of you do another one."

"I don't think so," another guys barks. "We're not going to fight each other while you wrestle with the *girl*."

"I should get the shape changer," someone else says. "I always take the smallest portion of food. I complain the least. I'm owed this."

My adrenaline slowly reveals itself for what it is — fear. *Why did I tell Ransom to go? What was I thinking?* Hoping they won't notice, I take small steps backward. If I can get a head start while they're quarreling, then maybe I can escape. I take another step, then another. The guys' voices raise and they move toward one another.

"Maybe I should take out *your* Pandora," one says to another. "You've always been a pain in my ass."

"Oh, so you're a tough guy now?" the guy responds. "Try it and see what happens."

"Both of you shut up," a new voice growls.

"Don't tell me to shut up. You're the one always running your mouth."

"Yeah?"

"Yeah!"

I steal another few steps. Then two more. Then three.

Finally, after enough verbal threats, someone throws a punch. Before I can think, the guys are rolling over one another in the sand, growling and kicking and throwing blows. I don't wait. I know I have to bolt.

Right.

Now.

Spinning around, I manage four long strides before I slam into something solid.

"Hey, sweetheart," Titus whispers. He jabs his knife toward my stomach. The point breaks the skin and keeps me from moving for fear of making it worse. "If you're smart, you won't say a word. You'll just circle around me real slow-like and start walking."

Even though I'm a few paces from the fire, there's enough light to see Titus's face . . . and the grizzly bear looming behind him. I nod my head like I understand what he's telling me. My heart feels like it's going to explode as I circle around him. I arch my back when I feel the knife slide between my shoulder blades. And then we walk.

Titus forces me to travel quickly, almost at a jog. It isn't long before I can't see anything at all. My terror builds until I can hardly stand. Titus doesn't want me dead. He wants me to join him in this race. *Titus doesn't want me dead.* I repeat this over and over in my head, though it does nothing to slow my pulse.

Below me, I can hear Madox whining. He must have changed back into his fox form. I know he wants to do something to help, but he must realize how risky it'd be to try anything while there's a knife pressed against my back.

Titus talks to me the entire way, though I don't start listening until now.

"I know you understand what I'm saying," he coos. "This will only work if we're alone. Those morons wouldn't know how to find the Cure if someone sewed it to their foreheads."

His free hand brushes the back of my neck, and I shudder.

"You'll see that this is for the best. Just you and me, Tella. Just me and my girl."

I hear something. It's a rhythmic sound. The sound of something hitting the ground over and over. *Footsteps!*

Titus's knife pulls away from my back. I spin around and my arms flail. Then fire floods my vision. In that moment, I see three things. A lion. A sociopath flat on his back.

And Guy, vengeance burning in his eyes.

The flames vanish and I hear the unmistakable sound of fist meeting muscle and tissue and bone. Titus screams and calls out for his Pandora to help. Another bolt of fire shatters the night and I see Madox biting into Titus's flesh, releasing built-up fury. I grab my fox around the middle and pull him away. Before the light vanishes for the second time, I also see Titus's bear swiping his enormous paw at M-4. In the pitch-dark, I hear the bear's roar.

What I don't hear is Titus.

"Guy?" I ask, setting Madox down.

Two strong arms pull me into an embrace. He says quickly, "Tella, you have to run. Base camp is on the other side of the rocks. I know it." He pauses. "Have you killed one yet? A Pandora?"

"Why would I do that?" But as soon as I say it, I know. My teeth snap together.

"It's a requirement to get into base camp. To continue the race." Guy sucks in a sharp breath. "We'll figure out something for you. But for now I need you to go. The Triggers are following Titus. And I have to hold them off."

"I won't leave you," I say, tears breaking my voice.

"Yes, you will. If you stay, I'll be too busy worrying about you to defend myself. And I'll get hurt. Do you want that?"

I shake my head.

"Tella, you have to answer aloud. I can't see you well enough."

"No," I say through my tears. "I don't want you to get hurt. But I don't want to be away from you again."

That's not all I'm thinking, though. I'm also thinking, *This is a race. What if Guy is making choices based on saving his cousin, and this is one of those choices?* And then I think, *Cody.* I don't know what to do. My head is spinning and I don't know what to do. Stay or go, stay or go?!

And then —

Guy pulls my face close and searches for my lips. When our mouths find each other, my body explodes with pleasure. I don't ever want him to stop kissing me. I don't ever want him to let go. But he pulls away. And I soon learn why. I can hear the sounds of approaching footsteps. The same sound I heard when Guy was closing in, but this time, it's louder. There are more of them — five of them — and two of us.

"Go," Guy says. "Go *now*."

"Promise I'll see you at base camp." I grab his hand. "Swear it."

"You *will* see me. Now run. Hurry!"

I turn and race into the desert with Madox at my side, my heart breaking with every step. Behind me, I can still hear the sounds of a lion and grizzly in battle.

CHAPTER THIRTY-FIVE

When I wake up, my body feels broken. Like maybe I swallowed glass, lit myself on fire, and leapt off a bridge. Though not necessarily in that order. Reaching a hand out, I find Madox and pull him against me. His body wiggles side to side and his ears press against his head.

Pulling myself up, I realize Guy would be disappointed in how I slept — sprawled out in the middle of the sand. No fire. No foliage bedding. But last night, I couldn't help it. When Guy told me to run — I ran. I ran until I couldn't feel my legs. Until I was sure my lungs would implode. And then I collapsed.

My eyes burn as I think about Guy. About how he saved me from Titus. And how he took on the rest of the Triggers once I fled. Though I know he's right, that I may have gotten in the way, I feel disgusted with myself for leaving him, even if it was for Cody. When I think about how he may be back there, hurt, it's all I can do not to scream.

"Maybe we should go back," I tell Madox.

Though I know he doesn't understand me, my fox grunts like I'm crazy. And maybe I am, because I'm seeing a flashing light that can't be real. Pressing a flat hand against my forehead to shield my eyes, I look closer. There it is again. A quick *flash — flash, flash — flash.*

When Madox cocks his head in the direction of the light, I know it's not a mirage. Standing up — and nearly buckling from pain and dehydration — I move in the direction of the sparkle. I try to imagine what I'm seeing and decide it must be a Contender. That perhaps it's the glint of a knife in the sun. Or even a canteen.

Finding someone with a canteen is more than enough motivation to start hiking, but then I remember something else. Something Olivia said at the start of the desert race:

This canteen could be used as a signal to each other. Wouldn't that be cool?

Once the seed of hope is planted, it starts to grow. And grow. And *grow*, until the legs beneath me begin moving faster. Could it be one of the Contenders from my group? Do they remember what Olivia said, like I do? Soon, I'm running toward the glinting light, my boots kicking up clouds of sand. Madox trots beside me, jaw hanging open as he pants.

Please don't stop, I pray. *Keep showing me where you are.*

At last, after running for what feels like half an hour, I come upon a tree. It's one of the largest I've seen in the desert. And it actually has leaves that grow green in the blistering sun. Beneath the tree's bough, I spot someone leaning against the trunk. I slow my pace and creep closer. I'm out in the open and there's no way I'll see them — hidden by the shade — before they see me. But I can't be afraid. So I take a breath, stand tall, and walk toward them.

While I can't make out what the person looks like, I can pinpoint the moment they turn in my direction and straighten.

"I'll be damned," a female voice croaks. "It's Dorothy and her little dog, too."

I don't need to hear more than that. And I don't need to see the person. I know *exactly* who this is.

"This girl and her dog are coming to save your rear," I tell Harper.

"Thank God you're okay." She hangs her head and sighs heavily. "I didn't know what Titus would do to you."

"Yeah, I'm fine. And Titus didn't do much," I tell her as I plop down. "Just psyched out a few times before Guy got there." I refrain from telling her about Nick, about the fact that Titus moved from creeper category to killer.

"So Guy made it." There's a look of regret in her eyes, and I want to tell her it's fine. But I don't. Because the truth is I'm a little curious as to why they didn't all come. So I just look her in the eye and nod. "And Titus?" she asks. "Is he still —"

"Yeah," I answer, glancing over my shoulder. "I think that freak's still out there."

She leans toward me, a new look on her face. "Do you have any water?"

I shake my head. "Guessing you don't, either."

Harper presses her lips together in frustration. I take that as a no.

I look her up and down and decide it's time to confront the obvious. That she's not wearing a shirt. Just sitting beneath the tree in her pink bra. "Going streaking later?" I'm joking with her, but all I want to do is squeeze her into a hug and never let go. Titus made it seem like she was dead. But I was sure she wasn't. Not Harper. Not the girl I saw fight like a gladiator. Finding her here, however impossible it feels, is a stroke of good luck I'm not about to question.

My friend pulls her arm up and I notice a white shirt wrapped around her right forearm. It's spotted with blood. I gasp, and then reach to inspect her wound. She pulls her arm back against her before I can try and help.

"From when the Triggers attacked us?" I ask.

She nods. "From the night Dink died."

A lump forms in my throat. One I can't quite swallow down. "He was a Pandora. The whole time, he was a Pandora."

"Yeah," she says. "Guy told us what he did. I don't blame him. Something was wrong with the boy. The Creators went too far. Trying to make a Pandora that looked and worked like a human? It's disgusting."

"Caroline?" I ask.

"After we fought off the Triggers, and she saw him . . ." Harper shakes her head. "She was inconsolable. I mean, we could tell she knew he was a Pandora. He must have hatched from the egg she chose, for crying out loud. But I think she started to think of him as her son or something. Maybe it's why she never told us."

I run a hand over my curls, which have grown longer since the start of the race. "Where is she? Where is everyone?"

"Caroline took off. Wouldn't let anyone follow her. Then Guy left, saying he was going to find you, that he couldn't have the rest of us slowing him down." Harper licks her dry, cracked lips. "Guess he really meant Olivia. But that's okay. She has Jaxon, who acts like her friggin' father. That's why I had to leave. I couldn't be around that. Not alone."

I zero in on the fact that Guy wanted to find me on his own. Insisted on it. That makes me feel better about the others' not coming for me. I mean, I know we're here for our families and friends back home, but thinking they'd left me with the Triggers hurt. I watch Harper pull into herself. She doesn't want me to ask what she means about not traveling with Jaxon. So I don't. Instead, I ready myself to ask why she's here, under this tree. But she beats me to the punch.

"Tella, do you think . . ." She pauses. "Do you think you could help me?"

"Of course. I'm not going to leave you. I'd never do that." *Not like I did to Guy* is what I think to myself. I go to slide my arm beneath her, but she stops me.

"That's not what I mean." Harper scoots away and points at the rock formations, which are now only a few hundred yards away. "My Pandora is up there. I heard her last night, screeching. I know that sound. I know *her* sound. She's caught up there somehow and I can't climb up and get her." She raises her injured arm as proof.

Then she looks at me with such desperation that my stomach churns. "Could you go and get her for me? Please, Tella?"

I listen to Harper as she begs me to rescue her eagle. As she explains that she won't have a chance to win without her. And that I'm not so stupid for naming my Pandora, because RX-13 is pretty awesome.

Guy said base camp was right on the other side of the rock formations. I have no idea how he knows that, but I trust him. And that means base camp is so close that I could have a chance at arriving first. I can't know for sure, but I haven't seen any other Contenders passing us. Not like I did in the jungle.

Five years.

I could give Cody *five* healthy years.

If I tell Harper no — that I'm here for my brother — I could keep him alive. But then I remember something else Guy told me — that I have to kill a Pandora to continue the race. My stomach sinks just thinking about completing the task.

I quickly decide to help Harper, because I can't *not* help her. And because her strength will help when it comes time for me to . . . destroy . . . a Pandora. Part of me wants to ask if she's already killed one. But right now she's staring at me, waiting for an answer.

Nodding, I wrap my hands around her upper arms. "I'll go and get your eagle. You walk with me to the formations and then wait while I go up."

Harper's face pulls together like she's going to cry. But, of course, she doesn't. She just waves me away like, *How dare you make me emotional*, and drags herself to her feet. I loop my arm around her waist and again she shoves me off. "I'm not crippled," she says. And then quieter, "Thank you, Tella."

Though the formations are close, it takes a while to get there. We both have to stop often; Harper because of the pain in her arm, and me because I feel damaged all over. But eventually, at snail's pace, we arrive.

Harper humphs, and I ask what she's humphing about.

She pats her hand against the stone. "It's not so big up close. You'd think as we got nearer, it'd get bigger. But turns out, it's not that high."

"Maybe they looked so big from afar because there was nothing else to look at," I say. She nods like this is true, but I can tell she's distracted. "It's okay, Harper. I'll be up and down in no time."

Looking up, I imagine I believe what I'm saying. The closest formation can't be any more than forty feet high — about the equivalent of a four-story building. And I've become quite the athlete over the last several weeks. Climbing up should be no problem. But glancing at Madox, I realize I'll have to leave him behind. I know I won't be long, but it still makes me nervous to go anywhere without him.

"Will you watch him?" I ask.

Harper wraps her arms around her slender waist. "Of course. Just be careful."

"Nah, I'm gonna intentionally try to get myself killed." I grab hold of a rock and bring my boot up onto the first flat surface I find. Behind me, I feel Harper slip something into my back pocket. "Harper?"

"That's my switchblade," she says. "I sharpened it while I was sitting there all night. I'll bet yours is about as dull as a butter knife."

I don't tell her the truth. That I lost my knife to Titus. I just reach out again, and pull myself up.

"Tella," Harper says suddenly, loudly.

"Harper," I mimic. "I'm scaling a mountainesque object, so can you not scream my name?"

"I hardly screamed it." Though I can't see her, I know she's rolling her eyes. "And anyway, all I was going to say was that while you climb that thing, I'm going to trek around it. Then you can come down the opposite side and we'll save time."

"But you don't know how thick this thing is." I grunt like Braun's pig as I find another handhold and ascend higher. "What if we get separated?"

"I can't just stand here all day." Harper doesn't say anything for a minute. When she finally speaks again, she says, "I'm going to do it. See you on the other side."

At this point, I'm not about to argue. Or explain how I haven't killed a Pandora. I'm about five feet off the ground. I need to cease talking and start focusing. So I do just that. I look up the side of the formation. I fill my lungs.

And I climb.

CHAPTER THIRTY-SIX

I've almost gone into cardiac arrest by the time I near the top of the formation. Heights have never been an issue for me. But I guess that was before I decided to go rock climbing with no training, little sleep, and severe dehydration.

Running my hands over the ledge, I grab hold of a fist-sized stone and flip myself over the side. Then I lie on my back and wheeze like a pack-a-day smoker. I decide I might take up smoking after this thing is over. And any other recreational drug that'll help me forget the things I've seen. On second thought, drugs make you ugly. Scratch that. I pledge to get weekly massages instead.

After catching my breath, I get to my feet and realize the formation isn't all that wide. It's maybe five football fields long, but only about thirty feet across. Overhead, the sky is a crisp shade of blue. And from here, the sun seems even bigger, like it's preparing to swallow me whole. I smell fresh soil and the faint scent of metal. It's refreshing, considering the only thing I've smelled in days is BO. Plenty of it mine. Superhot.

Carefully, I cross the distance to the other side of the formation, and look out across the desert. A tidal wave of excitement rushes through my body. There, on the horizon, is base camp. Torches are lit in a circle and small huts dot the interior. My eyes widen when I notice green grass growing within and around the camp. But that can't be possible unless . . .

And then I spot it.

Water.

A thin stream runs between the huts and past the circle of torches. My throat tightens just thinking about having a taste. For the past twenty-four hours, it's felt like I've had cotton balls shoved into my mouth. And now I see so much *water*.

I'm so close, I realize. *Maybe a half-hour walk. Fifteen minutes if I run.*

Stepping closer to the ledge, I look again. Just as I suspected, I don't see anyone walking around the camp. Sure, there could be people inside the huts. But something tells me there aren't. Glancing down the side of the cliff, I wonder how quickly I could make it down.

I could win this leg.

I'm so close, I can taste it.

My heart sinks when I remember the promise I made Harper. I have to free her Pandora. And I will.

But then I will grab Madox and *run*.

Spinning around, I scour the formation, searching for RX-13. It doesn't take long to find her. The rope that was tied around her left leg is tangled in some foliage growing between the stones. When the eagle spots me, she squawks and beats her wings.

"It's okay, girl," I say, bending over the Pandora. "I'm going to cut you loose."

"No, you're not," a voice says from behind me. I bolt upright and goose bumps race along my arms. It's him.

I reach for the blade in my back pocket, then slowly turn around.

Titus stands twenty feet away, his hair matted with blood, face swollen and bruised. "We're going to need that Pandora."

I back up so that I'm blocking Harper's eagle. My mind spins with surprise, but one thing remains clear — I can't let him hurt RX-13. Though if it comes down to me against him, I'm not sure what I'll do. He's hurt, but so am I. And he easily has eighty pounds on me.

"Back away from her." Titus tips the point of his knife toward himself. "We don't want to hurt her quite yet. Unless you're eager to get on with it."

"What are you talking about?" I snarl. There's no use pretending anymore. I hate Titus. And it's high time he realizes that.

"Well, we each have to kill a Pandora that isn't our own. So I'm going to kill that bird. And you're going to kill mine." He points over his shoulder, and I spot his bear on all fours some distance away.

AK-7 jerks his head like this is the first he's hearing of this plan. Pain and anger fill the animal's dark eyes, but mostly, the bear looks defeated.

"I've gotta tell ya, I've had nothing but good luck since that dick sucker punched me last night." Titus squares his shoulders. "You know I could've taken him, right? I mean, if he'd fought fair?" He shakes his head. "Anyway, once my boys — sorry, my *ex*-boys — distracted Guy, I headed toward these rocks. And when I got here last night, I heard that bird making a racket. So I waited until morning so I could see, and I crawled my ass up here. And there" — he gestures toward RX-13 — "was a Pandora just waitin' to be killed."

Titus bites his bottom lip to hide a smile. "But you know what? Things just got better from there. Because right as I was about to slice that yappy bird's head off, I saw your bitch friend beneath that tree. And *then* I look out across the desert, and you know who I saw?" He nods his head toward me and mouths the word *you*. "I couldn't believe you were coming to find me."

I toss the knife in my hand and catch it so that the blade faces downward. "I wasn't coming to find you, Titus. I'd rather leap off the side of this thing than be anywhere near you."

He tilts his head and shrugs. "That's always an option."

Titus strides toward me, his arms outstretched like he's going to give me a hug. It's a show of safety, but I don't miss the knife still gripped in his palm. I take another step back and hear RX-13 shriek behind me. Without thinking, I glance over my shoulder to see what's happened.

It's a terrible move.

Titus crosses the distance between us. He grabs me around the middle and shoves his knife against my neck. "Always worried about those damn animals," he growls, thrusting me against him. He looks me up and down, then meets my eyes. "It's your Achilles' heel, sweetheart. But don't worry. I'll make sure it doesn't get in our way. We're partners, see? Now give me your knife."

Gritting my teeth, I let him steal the blade from my hand. As soon as I release it, he spins me in front of him and presses his own knife against my back. Flashbacks of last night torture me. I can't believe I'm in the exact same position again, Titus behind me with a weapon to my body. Again.

He shoves me toward AK-7 but keeps an arm around my waist. "Let's get this over with." Seeing us coming, the bear lifts his head. The creature's ears perk, and he starts backing up. But Titus just moves faster and yells out, "Stop moving, AK-7. You stand still."

Titus pushes me so I'm inches away from the bear. I can feel the grizzly's breath hot against my face. The Pandora searches my face, then glances at Titus nervously. My head jerks back suddenly and I feel Titus's hand beneath my neck. He presses his mouth against my cheek and says, "I'm going to help you win, Tella." Then he slips a knife into my hand and closes my fist around it. "I want you to plunge this into my Pandora's heart."

AK-7 jerks backward, and Titus pushes me forward to match his steps. Then he slides the other knife up my back and presses it against the base of my scalp. "Kill my Pandora, or I'll kill you."

Ten minutes ago, I had thought I could win. That I could make it to base camp first. But now I realize it wouldn't have mattered. I hadn't killed a Pandora. And I'm not sure I can now. Or ever.

Titus guides my hand toward his Pandora, and the bear drops down on his haunches, like he's already given up. I stifle a sob and look at the great beast before me. If Titus broke an animal this powerful, then how do I stand a chance against him? Feeling him behind me, I know my only chance to escape is to do as he says.

I don't want to hurt AK-7, but this moment will last only minutes, maybe seconds. And I have to kill a Pandora if I want to continue the race. What if this is the only chance I get? What if saving the grizzly means killing my brother?

I move the knife slowly toward the bear. His eyes widen when he realizes I'm going to do it. But that doesn't stop me. I move the knife closer — my hand shaking — and the bear groans deep in his throat. That doesn't stop me, either. But when I spot the open wounds along the animal's stomach — I freeze. Pus and blood ooze over his muzzle, and I imagine the things Titus has done to this creature. The animal who has protected him. The animal who didn't ask to be born into this. Finally, I think of Cody, imagine he is here telling me what to do.

I raise the knife in my hand.

The Pandora closes his eyes.

And I drive the blade straight into Titus's thigh.

The scream that erupts from him rattles me to my core. I feel him drop to the ground, and I don't hesitate. I spin around and race toward the eagle. It takes longer than expected, but I'm finally able to pull her leg from the rope. The moment RX-13 is free, she spreads her wings and soars into the sky. She releases a wild call and dives down the side of the formation. Running to the ledge, I search for Harper.

She's there! Oh my God. I can see her!

"Harper," I scream.

She whips her head in my direction, and when she sees her eagle, she offers her uninjured arm as a perch. The Pandora lands gracefully. I expect her to ask me what's happening. To say she heard someone scream. But she doesn't. She just looks at me for a moment, glances at base camp — and starts racing toward it.

"Harper, no!" I yell in a panic. "I need help. Titus is up here."

She stops dead and whirls around. Though she's already far away, I can see how her head falls to one side like she's in pain. Tilting her chin up, she calls out, "It's my daughter, Tella. My *daughter*." And then she's gone.

My mind reels. Harper has a daughter. I never imagined — knowing her only as a fierce teenage beauty — that it was possible. But of course it is. It explains why she was so weird around Jaxon and Olivia. And around Caroline and Dink. They reminded her of her own child. I hate her for leaving me, but I can't pretend to understand how she must feel.

Watching her sprint toward base camp, I wonder if she'll be able to get in. Has she killed a Pandora? Then I remember something Titus said while debating rescuing Nick from the quicksand: *He let your little friend with the bird kill his Pandora.*

My friend with the bird — Harper.

Harper killed Nick's Pandora.

And now she's eligible to win. But where is Madox? I start to search for him, but I hear something behind me that demands my attention. I spin on the balls of my feet and find Titus standing inches away. He's pressing down on his bleeding thigh with one hand and pointing his blade toward me with the other.

"I'm going to kill you," he says. And I can tell from the fury contorting his face that he may be right.

That I may die today.

CHAPTER THIRTY-SEVEN

My first instinct is to move away from the ledge. Falling would be worse than facing Titus. I manage to take a few steps toward the middle before his open palm whips across my face.

The blow makes everything disappear. Sound. Smell. My vision. It's all gone. All that's left are the rocks digging into my cheek. And then everything comes back *louder*. Titus screaming. Titus reeking.

Titus standing over me with two knives in his hands.

I scramble for my blade like I can't accept that he has them both. Harper would never have been beaten this easily. But she's gone. And so is Guy. And everyone else along with them. Now it's just me and him. I have no chance, I realize. I'm not a skilled fighter. I'm not an analytical whiz who can outsmart my opponent. At least not when they're hovering over me. I'm just a girl who loves purple and Greek food and mani-pedis and singing out of tune. A girl who would give almost anything to be away from here and magically back in Boston, hanging out with her best friend, Hannah. I'm just a girl who thought she could save her brother.

Titus raises his boot into the air — the same one he killed Nick with — and brings it down on my ankle. I scream in agony as my foot twists in an unnatural direction. But my cries don't stop him. He only swings his boot out and slams it into my ribs.

I have to get away from him!

Turning onto my stomach, I rise up and try to crawl, my damaged ankle dragging behind me. Something crashes into my butt and I sprawl out onto my belly.

Faster, Tella!

Adrenaline kicks in, the desire to survive despite all odds. I spin around and bring myself to my feet. Pain rips through my body and nearly blinds me. I don't have much time to think before I feel Titus's fist connect with my jaw.

For some reason, after all the ways he's hurt me, I still can't believe he punched me. *Punched* me. I always wondered what it would feel like. To get socked in the face. And now I know. Something about this makes me laugh.

"What the hell are you laughing at?" Titus pauses. It must intrigue him, hearing someone laugh while they're down. I smile up at him from my stone grave, knowing my teeth are laced with blood.

"You're just so pathetic." I laugh until my sides ache. Until tears fill my eyes.

And then I lunge at his legs and bite into flesh.

Titus howls and brings his elbow down onto the back of my neck. I don't care about the pain anymore, though. I'm hysterical with adrenaline. Drunk with it. I spring to my feet and hold up my fists.

Titus eyes me. "God, you *are* amazing, Tella. A girl filled with surprises. If only you'd been smarter about your alliances." My heart kicks faster as he raises the blade in his right hand. I don't know where the other one went. I guess it's in his back pocket. If I can get to it, then perhaps I stand a chance.

Mad with fear, I dive toward him, my hand seeking the second knife.

Then I stop dead.

I glance down.

I found a knife!

It's right here — buried in my abdomen.

Titus pulls the blade out slowly and I slump to the ground. Amazingly, I don't feel a thing. I just stare at the wound and back at him with the wonder of a small child. The muscles in my face relax, and my whole body goes numb.

I know I should lie still and not move an inch; it'll keep the blood in longer. But I also know it's over for me. And though I've never thought about my death before — not *really* — I know I want to die on my feet.

I struggle to stand and Titus takes a few steps back, like he can't believe his eyes. Then his face changes, twists with a sinister shadow.

"Your will to survive was cool at first, baby," he says. "But now it's getting irritating." He tosses his bloodied blade to the ground. "As much as I'm starting to hate you, I'm not sure I can kill you myself. But I can let gravity do that for me."

I stumble backward, but pause as a thought occurs to me. I don't want to fall to my death. But maybe if he shoves me off the ledge, I can take him along. Give the other Contenders a chance to finish the race without him . . . out there.

Titus rushes toward me. But before he can cross the distance between us, something blocks his path.

His claws are four inches long.

He weighs over eight hundred pounds.

And he's moving toward Titus, a terrible growl building in his throat.

"AK-7, stand down," he says, trying to step around the bear. But the bear cuts him off. "I said, get the *fuck* out of my way."

The grizzly bear rises up on his hind legs. His back swells. And he releases a roar that makes my blood run cold.

He's protecting me, I realize. *AK-7 is protecting me.*

I can hardly make out Titus behind the beast, but I can see his face — and the moment he understands. He reaches behind his back and withdraws the last knife. The other is still on the ground, too far away for either of us to reach it.

"Come on, then!" Titus screams. "Come at me!"

The bear lands on all fours and races in his direction. And even though Titus is insane, he does something that surprises me still — he runs *toward* the bear. At the last second, before they collide, Titus lays himself out like he's diving for home base. He slides beneath the bear's legs and comes out the other side — directly in front of me. Bolting to his feet, his thigh gushing blood, he grabs me by the neck and drags me toward the ledge.

AK-7 roars again, but stops when Titus jabs his knife under my chin. My feet all but dangle off the side of the formation, and I squeeze my eyes shut.

This is it, I think. My last thought isn't of my brother. Or my mom or dad. It's of Guy. The way his face changes when he smiles. The way he never cracks his damn thumbs. I think about his love of newspapers, how he likes the way the pages sound in his hands. And I admit, for the first time, that when he said that, I imagined one day we'd sit at a breakfast table together — me in my leopard-print slippers and Guy crinkling his beloved paper. That we'd be together. Away from the race and the fear of losing those we love.

A breeze blows across my face and I snap my eyes open, expecting to be falling. To be one heartbeat shy of death.

But I'm not falling.

And when I realize what I'm seeing, my whole body shakes with excitement.

It's RX-13, flying three feet away, her wings beating the hot desert air. But then I realize I'm not quite right. And I laugh aloud again when I notice the burning green eyes.

My little Madox.

I clamp a hand over my wound, suddenly fighting to stay alive. At that exact moment, Titus slams his hand over my mouth.

"Don't think because Green Eyes came back, you're going to live," Titus snarls. "Then again, maybe you will. Let's see! Why don't you give him a command? Tell him to save you. And if he does, we'll all live happily ever after." Titus roars with laughter and presses his hand down harder. "Go ahead, tell him what you need."

Titus doesn't know Madox can't understand me. That he's *never* understood. But then again, that's not exactly true. More than anyone, my fox has gotten me. He always knew what I needed without my saying a word. With only a thought, it seems.

Something boils deep within me. It splits me in half, mends me back together. A calm slides over my body, and for the first time in days, I think clearly. I look at Madox, and I speak directly to him — using only my mind.

Tear his eyes out.

Madox screeches and dives toward Titus's face, talons outstretched.

Behind me, my captor screams with pain. The knife beneath my chin drops away and I twist around. Madox is beating his wings and tearing at Titus's face. It's like my Pandora had the same idea — to blind him — but was waiting for me to *think* the order. I wonder quickly how many other times he's waited for orders I never gave.

After Madox swoops away, I gasp with horror. Titus's hands cover his eyes, but I can still see the bright red blood dripping down his cheeks like wet fingers. He teeters toward the edge, and without thinking, I reach out to keep him from falling — then stop myself. But can I really let him fall? And if I do, is it me who kills him?

Titus steps closer and closer to the edge, growling in anguish like a monster. I cover my mouth as hot tears sting my eyes. *He's going to fall. He's going to fall to his death. Not me.*

Titus's foot hits the ledge and his arms pinwheel. He knows he's going down. I can see it in the way his mouth forms a perfect circle.

But then he stops. Manages to right himself.

And he takes a step toward me, his arms outstretched, eyes bursting with red flesh and blood. Suddenly, I'm not afraid of him falling. I'm afraid of him *living*.

No sooner than I think this — Titus flies off the side of the ledge.

His body plummets to the earth.

Seconds later, I hear a sickening, wet thud. AK-7 stands where Titus once did, looking down over the ledge. The grizzly shoved him off. And now the creature gazes at me with fear, backing away, afraid I'm going to hurt him for what he did. But all I want to do is throw my arms around his neck.

So I do.

The animal grunts when I fall against him. His muscles tense against my embrace, but then the creature relaxes and nudges his head into my side. Seconds later, I feel a second head nudging my other side. When I turn, I see Madox dressed as a twin bear. He must think this is what I want. I laugh and hug my Pandora, overwhelmed with love for these animals who have saved me.

Pulling away, I press down on my stomach. I can't inspect the wound again. I'm afraid I'll faint if I do. I also know I don't want to look at Titus's body, but that I must. Stepping toward the side, I glance over. One look is all it takes. He's facedown on the ground, his head turned to the side. A stream of blood flows from his open mouth and from his leg.

He's dead.

I step back and — after suffering a wave of dizziness — nearly tumble over the side myself. Touching a sticky hand to my forehead, I realize I have to get to base camp. Titus stabbed me only minutes ago, but already I feel light-headed and weak. He must not have hit a major organ or whatever. Otherwise, I'd already be toast.

Adding to my wooziness are raw nerves. My stomach twists when I think about saving Cody. With my injury, I don't have much choice but to seek medical attention. But I pray Guy gets to base camp soon. And that he'll help me find a way to continue the race without having to harm a Pandora. I have to believe it isn't over. Not when I chose to do what I believe is right.

I look at the Pandoras. *My* Pandoras.

"Can you climb down?" I ask AK-7.

Can you climb down? I think to KD-8.

Both bears flex their paws and their mammoth nails begin to grow until they're nearly a foot long. I'm guessing the talons can be used for climbing almost any surface.

"Of course you have Wolverine claws. Of course." I shake my head and move away from the ledge Titus fell from. When I find a place that seems easy to descend, I nod at the bears. Then I swing my leg over the side.

What goes up . . . I think.

CHAPTER THIRTY-EIGHT

When my feet touch the ground, I nearly collapse. It doesn't take long to right myself, but I'm worried about how I'll get to base camp. The bears descend behind me and then watch as I peer into the desert.

I believe I was correct. About a half-hour walk. It doesn't seem like much. Not after everything I've been through. But with more blood leaking from my wound and dripping down my leg — the distance seems infinite. My biggest worry is that once I get there, I won't find a way to continue the race. But I clench my fists and I grit my teeth and I vow to try.

"It is you," a small voice says.

I spin around — still on guard — and spot a figure leaning against the formation. The person is only about twenty feet away. Close enough so that when I narrow my eyes, I realize who it is.

"Ransom!" I yell, rushing toward him. My steps slow as I close in. DN-99, his raccoon, is sleeping in his lap. Or maybe it's just closing its eyes, trying to shut out what's happening. "Oh God." I note the ram at Ransom's feet and crouch down beside the animal, one hand covering my stomach. G-6 is gasping for air and lying flat on his side. Looking at Ransom, I grasp what he's trying to do. The knife is poised over the ram's heart, but he doesn't move an inch from there.

Ransom glances up at me with tears in his eyes. "I already killed a Pandora," he explains. "That's not why. It's just he's . . . He's in so much pain."

I nod and sit down next to him. My head swims from pain and loss of blood, but I can't leave him. Not like this. Ransom glances over my shoulder and spots AK-7 and Madox, who's back in fox form. He flinches. "It's okay," I tell him. "AK-7 helped me. He won't hurt us or Madox."

He shakes his head and lowers the knife. "That blasted fox. I tried to keep him still. When Harper came rushing around the corner earlier, I didn't know what was happening. She took one look at me and tossed the fox in my direction. Told me to watch him. To not let him go." He sighs and runs a hand through his red hair. "But that Pandora nearly took me out trying to get loose. He mimicked that eagle and wanted to go up the formation, see about the commotion. It was you up there, huh?"

I nod. Ransom looks only half there, like a part of his mind was lost somewhere in the desert. Seeing him this way, I can't bear to tell him what happened.

"You're hurt," he says.

"I'll be fine."

"Harper has a daughter," he adds.

My eyes widen. "She told you?"

"She told everyone. She screamed it." Ransom points to where Harper stood, where she yelled out to me. "Think I'm the father?"

I laugh and then cringe with agony. Darkness lurks at my peripheral vision, threatening to pull me under. I drop down onto my butt and hang my head. "No, I don't think you're the father," I tell the boy.

Ransom looks at me with clarity. Like some of the fuzziness in his head has subsided. He glances down at his hands, at the knife he's holding. Then he slips it into my palm. "You have to do it," he says in a whisper. "That's why you're here."

I close my hand around the blade, but shake my head. "No, Ransom." Though I already know I *will* do it. Not only because of Cody, though I feel a sting of guilt that this may be the opportunity I wanted. But because every breath the beast takes rips out my heart. I want it to end. I want the ram to go with his Contender. To be at peace. And, yes, because I want my brother to survive.

"I'm going home. I need to tell my family about Levi and be with my sister," Ransom says suddenly. "But I need you to do this first." He pulls himself up and moves closer to G-6. The raccoon startles and then crawls away. Ransom cradles the ram's head in his arms and closes his eyes. "Please do it now, Tella. Please. Please don't wait. Make it fa —"

Ransom's voice breaks in a sob. Another wave of dizziness washes over me, but I fight the urge to succumb. There's something I must do first. Getting to my knees, I hold the knife over the ram's heart — or where I hope it is. Ransom lowers his mouth to the ram's ear and whispers into it. Tears burn my eyes and I squeeze them shut. I want to make this all slow down. It seems ever since I climbed the formation — ever since I tossed my backpack on the passenger seat of the car, really — everything has moved too quickly. But I can't draw this out. Not when both Pandora and Contender are in so much pain. I wonder if I will ever forget what I'm about to do.

No, never.

I thrust the blade in and cry out. When I look up, Ransom is staring at G-6. His face is relaxed, but his eyes seem more empty than ever.

My body shakes with disbelief. I've never killed anything before. The grief is instant and crushing. It wasn't my Pandora. But it's the last piece of Levi I'll ever know.

"Thank you," Ransom says. When he looks directly at me, his expression changes from sorrow — to concern. "We need to get you to base camp."

It's the last thing I hear before I lose consciousness.

What happens next comes only in fragments. It's like I'm lying near the ocean; one moment, I see things clearly, the next, I'm smothered by the tide.

I feel a rocking, jerking sensation and realize I'm being carried. The person holding me is about the size of a mattress. He's talking about his nails.

Beside him, I spot a blur of yellow curls. In focus. Out of focus. It's like a flower blooming, then fading to black.

The mattress carries me farther.

I sleep in his arms, and when I wake again, there are men hovering over me, tending to my wound. I feel the sting of a needle sewing flesh. When I groan, one of the men stops and speaks to the other. Something pinches on the inside of my arm, and my mind goes blank.

And then, sometime in the night, I hear him.

Him.

He leans over me and whispers in my ear like Ransom did to Levi's Pandora. His voice sounds like it's coming from a wind tunnel, and I can barely understand what he's saying.

". . . don't need to know everything now. Only that I'll never leave you again," Guy says. Though I can't see him, I know he's thinking. Wondering how much to say. Finally, I hear his voice continue. His words slide over my body like silk. "You asked about my tattoo." Guy pauses, chooses his words carefully. "Do you know what hawks sometimes eat? Do you know what they *hunt*?" My heart beats faster, but I can't open my eyes. *Open your eyes!*

"They hunt serpents, Tella," he finishes. "Serpents, like the ones running this race."

My heart thumps so hard, I'm afraid I'll die in this moment. But no matter how hard I try, I cannot open my eyes.

Even as Guy tells me his secret.

That he is here for more than just his cousin.

"She's definitely looking at me," someone says.

I hear a long sigh. And then, "You're imagining things. Again."

I know the voice. I know both of these people. My eyelids flutter and the room spins. Someone's face comes within inches of mine. I see teeth. So many teeth, I'm afraid it's a monster. That Titus is back with his ever-present smile.

"Get back, Jaxon. If she *is* awake, you're going to scare the crap out of her."

That's it. That's the face — and the owner of the teeth. "Jaxon," I croak.

"Hot damn, I knew you were awake," Jaxon cries.

A chair groans and seconds later, Braun leans over the cot I'm lying in. "Hey, Tinker Bell. You passed out. I carried you. Did a number on my nails." He glances at his fingers and his eyebrows knit together with concern. Then he looks up and smiles. "Thought we might lose you."

"Where's Madox?" The first thing I want to know about is Guy, but I can't bring myself to ask. His name conjures too many questions. So for now I think of my fox.

"Olivia is with him outside," Jaxon says. "Him and the *bear*."

"Is Olivia okay?" I try sitting up, but Braun lays his enormous palm against my shoulder and guides me back down. "And AK-7 isn't bad."

"She's fine," he replies. "And we know the bear isn't bad."

"The bear killed Titus," I add. What I don't admit is how I helped. But I doubt they'd blame me for my part.

Jaxon rubs the back of his neck. "Uh, we didn't know *that*. We figured something went down, but no one knew what."

"Is Ransom here? Maybe I should tell him about Titus, too. I haven't yet." I reach down and touch the place where Titus stabbed me. Just as I suspected, I feel stitches running along my abdomen.

"Um, you should ask Guy about Ransom. He insisted he be the one to tell you." Braun rubs a hand over his shaved head.

My muscles clench upon hearing that Guy is here, at base camp. Perhaps right outside the door. But I guess I knew that. I remember . . . I remember what he said to me.

"Are you sure Titus is dead?" Braun continues.

I think back to how far Titus fell, almost four stories. I think about the tilt of his head and the blood streaming from his mouth and leg. "I'm sure."

Braun's shoulders fall with relief and he nods. "I didn't want to let those things happen to you. I didn't want to —" Something catches in his throat. He looks down and presses his lips together, breathing in through his nose.

I can't stand the thought of Braun feeling guilty. Not after he carried me here. But mostly, I don't want to hold on to anger or resentment. This race is hard enough on its own.

"It's fine." I take his hand and give it a squeeze. Jaxon takes my other hand and we have a total bonding moment. I could stay here for hours, just relaxing and chatting with these two. But there are others I need to ask about.

"Where is Caroline?" I swallow hard. "And Harper?"

Jaxon and Braun exchange looks. "You should talk to Guy about them, too," Jaxon answers.

I want to demand answers, but decide since Guy is the only person left to ask about, I'll do as they say. "Then can you send him in?"

They glance at each other and nod like they have to agree on this together. I wonder how long I was out for these two to have become such close conspirators. "Yeah, okay," Jaxon says. "We'll be right outside if you need anything."

They leave quietly, and I glance around for the first time. I assume I'm in one of the huts I spotted from the formation. The walls create a perfect circle and the roof is pitched to a single point. The entire thing — except the dirt floor — is made of dried grass. Over the door hangs a thick green-and-blue plaid blanket. I have a similar one over my legs. Hanging across the room is a small, round mirror, and below it is a rickety chest. There are three other cots besides mine. And only one chair. The one Braun was sitting in when I woke up.

I stare at the empty chair and suddenly feel very alone. The sensation doesn't last long. Because when I turn my head — I see Guy standing in the makeshift doorway. My chest splinters and my ribs stretch open.

All that's left is my heart.

CHAPTER THIRTY-NINE

He runs a hand over his jaw like he's not sure what to do. A shiver works its way down my spine and my skin tingles. If he doesn't touch me, I'll burst from anxiety.

I will crumble.

He takes a step in my direction, and I open my mouth to say something, *anything* that will bring him closer. But he crosses the room without encouragement. He sits down on my bedside like he's not sure if I want him there. Like he's afraid I'll shove him off at any moment. I'd rather tear my insides out.

Guy swallows.

His fists tighten.

His jaw clenches.

"Say something," I tell him.

He turns and looks at me. His eyes swim with fear. My breath catches. "Jaxon tells me Titus is dead."

A knot forms in my throat. I suddenly feel like a child again, like I need to be rocked in someone's arms. On the formation, I was brave. I faced Titus and I lived. But here, with Guy sitting so close, the terror I felt devours my soul. Tears streak down my cheeks. I'm in awe of them, surprised that I can cry after being so dehydrated. It's then that I realize I'm not thirsty, and that the men who work for the race must have given me fluids.

Guy wipes away my tears and shakes his head. "He got away from me, Tella," he explains. "I knew when he ran . . . I knew he would go after you." Guy looks into his lap and bites the inside of his cheek. "I tried to find him before he found you. I tried." He squeezes his eyes shut. "I would have killed him."

I sit up — gritting my teeth against the pain in my abdomen — and throw my arms around his waist, bury my head into his chest.

Beneath me, I feel him draw in a deep breath. Then he wraps his arms around my shoulders. "Tella," he whispers into my hair. "It's okay. I'm here."

I bite my lip and press my cheek closer to him. "I remember what you told me."

He stiffens. "What do you remember?"

Pulling away, I sit up and stare into his face. "That tattoo on your back. It stands for something," I say. "You said hawks *hunt* serpents."

Guy looks at me for a long time, then nods. "That's right."

I clasp my hands together like Caroline does when she's nervous. It doesn't help. "You're here to take down the people running this race."

He glances over his shoulder at the door. When he looks back, he squares his shoulders and straightens. His silence is admission enough, but I want to hear him say it aloud.

"Tell me," I say. "Tell me I'm right."

New tears escape my eyes. I'm more afraid in this moment than I have been the whole race. Afraid Guy will die trying to find these people — and of the things I'd do to prevent that. He rubs his thumbs over my cheeks and says, "You're right. I'm here to destroy the Brimstone Bleed. To ensure no one ever suffers through it again. I've been training. . . ." He trails off and touches a hand to his mangled ear absently, as if remembering this training. Then he moves his hand to my chin, holds it so that I meet his eyes. "Tella, do you remember what I told you about Gabriel Santiago's daughter, Morgan?"

I nod. How could I forget?

Guy breathes through tight lips, and I realize he's about to tell me the rest of the story. My muscles tighten as I anticipate his words. "After Morgan died," he says gently, "Santiago found out that the Pharmies were the ones who started the fire. And he sought vengeance. He wanted the Pharmies who killed his daughter, the same ones who destroyed *his* work, to pay for what they'd done. He threatened their families, said he'd murder their children and spouses and parents unless they agreed to his terms." Guy swallows, and then he says to me, "Santiago was a powerful man, with powerful friends. He could've done what he promised."

My eyes fall to the floor, wondering what I'd do if someone threatened to kill my entire family. Someone I thought could follow through with it. "What did he want them to do?" I ask in a whisper.

Guy rubs a hand over the back of my neck. I close my eyes as his fingers trace circles along my skin. "He asked them to choose. He asked them to choose one person in their family to compete in a race."

My eyes snap open.

"Santiago then told them to choose someone else. Someone to be injected with a virus they'd create. That family member would be used as motivation for the person competing in the race." Guys stops rubbing my neck. "As punishment for having a hand in his daughter's death, Santiago created a race. And every six years, he made the Pharmies choose two people from their families. One to compete and one to become ill. Cousins, brothers, great aunts . . . they could choose anyone. But they had to choose. And the only thing they could do to help was create animals to assist them in the race."

After everything I've been through, I almost can't handle this last piece of the puzzle. The knowledge that nearly sixty years ago, someone in my family had a hand in Morgan's death. And that my being here is a consequence of that. My body starts shaking as my mind snaps hold of something else. . . .

Creator Collins.

The one who created Madox.

He could be *family*.

"How is this still going on? Isn't Santiago dead?"

"Others have taken his place," Guy says quickly, and I can hear the spitefulness in his voice. "It's bigger now than Santiago ever thought it could be. There are people out there ignorant of the details, gambling on what they believe is an illegal horse race. And others who help the Pharmies decide who out of their families should be infected and who should compete. And there are managers, too. People who oversee the actual race and keep the gamblers informed on how their *horse* is performing."

I'm overwhelmed with everything Guy's telling me, and part of me wonders, *Why tell me this now?* "Is that everything you know?" I ask, defeated. "Is there more?"

"There's more. Details that aren't important." He squeezes my hand.

"You're really going to try and end this race?" I ask. "For good?"

Guy makes a fist and beats it twice against his knee. "My father told me that the people running the race recruit the top five Contenders to work for them." Guy pauses, licks his lips. "I'm going to win, and then I'm going to take the job."

"You'll try to take them down from the inside," I speculate.

He squeezes my hand again as if to say, *That's right.*

"If Harper stays, maybe she can help us," I tell him, my heart beating faster. "Did you see her fight the Triggers the night they attacked our campsite? She was like this —"

"Tella," Guy interrupts. "You're not doing this with me. I'm only telling you so there aren't any more secrets."

"But with me and Harper —"

"Harper is gone."

I let go of his hand. "What are you talking about?"

Guy cups my face in his palm. "You've been out for almost a full day," he says. "Harper left last night. She took Caroline and Ransom with her."

"How could she do that?" I put both hands on my head, trying to come to terms with what he's telling me. "They don't give us the choice to leave until the last day of base camp, right?"

"She was the winner," he explains. His voice lowers into a whisper. "She made a request because of her circumstances." My brow furrows and Guy runs his thumb over the crease. He avoids my eyes when he says, "Harper's daughter died."

I cover my mouth and choke on a sob. Shaking my head, I think of how she told me only yesterday. How I went from seeing Harper as a friend and comrade — to a mother.

Guy slides his hand inside his cargo pants and withdraws an envelope. "She left this for you." Before I can ask what it says, he presses his lips against mine. The letter flutters to the bed and I twine my arms around his neck. Guy pulls me closer and kisses me deeper until all thoughts of the race vanish. He kisses me until there is only him and me and the feel of our skin. I shiver as his hands move up my back and wrap around my neck. His tongue slides into my mouth and heat floods my body. I want to live here, in this moment — with him this close and me in his arms.

When we break away at last, both gasping for air, our hands continue to roam. They touch thighs and lips and cheeks. It's as if our minds have released each other, but our bodies can't dream of stopping.

"Read her letter," he says finally. "I'll be outside."

He heads for the door and even then I reach out for him. I want to scream for him to stay. But instead, I look down at the envelope. The one Harper left me.

I fill my lungs, run my finger under the sealed flap —

And I pull out the letter.

Tella,

I'm leaving tonight, and I'm taking Caroline and Ransom with me. You should know I'm giving my small portion of the Cure to Caroline. She deserves a chance at a real relationship with her mother. As for me, I need to go home. I need to be with my family. I have to see my daughter again.

I will never be the same, Tella. Not without her. But listen when I tell you this - I'll be back. I'm going to make sure what happened to me doesn't happen to you.

I'm going to help you win the Brimstone Bleed.

- Harper

Reading Harper's letter is too much. I pull myself out of bed and double over with pain. The stitches in my stomach are tender and raw, but I can't lie here any longer. I right myself and move across the room. I shuffle like an old man and my mind spins. I think about the race and the things I've done. I think about Madox and how I'd dissolve without him. I think of Caroline and Ransom and Harper — who are all on their way home. I even think about Jaxon and Olivia and Braun, my new friends.

And I think of Guy.

I remember he's here for more than just his cousin — that it's bigger than a sister or a mother or a daughter. That he'll try to destroy the Brimstone Bleed. I wonder if I'm strong enough to aid him — if I can let this be bigger than Cody. If I can help save more than just my brother.

Madox trots in and I scoop him into my arms, careful not to strain myself. The fox nuzzles my neck, and my heart sings.

Holding my Pandora, I realize there's more at stake than our loved ones back home. There are also the animals the Creators — the *Pharmies* — generated. What happens to them when the race ends? Are they destroyed? If so, do they go willingly to their deaths, or do they fight? I gaze at my fox and my body trembles.

When I glance up, I realize I'm standing before the oval mirror.

My gut twists when I see myself. "Good God," I tell my Pandora. "I need a friggin' bath." There's sand in my curly hair and my face is covered with grime. My white shirt is nearly brown with sweat and dirt, and I have a purple bruise blooming across my cheek. But my lips form a small smile when I see that the green-and-blue feather still dangles over my shoulder.

Finally, I see my eyes. My *mother's* eyes. And I suddenly grasp what she meant. Running my thumb beneath them, I notice they hold strength I never recognized before. The same strength I always saw in her.

Understanding — or maybe *acceptance* — showers over me.

My mother took us to Montana to try and save my brother. To hide him from the race. To hide *me.* But they found us anyway. She knew all along. It was right there in her eyes: knowledge and determination and strength.

I know what she was telling me when she said I have her eyes.

You have my strength, too.

The feather in my hair is more than what it appears, I realize. *This was my mother's,* she'd said. But it's what she didn't say that haunts me. The questions I never thought to ask. The questions I'd ask now if she were here: When *did she wear this feather, Mom? Did she wear it in the jungle? In the desert? Did she wear it as a* Contender?

But perhaps there's another question I'd like answered even more.

What happened to her?

I look down at Madox. My mother never wanted me to be here, but she knew I was going anyway. And she knew I could win.

I *will* win.

I'll save Cody.

Then I'll help Guy bring down this entire race.

ACKNOWLEDGMENTS

Thank you first and foremost to my sister, Tyse Kimball. Tyse, this book wouldn't exist without your support. From titles to Pandoras to critical moments in the story, we discussed it all. Thank you.

To my editor at Scholastic, Erin Black, our brains are so similar it's scary. You rock my world with your mad editing skills. Thank you for loving Tella, Madox, and Guy from the start. I'm mailing you a Pandora egg ASAP!

To Nina Goffi, Rachael Hicks, Esther Lin, and everyone else at Scholastic who helped *Fire & Flood* along the way, thank you. Also, to the Scholastic sales peeps, I used to be in your shoes and I know how hard you work to make it rain. Hugs!

Thank you to my agent, Laurie McLean, for selling *Fire & Flood*. You were the first person to read the manuscript and say, "It's absolutely perfect." Also, a big thank-you to Rachel Harris, Jenny Martin, and Trisha Wolfe; all brilliant writers who've helped me on this journey.

Thank you to my grandma for always being so excited to see me; to my mom for being a meticulous early reader; to my dad; to my brother; to Jeremiah Kimball; to friends Angee Webb, Gianina Bailey, and Laryssa Rastrelli; to the Dallas crew of writers, bloggers, and librarians; to the Scotts and the Wittmanns for their continued support; and to all my nieces and nephews on both sides — you kiddos are awesome.

And, finally, to my husband. You are my best friend and soul mate. I make up silly songs about you and sing them while you're at work; that's how much I hate the hours we're apart. I've been married to you for five years and it isn't enough. It will never be enough. I love you, Lion.

ABOUT THE AUTHOR

Victoria Scott is the author of the Dante Walker series. She lives in Dallas with her husband, and is currently working on the second Fire & Flood novel. Victoria adores getting to know her readers. Visit her online at www.VictoriaScottYA.com.

Don't miss the stunning sequel!

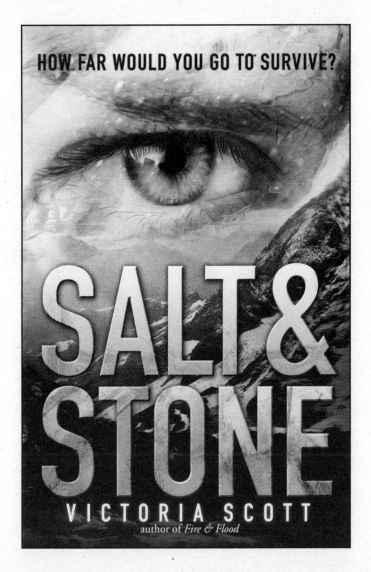

this is teen

Want the latest updates on YA books and authors, plus the chance to win great books every month?

Join the conversation with This Is Teen!

Visit **thisisteen.com** to find out how to reach us using your favorite form of social media!

TEEN2